Noah Clue, P.I.

Noah Clue, P.I.

(a novel)

by Jason C. McDonald

This book is set in Arapey and My Underwood fonts.

Noah Clue, P.I.
Published by AJ Charleson Publishing LLC
Hayden, ID
ajcharlesonpublishing.com

This is a work of fiction. All of the characters, organizations, and events portrayed in this novel are either products of the author's imagination or are used fictitiously.

ISBN 978-1-7323680-3-3

Library of Congress Control Number: 2019948665

2019—First Edition

Contents

How To Get Murdered In Three Easy Steps

Murder In G Minor

Introduction

I have always loved detective fiction—the works of greats like Sir Arthur Conan Doyle, Agatha Christie, Tony Hillerman, and the like. I've spent many an evening sipping chamomile tea, while reading about master detectives untangling maze-like crimes. Growing up around authors, I learned to dismantle and recreate the complex workings of the human mind, so my fascination with both crime and psychology was almost inevitable. I loved to pit my wits against the likes of Sherlock Holmes, Hercule Poirot, Miss Marple, and Joe Leaphorn, trying to solve the case before they could.

Yet the writer in me enjoys turning things sideways and inside-out. All the great detectives, aided by their slack-jawed companions, would solve crimes by piecing together dozens of seemingly unimportant details. Where then was the not-so-great detective, the last person on this rock who should have ever obtained a P.I. license, who could overlook the painfully obvious? Where was the sharp-minded (and sharp-tongued) assistant who missed no detail, and got no credit? What if every stock character of detective fiction was inverted and amplified to the disproportionate absurdity that is real life? I humbly submit for your consideration, *Noah Clue P.I.*

As comedian Mark Russell once pointed out, the lines between reality and satire are very thin indeed.

—Jason C. McDonald

Notes, Apologies, and Thank Yous

Of all the cities I have lived in and near, Seattle truly stole my heart. Many locations described herein either truly exist, or are based on real places. Seattleites are likely to enjoy trying to identify many places described. However, Noah's alma mater, Lake Union College, is entirely fictional. The Salish Music Conservatory is likewise purely a work of fiction.

Nearly all the characters are products of my imagination, with a few notable exceptions. My psychology professor, Dr. Randy Ware, helped with a few technical points, and I drew a lot of inspiration from his lectures, so he naturally deserved a cameo. My adoptive sister Allie Lingard, whose "Curse of the Joke Clairvoyant" is anything but fictional, appears as a forensics chemist. The incorrigible Lee Fox and publicist Isaac Juniper are cameos of two of my closest friends. You know who you are. One of my best friends from grade school, Samantha, inspired the forensics analyst of the same name.

I also probably owe an apology to my fellow college alumnae Bryan, whose snappy secretarial snark inspired many a real-life cadence of "shut up, Bryan." I threatened to put you in a book, and I did it!

Many thanks to Detective Mark Jamieson of the Seattle Police Department for insight into police procedure and structure, especially around the time of this book. Thank you to Mark Barbieri of Washington Holdings for his assistance in ensuring historical accuracy of some real estate details.

Gregg Warren in all his ranks is purely fictional, as are Detective Thomas M. Jones and the unnamed Chief of Police. No part of this story should be taken as a commentary on the Seattle Police Department. Some real events and timelines are borrowed, as convenient to the story, and some are mangled to fit my purposes.

I'm a stickler for research and accuracy, but a few points of police procedure are intentionally fudged for plot convenience. The "police advisor" has been a trope of detective fiction since Sir Arthur Conan Doyle, and I happily carry it forward despite its inaccuracy. In the real world, P.I.s don't get the same breadth of information from the police that Noah does, but that fabrication makes the stories more enjoyable to read.

Thanks to Rene Gutteridge for introducing me to the humor in the awkward through her books over the years.

I also want to thank everyone who made this book possible. Special thanks to my mother, Anne McDonald, for being my tireless editor, sounding board, co-conspirator, cheerleader, and test audience. I literally couldn't have written this book without you.

A special thank you to my dearest Auntie Jane McArthur for being my self-proclaimed biggest fan and most enthusiastic test reader over the years.

Thank you to Barbara Warren, Joanne Dearman, and Kat Beecham for their editing skills and invaluable input.

Thank you to David Bush, Dan Harrington, Allie Lingard, Lane Mattis, and Zahran Sajid for being my test readers. Your encouragement keeps me going.

A warm thank you to all of the family and friends who have been sucked into the swirling vortex of my imagination. Your tolerance for (and encouragement of) my madness makes this possible. Writing really is borderline schizophrenia for fun and profit!

Te quick brownfox jumped over the lazy dog The quick brown fx jumped over the lazy dog. The quick brown fox juumped over the lazy dog. The quick brown fox jumped over the layz dog. The quick brown fox jumped over the lazy dg. The quick brown fox jumped over the lazy dog.

Red Herrings

and

Referrals

To Rondi Downs,

The original "Dee" to my "Noah."

Your mark on this story is lasting.

I must say, you're saner than she is.

1

I Get Fired

Thursday, March 11

Staying to the early morning shadows, I crept down the damp, dark alley. Days of investigation were about to pay off. I mounted the fire escape and crept up the steps to the third floor. I threw one leg over the wet balcony rail and pulled myself onto the other side. Sometimes it paid to be a vertically challenged male.

Creeping up to the sliding glass door, I peered inside. By the light of the living room lamp, I could see my target laying fast asleep on the couch, his broad frame sprawled across the sofa. His white shirt and tie were rumpled and his dust-colored bangs partially covered his eyes. I tried the door, and found that it had been left unlocked. How convenient.

I moved to the arm of the couch and peered down at the man. "Good morning, Mr. Fredrickson."

Nicholas Fredrickson's eyes popped open, and he stared at me. "Who are you? How did you get in here?"

"Your sliding glass door was unlocked. I let myself in." I pulled one of my cards from my pocket and tossed it onto his chest. "The name is Clue. I'm a private eye. The name Thompson ring any bells, pal?"

"Ye-ah." Fredrickson gave me a puzzled look. "Buddy of mine."

"His flat was robbed two weeks ago, Thursday. You know anything about that?"

"Now, wait just a blasted minute!" He swung his legs off the couch and towered over me. "Are you accusing me of something?"

I crossed my arms. "The evidence leads straight to you. Now, you can come with me peacefully downtown and you can turn yourself in, or we can do this the hard way."

"You'd better have a warrant on you, buddy, otherwise," Fredrickson pointed a meaty finger in my face. "This is going to get ugly, fast. The nerve of you, accusing me! I was in Toledo, for goodness' sake."

As if he could intimidate me. "You and Thompson were business partners. When he left the organization, you went out of business. What better way to get back at him for ruining your life then by robbing his flat?"

"For your information, we decided together to call it quits and go our separate ways. And I'm making twice what I was with my new investments."

"It must help, having a little extra cash from the robbery, huh?"

Fredrickson glowered. "I don't believe this. You really beat all."

"So you admit it?"

"I'm not admitting anything." He pulled out his cell phone and fingered the buttons. "Do you have a warrant or not, Clue?"

I raised an eyebrow. He really wanted to play this game? "No. I can't get those, and it would involve breaking my client's confidentiality agreement anyway."

"Then I'm calling the police."

* * *

"We're getting tired of dealing with you, Clue." Lieutenant Gregg Warren rubbed his thick strawberry blond crew cut with one hand. "I can't decide if you're a complete imbecile, or just plain mule-headed. Lucky for you, Fredrickson decided not to press charges, otherwise you'd be looking at 'trespassing' and 'harassment'."

Just my luck I'd get this guy. The brass who would ordinarily be giving me this talk was out of the office, leaving the crabby Homicide Lieutenant as next in line to do the job. Best I could tell, Warren couldn't stand me. "Look, Lieutenant, it isn't my fault that I hit a red herring or two."

"Hit a red herring or two!" Warren's icy blue eyes mocked me. "You dug up enough to open your own fish market. And what you didn't stumble on, you made up. Your methods are sloppy, disgraceful, not to mention outright illegal half the time. It's a wonder you didn't get your license yanked and your rear planted in county lockup months ago. At this rate, you may yet manage both."

I snorted. "If you're quite finished, I have a case to investigate."

"Since no charges were filed, there isn't much to stop you, I'm afraid." Warren leaned back in his office chair, his thick mustache accentuating his frown. "But, by golly, stay off private property without proper permission! Next time, you might not be so lucky."

"I'll keep that in mind, Lieutenant, and have a wonderful day." I snatched up my black Stetson from the desk and left his office. The grump. As I stepped out of the station into daylight, Bob Thompson, my client, approached me.

"What on earth do you think you're doing?" he shouted.

"A bit of a misunderstanding, that's all."

Thompson's plump face reddened as he glared down at me. "You accused one of my closest friends, numb-skull! Did it ever occur to you that the guy was in another state at the time of the crime?"

"A slight oversight on my part. My apologies."

Thompson shook his head as aggravation filled his bloodshot eyes. "If anything, you are a master of the understatement."

"I am truly sorry about the misunderstanding, Mr. Thompson. I'll review my notes before continuing the investigation."

"Add this to your notes, Colombo." Thompson stuck his finger in my chest. "You're fired."

I squeezed my eyes shut in disbelief. "What?" I opened them again, but Thompson was already gone. I couldn't believe this. Out of the fourteen cases I had taken in my short career, I had been fired from all of them. Not exactly what you would call a spotless record. I trudged back to my office. Maybe I should have taken more criminology courses before I left college.

Of course, my main problem was probably disorganization. After all, I hardly had time to keep track of the three-hundred-and-twenty some-odd sticky notes and take-out napkins that comprised my case notes. Not to mention my desk drawers, which were filled with enough dead pens and candy wrappers to blanket Seattle twice.

The clanging bells of the nearby train station jolted me out of my reverie. I glanced up at the King Station clock tower. Nearly seven in the morning. I had a whole day ahead of me, and basically nothing to do with it. I might as well catch up on sleep.

At last, I reached the brick building where my combination apartment and office were located. My career was such a cliché. Sam Spade, Nick Carter, Richard Diamond, Johnny Dollar. The only difference between them and me was that they had good reputations.

I slammed my door shut, locked it, and threw my trench coat on the worn office chair, right on top of an old Dick Tracy comic. Who was I kidding? Maybe my father was right. How could I expect to be a decent private investigator with a name like Noah Clue?

I hung my Stetson, a gift from my Uncle Denby, on a nail in the wall beside my bed. I owed a lot to the old Texas rancher. Without his continued help, I wouldn't even be able to afford this place. Worse yet, I'd still be stuck in Decatur, Texas with my lunatic parents. Would he be disappointed if he knew how things were going for me right now? Probably.

After removing all but one bullet from my antique Smith and Wesson Model .38 Special, I ensured the engagement of the safety, and set it in my bedside drawer. My Washington state concealed weapon training taught me to remove all ammunition for safety, but my homegrown Texas training told me that life didn't always give you a chance to load. I knew how to make one shot count. As my Uncle Denby had always said, "Semi-automatics are only for people who miss."

My hat, gun, vintage answering machine, and manual typewriter were the only things to my name worth anything to me, all gifts from the relatives who *did* love me.

I rolled into bed. The hard mattress greeted me, with its usual gaping depression in the middle just waiting to swallow me up. I'm sure Spade bought a new mattress once in a while. Not me. The best I could manage was the leftovers at the consignment shop—the junk they couldn't sell to anyone else.

At least I didn't have rats crawling all over the place, although that was probably because no self-respecting rodent would be caught dead in this dump. The bedside clock flashed 6:54 a.m. in red, digital numbers. I rolled over to try and get some rest.

I hadn't been lying there long when a knock startled me out of bed. A blinking neon hotel sign outside my window pierced the darkness. I dragged myself to the door, unbolted it, and opened it a crack. "Yes?"

A gorgeous, five-foot-something brunette stood on the other side, purse clutched in both hands. "Detective Noah Clue?"

I opened the door wider to admit the dame. "Yes, that's me. Can I help you? Come in."

She strode past me and sat down in one of the chairs in front of my desk. "My name is Lola Sterling. I need help." She adjusted her feather boa.

"Of course." I threw my hat, coat, and comic book off my office chair and took a seat. "What can I do for you?"

"Oh, Mr. Clue, it was horrible. Someone murdered my fiancé!"

"I am so sorry to hear that."

"I have come to hire you." Lola set a stack of cash on the table. "Find the killer, and I'll give you a handsome reward." She sniffed back tears. "I know you can do it. I've heard so much about you."

I did a double-take. "Come again?"

"Yes. You're one of the most brilliant detective minds in the country." She dabbed at her eyes with a lace handkerchief.

My mind raced. Murder. Rich, single, female victim. Everything looked so much like a movie. Either this was some sort of sick prank, or I was dreaming.

Which would explain why everything was in black and white, and why my desk was clean.

My eyes popped open, and I sat up in bed. There was my hat and trench coat, right where I had left them on my office chair. That had to be one of the worst dreams to date. I'd rather have nightmares about getting eaten than those master detective fantasies. They only made my current reality that much more painful. At least, in those monster dreams, you can wake up and find comfort in the fact you're still breathing. Often halfway to hyperventilation, sure, but still breathing.

It was obvious that my office needed organization if I were to have any chance of success. So far, my methods were too scattered. I got out of bed, pulled a Seattle area yellow pages off the bookshelf, and flipped to the "secretarial services" listing. I checked my watch. Eight-thirty in the morning. Everyone should be open.

I skimmed the page, bypassing anything with a flashy ad, an automatic tip-off to me that they were too expensive for my budget. Freda's Secretaries looked just about right.

I grabbed the receiver off my outdated rotary phone and dialed the number. A woman with a thick southern accent answered. "Hello. Freda's Secretaries. This is Freda."

"Hello, Freda, my name is Noah Clue. I'm a P.I, looking for a secretary to help me get organized and stay organized."

"Of course, darlin'. Did you have a specific price range in mind?"

"Say...thirty-five bucks a day?"

"Honey, you ain't gettin' a trained lizard for thirty-five."

I rubbed the back of my neck. "How low can I get away with?"

"Only one will work for less than seventy a day."

"How much?"

"Sixty-nine."

"I guess I'll have to rethink my options. Thanks anyway." I hung up the phone.

After trying about four other agencies to no avail, I plopped the yellow pages back on the cluttered shelf. Perhaps I'd have a better chance with the classifieds. I dug through my office drawers for a couple of quarters.

I retrieved a copy of the Seattle Times from the kiosk on the corner and returned to my office. I scanned through the careers section, and circled possible candidates. I had no sooner narrowed down the list to six entries than my phone rang. Maybe Freda had thought of someone else. I snatched it up. "This is Noah Clue."

"Where are you?" the voice demanded.

"Huh?" I paused. "Uhh, Pioneer Square neighborhood. Are you calling about the secretarial position?"

Silence. "Sure, let's go with that. How much are you paying?" Her voice sounded familiar, but I couldn't place it.

"Thirty-five bucks a day."

"Less than minimum wage. You really are broke."

I struggled to place that voice. "I'm sorry, who is this?"

"Eight years, and you can't remember your favorite cousin?"

No way. I held the earpiece closer, half wondering if I had mistaken the voice. "Dee?"

"That's me. I'm here in Seattle, trying to find you."

I snorted. "Favorite cousin? You're my only cousin." Her words sunk in. "Wait, why are you in Seattle? Did something happen to Uncle Denby?"

"No, he's fine. Actually, it was my father's idea." Her voice faltered. "See, ah...Dad cut me loose. Pushed me out of the nest, so to speak. He said thirty-three was too old to be living at home."

All these years, I'd assumed Dee had been living independently. "I thought you were working as the head secretary for his law firm."

"Yeah, for room, board, and stipend, until he told me enough was enough. And then he informed me that, until you succeeded as a P.I, I wouldn't see a dime of my inheritance."

I winced at the inheritance card. My father had made basically the same threat with me. Unlike him, my uncle meant well, but why did he have to saddle me with his bossy daughter? "So, what, you want to make sure I succeed?"

"That's right. I don't plan to be buying clothes off the rack at Goodwill for the rest of my life, thanks. So, what do you say?"

Given our turbulent history, why should I make it easy for her? I glanced down at the newspaper. "Well, I have a few other candidates to call first..."

Exasperation laced her voice. "Fine with me. You know, I was thinking of calling your mother. Bet she'd be real interested in how everything's going with you."

Oh great, blackmail. The last thing I needed was for my parents to learn of my latest failure. "Well, whaddaya know, the other five people aren't available for the job. You're hired."

Her tone turned congenial. "Excellent. Let me come by this afternoon, about 2:30, and we'll discuss the job in more detail."

I rattled off directions to my Jackson Street address before I hung up the phone.

I leaned back and looked around the office. Piles of papers and unopened seasoning packets covered every flat surface, including the floor by my bed and the desk. My cousin would kill me when she saw this mess. I grabbed my last three plastic trash bags and started filling them. When I ran out of room, I tossed the remainder of the notes and napkins into the file cabinet and called it good. The plastic bags barely fit under my bed. I scurried to arrange my sheets and blankets to cover the opening—my tried and true method of cleaning.

The arranged time came and went, with no sign of Dee. I tried her phone, and got the message. I hung up before the beep. She was probably on the road. The one-way signs in downtown could drive anyone out of their minds.

Just around three, a knock sounded. I left my pacing spot by the window and threw open the door. "When you start a new job, it is courteous to show up on time!"

The delivery guy blinked. "What new job?"

My shoulders dropped. "Never mind. I thought you were someone else."

"Uh huh. Package for a Mr. Morris."

Couldn't these people read? My irritation spilled out. "I don't know what it is with your company. For the hundredth and first time, Morris lives in three-oh-five." I pointed to the numbers on my door. "This is two-oh-five."

"Of course. My apologies." The delivery guy waved and headed for the staircase.

I shut the door and shook my head. Somehow, I had become an expert at making a complete idiot of myself.

A few minutes later, I answered another knock and opened the door to my cousin. Her nut brown hair had been pulled back in a tight ponytail, except for that one surly curl falling over her forehead like it always had. I hardly recognized her in her dark blue business suit. She carried a black briefcase in one hand, and her matching purse in the other.

It irked me to notice that she still had half-an-inch on my height despite her flats. "You're late."

Dee's brown eyes held some resentment. "I take it you don't drive much, Noah."

"Why bother? The Union Station bus stop is practically right across the street." She didn't need to know that I couldn't afford to replace my old car when it died two years before. I'd never enjoyed driving in Seattle anyhow.

"That would explain why you didn't bother to tell me about the dismal parking around here. I had to drive in circles for the past half hour before I could find something." Dee looked around me. "So, this is your office."

"And apartment." I stepped aside. "Come in."

She set her briefcase on one of the chairs in front of my desk and peered out the front window. A strip of dust streaked the sleeve of her tailored jacket. She brushed it off in distaste.

What happened to the carefree jeans-loving girl who gave as much thought to dust as she did the dangers of climbing huge trees or jumping desert ravines? In my mind's eye I could still see her triumphant dirt-streaked face after she'd beaten me in a horse race across the back acreage of Uncle Denby's Marietta, Texas ranch when we were in our teens.

Her voice dragged me into the present. "What exactly is involved in being your assistant?"

"Uhh...helping me stay organized while I'm working on my cases. Running errands. Managing the office while I'm gone."

She peered into my adjacent bedroom and kitchenette, and nodded at the cut-off point between there and my office. "My responsibility stops at that threshold. I'm not a maid."

"Of course."

She crossed the room to stand in front of the file cabinets. "How much organization are we talking about?"

"I...uh..." I stammered.

Dee opened the file cabinet drawer and clicked her tongue. "You bachelors are all alike. No wonder you're desperate." She pulled a handful of scribbled sticky notes out of the drawer and held them up. "Don't you have a computer, Noah?"

"Just my typewriter."

"Yeah, I see that," she mocked. "Isn't that the one my dad gave you when you ran off to college?"

"It sure is." I patted the faithful Royal Heritage manual typewriter. "But it needs a new ribbon."

"What do you have against modern technology? Typewriters are so old school." Dee crossed into my bedroom.

As if she didn't remember. I scowled, "Typewriters don't eat a week's worth of research."

She rolled her eyes. "That was high school. You're still harping on that?" Dee lifted my bed covers and pointed to the hidden bags. "At least you've started using containers. That's an improvement, Noah. Work hours?"

I sat down in my office chair and leaned back. "Eight a.m. to six p.m, Monday through Friday."

"What does your client base look like now?"

I sighed. "Nonexistent."

"You really do need the help." Dee gestured to my desk chair. "May I?"

"Of course." I surrendered my spot. My new assistant took a seat and began searching through the drawers. "They're empty. You cleaned them out before I came."

She was good. I shrugged. "Guilty as charged. I didn't have much worth keeping."

"Client history?"

"Only fourteen cases so far."

Dee quirked her lips. "You got fired from all of them."

I stared at her. "How do you know?"

"You order Chinese takeout from Hot Wok almost every night. You must not have much money to go that cheap."

Her instincts always had been uncanny. "Okay, but how did you know about the food?"

"You have soy sauce stains all over your desk. Plus a lone branded chopstick here." Dee grabbed the object from under my desk and held it up.

My cousin had quite the observation skills. I grinned to myself. With her in charge of keeping my case notes organized, I wouldn't hit a red herring ever again.

2

I Get Organized

I tossed the new typewriter ribbon on the desk. How my cousin had managed to rope me into going to the office store for her, I will never know.

"Thank you." Dee installed the ribbon in my typewriter. "How many of those old case notes do you need, Noah?"

I opened the file cabinet drawer and began digging through. "You know something? I might as well toss all these. Start new."

Without a glance, Dee held up the recycle bin, and I tossed the drawer's contents in. She set aside the bin, loaded a piece of blank paper into the typewriter, and began typing.

I studied my newly-organized office. My secretary certainly worked fast. Every surface had been cleared, dusted, and decorated with office equipment, most of which I had never seen before in my life. A black combination printer/fax machine sat on a stand near the window. "Where'd you get all this stuff, Dee?"

"Some you had stashed around here. Most of it I brought from my apartment. I habitually stock up to avoid extra trips to the office supply store. It's all in boxes now anyway."

I fiddled with the stack of my business cards that Dee had placed in a brass holder. "I'm impressed."

"Glad you like it." Dee pulled the paper out of the typewriter and handed it to me. "Here's a template for how you should type out case notes. Judging from the previous state of your office, I figured you'd need it."

I scanned the page, determined to quell my rising frustration. Dee was already acting like she ran the place. Yeah, she had experience in this sort of thing, but I was the P.I.

Then again, I didn't have any choice. Last thing I needed was for her to call Uncle Denby and my parents to reveal what a dismal wreck I'd made of being a private investigator. Not to mention, there probably wasn't another secretary in Seattle who would work for the low wages I could offer, whereas my cousin had offered her services for free.

"Yeah, great." I handed the paper back to Dee.

She slipped it into a thin plastic cover and placed it in the center drawer of my desk. "It's right here when you need it."

This half of my place looked quite professional. "Anyway, I really like what you've done with the office."

Dee shrugged. "First impressions are important. Not many people will want to hire a P.I. with a messy office."

"Well, I'm sure this all will help business."

"Not with your living quarters the way they are."

I squared my shoulders, determined to hold my ground against Dee's overbearing interference. "Pardon?"

Dee pointed to my bedroom. "It's unsightly. You'll need to either clean it up or put a curtain across the doorway. Same with the kitchenette, though I'd highly recommend cleaning there. Fresh coffee tends to please potential clients."

I snorted. "I don't recall signing up for Dee's School of Business."

My cousin narrowed her gaze. "Look, do you want help or not?"

"Yes. And no." I crossed my arms. "I'm perfectly capable of holding my own around here."

"Oh, yeah, I can see that," She leaned back in the chair, her hands behind her head. Sarcasm laced her voice. "I'm impressed by your extensive client base, Noah. And you must be so respected by your peers."

I hated her condescending tone. "Well, there's no need to get nasty about it."

Dee stood. "Let me put it this way, Noah. If you want to survive in this business—in any business for that matter—there are certain things you have to do. Ask anyone successful."

As much as I hated to admit it, I couldn't argue with that.

Dee looked at her watch. "Well, it's six. I'd best be going." She picked up her briefcase and purse, and headed for the door. "Goodnight, Noah."

I handed her my spare apartment key. "Eight o'clock Monday?"

Dee stopped and looked over her shoulder. A smirk crossed her face as she took the key. "See you then."

I shut the door and surveyed my orderly office. I could really get used to this. I could even get used to Dee. She'd always been bossy as a kid, but I'd survived every summer of my childhood with her. I could survive this, too.

First things, first. I jury-rigged rope and a set of tan flat sheets across the entryway to my bedroom. After surveying the effect, I decided to leave the make-shift curtains closed. There was no real sense in exposing my bedroom to the world.

I turned my attention to cleaning up the kitchenette. Just as I started washing the dishes, a knock sounded at the door. I muttered a few words about Murphy's Law, dried my hands on the towel, and unlatched the door.

My best friend, David Sigfeld, leaned against the door frame. His short black hair stood at weird angles, as if he'd slept on his head. "What took you so long?" He glared at the towel draped over my shoulder. Amusement twinkled within his dark blue eyes. "You're washing dishes?"

"Yeah, so I decided to tidy up a little."

He raised his bushy eyebrows, a dead giveaway of his Italian roots. "O-kay. Reception's lousy at my place. Mind if I watch the game on your TV?"

"Sure, but I guarantee nothing." I stepped aside to let him in. I never felt inferior around my friend, perhaps because he was one of the few people I knew that wasn't taller than me.

David remained in the doorway, his mouth hanging open.

I waved my hand in front of his face to get his attention. "Base to Sigfeld. Come in Sigfeld."

"A *little* cleaning?" His gaze darted around.

"Oh, that." I turned around to survey the space. "My secretary set up the office."

He snorted. "Man, you have a secretary, too?"

"Uhh, yeah."

"When did you get so fancy? Is she hot?"

I smirked. "Not by your standards, Mr. Bogart." I pointed to my bedroom. "TV's in there."

"Thanks." David pushed the makeshift curtains aside, revealing my unmade bed. "Well, at least some things stay the same." He tucked one of the curtains behind the TV stand to keep it pinned back, flipped on the television, and began adjusting the antenna. "I tell you, digital TV is such a headache, but I refuse to pay for cable. Why didn't they just leave analog in place?"

"I still say money exchanged hands in that deal." I reached into the dishwater and pulled out one of the bright orange plates I'd purchased from Goodwill years ago.

My friend brushed something from the edge of my bed. "So, what possessed you to clean up your apartment?"

"It's good for business."

He narrowed his eyes. "Says who?"

"My secretary, if you must know." I dumped the container of dirty plastic utensils into the dishwater. "She said that it reflected on my reputation, or something along those lines."

David tisked. "Noah, I think you fail to understand the definition of 'bachelor'."

"I understand it perfectly. Just a fancy term for single."

He shook his head. "No, 'bachelor' means that women don't tell you what to do."

"Look." I stuck my head around the edge of the tan curtains to make eye-contact with him. "For one, she's my cousin."

My friend grunted. "Oh, like that makes a difference."

I cleared my throat. "Two, I kinda need the help. Being fired from every case you've ever taken isn't exactly an accomplishment."

He gave me an incredulous look. "Seriously, man, I keep telling you to use the resources you have at your fingertips."

"Like what?"

"Remember Sammi Keppler from college? You helped her pass a psychology final?"

I tried to think back, but I couldn't really place the name. "David, I tutored so many people. I can't keep track of them all."

"Well, anyway, she never forgot it. She works for SPD as a forensics tech now. I go to game night at her house the third

Tuesday of every month." He pointed at me. "The same game night you've been turning down invitations to for the past year."

I shrugged it off. "I don't really have the time for that." My ears burned. "Anyway, it feels wrong to ask for favors from someone just because I helped them pass some test."

"It's more of a strategic friendship. Goes both ways, anyhow." He nodded to my television. "I drop in to watch the game, you hang out at my place for movie night."

I couldn't imagine having to rely on other people to do my work for me. "I just can't, David. I appreciate the thought, but I have to stand on my own two feet."

"Have it your way." David turned up the television volume. The excessive stutter in the announcer's voice indicated a not-so-clear signal. My friend blew a raspberry, got up, and began adjusting the antenna again.

"Sorry, I told you no guarantees." I returned to the sink and sloshed my hand through the dingy, lukewarm water to stir up more suds. The soap had virtually vanished by this time.

David patted the television. "Finally. I got a signal that doesn't cut out every ten seconds." He paused. "Cuts out every twenty seconds, instead. Big improvement."

"Try muting it and just watch the plays. The lapses don't really affect the picture much."

"Good idea."

Another knock at my door. "Oh, good grief." I proceeded to dry my hands on the now-crusty towel.

David came out of the bedroom. "I'll get the door. It's probably for me anyways."

"How's that?"

He proceeded to open the door and converse with the guest. The smell of pepperoni answered my question to the person's identity.

Finally, my friend shut the door and set two large pizzas on my desk. "Hungry?"

"I'm hoping that was on your tab."

David scoffed. "Like I'd stick you with the bill."

"You did at Anchovies & Olives."

"That was two months ago." David arranged the complementary napkins. "Pepperoni, olives, and mushrooms, just like you like it."

"I hate mushrooms." Strange for David to forget something like that. He always remembered everything. Literally.

He opened the box and pulled out a slice. "I'm just messing with you, Noah. It's the usual pepperoni, olives, and sausage." He bit into the crust side first. "You're really too gullible."

I plucked a napkin off the desk, and served myself. I glanced over at David. "You're dropping stuff on my floor."

"Oh, um..." He looked down. "I'll wipe that up in a sec." He finished off his pizza slice and licked his fingers. "I can't stand for my apartment to be clean. It would totally ruin my image as a broke, single computer nerd."

"Hopefully by changing my image, I won't be broke for long."

"Don't count on it."

I glowered at the tan sheet curtains. "Those really do look tacky, don't they?"

David raised an eyebrow. "You're working out of a low-end apartment on the fringe of the Stadium district. What were you expecting exactly?"

"I don't know. Something that makes this place look less like a residence, and more like an office." I chewed my pizza thoughtfully.

"Well, if you want to go that route, there's a weekly flea market up in Fremont on Sunday. You could probably find a good set of proper curtains there."

I frowned. "How much money is involved?"

"I'd say, bring a twenty. I'll cover lunch."

Sunday, March 14

The sounds of live bluegrass mingled with the chatter of excited visitors as David and I strolled along the Fremont Sunday Market. The few scattered rain clouds did little to dampen spirits. I gnawed on my piece of apple cinnamon fry bread and scanned the white tents for anything resembling curtains. David, meanwhile, seemed intent on exploring every single item for sale in the whole market.

"Hey, Noah, check these out." David waved me over to a furniture booth. "I've been needing a new occasional table for my apartment, after my brother's Bullmastiff broke the last one."

I remembered that afternoon. A laser pointer, a huge dog, three bored guys, and insufficient caffeine to get our brains going. "That dog was all bull, no mastiff."

"Not a bad table. Sturdy, not too much wear." David picked up the occasional table and turned it over. "Thirty-eight bucks. Shoot, for solid walnut?" He knocked on the underside. "I'll take it." He hiked it over his shoulder.

I studied a set of wooden, wicker-top footstools. "These don't look too comfy, do they?"

David set his prize down and pushed on the top of one of the ottomans. "It's solid enough. These might go nicely with the table."

"Solid or not, I wouldn't want to rest my feet on these. Super uncomfortable."

"Dude, that's what they invented cushions for." David searched the ottoman for a price tag. "Thirty bucks a piece. Eh, I'll buy one. I've got enough pillows around, I can just throw one on top."

"With a design like that, you'd think they would come with cushions already attached."

"Well, you know how designers are." He twirled a finger in the air. "Form over function." He picked up the footstool with one hand, and the table with the other. "I'll go pay for these. Maybe you can find some curtains here."

"Maybe." I scanned the booth and caught sight of Bob Thompson, my former client, talking to another customer. This was his booth? I backed towards the entrance. "On second thought, I'll...be over at the next tent."

"Hmm?" David looked at Thompson, and then back at me. "Oh, okay, suit yourself."

I ducked into the next tent and immersed myself in the collection of antique books. Caressing the worn leather and cloth bindings, I searched for any familiar names or titles. I loved old hardbacks, a passion I shared with my Aunt Elizabeth, Dee's mother.

The young lady running the booth approached me. "See anything you like?" Her short copper-colored hair bounced in tight ringlets as she looked from me to the books and back again.

"I'm not sure yet." I pulled a random book off the shelf and thumbed through it. "I always expect to find some great masterpiece, but honestly, I usually only find first editions that weren't deemed worthy of a reprint."

"Well, this one's particularly interesting." The lady took down a beige hardback, with an image of a broken chain on the spine. "*Paris Underground* by Etta Shiber. This is a true story published during World War II, by a woman who was involved in smuggling Allied airmen out of Nazi-occupied France. It's a first edition, so it has some interesting notes inside the cover about war time paper rations, et cetera."

I took the book. "Interesting. I studied World War II history a bit back in college."

"Well, I'll tell you what—if you ever happen across a book called *Lest They Die* by this author, buy it." Her emerald green eyes sparkled. "That's the true first edition of this book, but she used some of the real names. When she realized that the Gestapo could use it as evidence against her friends, the publisher stopped printing and destroyed all the copies they could find, but a few slipped past. They're actually pretty rare, but no one realizes it."

"Huh." I handed the book back. "I'll bear that in mind."

"Table acquired!" David entered the tent, carrying his new furniture. "So, what's with the harried bug out, anyway?"

I cleared my throat. "Former client."

David's eyes expressed understanding. "Ahh."

I tilted my head and started at my friend. "Do you need to find a wagon or something for those?"

"Nah, they're pretty light." David adjusted the position of the table slightly. He turned to the lady running the booth. "Say, do you have curtains here?"

She shook her head. "Afraid not. I think there's some at a tent on the other side, down that way a little." She pointed towards the right. "You could check there."

"Thanks." My eyes fell on a telltale black case. "Say, what's this?" I bent down and opened it, revealing a Royal Quiet De Luxe typewriter.

"It's just a manual, I'm afraid," the lady replied. "I've had that thing in the booth for two months, and no one has wanted it."

I tapped a couple of keys. "It's in great shape."

"The ribbon is worn out, I'm afraid, and I don't know where you'd even get one now." The lady shrugged. "But it makes for a nice museum piece."

"Museum piece my foot! I still use these." I tapped the space bar until the bell sounded, and then slid the carriage back.

The idea seemed novel to the booth lady. "You actually *use* manual typewriters?"

"Yeah." I knelt down and lifted the typewriter out of its case. "No electricity, no cables, no software glitches eating your research. They just work." I set it down again.

"I suppose so." She leaned to look over my shoulder. "But, I mean, how do you even erase on them? If you make a mistake, you have to start over, right?"

"Not necessarily." I tapped the Royal logo to open the top, and then pointed to the worn out ribbon. "These are pretty standard, and you can buy it with a strip of correction tape on the upper half. And then, this switch in the front..." I flicked the lever to the right, "...that will change where the key strikes the ribbon, so you can erase things."

David sniggered. "And I thought I was a nerd."

I closed the top on the typewriter and glared at my friend. "I just really love analog technology, that's all."

"Well, it looks like this old typewriter just found a new home." The booth lady's voice held a hint of begging. "Like I said, I've been trying to sell this thing for months. How's five bucks sound?"

I gingerly closed the typewriter into its case. "Sold."

3

I Take On A New Case

Monday, March 15

"Noah, you'd better not still be in bed."

I groaned and rolled over. "I'm not, mother."

"Excuse me?" My mother's voice morphed into Dee's.

I rubbed my eyes and glanced at the clock on my bedside table. "Sorry. I'm still half asleep."

"Well, are you?" Her impatient voice floated through my new, pale gold drapes.

My eyes tried to focus on reality. "Am I what?"

"Still in bed?"

I grumbled and got up. "Not anymore."

Dee persisted. "So you *were* in bed."

A groan escaped me. "Yes." I proceeded to get dressed.

"I would think that, since you set the daily opening time, you'd abide by it." Her voice grated against my nerves.

I fastened the top button on my shirt and slid open the curtains. The tension rod David suggested really worked wonders here. "I was tired, okay?"

She stood with her hands on her hips. "What time did you get to bed, anyway?"

I dropped into my office chair, still rubbing my eyes. "Oh, midnight, one, somewhere around there." I looked up at Dee. "I suppose you want to set a bedtime for me now, too?"

"You should be old enough to set one of your own." She turned towards the kitchenette. "I'll start the coffee."

I yawned. "You might consider not staying the whole day. Business is usually pretty slow around here."

"Won't be for long," Dee replied from the other room. "You're going to be placing a few ads today. One in the Times, another in the yellow pages, and a third in an online directory."

I sat up. "Are you kidding? Those are expensive. I don't have the money for that sort of thing!"

"I'm perfectly aware of that, Noah." Dee came out of the kitchenette, munching on a muffin.

My stomach roared and I licked my lips.

She sighed and nodded towards the kitchen. "I brought them. They're on the counter."

"Thanks." I got up and proceeded to retrieve my breakfast. Hopefully she'd gotten some with chocolate chips.

"Anyhow, I'm paying for the ads. At least until you have enough to cover them yourself."

I grabbed a muffin from the plate and peeled away the paper liner. "What about my not-so-spotless track record?"

"They don't ask, you don't tell. You're starting over, remember?"

Made sense. "Right. Go for it, then." I opened my mouth to take a bite of muffin.

"Oh, I'm not the one placing the ads, Noah. You are."

I stopped mid-bite and peered around the corner at Dee. "I thought you were my secretary."

"Very well." She sat down and loaded a fresh piece of paper into my typewriter.

"Thank you." My lips brushed the edge of the muffin.

"You'll have to dictate since I'm only typing for you."

I lowered the muffin. "Doesn't the secretary usually do all the composing for her boss?"

My cousin's stubborn streak flashed in her eyes. "Nope. She usually only does the typing for him." Her attitude mocked me. "I'm waiting, Boss."

I groaned in defeat. I hadn't even eaten yet, and she expected me to dictate an advertisement for the Times. "Um...I really don't know where to start."

"Try your name."

"Fine. Noah Oswald Clue, P.I." I dared to bite the muffin. Its grainy texture sucked the moisture out of my mouth, making it impossible to swallow. I coughed violently.

"Noah, put down the muffin."

I tossed the offending object into the trashcan and gulped down some coffee. "Dee, sawdust is not edible. You should have learned that by now."

She rolled her eyes. "Those happen to be my favorite brand of organic bran muffins."

"The paper liners would have tasted better." I dug out a half box of pastries from the back of the fridge and slid them onto a plate.

"Can we get back to the ad?"

I helped myself to a jelly donut before setting the plate on my desk. "Fine. How about 'A standard in excellence?'"

Dee pulled away from the typewriter. "This is an advertisement, not a fantasy story."

"Oh, ha ha." I resisted the urge to pitch my jelly donut at her, deeming it a waste of a perfectly good pastry. "Can you do better?"

"Probably." She sat silent for a few moments. "Well, try again."

I held up a finger and took a large bite of my donut. The jelly filling proved harder to swallow than I had expected. "Move over, Joe Friday?" I mumbled.

She glared at me. "Not even."

"Then, I'm fresh out of ideas."

Dee shrugged.

My cousin's behavior infuriated me. Why wouldn't she give me a hand? A long-forgotten quarrel came to mind. I sighed. "Can you please help me, Dee?"

"Well, I thought you'd never ask." Her mouth curved into a smile. "How about 'Solving every case with first-class service'?"

I pondered her suggestion. "Not bad. But can I really say that?"

Determination glinted in her eyes. "Oh, you can be sure you'll be giving them first-class service from now on, Noah."

I got the hint. I had to completely change my approach if I wanted to succeed. "Anything else?"

"Contact info and rates."

"Use the information on my card. That should work well enough."

"Okie-dokie." Dee pulled a card from the top of the stack and resumed typing.

Within half an hour, we had placed ads in several online directories, the Times, the Seattle area yellow pages, and a free classifieds paper for good measure.

Dee insisted on staying the entire day, so I broke out the Uno deck. With my plate of pastries nearby and a fresh cup of coffee, I felt in good form. Having my cousin here took me back to our summer vacations at Uncle Denby's ranch. Life seemed so simple back then.

"That's two games for me, two for you." Dee added a line to our tally sheet. "This one decides the tournament." She slapped the shuffled deck in front of me. "Your deal."

"I dealt last time."

"No, I did. And I know that, because the top card turned out to be wild, and you got to pick the color. Your deal."

"Fine." I snatched up the deck and dealt each of us seven cards.

Someone knocked at my door. Dee shifted into her secretarial role and answered it.

A middle-aged African-American man in a black business suit and striped tie stepped inside. "I'm looking for Noah Clue."

I tossed my cards face down on the desk and stood. Those online directories sure worked fast. "That would be me." I shook hands with the newcomer. He might have been a tall, impressive fellow if he wasn't so hunched over.

"Christopher Reilly, senior vice president of Sanford James Fine Furnishings." Short, tight curls of salt-and-pepper hair framed his high forehead. "I wish to hire your services."

Dee slipped behind me and whisked the Uno cards into one of the desk drawers.

"Of course." I motioned to the chair in front of the desk. "Have a seat. Would you like some coffee?"

"Yes, thank you. Black, no sugar."

Dee strode into the kitchenette. I slid my typewriter aside and took my place behind the desk. "So, tell me what I can do for you today, Mr. Reilly."

The businessman sat down. "My company is an importer of the finest home furnishings and decor. We have a showroom in the Seattle Design Center on Sixth Avenue South. You should check it out. Anyhow, several of our company trucks were recently hijacked, and we have lost quite a bit of valuable merchandise."

Dee handed Reilly his cup of coffee and went back to the kitchen. He thanked her before continuing. "I need you to figure out who is responsible for these hijackings, and where our goods have gone."

"How many trucks are we talking about, and how much is the missing product worth?" I opened the top drawer, pulled out a pad of paper, and began taking notes.

"Four trucks hauling about four hundred and eighty-six thousand dollars' worth of merchandise, coming from our warehouses in Portland."

I couldn't hold back my whistle. "That's quite a loss. Do the police have any leads?"

Reilly gave a weary shake of his head. "No cops. The last thing we need is for this to hit the news. Our designer clientele could lose confidence in us." He leaned forward. "We have another large shipment due in less than two weeks. I'm willing to pay your fifty dollar hourly rate to get to the bottom of this."

Dee nodded at me from the kitchenette doorway.

I took a breath. "All right. We'll need more details to get started: where the merchandise was headed, where the trucks were hijacked, and what specific products were stolen."

"Right. As I said, these shipments were coming from our Portland warehouses, headed for Sanford James showrooms in this area. I have copies of the manifests and the hijacking details." He patted the pockets of his suit, and then reached inside his jacket. "Ah, here they are." As he unfolded the papers, confusion washed across his face. "I could have sworn..." He shuffled through the pages before handing them to me. "I must have left some of the information behind. I'll have to call my office to have the specifics of the hijackings faxed over. Organization is not my gift." He flipped open his phone and dialed.

I glanced through the papers. Each page was filled with lines of numbers accompanying what looked like various abbreviations for items. I'd need some kind of translation guide to convert this into readable English.

Reilly shut his phone and gave me a weak smile. "I'm so sorry. I'll have to get that other information to you later."

"Not a problem," I responded. "Could you possibly help me decipher the descriptions of the stolen items?"

He cleared his throat and took the papers from me. "Sure. This could take a while, if you don't mind."

"My time is yours, Mr. Reilly." I held up the plate of pastries. "Would you like one?"

"Yes, thank you." Reilly reached for an éclair.

Dee stopped him. "You probably don't want that one, sir. It has a crème filling."

"Oh." He selected a Danish instead. "How did you know that I couldn't have cream?"

"When I brought your coffee to you, it was black. Now, it is light brown, which means you added your own creamer. A common reason for that would be that you either had an aversion or intolerance to milk."

Reilly looked down at his coffee, then back up at Dee in amazement. He smiled. "Excellent observation skills, my dear. I am, indeed, lactose intolerant."

Wow. My cousin was sharp.

After about an hour of manifest translation, we narrowed the stolen items to dressers, dining room sets, and living room furniture. Reilly headed out, promising to get the hijacking details to us as soon as possible. I stayed silent while his footsteps faded down the hallway. "So, Dee, what is your impression of the guy?"

She began gathering up the empty coffee mugs and used napkins. "Not sure yet. Want another cup?"

"Um, sure." I opened the center drawer of my desk and peeled the typed template from its place.

"Cream and sugar?"

"No, just black, please."

She grimaced. "How can you stand it? I can't stomach the bitterness of Seattle roast, myself."

"It's pretty good stuff once you're used to it. Strong, too. I fall asleep with the cheap brands. It's the one thing I splurge on."

Dee set the coffee in front of me and retreated to the kitchen.

I took a sip and began to type out my notes. "Apart from Mr. Reilly, do you have any ideas about the case?"

"Can't say that I do. Not enough information, yet."

I glanced up at Dee, who stood at the sink washing out the used mugs. "I thought you said you weren't going to be a maid."

She dried the mugs and set them in the cabinet. "I'm not. But keeping the office and kitchenette clean during office hours is part of my job. You'll need to be able to focus on solving the case."

"I see. Thank you." I scanned through the manifest pages again, setting them on the desk. "Dee, could you start a file on this case?"

"Sure thing." My cousin wiped her hands on a towel and crossed the room to stand in front of the file cabinets. "Do you want it filed under 'Reilly, Christopher' or 'Sanford James?'"

"Well, 'Reilly' is a little easier for me to remember."

"Good call." She pulled a new file out of the back of the top drawer, labeled the tab, and set it in front of me. "You'll want to keep both the typed and written versions of your notes, just in case of a transcription error."

I nodded and began reading through my handwritten notes again. "Four-hundred eighty-six thousand dollars. Must be one doozy of an apartment they're furnishing." I took another sip of coffee. "Perhaps we should start with the product itself. He said 'fine home furnishings and decor'. Does he mean 'fine' in context of appearance, or price?"

"I would assume price, though we'd best look it up." Dee pulled a laptop out of her briefcase and flipped it on.

I stared at her. "You have a computer?"

She smirked at me. "Yes, and you stick to your typewriter, Mr. Spade. This baby's for my personal use only."

"Good, I hate those things."

"I know. Also..." She held the computer, turned in a complete circle, and walked toward the back wall. "...you don't have the slightest hint of Wi-Fi up here."

"My reception is lousy for just about everything, actually. At least I get radio."

Dee sighed. "There's a coffee shop on the corner. They'll have Wi-Fi, so I'm going to hike down there and dig up what I can."

"Okie-dokie."

Dee tucked her precious laptop into her briefcase and marched out, leaving the door open behind her.

Grateful for the quiet, I reviewed the case notes for a third time. Reilly certainly hadn't given me much to work with. I'd have to wait to get the hijacking details. While I understood his not wanting his clientele to find out about the thefts, it seemed rather odd that Reilly didn't want to involve the police. Still, my orders were to keep this hush-hush. After my previous failures, I needed to make sure I handled this case correctly from the get-go.

By the time I had typed out my musings, Dee returned.

"Anything?"

My cousin set her briefcase down next to my desk. "From the looks of their website, their products are expensive. But…" She shrugged. "…no listed prices."

"Ouch. I wonder how companies can get away with those kinds of profit margins."

"It may also be a clever marketing ploy to get interested buyers into the showroom." She hung her purse over one shoulder. "In this case, it worked. Come on, Noah. We're going shopping."

4

I Buy Ugly Home Decor

I held the door open for Dee as we entered the Sanford James showroom in the Seattle Design Center. The air hissed as I let the door shut itself behind me. This place even smelled expensive.

I whistled. "Okay, we are officially out of my price range."

"Just pretend you have money." Dee straightened and plastered a smile on her face as a well-dressed salesman in his late thirties approached us. I envied his thick, red hair. At least he stood out in a crowd, unlike me.

"Welcome to Sanford James Fine Furnishings. I'm Ben." He loomed above me as he shook my hand. "And you are?"

I should have been better prepared. "Noah...Smith, and this is my fiancée, Dee."

My cousin shot me a dirty look, then turned back to Ben, still maintaining a cordial tone. "How do you do?"

"Excellent. What can I do for you today?"

Dee gave me a sly side glance. "We're looking to redecorate. You know how some guys can be. No decorating sense."

Ouch.

The salesman simpered. "Of course. What kind of space are we talking about? Apartment, single-family home...?"

"Small condo," I cut in.

Ben's smile held a hint of condescension. "I see. Small spaces are full of decorating potential. Are you looking at new furniture, or just changing out decor?"

I couldn't resist leading him on. "Both. We need to completely re-do a living room, kitchen, bedroom, and bathroom."

Ben's attitude shifted. I could practically see the commission check flashing in his eyes. He put a hand on my back and led us deeper into the showroom. "Let's start with the living room, then."

I scanned for price tags, but none were evident. We stopped in front of a model living room, complete with cardboard plasma screen TV. Ben moved to stand in front of us. "This is a part of our 'Simple Living' collection."

I failed to follow the logic behind the name, considering the glaring coffee brown and cream zebra striped upholstery.

"The cherry wood finish both accents and contrasts the furniture, and the glass elements tie everything in." Our salesperson gestured to the decorations atop the entertainment center. "Two old-world style figurines tie in with the cream on the upholstery, and the blue vase draws interest and stands out."

"If you ask me, the whole thing stands out," I whispered to Dee. The ottoman caught my eye. I lifted the rectangular overstuffed cushion, revealing a woven wicker top. This looked exactly like the one David had bought at the flea market.

Dee continued her conversation with the salesman. "Do you have anything more neutral?"

"Indeed. Follow me." Ben ushered my cousin through the furniture display to the other side of the showroom. I replaced the bulky ottoman cushion and trotted after them. A glaring electric lime and orange living room set caused images of John Travolta and disco balls to flash through my mind. To save my sanity, I rushed past the mock-up.

Ben stopped and diverted our attention to a simple white sofa and glass-top wooden coffee table. "This would go nicely with a set of light oak furniture."

Dee nodded. "It's nice."

I seized the opportunity to get her back for that jab at my sense of style. "Hon, this is exactly what we have now."

She shrugged. "Didn't recognize it without the pizza stains and cat hair." She faced the salesman. "Do you have anything a little darker? My fiancé has a Persian that sheds quite a bit."

Ooh, a double hit. I hated cats anyway, especially Persians, and Dee knew it.

Ben escorted us to the other side of the aisle. "We have this wine red set over here."

"Now, that is nice." Dee ran her hand along the back of the sofa. "May I try it?"

"Of course."

She took a seat, placing her feet on yet another large, rectangular ottoman. Could the cushions be customized?

"Very cozy," Dee crooned. "What do you think, sweetums?"

My mind raced to find a snappy comeback. "The couch is a little too sophisticated for my tastes." So much for a comeback. "But, I am interested in the ottoman."

Dee rolled her eyes. "This would outclass what we have now. Like I said, he has no sense of style," she complained to our guide.

"No," I insisted, hoping she'd catch my hint. "I *really* like this ottoman, hon."

The salesman interrupted. "I'm so sorry, but that's out of stock."

No wonder, since they were being fenced at a flea market.

My cousin got up and sauntered over to the mantle, where a pair of small, two-toned bronze elk stood. She picked one up and looked it over. "I love these statuettes. How much?"

"I'm sorry, ma'am. Those are out of stock, too."

"Oh," she pouted. "Do you have anything similar? I just love the rich colors."

Ben sighed. "I'm afraid all the shipments for statuettes, pots, and ottomans were delayed. We should be getting them next week."

"I see." Dee glanced at me and mouthed something.

Lip reading wasn't my strong point. I mouthed "what" back.

My cousin rolled her eyes, sidled over, and whispered in my ear. "We need those statuettes. Ask if you can buy the displays."

"I need to talk to you about the ottoman," I whispered back. "I have reason to believe it is important."

Dee sighed. "Get the price on all three, but remember: I'm not made of money."

"Understood." I turned my attention to Ben. "Sir, we're interested in the pair of statuettes and that burgundy wicker-top ottoman. What would you charge for them?"

The salesman blinked. "Well, uh, our sample sale isn't for two more weeks."

Dee subtly poked me in the side.

I caught her meaning. "We hate to be a bother, but we've got our hearts set on taking them home with us."

Ben looked at us, and then the three items. "I'd...have to ask a manager. Excuse me." He departed.

I turned to Dee. "What are you thinking?" I asked her just under my breath.

"We'll compare notes later," she whispered back. "But we need those statuettes. I'll pay for them."

"Got it."

A tall, thirty-something man in a black suit approached us. "I'm Frank, the showroom manager. What can I do for you?"

I pointed to the mantle. "My fiancée really likes those little statuettes, and I want that burgundy wicker-top ottoman. One of your sales associates, Ben, said that they are all out of stock."

"Ah yes. These are some of our more popular items."

I let his obvious fib slide by. "Would it be possible to purchase the display samples?"

"Well, if it is color you're after, I'd recommend the bookends on the desk over there. We have plenty of those available."

I stood my ground. "No, we really want these, and the ottoman."

Frank sighed and picked up the two statuettes. He pondered our request for a moment. "How does seventy-five a piece sound for these? The ottoman I can let go for one-twenty."

Yikes! So much for this plan. I glanced at Dee. To my surprise she nodded.

I hoped she didn't plan on having me pay her back anytime soon. Despite my anxiety, I forced a smile. "We'll take them."

"Good. Anything else?"

I shook my head. "Not at this point. I think we need to talk more and get a better idea of what we want."

The store manager perked up. "If you need help deciding, we do have design consultants available."

"We'll get back to you." I handed the statuettes to Dee, and picked up the ottoman. "Thank you very much."

As soon as Frank moved away from us, I quietly confronted my cousin. "You can't use your bank card without blowing our cover, so how are we going to pay for these?"

Dee calmly opened her purse and took out a wad of cash. "No worries, I've got it under control."

My cousin was certainly full of surprises today.

After checking out, Dee and I began our drive back to the office.

"Frankly, I think the statuettes look rather cheap." I turned the figure over. "They're made of some kind of plaster, and there's a large hole on the underside."

Dee nodded without taking her eyes off the road. "Exactly. So why would someone steal them?"

"Unless, the thieves were actually after the ottomans. David bought one exactly like it at the Fremont Sunday Market for thirty bucks, only it didn't have the cushion. The seller had a whole stack of them for sale."

"Really?" Dee's eyebrows shot up. "Brand new?"

"Looked like it."

"It could have come from one of the shipments. Reilly did say that ottomans were among the stolen items, and flea markets are infamously useful for pawning off stolen goods."

I hesitated. "Sure, but, two problems. First, why would they sell it without the cushion?"

"Hmm."

"Second," I continued before she could respond, "This isn't just any flea market we're talking about. It's Fremont Sunday Market. They've got rules about that sort of thing."

Dee flicked on her turn signal to pass a slow vehicle. "I wonder who the vendor is."

I replayed that day in my mind. "You know, that's the strange part. The guy running the booth was Bob Thompson, my last client. I don't think he saw me, though."

"That's very interesting, actually." Dee's voice trailed off. Neither of us spoke for the rest of the ride home.

A parking spot presented itself in front of my building. I grabbed the ottoman, opened the door with my free hand, and then held it with a foot. "After you."

Dee passed me with statuettes in hand and trotted up the stairs. Once back in the office, she shut the door behind us. "There has to be a reason why those particular shipments were targeted." She set the elk on the file cabinet and checked the answering machine. Nothing. "While I take a look at these, call Reilly and get the information on the hijackings."

I nodded, vaguely sensing that my cousin had just reversed our roles. Ignoring my growing agitation, I picked up the receiver, and dialed my client's number. Two rings, and then the line clicked. "This is Christopher Reilly."

"Hello, Mr. Reilly, this is Noah Clue."

"Ah, Mr. Clue, I was just about to call you. My papers are still missing, but I've got the names and phone numbers of the drivers. They'll be able to give you the details you need."

I opened my notebook and scribbled as he read off the information. Four different truckers all apparently hijacked on the same route from Portland. "All right," I said, "I'll follow up on this and see where it leads."

"Thank you. Keep me apprised of what you find."

"Absolutely." I hung up, leaned back in my chair, and pondered the evidence I did have. "Dee, according to the shipping manifests, the hijacked shipments contained dining room sets, dressers, and living room furniture. Yet, the guy at the store said the ottomans, statuettes, and pots were affected."

Dee frowned. "Someone either doesn't know what they are talking about, or they're lying."

"Except the smaller items are tangibly delayed."

She went back into the kitchenette. "True. Something could have gotten lost in translation."

"How can someone mistake a couch for book ends?" I argued.

The refrigerator door creaked as the magnet released its hold on the frame. Dee tisked. "Boy, don't you have a thing to eat?"

"Yeah. I can call up Hot Wok..."

"No, I mean here."

"Ramen Noodles up in the cupboard."

She shut the fridge and came to the kitchenette doorway. "I'm talking about food, Noah. Eat enough of that preserved stuff, and they won't need to embalm you when you die."

"I can't afford any of the fancy stuff, Dee." I left out the detail that a good part of my food budget went to coffee. I couldn't survive on budget beans.

Dee's lips flattened. "I still have extra grocery money set aside for the week. I'll give you forty dollars, and we'll get some food tomorrow." She opened her purse and took out two twenties. I was surprised she had any cash left after our foray into the world of over-priced decor.

Dread nagged at me as I accepted the money. "You mean... grocery shopping?"

She raised an eyebrow. "Yes, shopping. You know, grocery store, baskets, check out lines."

"I've heard of it." Memories of childhood disasters with Miss Bossy Boots flashed before my eyes. She definitely lived up to Uncle Denby's nickname for her.

"Good." She disappeared from view again. "I need to teach you about food. Get some vegetables, twelve grain bread, some whole grain pasta, a few spices."

"No hot dogs?" I ventured.

"Definitely not! Do you know what is in those things?"

My mouth went dry with anxiety. "No."

"Well, neither do I. But I do know, it isn't meat."

Oh, boy. "Am I allowed milk?"

"Skim is fine. And some fat free yogurt."

My stomach turned over twice. "Sounds great."

"Indeed." Dee looked at the clock. "And it is just about closing time. I'm going to head home. Call me if you need anything."

"Right-o." I preferred to ship her back to Texas.

"We'll go shopping bright and early tomorrow."

I faked enthusiasm. "You got it."

"And don't you dare spend any of that money without me." She chuckled and opened the front door. "See you tomorrow, Noah."

"Yep. Tomorrow."

She shut the door. I waited a few moments, and then watched her out my window until she walked down the street. I snatched the phone off its stand and dialed my best friend's number.

The phone rang twice. "Yo? David here."

My desperation spilled out. "David, you gotta help me, man!"

"What's goin' on?"

The nightmare replayed itself in my head. "She wants to take me grocery shopping," I hissed through clenched teeth.

"Who?"

"Dee! My cousin-turned-secretary."

He snorted a laugh. "Is she buying?"

"Yeah, but that's not the point." I took a deep breath. "She wants to get health food."

David seemed unconcerned. "Uh huh?"

"You don't get it. She wants to fill up my fridge. I'm gonna be forced to eat this junk!"

His tone changed. "Oh dear."

"Man, you gotta help me. I need your car and forty bucks. I'll pay you back as soon as I can, but I need to fill up this fridge before tomorrow morning."

"Didn't she leave the money with you?"

I hated to grovel, but I was desperate. Borrowing money just wasn't my thing. "Please, man, I really need the cash and the ride."

David hesitated. "Well, I dunno about the forty."

Seriously? "You still owe me after the Anchovies & Olives bill."

"I bought lunch at Fremont Market on Sunday."

"Fifteen dollars is hardly equal to what I shelled out. And, if you ever want decent food around here again, I need help. I think she's going to ban every pizza chain in Seattle from my apartment."

David lost his hesitation. "Fine, you got it. I'll be there to pick you up in five minutes."

True to his word, my friend pulled up outside in the allotted time. I climbed into his gold Mercury Sable. "I don't know what Dee does after work. If I run into her while we're out, it's all over."

David shrugged. "There's an unfashionable twenty-four-hour grocery market in downtown. I doubt she'd go there."

Another worry surfaced. "Uh oh. When she sees that full fridge in the morning, she'll have me take it all back."

David scoffed. "Easy. Just shred the receipt."

5

I Take Control

Tuesday, March 16

"Noah! You didn't."

I groaned and rolled over in bed. "Yes, I did, Dee. Now dry up and let me sleep."

My cousin threw back the curtains to my bedroom. "You went and bought groceries without me. And just look at the garbage you got! What do you have to say for yourself?"

I sat up, rubbed my eyes, and grinned. "P.I., one, secretary, zero."

Stony resolve covered her face. "I can take that junk down to the food bank just as easily, you know."

I snorted a laugh. "Actually, you can't."

She locked one of her knees as she put her hands on her hip. "And, why not?"

"Because my buddy gave *me* a loan to buy it. It's mine." I pulled her forty dollars from my wallet. "Like I said. P.I., one, secretary, zero."

Dee reluctantly took back her money. "You really take the cake."

"Yeah, lemon pound cake, and I think there's a blueberry pie in that fridge, too." I grabbed my work clothes and headed for the bathroom. "Real food. You can keep your packing material lunches, thank you very much."

Dee turned her back and threw her hands in the air. "You're absolutely hopeless!"

"No, I actually feel a whole lot of hope right now, knowing my cousin's plot to starve me didn't work."

After I got dressed, I started for the kitchenette. "I'm gonna get my coffee and breakfast, now."

"Don't bother with the coffee. We're meeting one of the drivers of the hijacked trucks at Starbucks in half an hour."

I cut a piece of blueberry pie. "Good. I'll ask him about what he was carrying, and anything leading up to the hijacking."

"Be sure to ask him if he had any truck problems, changes in route, delays."

"What are you thinking, Dee?" I bit into the pie and savored the sweet fruity flavor.

My cousin picked up her notebook and pen. "I'm not sure. If we interview all the hijacked truckers, we may find a pattern that will lead to the perpetrators."

Before long, I found myself seated outside at Starbucks on First and Walker. Heavy traffic and the train freight yard blocked any view of Puget Sound. I zipped my jacket against the brisk March breeze. Dee set a large cup in front of me. "Here's your grande Caffè Latte." She set it on the table, took her seat, and sipped on her cappuccino. After a moment, she pulled the notebook and pen from her purse. "All right. I'm ready to take notes when he arrives."

"What's the name of our guy, again?"

"Martin Steele." She nodded down the sidewalk. "Right there. Gray ball cap, scruffy face, jeans, gray shirt."

As the bulky man drew close, I stood to greet him. "Mr. Steele. Thank you for joining us." I held out my hand and tried to ignore the scorpion tattoo on his neck. "I'm Noah Clue, private investigator. This is my secretary, Dee."

The trucker's strong grip squeezed the blood from my fingers. "Pleasure to meet you."

I gestured to the seat across from me as I flexed my hand, willing the feeling to return. "Please, have a seat. Would you like anything?"

"Yes, thank you. Double shot espresso. Two cream, no sugar." Steele seated himself.

"Coming right up." Dee set down her notebook and went back inside to order.

Steele leaned forward. "I understand you're investigating the truck hijackings." His face seemed sunburned except for the white ring around each eye, no doubt from sunglasses.

"That's right." I fished my own notebook and pen out of my jacket pocket to take notes in Dee's absence.

He scowled and shook his head. "Glad someone is. My boss wouldn't let us call the cops."

It still seemed crazy that Reilly wouldn't involve the police. "Did he say why?"

Steele shrugged. "Not much, other than that it would interfere with regular business."

Dee came back and set Steele's order in front of him. She took her seat and began her secretarial role again.

I continued to jot down my own notes. "Do you know what you were carrying?"

Steele sat back and crossed his legs. "If I remember correctly, it was mostly decor. Statues, figurines, pots."

Another mismatch with the manifest. "Did anything unusual happen that day?"

"Other than being hijacked?" He sipped his coffee.

I glanced at Dee, and then back at Steele. "Yes, other than that."

The trucker thought for a moment. "Well, there was a short delay in loading. About ten or so minutes over schedule."

"Anything else?" I hoped he could give me some new clues I could follow, because so far, interviewing the truckers hadn't gotten me very far.

He paused for a moment, tapping his coffee cup. "Not that I can think of."

"What happened during the hijacking?" I needed details if I had any hope of solving this crime.

Steele shrugged. "Nothing much I can tell you. I went into the truck stop to...well, use the can. Anyhow, I was only gone for about fifteen minutes, and when I came back out, the truck was gone."

I raised my eyebrows. "Wait, you left the keys in the ignition?"

Steele jeered. "I'm not that stupid. Someone probably hot-wired the truck."

"I'm not meaning to insult you. I just need to get all the facts. Is this the first time you've been hijacked?"

"Yup." He took a large swig of coffee.

Somehow I felt this interview had yielded a fat nothing. Still, I pressed on. "How long have you worked with this company?"

His jaw clenched. The scorpion tattoo on his neck seemed to twitch. "Two and a half years, and I've been driving trucks for over fifteen. I haven't lost a shipment before in my life."

* * *

Two of the other truckers had more terrifying recollections of their hijackings. One had stopped to help a woman with a flat tire and ended up unconscious in a ditch. Since he'd been hit from behind, he never saw his attacker. The other had been run off the road by two cars working in tandem. The three gunmen that boarded his truck wore black ski masks and yelled for him to get out or die. He opted to live, and was tied up and left in a ditch. Both truckers were forbidden by the company to involve the police in any way.

Dee tapped her pen on the desk. "I'm really uncomfortable with this. Why would Reilly forbid even the injured trucker to talk to police? It doesn't make practical sense to keep the lid on this case."

I got out of my office chair and paced back and forth between the window and my bedroom curtain. It didn't really help, but it made me feel smarter somehow. "What are you saying? Inside job?"

"I'm not sure. It doesn't make sense why an executive would want to steal furniture and decor, considering his salary. Yet, I'd think the company would call the police, given the violent nature of at least two of the hijackings. It isn't like you have the authority to place anyone under arrest—except maybe citizen's arrest."

"True, though Reilly did say he was fearful of losing his designer clientele if word got out."

Dee began clicking her pen, a habitual sign of mental agitation. "And, with all his money, why would he hire a P.I. with little experience, and no solved cases under his belt? Furthermore, how did he even find out about you? We placed the ad only a few hours before Reilly hired you."

I bristled at the reminder of my string of failures. "Maybe someone referred him."

My cousin smirked. "As if there were a single person in the entire state of Washington who would recommend you."

"Dee, will you stop that incessant pen clicking?" I snapped. "It's driving me up the wall."

"Sorry." She set the writing implement down. "It just doesn't make sense to me."

"Well, thankfully, it doesn't have to." I pointed to myself. "I'm the P.I., so I'm the one who has to solve the case. You just have to take notes, nothing more."

Dee rolled her eyes. "Well, excuse me for intruding, Sherlock. If you recall, I've worked at a law office for several years. You've been a professional student for most of your adult life."

"Six years typing up legal affidavits doesn't automatically make you a brilliant detective."

"Getting a P.I. license doesn't make you one, either." Dee took a sip of coffee, clearly savoring her rhetorical victory. "Now, if you have any sense in that head of yours, you'll have me call Reilly and get the correct phone number for that fourth truck driver."

Her know-it-all attitude irked me. "If you're suggesting it, why don't you just do it?"

She shrugged. "Like you said, you're the P.I. I'm just here to take notes." Dee punctuated her statement with sarcastic jazz hands.

"Go ahead and call him," I grunted. "Maybe he'll have something we can use."

Her hand flew up to her eyebrow in a mock salute. "Sir, yes, sir."

Much more of this, and I might just change careers. At least my dropping the P.I. gig would mean Dee wouldn't get her inheritance.

Still, I rather wished someone could give me some less patronizing feedback. Neither Dee nor I had any experience investigating crimes. Maybe David's idea about having some "strategic friendships" wasn't such a bad one. It might be useful to know a forensics technician, and David wasn't the type to hang out with boring people. Anyhow, it was the third Tuesday of the month, which meant Game Night. I decided I'd give him a call as soon as Dee was done making her phone call.

* * *

A light rain pattered on my Stetson as I knocked on Sammi Keppler's downstairs apartment door. The sounds of laughter and light jazz music sounded from within. Dee tucked her hands under her arms as another gust of wind blew against us.

Perhaps it was just the weather affecting my mood, but I rather resented having to bring Dee. David had insisted on meeting her, and it was nearly impossible to say no to his charisma once he got going. Now I found myself standing out in the rain, next to my crabby cousin, and I couldn't hear anyone coming to let us in.

Dee cleared her throat and nodded to the doorbell. "Ring?"

"Ah." I pushed the button. A bell buzzed inside.

After a moment, David threw open the door. "There you two are!" He ushered us inside. "I was worried you had changed your mind, Noah. We have lasagna."

I took Dee's jacket. "David, this is my cousin, Dee Ann Tindall. Dee, this is my best friend, David Sigfeld."

Dee extended her hand. "Ahh yes, the accomplice to Noah's culinary delinquency."

David gave her a look of feigned suspicion, which almost concealed his amusement at the new title. He shook her hand. "Charmed, I'm sure."

"Noah! I would recognize you anywhere." A wiry young woman with bright red hair bustled up. "You haven't changed a bit."

I stumbled for the appropriate response. I had never been good with faces, especially years after the fact. The woman's claim to recognize me came as a second surprise; my unremarkable looks made me blend into virtually any crowd. "Good to meet...you...again? Hi." I swallowed.

"You don't remember me." Mischief sparkled in her green eyes. "Well, it has been nearly a decade. You tutored me in psychology back in college."

"Spring of '01," David prompted me.

"I wouldn't have graduated on time if it hadn't been for you," the redhead added.

"Psychology?" I stumbled over my thoughts. "Okay, so...you would be Samantha Keppler?"

"The one and only." She held out her hand. "Good to meet you again, then."

I shook her hand. "This is my cousin Dee."

Samantha turned to her. "Dee, it's very nice to meet you at last. I remember Noah's stories about you."

"Oh, really?" Dee raised an eyebrow in my direction.

I shoved my hands in my pockets. "It's been a decade. I can scarcely remember what stories I told back then."

"The thing with the wedding cake, for one." Samantha prompted.

Drat, I had told her *that* story? I made my escape towards the kitchen. "I hear you made lasagna."

"Yeah, Allie made it." Samantha slipped past me and stood next to a young lady with a huge grin and long blonde hair. "Noah, meet Alexandra Meyer. Allie, this is Noah Clue and his cousin, Dee Ann Tindall."

Allie shook my hand vigorously. "I think I remember you. Didn't you tutor history, too?"

"Ah...yeah." How many of my former students did David know? "It's nice to see you again."

She laughed at my bewilderment and led the way to the breakfast bar. "Here, have some food. I'll get you a plate."

Before I had much of a chance to figure out what was going on, Allie and Samantha had loaded me and Dee down with generous helpings of four-cheese lasagna, garlic bread, and lemon-lime soda. I balanced the paper plate in one hand, trying not to splatter marinara sauce all over the floor. I eased myself into a chair at the end of the coffee table, where David had begun setting up Scrabble.

"This is my kind of party." Dee set her plate down. "Scrabble is one game I never lose at."

"Well, this is a little different." Samantha handed a refilled cup to David. "Ever heard of 'Nonsense Scrabble'?"

Dee blinked. "Nonsense?"

Allie giggled as she took a seat on the sofa to my right. "It's quite simple. You have to make up the words; they can't be in the dictionary."

"You have to pronounce them," added Samantha. "And come up with a definition for them."

"Oh." Dee looked lost. "Huh, I just noticed, there are five of us, and Scrabble is for four. I'll just sit back and watch."

"Nonsense. We always combine two sets." David wiggled an extra tile tray in his hand. "Come on, Dee, it won't be as much fun if you just watch."

I'd known David long enough to recognize that he mostly wanted to watch my cousin flounder at something. Dee exuded such a sense of superiority, it was rather fun to see her out of her element.

She took the tray with some reluctance. "Well, if you insist."

Samantha shook the bag of tiles. "Everyone take one, no peeking, and we'll see who goes first."

As the bag passed around to me, I plucked one out. "So, Allie, what do you do?"

"Forensic chemistry, county medical examiner's office. Sammi and I are both science nerds." She set her tile down. "N. Not bad."

David frowned. "U, I'm definitely not first. And Dee's got an E."

"At least this is the same," Dee remarked.

"L here." Samantha tossed her tile on the board. "What about you, Noah?"

I turned the tile over in my hand. "Huh. It's an A. I guess I go first." I set it down and picked up the bag of tiles, drawing seven and perching them on my tray. V, C, B, A, D, E, R. "So...I have to make up the word, right? Nothing real?"

"Exactly." David pulled a pen out from behind his ear. "I'll write down the words, and Sammi keeps score. Standard rules otherwise, except a challenge means you think the word is real."

"So, what's your career, Noah?" Allie set her tiles in place and began shuffling them around. "David is always vague on details."

Good old David, shielding me from scrutiny as always. "I'm a private investigator." I pondered my letters, hoping to avoid further questions just yet. This whole "nonsense" angle was proving tricky for a practiced Scrabble player like myself. I dropped the V in the middle of the word "BAD", to try to get my mind off of real words.

Allie grinned. "That's cool. Clue's a pretty ironic name for a private investigator, isn't it?"

I shook my head. "It's not a coincidence." I determined not to fill in the rest of that history right now. My family wasn't a great conversation topic, unless you were into abnormal psychology.

"What are the chances of us all going into different branches of investigation?" Samantha began writing the names in at the top of the score sheet. "Well, except for the computer nerd over here."

"Technically I do network security, so that's kinda sorta similar." David handed the bag of tiles to Dee. "You still have to think like a criminal would."

"What sort of stuff do you investigate, Noah?" Allie continued.

"Oh...the usual stuff." I didn't want to have to explain that I took whatever I could get. A P.I. with my reputation couldn't afford to be choosy. My eyes caught sight of CRED spelled out on the tray. I superimposed the B on the end.

"Come on, Noah, you're making something up." Dee nagged. "It's not even as hard as those three-letter words you usually play."

I shot her a look of annoyance. "Easy for you to say, cuz. You haven't had your turn yet." Without thinking, I dropped C-R-E-B into place onto the board. After staring for a moment, I added the A-D for good measure. "There. Crebad—a reputation that is falling apart."

"Not a bad start." Samantha leaned towards the board. "That's three, four, five, eight, nine, eleven, times two. Twenty-two points."

I flashed a superior grin at my cousin. "Your turn, Miss It's Easy. Let's see you beat that."

"Ah, oh..." Dee glanced down at her tiles. "Play does go clockwise, doesn't it?"

I chuckled at her unpreparedness. "Always and forever."

"You working on anything particularly interesting right now?" Samantha took a sip of her soda, her green eyes trained on me.

I hated to admit it to myself, but that question basically summed up my entire reason for coming. "Yeah, one case. A bunch of truck hijackings at the same company. We can't even figure out for certain what's been taken. The reports don't match the tangibly absent inventory in the store."

"I even picked up what might be a stolen ottoman at the Fremont Sunday Market!" David volunteered. In his usual weird manner, the connection to a crime seemed to excite him. "That'll make a cool conversation piece, assuming I get to keep the thing when all is said and done."

I glanced over at Dee. "Having trouble, cousin dearest?"

"Shut up," she snapped.

"The weirdest part is that this company, which sells expensive furnishings, hired me instead of going to the police." I debated how to ease into the unavoidable situation of my non-reputation.

"Fine!" Dee dropped three tiles into place with some frustration. "*Slud*. A sled for mud."

"Let's see." Samantha lifted a tile out of place. "Triple letter score, so that's three. And...four, five, seven points."

Dee grumbled under her breath as she drew three new tiles. I had to admit, it gave me a bit of pleasure watching her struggle through a game for once.

"I can imagine the company that hired you just wants to avoid bad press, Noah." Allie began moving her tiles around again. "It's not all that uncommon."

"Oh, I've got a good one." David dropped his tiles into place with a flourish. "Cofean—a person who subsists purely on coffee. And, that's a double word score."

"Well, that's the trick, Allie. I'm not very...well known. Like, at all." I took a long look at my tiles. Darn, no vowels, and some pretty high scoring letters. V, X, R, W, D, R, T? At least I didn't have to think of a real word.

"Anyway, the hijackings almost always involved assaults," Dee added. "Getting hit from behind, et cetera."

"Twenty-two points, David." Samantha turned to Dee and furrowed her freckled brow. "Almost all? That doesn't sound right. If a criminal has a violent M.O, why change it partway through?"

"Tell me about it," I muttered. "This whole thing doesn't make much sense."

"It's almost a shame no one's been killed yet, or I could seriously help you out," Allie quipped.

"Allie, hush!" Samantha backhanded her. "Don't you dare."

I blinked. At least she'd made the offer, although Samantha's reprimand had me worried.

"It wasn't a joke, Sammi," Allie pleaded. "I'm just saying."

David grimaced and leaned forward. "She's got this weird superpower-like thingy. We call it The Curse of the Joke Clairvoyant. Just about every time Allie makes a joke or pun about something happening, it happens."

"Her then-boyfriend got a staph infection because of it, once," Samantha added.

"Wait, what?" Dee paused in the middle of rearranging her tiles. "Seriously?"

Allie hung her head. "I made a pun off of 'staff parking,' and the next week..."

"Yeah, watch where you point that talent, Alexandra," Sammi scolded. "You could get somebody killed one of these days."

"A-hem. It's your play, Sam." Allie nodded to the board.

"Right." Samantha fell into deep meditation over her tiles.

"So, what angles have you covered already, Noah?" David twirled the pen between his fingers. "Inside job, maybe?"

"But why hire a guy to investigate the crime you committed?" Allie returned.

My friend held up a finger. "What if you wanted to avert suspicion from yourself?"

Allie didn't miss a beat. "Wouldn't that be a bit risky?"

"What if the risk of being suspected is greater?" David ventured.

"Wouldn't the P.I. be suspicious too?" She tucked a stray lock of blonde hair behind her ear.

David made a face. "Would he really suspect the guy who's paying him to investigate?"

I watched this back-and-forth with some amusement. I could definitely see a benefit to coming here more often. Not only could these three provide me with fresh insight, but it brought a rare occasion to watch my cousin struggle for points.

"Stranger things have happened..." Allie trailed off.

"Ha!" David leapt to his feet. "Statement! Fifteen-love, my favor."

I sniggered at the reference to *Rosencrantz and Guildenstern Are Dead*. It felt good to be among fellow nerds again.

"Here we are." Samantha began placing her tiles. "Trejib—to poke incessantly in the ribs." She demonstrated with a friendly jab in Allie's side. "Like that."

Allie recoiled with a giggle as Samantha began counting up her score. "Double letter here, so, that's two, three, four, twelve, thirteen, sixteen points." She scribbled it down on the score sheet.

"Well, I've got a good one. *Roo-sed*! R-U-C-E-D." Allie grinned. "A slightly reddened complexion."

"One, two, five, six, eight points." Samantha wrote it down. "Your turn, Noah."

I frowned. "Give me a minute. No vowels." I moved my X to the end of the tray. I doubted I could get away with using it here at all. "Honestly, I don't know what anyone would want with half the stuff that appears to have been stolen from the trucks. Wicker ottomans and cheap statues?"

"If they're being fenced, it ain't going to bring in much. Thirty bucks for that ottoman, that's it, and it was missing the cushion from what Noah tells me." David looked up from his notebook. "By the way, nice word, Allie."

I decided to build around the U in *ruced*. "D-V-U-R-X, and that's a double word score."

"Two, double letter, so that's four. Eight, nine, ten, eighteen. Twice is thirty-six points! You're definitely in the lead, Noah," Samantha declared with a smile.

"Uh-uh!" Dee's gaze challenged me. "Not until he pronounces it."

"*Da-vurks*." I returned the look. "Deal with it."

"And it means what?" Dee persisted.

"Well..." My mind raced for a definition. We'd all gotten so caught up in the conversation about the missing merchandise.

An idea popped into my mind. I grinned. "A worthless object that everyone wants to steal."

6

I Hit Yellow Tape

Wednesday, March 17

Dee's voice held a note of professionalism that she rarely used with me. "Uh huh. What's the nearest major cross street? Highland Drive. All right. No, thank *you*. Uh huh. See you soon. Yup. Bye bye." She hung up the phone. "Mr. Hampton gave me his address. He's more than willing to talk about the hijacking, but not over the phone. We're to meet him at his house as soon as we can get there."

"That's good. Maybe this interview will lead to a break-through." I chugged down the rest of my coffee and set the mug on the old compact disc I used as a coaster. The light from the window shone on the shiny surface, reflecting a rainbow back onto the cup. "Where's he located?"

"South Lake Union. He said he thinks he may have recognized a tattoo on one of the gunmen. He hasn't told anyone before this, since his boss didn't want him calling police."

"So, it could be an inside job." I slipped on my jacket. "The traffic in that neighborhood is notorious. It's going on five o'clock now, so if we want to get there in under an hour, we have to get moving."

Dee grabbed her purse and jacket as she followed me out.

As I expected, as soon as we made it to the I-5, we hit heavy traffic. I leaned back in the leather car seat and groaned. "What are we paying the city to do, anyhow? If they quit all their fussing about that tunnel, maybe they'd start paying attention to more important things. Like, I dunno, widening the existing roads?"

Dee grunted and turned on the radio.

"There are several factors we have to consider, here," came the male commentator's voice. "The Alaskan Way viaduct obviously needs to be replaced..."

"But," interrupted his co-host, "the city budget is already under strain. And now, they want to overhaul the system. And then there's the light rail."

The commentator butted in, "—which would help alleviate the traffic problems."

"Not if there isn't any parking for it! Which is even more tax payer dollars down the drain."

My irritation increased with the vocal reminder of the city's lack of leadership. I punched the "two" on the radio. The bickering over the traffic issues continued. Three, four, five, six. No change. "What is going on here?"

Dee shrugged. "I filled up my presets. All I really listen to is talk radio, anyway."

I growled and spun the tuner knob until I came to 98.9 KWJZ, the smooth jazz station. "The whole reason they invented radio was to drown out stupid political discussions on car rides like this."

"You started it."

Her patronizing tone irked me. "I don't need some underpaid deejays to continue it! Now, will you be quiet? I like this song."

The remainder of the car ride continued in relative silence. I kept my eyes closed, to keep from losing my temper. At last, around 6:30, we turned down the street where Dale Hampton lived. Flashing red and blue lights caught my eye. I hoped the emergency crew wasn't there for our witness.

Dee pulled up to the curb a block away. "You have got to be kidding me."

One glance at the mailbox confirmed my suspicions. Yellow tape surrounded Hampton's yard and porch. "Just great." I spotted Warren in his two-tone blue uniform speaking to another officer on the curb. I pointed him out to Dee. "See that tall strawberry-blonde guy? Lieutenant Gregg Warren. He'd like to end my career."

Dee grunted acknowledgment.

I hopped out and approached Warren, who had turned away to talk to someone else. I decided to pretend not to know him. "Excuse me, officer?"

Lieutenant Warren spun around, one eyebrow arched. He groaned. "What in heaven's name are you doing here?"

I ignored his disgruntled tone. "We were supposed to meet Dale Hampton regarding a case I'm working on."

Warren nodded towards Hampton's house. "Someone already beat you to the breaking and entering this time, Clue."

Dee stepped forward and gave him her most brilliant smile. "Lieutenant Warren, is it? I'm Dee Ann Elizabeth Tindall. Mr. Clue's new assistant."

Surprise flickered in Warren's eyes. His formal demeanor wavered. He shook Dee's hand. "Pleased to make your acquaintance, Miss Tindall."

Her tailored gray business suit seemed to throw him. She kept up her Texas charm. "I understand this isn't the best time, but we really need to speak to Mr. Hampton. It's urgent."

Warren sighed, both eyebrows approaching his receding hairline. He seemed to hesitate. "I'm sorry to say, you're a bit late. Hampton is dead."

My mouth dropped open. "What? How?"

"We found the rear sliding glass door shattered and our victim on the kitchen floor. What did you need to talk to him about?"

I raised my chin a little. "It's confidential."

All of Warren's friendliness disappeared. "Mm hmm. Clue, just so you are aware, in a murder investigation, any confidentiality agreements are null and void. If you don't voluntarily help me out, I'll be forced to subpoena your files. It may be linked."

He certainly had a lot of nerve. I stood my ground and responded coolly, "I will keep that in mind, and I will be in touch if I am able to make any arrangements. Good evening." I turned around and headed back for the car.

Dee bit her lip as she slid behind the steering wheel and shut her door. "I cannot believe you just did that."

"If Warren wants my case files, he is going to have to fight to get them. The last thing I need is some nosy know-it-all officers putting me out of a job. I will cooperate with a court subpoena, of course, but nothing more."

"And what if this *is* tied to our investigation?"

I shrugged. "Then I'll do my own digging, and give Warren the information that is relevant. And then, if Reilly agrees, I'll turn over the rest of the files. But I absolutely refuse to violate my client confidentiality agreement."

Dee turned the car around and started back towards Seattle without another word. Once we had merged onto the highway, the talk radio went on. I left the dial alone, under threat of bodily harm.

* * *

I tossed my coat and hat on the chair and collapsed in my bed. Dee had dropped me off at home, without so much as a goodbye.

Where did she get off? It didn't matter what experience she had. The fact of the matter was that I had the P.I. license, and she held the secretarial position. Not the other way around.

I sighed and propped myself up against my headboard. I fumbled for a minute to grab the remote from the far side of my bedside stand, finally succeeded, and flipped on the television. As usual, a garbled reception greeted me. I muttered a few choice words about Congress and changed the channel. At last, I located a station with a relatively decent signal.

Just my luck. *Citizen Kane.* If I hadn't already seen the film about a dozen times, I would probably be interested. Now, I just stared past the television screen with half-closed eyes.

I had actually made some real progress on a case, for the first time in my career. And now both Warren and my cousin were trying to muscle in on it. The lieutenant probably took credit for upwards of twenty closed cases a week, and Dee had no place solving anything. How were private investigators supposed to make a living this way?

Except for the fact that Warren hated my guts, I could probably aim to become a police advisor like in so many detective novels. My P.I. gig was the only thing keeping me from winding up at Mickey D's, flipping burgers and filling orders for rude, impatient customers and their whining kids.

"I always gagged on that silver spoon." Orson Welles's voice broke through my musings, and I returned my attention to the movie. "You know, Mr. Bernstein, if I hadn't been very rich, I might have been a really great man."

"Don't you think you are?"

"I think I did pretty well under the circumstances."

"What would you like to have been?"

A dramatic pause. "Everything you hate."

I sighed and changed the channel. Amazing. Channel 5 was actually coming through tonight. The female news anchor gazed earnestly into the camera.

"One man is dead in a South Lake Union neighborhood this evening after someone apparently shot him through his back door. Now over to Chris for the details."

A twenty-something male reporter stood grim-faced in front of the police crime scene tape. "Thank you, Jean. Around five-thirty this evening, a neighbor called police to report gunshots. When authorities arrived on the scene, they found a forty-three-year-old man lying on his kitchen floor in a pool of blood, the rear sliding glass door allegedly shattered by bullets. We spoke to Lieutenant Gregg Warren on the scene earlier. "

I rolled my eyes as Warren's face appeared on TV. I saw enough of the man in real life.

"Our investigators are still processing the murder scene, but at this point we have no motive." Warren's typical no-nonsense tone seemed to be universal. He used it on officers, on suspects, on reporters, and on me. "We are treating this case as a homicide."

"Yeah, no kidding!" I shouted at the screen. "It doesn't take a genius to figure that one out."

"Do you have any suspects yet?" Chris returned the microphone to its spot in front of Warren's mustached mouth, in anticipation of his response.

Warren seemed to stare directly at me. "Not at this point, though we will be talking to a few people of interest. If anyone has any pertinent information, please do your civic duty and come forward."

I had a gut feeling that statement had been aimed at me.

The camera cut back to the live scene of Chris standing in front of Hampton's house. "A tragic end for one South Lake Union resident this evening. Viewers, Seattle's finest needs your help to solve this case. Anyone with information is urged to call..."

I shut off the television and let the remote slide out of my hand. As annoying as Warren was, he did have a point. Hampton's murder very well could have been tied to the Reilly case.

Thursday, March 18

"Dee, my life is enough of a cliché, without you sitting there, feet on my desk, filing your nails into oblivion."

My cousin glowered and tossed the emery board on the desk. She sat upright and placed her feet on the floor. "So, what do you want to do now, *de-tec-tive?*" Her voice oozed with sarcasm.

"Call Reilly again and see if he has those photos of the stolen merchandise. If the hijackers are desperate enough to kill a possible witness, they must be stealing something pretty darned valuable."

She raised her eyebrows. "Don't you find it odd that his office manager still hasn't provided the information we're asking for? It's almost like it isn't a priority for any of them."

"Well, Reilly did say his office was a disaster zone. Not those words, per se, but..."

My cousin scowled. "He's a wealthy CEO, for cryin' out loud! The man has to have a gaggle of secretaries at his beck and call. He's stalling." She picked up the phone.

"You know how bureaucracy works. Papers get lost."

Dee snorted. "That high up in an administration, papers only get lost when someone wants them lost." She dialed the number.

I shrugged and turned to the coffee maker for a refill. "I'm becoming a regular cofean, I suspect," I quipped, hoping Dee would remember the Nonsense Scrabble game and lighten up. She didn't. Even so, my cousin had a good point. Reilly hadn't been too forthcoming with information. Still, it didn't make sense. Why would someone involved in a crime hire a P.I. to solve it?

I tuned out Dee's voice as she spoke into the phone, and turned over the situation in my mind. With one witness dead already, I'd have to be careful not to trip on any of those red herrings I always seemed to find. Whoever I was up against was undoubtedly getting desperate if he'd escalate to murdering a possible witness.

I turned my attention back to Dee.

"Uh huh, thank you. You too, sir." She hung up the phone. "Reilly finally located the photos. He said his office manager will have them down here within the hour."

Progress. "At least he found them, right?"

She shrugged. "I suppose so."

"What is that supposed to mean?"

Dee vacated the office chair. "I don't know. Right now, none of this is adding up."

Didn't she know the function of a secretary? "Thankfully for you, I didn't hire you to do the adding. Let's keep roles straight, here."

My cousin crossed her arms. "What, an official moratorium on my being allowed to think, now?"

"Don't get sarcastic with me. I'm starting to feel a little crowded out by you. I'm no Hercule Poirot, but I'm no moron, either."

"As evidenced by your client base."

Bossy Boots was getting close to the line. "Believe it or not, they don't go handing out P.I. licenses to just any idiot that walks in, Dee."

"No, they singled you out for that privilege."

I slammed my mug down, splashing coffee on the counter. "I've had just about enough of you! The only reason I have you here is to help keep me organized, and I'll be the first to admit I need the help with that. But if you wish to retain your post beyond this case, I suggest you stick to your job, and I'll stick to mine!"

Amusement crossed my cousin's face. "And who else in Seattle would possibly want my position?"

"Plenty of secretaries, all of them a far cry more tolerable than you!" I pointed my finger at her. "And another thing, don't even bother threatening me with calling my parents. I am immune to that idiocy. They've never supported me in anything, and I know that my success or failure at this job won't change that."

"Well, if you don't care about succeeding, then there's certainly nothing keeping me here," Dee shot back. "There are scores of better positions in this city for a well-organized secretary, and one with a paralegal degree to boot! Pardon me for doing you a favor."

"A favor? You're taking over my career! A wreck, a disaster, granted, but MY career! You're no favor, you're the booby prize!"

Dee scooped up her bag. "I shouldn't be surprised you don't appreciate my skills. My own father certainly didn't. I hope you both wind up paying through the nose for secretaries that can't do half as well as I can."

"Where are you going?"

"Down to Zeitgeist for a coffee, as if you'd really care. I'll be back to play stenographer for you in half an hour, boss." Dee let the door slam shut behind her.

I decided to drown out my anger with a distraction. However, the TV announcer's voice had started in on the signature stutter that indicated I'd lost the signal yet again. I flipped off the set and threw the remote on the bed.

The apartment door swung open, and my cousin stormed in.

"Dee."

"*Él Líder.*" She threw her bag in the corner. "Reilly's office manager still hasn't arrived?"

"No."

"Glad I'm on time for you, *Él Líder.*"

She really knew how to get on my nerves. I shut the curtain to my bedroom behind me. "Shut up for once, will you?"

A knock at the door. I straightened up, plastered on a cordial smile, and threw the door open. Reilly stood on the other side.

"Why, hello, Mr. Reilly. Come in."

He brushed past me and set his briefcase on the desk. "I found all the files you wanted, Mr. Clue. I apologize for the delay. They were in the recycling bin of all places!"

Dismay covered Reilly's face as he sat down and opened the briefcase. "I'm totally overwhelmed. The police questioned me about the death of one my truckers, my clientele are up in arms because their orders haven't been delivered, and now my office manager has up and quit." He furrowed his brow and sat down. "Did you ever get to talk to Hampton?"

I shook my head as I seated myself behind my desk. "Dee spoke with him briefly on the phone. We were going to meet, but someone else got to him first."

Reilly's shoulders sagged as he rubbed his short salt-and-pepper curls with both hands. "Obviously, with Hampton's death the cops are now involved." He sighed and straightened. "But, I'm a man of my word and will stick with you. You need to know, the police said there was something drawn in his palm with a marker—an insect of some sort."

Insect? Hampton had told Dee on the phone that he had recognized one of the gunmen's tattoos. Perhaps this was a connection. "Did the police show you any photos of Hampton's drawing?" I hoped he had more information.

"No, they said the crime scene was rather gruesome, and they had to identify him by his fingerprints." He pulled a stack of papers from the briefcase and handed them to me. "Here are the product photos, the hijacking reports, and a copy of our freight schedule. I hope this helps"

I found Hampton's eyewitness account and skimmed through it. According to his statement, a motorcycle lay across the center line of the north-bound lanes of I-5 near Centralia. When he stopped his rig, three masked gunmen gained access through the passenger door which he thought he had left locked.

Dee picked up some of the papers from my desk and studied them. Where did she get off? I pushed back my irritation and fought to keep my demeanor professional.

After a few moments, my cousin spoke up. "Is this your usual shipping schedule, Mr. Reilly?"

"Yes, it is. Every man must stick to it. Our company believes the most efficient plan is mapped out to the last second."

Dee raised her eyebrows. "Interesting you say that, Mr. Reilly. Two of the truckers reported a delay in loading."

"Really?" Reilly looked shocked.

She nodded. "A fifteen-minute delay once, and almost half-an-hour the second time."

The businessman shook his head. "My staff assured me that every shipment was getting out on time with no delays."

Dee's voice turned skeptical. "So this is news to you?"

What was she doing, questioning my client like this?

"Absolutely." Reilly closed his briefcase. "Well, I do have to get back to the office. I don't know how I'm going to cope without an office manager."

Before I could stop her, Dee grabbed the manifest from the file cabinet. "Just one more thing. This says Mr. Steele was transporting mostly wood furniture. However, he said he was hauling statuettes, ottomans, and such."

Reilly shook his head. "I can't imagine how the paperwork could be wrong. Those truckers do confuse their shipments from time to time." He seemed in a hurry to leave now. "Anyhow, I really must go. My entire department is in an uproar and I must get things wrangled back into order. Until later, Mr. Clue."

After he had left, I turned back to Dee. "Who gave you the right to attack my client that way?"

Dee glowered. "I merely asked clarifying questions."

"It wasn't the words, it was the tone. Anyway, why would anyone need to lie about what the truck was carrying, Dee? Money is money is money. As it is, furniture would be worth more than some cheap clay and wood decor from, where, South America?"

Dee picked one of the elk off the file cabinet and turned it upside down. "Made in Nicaragua, to be specific."

"Same difference. Isn't worth the paper they use to print the hefty price tag for it." I shook off the effects of the rabbit trail. "The point is, you actually insinuated that my client was involved. May I remind you, he hired me to investigate this case?"

Dee's expression remained stoic. "Pardon me for thinking. I'm merely becoming uncomfortable with the company's lackadaisical response to this whole case, especially now with a murder involved."

"Lackadaisical how? They're cooperating with the investigation, and again, Reilly hired me. What more do you want?"

Dee began clicking her pen against the file cabinet top. "Missing paperwork, and then the office manager just happens to quit. I'm still thinking inside job, here."

Had she lost her ever-lovin' mind? "Dee, that doesn't even make sense! Why would Reilly kill someone, and then put us on a trail that could very well lead straight to him?"

"We've already discussed his possible connections before."

My anger surged. "No, *you* discussed it. I never got a thought in edgewise until now, between your prattling and clicking that stupid pen." I narrowed my eyes. "Much like you're doing now."

"Nervous habit." Dee dropped the pen onto the desk. "Since you're so clever, do you have any other suspects in mind?"

"The maid did it." I stood and crossed the room to the kitchenette. "I don't know, Dee. Unlike some people, I need facts before I can make any conclusions."

"Judging from your botched cases, that's a new method of investigation for you."

I pointed to the exit. "There's a door over there, Dee. You're welcome to use it."

She narrowed her gaze. "Are you throwing me out?"

"Certainly sounds that way."

"Very well, Mr. Clue." She retrieved her bag from the corner.

"And don't expect me to call you later in desperation!" I shouted after her.

Dee shut the door without another word.

"Good riddance." I collapsed in my office chair and began reviewing the case notes.

Three hijackings shared similarities—being attacked and left in a nearby ditch. Two encountered masked gunmen. Another was knocked out when he stepped out of the truck to help a stranded motorist. Only Steele said his truck had been hot-wired, at a truck stop near Chehalis.

My thoughts focused on Dale Hampton. What significant detail had he alluded to? Did the drawing on his hand have anything to do with the hijacking? Part of me wished I hadn't burned my bridge with Warren, so I could have access to the crime scene photos. A police connection could come in handy in this field.

I read through all the current case notes. For a stack of orderly, meticulously typed facts, something vital was missing. Perhaps Dee could...

Good grief, what had I just done?

7

I Get Clever

"Hello. Freda's Secretaries. This is Freda." The same southern-accented woman from before answered the phone.

I cleared my throat and assumed my professional voice. "Hi, Freda, this is Noah Clue, P.I."

She didn't miss a beat. "Yes, the one who wanted somethin' for thirty-five bucks a day."

Ouch, so she remembered me for the wrong reasons. "Well, circumstances have changed. Is Leah Lee still available? I can pay her rate."

"As it happens, darlin', she was hired two hours after you called."

"Oh." I tried to hide the disappointment in my voice.

"An' then the man that hired her fired her the next day on account of her havin' the wrong color eyes. He must be lookin' for rental arm candy."

I perked up. "How good is she at adapting to an existing organization system?"

"Oh, you'll have no problems with her there, Mr. Clue. Miss Lee is a bright li'l thing."

I kept my tone neutral, but inside I was jumping up and down with excitement. Who needed Dee, anyway? "Same rate of sixty-nine dollars a day, yes?"

"Yes."

"Good, I'll hire her. Can she come by right away?"

"That can be arranged, Mr. Clue."

I gave her my address. A half hour later, I answered the door to a drop-dead gorgeous gal somewhere in her mid-twenties with platinum blonde hair. She sported a neat white blouse beneath a floral print blazer, and wore a simple, knee-length black skirt. "Are you Mr. Clue?"

"Yes, and you are Miss Leah Lee?"

She clutched her handbag in exactly the manner you might expect from a secretary in the movies. "I am."

"Excellent. I'm in the middle of a very important case, so let's get right down to business." I took out the template Dee had typed up. "I'll show you the organizational system I have going. We had best not change anything right now, lest it throw me off my game."

Her large blue eyes scanned the office. "My, you must be quite the detective."

Oh dear, had I just hired the quintessential dumb blonde secretary? "I don't know if I'd put it that way, Miss Lee. I just tend to be a bit disorganized, that's all."

"I understand, Mr. Clue." She looked around the little space. "Though I must say, your office looks like something out of an old detective movie."

I wilted. "Please don't remind me."

"A typewriter and everything."

My gaze drifted to my ever-faithful Royal Heritage. "You know how to use a manual one, correct?"

"I'm better with computers, but it can't be too hard." She sat down at the desk. "So...I just start typing to make it work, right?"

"Yes, though it requires more accuracy than typing on a computer. Accuracy matters more than speed to me."

Miss Lee rolled a piece of paper into my typewriter. "Well, I type at ninety-eight words per minute, Mr. Clue." She stretched her fingers and put them in their places on the keys. She seemed fascinated with the machine. At least her nails were sensibly trimmed. "Did you need anything typed up right now?"

I resisted the urge to rub my eyes. "Nothing at the moment, Miss Lee." Heaven help me. This was going to be a long afternoon.

After getting my new secretary used to the system, I began reviewing the case again. I mused over every statement, report, and angle until my head hurt.

Two hours later, I slammed the case file down and rubbed my eyes. "I give up, Miss Lee. Four shipments, all from the same company, hijacked on different days on the same route. The hijackers had to know which trucks to hit, and when. What am I missing?"

She began typing. "I wish I knew, Mr. Clue. You're the detective."

I stared at her for a moment. "Yes, you're absolutely right." I never thought I'd actually miss my cousin's uninvited input.

"It could be an inside job," I continued. "But I can't see Reilly involved. His salary depends on company success."

"...company success." Miss Lee finished typing and glanced up.

I blinked. "You really don't have to type everything I say."

She shrugged. "If you wish, Mr. Clue. I do it out of habit. My last boss liked everything he said being typed up, so he could review it."

"Ah, yes, good thought." At last, some feedback! "Carry on."

"Yes, sir." Miss Lee returned to typing.

I folded my hands behind my back and tried to look the part of the competent detective. "What is most confusing of all is the value of the stolen items. Most of it isn't actual furniture."

"Furniture."

"That was what is reported on paper, but the truckers and the out-of-stocks tell a different story. They keep saying that the hijacked trucks were carrying ottomans and small decor items." I laid Dee's notes regarding the shipments next to the typewriter.

Miss Lee glanced down at the paperwork. "Ah, yes, that." She ran her finger along it, skimming the details. "According to the truckers, they were carrying pots, statuettes, and ottomans."

I picked up the two-tone elk statue from on top of the file cabinet. "Who'd want a *dvurx* like this?" I recalled my invented word from the Nonsense Scrabble game.

Miss Lee gave me a blank stare. "A...what now?"

I frowned. "Sorry, inside joke." I turned the figure over. "These couldn't be worth very much. They're pretty cheap quality. Imported."

"From where?"

"Nicaragua."

"That's what you get for outsourcing, I suppose." She resumed her typing.

Leah Lee might not look like the sharpest knife in the drawer, but she was an excellent typist.

I returned the elk statue to its place on the file cabinet. "Let's call it a day, Leah. I'll see you at eight tomorrow morning."

Friday, March 19

My alarm clock flashed 3:27 in the morning. Sleep had been fitful. The details of the case kept whirling around in my head, invading my dreams. Hijackers murdering a trucker over a load of cheap decor. Imported from Nicaragua.

What angle had I not thought of yet?

The distractible part of my brain began to question why any company would want to outsource overseas. Cheap labor, less regulation. Mexico, Costa Rica, Taiwan, Nicaragua. What was so special about Nicaragua?

I tried to recall the class on South American culture. Nicaragua was the land of lakes and volcanoes, and home to the second-largest rainforest of the Americas. Managua, Granada, León, Puerto Cabezas. Nothing special about the economy, either. Major exports included bananas, great coffee, cotton, tobacco, beef, sugar...

And drugs.

I sat stock upright in bed. The hole in the bottom of the statuettes suddenly made sense. Why hadn't I thought of that before? The trucks were hijacked, not for the decor and furniture, but for the drugs hidden inside! The items were all things that could easily conceal plastic bags: statuettes, vases, ottomans with thick cushions. After retrieving the payload, the items would be passed off to a second-hand retailer. Of course, the cushions couldn't be resold without stuffing, which is why those ottomans at the Fremont Sunday Market had been sold the way they were.

Stumbling out of bed, I snatched up my flashlight and made my way to the file cabinet where the elk statuettes stood. I peered inside each, half expecting to find illegal drugs. While I could find none, the size of the hole and the space inside could certainly accommodate such cargo.

I fumbled around for the switch to my desk lamp, and shielded my eyes as the blinding yellow light flicked on. I snatched Reilly's card up from beside the typewriter. He had scribbled his personal cell phone number on the back. I dialed the number and prayed he would answer.

A groggy voice spoke on the other end of the line. "This is Christopher Reilly."

"Mr. Reilly, this is Noah Clue." I couldn't suppress my excitement.

"Mr. Clue!" Reilly seemed to wake up at the sound of my name. "What's the matter?"

"I believe, sir, that I solved why your trucks were hijacked."

His voice perked up. "Do you know who is responsible yet?"

I suppressed the urge to state my working theory. "That's only a matter of time, but I believe that the 'why' is reason enough to call you in the middle of the night like this."

Reilly laughed. "Don't worry about the time. I fell asleep at the office anyway. I'm surprised you're awake, though. What have you found out?"

"I have reason to believe that someone in your company has been using your imports from Nicaragua as a means of smuggling in illegal drugs, and then falsifying the shipment paperwork to further cover their tracks."

Understanding dawned in Reilly's voice. "Actually, that could explain a few other logistical messes I've been trying to untangle for the past few weeks."

My mind snapped to Steele, the only hijacked trucker not to be assaulted. I remembered the scorpion tattoo on his neck. Was that what Hampton had drawn on his hand? "Someone in your company has to be involved."

"Interesting theory. Do you have any proof at this point?"

Proof. There was only one way to get that, and I hoped he would cooperate. "It is my professional opinion that a police investigation would be necessary to recover solid evidence, but I believe that the clues point to drug smuggling."

"And this is coming from within my own company, you say?" He paused. "It might explain my office manager quitting so suddenly."

"Yes, sir. Can you come by in the morning?"

Agitation filled Reilly's voice. "I can come by immediately, if that would be convenient, especially seeing as neither of us will be doing much sleeping now."

"That would be fine, sir. I apologize for the early wake-up call."

"No, it is quite all right. Like I said, I fell asleep at my desk anyhow. And if what you say is true, the sooner we figure out who is responsible, the better for all of us."

* * *

I set a cup of black coffee in front of my client. "I have to ask, Mr. Reilly, and I hope you won't be offended..."

"Ask anything you like, Mr. Clue." He took two packets of creamer out of his rumpled suit jacket pocket. "This is an investigation. If you didn't view me in the same light of suspicion as everyone else, I'd be disappointed in you."

"Why did you hire me? I'm not exactly well-advertised, and I don't have any recommendations floating around out there."

The businessman smiled. "You might be surprised, Mr. Clue. One of my business partners actually referred you by name. He said not to give you his name, lest you feel needlessly indebted, but considering the circumstances..." Reilly tapped his fingers on the desk. "Okay, his name is Fredrickson."

I coughed. Fredrickson recommended me? My heart thudded.

"Mr. Clue? Are you all right?"

I gripped the desk and leaned forward. "Mr. Reilly, are we talking about Nicholas Fredrickson, the investor?"

"Yes."

Suddenly, finding the ottomans at Bob Thompson's booth made sense. Was my former client involved, or just a convenient pawn? "I got fired from my last case for accusing Fredrickson of burglary without any evidence! He chose not to bring trespassing and harassment charges against me. I don't have a good reputation in this city; in fact, I barely have a reputation at all. I've never solved a case in my life."

Reilly lost color. "Then, if he recommended you to me, it was…"

The door swung open, revealing Fredrickson gripping a hand gun. "Hands in the air, both of you. Unfortunately, it looks like Clueless finally figured out how to run a proper investigation, and that means I'll have to mop this up."

I slowly raised my hands and mentally assessed the location of my Smith and Wesson. If only I had remembered to remove it from my bedside stand. I had to stall for time. "Mr. Fredrickson, if you kill us, it won't take much for the police to trace it back to you, especially what with Hampton's murder being under investigation, and Lieutenant Warren taking interest in my case files."

Fredrickson snorted. "Look at everything I've done so far. Do you really think I'd be that sloppy? My friend and I will take care of setting up the scene, and this gun has a silencer." He cleared his throat. "I assume you've met my friend, Mr. Steele?"

I held my breath, waiting for the trucker to appear.

My cousin emerged through the doorway, instead, and shoved her Smith and Wesson's muzzle in Fredrickson's back. "He's indisposed. Now, drop the weapon."

Lieutenant Gregg Warren rushed past her and disarmed the man. "Nicholas Fredrickson, you are under arrest for the murder of

Dale Hampton, breaking and entering, hijacking, grand theft, and illegal trafficking of drugs."

He handcuffed him and turned him around. "You have the right to remain silent, anything you say can and will be used against you in a court of law. You have the right to an attorney. If you cannot afford an attorney, one will be appointed for you. Do you understand these rights?"

Fredrickson spat in Dee's direction. "I should have guessed Clueless had an accomplice. He couldn't solve a case if his life depended on it."

"Actually, without him, we wouldn't have found all the evidence." Dee grinned in my direction.

Warren pointed at me. "Don't go anywhere, Clue. I still want to speak with you."

I winced, waiting for the other shoe to drop.

8

I Do The 'Firing'

"More coffee, sir?" Dee carried the carafe into the office area.

"Mm, yes, thank you." Warren held up his empty mug. "You're lucky you sent Dee over to my office when you did, Noah. I'm glad you finally came to your senses about not withholding evidence."

I opened my mouth to protest, but Dee caught my eye. She lifted a finger to her lips, and I nodded. She was really covering for me?

Warren continued. "That lead on Bob Thompson really blew everything wide open. We were able to get a search warrant for his second-hand store, where he also keeps the product he takes to the flea markets. We recovered a considerable amount of stolen goods. He told us he had no idea about their origin, only that he bought them from Fredrickson's niece. This led to our common denominator between Hampton's murder and the current hijackings. Incidentally--"

"Wait a minute," Reilly interrupted. "Fredrickson's brother-in-law worked as my office manager. No wonder I found my paperwork regarding the hijackings in the recycling. Some friend. My investor probably bugged my office, too, which is how they knew I'd be here."

The bit about the recycling bin struck me as odd. "Why take the risk with the papers? He could have just shredded them."

Reilly bit his lip. "The shredder's been broken for about a month. I kept meaning to replace it, but the hijackings kept me occupied."

"So they unknowingly preserved the evidence." Warren took a sip of coffee. "You were right the whole time about him being responsible for the robbery of Thompson's flat, Noah. When they broke up their business partnership, Fredrickson needed to recover some critical documents, so he had one of his associates rob the flat. You got the motive and half the evidence wrong, but…" He shrugged. "The right guy."

I leaned back in my chair. Everything made sense now. "Fredrickson spotted an excellent opportunity for drug smuggling in Reilly's business. Importing decor from Nicaragua, one of his major supplier countries, meant he could easily have the drugs slipped into various items: statuettes and vases, or packaged into thick ottoman cushions…"

Lieutenant Warren cleared his throat. "According to state police, once the shipments were en route from Portland, Fredrickson's crew would reroute it to his niece's storage facility in Toledo, just south of Chehalis. WSP raided the place today, and found the missing trucks and trailers."

"Toledo, Washington?" I blinked. "So, all of us, even Thompson, took it for granted that Fredrickson was in Ohio at the time."

"He had thoroughly planned that out." The lieutenant took a long drink of coffee. "Anyhow, Martin Steele's half-brother, Bobby, was supposed to be hauling the shipment Hampton ended up with, but had been arrested for DUI the night before."

"Steele was the intended target, then?" Reilly ventured.

"Oh, no, Martin Steele was very much involved," Dee replied. "If you look at the hijacking reports, he was the only one out of the four not to be assaulted. He also said that he had been a trucker for fifteen years, so the police looked up his employment records. His last employer ran a private semi fleet back and forth over the Mexican border, and that company was shut down for smuggling drugs, weapons, and immigrants."

"Definitely a nasty character," Warren added. "So, Steele had to pull an unexpected hijacking, and Hampton somehow saw the scorpion tattoo on his neck." He turned toward Reilly. "Why hadn't you called us when the first couple of trucks were hijacked?"

The businessman frowned. "I was going to, but Fredrickson kept insisting it would ruin our reputation and drive the upscale designers away. He said he'd just cover the loss of the merchandise himself. Finally, he agreed to let me hire a private investigator, and gave me Mr. Clue's card."

"Great," I groaned, remembering that I had flung that card on Fredrickson's chest the night I accused him in the last investigation. "So your investor hoped I would buy him more time. In the meanwhile the group somehow got nervous about Hampton talking to me, and killed him."

I handed Warren my entire file on the case. "You'll find all of the truckers' hijacking accounts in there. Steele told us everything he knew the other truckers would tell us, to prevent his standing out in our notes. But he let a little too much slip."

"And he underestimated our abilities," Dee chimed in, glancing down at the empty carafe in her hand. "Why am I still holding this?" She took the coffee pot to the kitchenette.

Lieutenant Warren stood. "I think that about wraps up this side of things. We're cooperating with WSP for a more thorough investigation." He set his coffee mug on the desk and headed for the door. "Thank you, gentlemen. And lady. Your assistance has been most valuable."

As Warren left, I turned back to Dee. "There's just one last thing I don't understand. You told me you thought Reilly was behind all of this." I glanced at my client. "No offense intended."

My client waved it off. "None taken."

Dee chuckled. "I said it was an inside job, never that it was definitely linked to Reilly. You misunderstood me."

"Here's my check for the full amount I owe you." Reilly ripped it out of his checkbook, and then shook my hand. "Meanwhile, I have to see about getting a new office manager. If you have any recommendations, I'd surely appreciate it."

I locked the door behind the departing Reilly and turned back to my cousin. "Dee, I don't understand it. I thought you quit."

"I let you believe that, Noah, but I only left the office to get out of your way." She began clearing the empty mugs from the desk. "And I realize now I had completely overstepped my bounds when I tried to take over."

I dipped my head in embarrassment. "I'm the one who should be apologizing, Dee. I'm really not cut out to be a P.I."

Dee smiled. "Actually, you did pretty well for yourself. The ability to link everything together is there. It's the matter of finding all the pieces that's lacking."

I had to agree with that. "Which is where you fit in. You know what questions to ask. Are you still willing to work for me?"

She shrugged. "Of course, if you'll have me."

"Are you sure you don't mind working for a second-rate P.I. out of a low-end apartment?"

Dee scoffed. "Of course I'd mind *that*, but I'm working for my cousin instead—a first-rate P.I. in the making."

* * *

Later that morning, a knock at the door aroused me from my feeble attempt at sleep. "Dee, would you mind terribly if I pretended I didn't hear that?"

"Go right ahead," came the muffled reply from the office chair.

I rolled over in bed.

Another fierce rapping. "Hello! Mr. Clue? Are you in there? I don't have a key!"

Oh, for cryin' out loud. I had forgotten about Miss Leah Lee.

"Who in tarnation is that?" Dee muttered.

I stammered. "My...ahem, my secretary. Replacement...well...former. For..."

"Yeah, I got the idea. Let the poor woman in."

"Me? You're closer."

"You hired her," Dee growled.

I rolled out of bed and dragged myself over to the door. "I'm coming, Miss Lee."

Her expression switched from concern to shock at seeing me in my disheveled state. "What happened to you?"

"Late night, you could say."

"I see!" She spotted Dee. "Is that your...oh!" Miss Lee blushed. "Am I, um, interrupting something?"

Awkward. "No, this isn't what it looks like. That's my cousin, Dee. Umm...my first secretary. I fired her. And then I hired her again."

Leah Lee raised an eyebrow. "Are you feeling okay?"

"Don't mind me, dear." Dee had managed to raise her head. "We had a misunderstanding, that's all. I'm his usual secretary."

Miss Lee looked disappointed. "So, I take it then, Mr. Clue, you are no longer in need of my services?"

I wrote out her final check. "I'm afraid not. That's pretty well in hand." I looked back at Dee, and then spotted Reilly's card sitting by the typewriter. "I do, however, know a businessman that will immediately welcome someone of your exceptional skills. Please tell him I sent you."

Miss Lee seemed all too eager to take the card, with my offer of a personal recommendation. With her gone, I turned to Dee. "What I don't understand is why, out of all the opportunities this city has to offer a skilled secretary like yourself, you come back here to work for free."

"I can't very well leave you to sink or swim by yourself, can I? We need each other to excel."

"True."

Her tone turned patronizing. "Anyway, I think of you as a project. A very, very large project."

I paused. "Normally, I'd have some sort of come back for that, but I'm too tired." I collapsed backwards onto my bed.

"How's about another four or five hours?"

"I'm all for it." I shut my eyes and let the sleep fog take hold.

Mere moments into it, another knock sounded at my door. Good grief! I dragged myself out of bed, closed the curtain to my bedroom, and threw open the office door.

A gentleman in a tan wool suit, sporting slick-backed auburn hair, stepped inside. "Mr. Clue? I am in need of your services."

I managed a professional response. "We've just finished an extremely long shift, sir. Any chance you can come back later?"

The visitor paused and stared at me. "How much later?"

"Tomorrow. We'll open just for you."

The man blinked in silence for a few moments. "I have to say, this is quite unconventional."

"You just summed us up in a nutshell," came Dee's response from the desk.

He turned to my secretary. "By that time, I'll have hired someone else. You do realize that?"

"Yes, sir," replied Dee. "But at least you'd be hiring someone halfway cognizant. I apologize for the inconvenience, but this office is closed for the day."

He frowned. "Hmph, I suppose I shall have to come back then. Good day." He donned the brown panama hat in his hand and departed. I shut the door behind him and locked it firmly.

"The way I look at it," Dee mumbled. "If he's worth working for, he'll be willing to wait until tomorrow. I couldn't type if my life depended on it right now."

"Indeed." I slipped behind my bedroom curtain and collapsed on the bed. "Goodnight, Dee."

"Goodnight, Mr. Clue," came her response from the chair.

It Reminds Me
Of A Game

To Lewis, Josh, and Audrey,

Who taught me to listen with my eyes and ears,

And to speak with my whole self.

Does typing count?

1

So Long, Sam Spade

Tuesday, April 27

"Noah, where in blazes are you?" My cousin's voice echoed through my apartment.

"Under here." I was on my back in the kitchenette, head and shoulders in the under-sink cabinet, with my flannel shirt sleeves rolled up past my elbows. Waves of rain splattered against the window pane.

"What are you doing?"

"I'm attempting to fix this sink." I pulled the badly clogged U-pipe loose, and sputtered as putrid brown liquid poured onto my face. I tried to slide out and sit up, banging my head on the edge of the cabinet. "In reality, mostly just eating rancid water and working on a concussion. Hand me that towel, will you?"

Dee tossed the rag to me. As usual she was dressed in a tailored business suit. "Isn't the landlord supposed to take care of that?"

I wiped my face with the rag. "Allegedly, but all I keep hearing is 'it's never done that before,' or the some such nonsense."

"Well, Uncle Denby you ain't."

"Don't I know it?" I slid the rest of the way out of the cabinet and dried my hands. "I kinda wish I had taken time to learn more handyman skills. Uncle Denby sure knows how to keep the ranch running smoothly."

"And profitably." Dee nodded. "Speaking of which, we really need to increase our client base."

"Hey, three closed cases in a month isn't bad, considering my record before you came along." I picked up the new grease trap.

She didn't agree. "We're barely clearing expenses with what our clients have paid us. And this dump doesn't help our reputation."

I hated the reminder of my past failures. "You know I can't afford a better place right now, Dee."

My cousin shrugged. "I'm just saying that an uptown office would bring in higher-paying clients, and make a better impression."

Had she lost her ever-lovin' mind? "So, we're barely eking by, and you want to rent a more expensive office? I'm not following your logic." I moved back under the sink to put the new trap into place. At least I wasn't a total idiot when it came to home repairs. And the library helped.

"I have quite a bit of money saved up, Noah. I could carry the full weight of the new office rent for a good six months without touching my personal budget. Anyway, I've got an extra bedroom in my apartment if you want it. But I'm not putting a red cent into this money pit."

I considered the proposal for a moment. In the best case, we'd be making much more in a few weeks' time, what with my climbing reputation and higher paying clients. In the worst case, Dee would be out a good chunk of cash, and we'd end up back here.

My cousin broke the verbal silence. "When's your lease up?"

"I'm on a month-to-month." Before I could fit the u-pipe in place, a clog further up the line came loose, sending another torrent of filthy water into my face. I slid out of the cabinet and grabbed the towel again. "Who cares about a thirty-day notice?" I flung the pipe under the sink. "The landlord will likely keep the damage deposit anyway, and I'm sick of making repairs in this dump for free."

"So, we start looking at new offices after work?"

"Better yet, let's start looking at new offices right after I lose my lunch and take a shower." I sighed. "And to think, today is only Tuesday."

* * *

Our real estate agent, Praveena Nayar, came to stand in front of the massive picture window. Her thick black braid swung behind her as she turned around in the space. "This one has new carpet, with an excellent view of the waterfront. One thousand and eighty-six square feet. And being in the Columbia Center has benefits, as I've mentioned before."

"We really don't need this much square footage." I looked around. "What's the smallest space for lease in this building?"

Praveena motioned to the room with her hands. "This is it."

Dee shook her head. "We really need something under fifteen-hundred a month."

"How little square footage are you willing to work with?" Praveena opened her binder, ready to search through the real estate listings.

I snorted. "I'm fairly certain there are janitor closets in this city that are larger than what we have now."

"Let me make a couple of phone calls. Give me a few minutes." Praveena stepped out into the lobby.

Once the door shut, I faced my cousin. "Dee, I'm still amazed you can afford any of this."

"Why? Just because you have no budgeting skills?" Mockery glittered in her brown eyes.

I rubbed the back of my neck. "Well, no. It's just...how much money can one possibly save up working as a lawyer's secretary?"

"When one is living with her parents? A considerable amount. No rent, no utilities..."

"Still, fifteen hundred a month?"

She curled her lip. "*Under* fifteen hundred."

"Still..."

"I'm frugal, okay?" Dee rolled her eyes. "Whereas you can blow through in a weekend what would be my grocery budget for the entire month."

"Yeah, that's the only problem with moving. I'm really going to miss Hot Wok Chinese Takeout."

She clicked her tongue. "I won't."

"Well, of course you won't. You're happier eating cardboard three square meals a day." I crossed to the window and stared out. Rain streamed down the glass, blurring my view of the dreary Seattle day.

"Whole grains aren't that bad."

I didn't even turn back. "The Italians never intended for pasta to taste like that."

Dee scoffed. "And the Chinese never intended for Chow Mein to have a ninety-eight percent fat content."

"Good news," Praveena called out as she entered the room. "There are some office spaces a few blocks away in the Colman Building, all of them under fifteen hundred a month."

My cousin started for the door. "What are we waiting for? Lead the way."

* * *

I turned around slowly in the open space. "The floor plan works for me. It's my favorite out of the five others we've seen so far in this building. I just wish there was a little bit more natural light."

Dee nodded. "I have to agree. We can make it work, but we'd better see that last one, just in case."

"It's just down the hall." Praveena led us out of Suite Four-Ten.

Dee marched shoulder-to-shoulder with me, her voice barely above a whisper. "I really like this building, Noah. It seems clean and well maintained. Upscale, but not in your face about it."

I had to admit, the prospect of working out of the Colman Building excited me. It would certainly give my practice a prestigious air. "Yeah. It's very professional."

"And that's precisely what we need."

Praveena stopped. "Here we are, Suite Four-Fifteen." She consulted her clipboard. "You're giving up about five square feet." She unlocked the door and held it open for us.

I surveyed the office. "Pretty good layout, and I love the extra large windows. What's the footage again?"

Praveena glanced down at her papers. "Five hundred ten. The furnishings are temporary, so you'll need your own."

I did the calculation in my head. "Less than a thousand a month, Dee. If there's a kitchenette, you want to take it?"

My cousin nodded "It works for me. Looks like a counter with a microwave over here," Dee replied as she continued around the desk by the front door. "Oh my...!"

I followed her. "What?"

"We'll be needing new carpet." Dee pointed to a dead body sprawled in a pool of blood. "Someone's been murdered."

* * *

I sat across the table from the manager for the Colman Building, trying to figure out how exactly I had wound up here. Praveena had apparently told someone that I was a private investigator, and I could only presume the knowledge had reached the manager somewhere around the same time as the news of the dead body had.

Curtis Daubney smoothed his navy blue tie and leaned forward, folding his hands on the table. "Have you ever solved a murder before, Mr. Clue?"

"Yes, one." I spotted a flash of disappointment in Daubney's blue eyes. "Private investigators don't generally work murder cases. That's typically handled by the authorities."

"Naturally." The businessman sat back and drummed his fingers on the table. "This incident creates a small problem for me, see. Many people don't want to lease space in a building if they think someone might knock them off."

"I'm fairly sure the police can handle this, Mr. Daubney." I glanced around. Dee had promised to rejoin me after a pit stop, but she hadn't shown up yet.

"Oh yes, I'm sure they can, but that does nothing for appearances." Daubney leaned forward again. "See, this is where you come in handy." He tapped the table in front of me. "If we hire you to look into the issue, that sends a clear message that we take this seriously. That it isn't a common occurrence."

"Fair enough." I pondered the last time I had been hired to solve a murder. "Pardon the question, but why me?"

Daubney looked puzzled at the inquiry. "Why not? You're a private investigator, aren't you? You've solved murders."

"One murder." I reminded him.

"Okay, one murder. Anyway, you also happen to be the person to find the body. Surely your investigator's instincts are aroused, no?" The building manager tented his fingers. "I'll tell you what: if you take the case, I'll give you your first two month's rent here free. If you solve the case…" He grinned. "I'll throw in a whole year at half the price."

Dee or no, this was an offer I couldn't refuse.

Once I'd finalized the arrangements with Daubney, I returned to the office where the body had been found. I wanted to find Dee and tell her the news of our latest case. Instead I ran headlong into Lieutenant Gregg Warren.

"Noah, fancy meeting you here." Warren sounded as thrilled about my presence as a restaurateur would be about a colony of rats. His blond crew cut had grown out a bit since our last encounter.

"We were merely looking for new office space when we found the body." I frowned at the ribbon of yellow crime scene tape across the door of our dream office. This would certainly put a damper on moving for the time being.

"And here I was worried you had been called in to investigate." Warren's tone gave me no hint of whether he was serious.

I gave him a wry smile. "As a matter of fact, the building manager just hired me to do exactly that."

Dee's most charming Texas drawl sounded behind me. "Why, Lieutenant Warren, good to see you again."

I watched Warren's tough demeanor waver. He gave a nod of his head. "Miss Tindall. I trust you're keeping your P.I. on a short leash?"

I narrowed my gaze. "Excuse me?" Being a ranking Seattle police officer didn't give him an excuse to be rude.

My cousin gave him a tight smile. "I'm his secretary, not his handler, Lieutenant. Noah is capable of handling his own leash."

I raised my chin a little. "Three satisfied clients this month. I think I've finally hit my stride. Dee and I make a pretty effective investigative team."

"Three cases, and you're moving operations to downtown already?" Warren raised his eyebrows. "Pretty ambitious, wouldn't you say, Noah?"

Dee studied her fingernails. "It was my idea, actually. I'm footing the bill."

Bewilderment drifted across his face. "You're the secretary, and… how much does he pay you, anyway?"

"Never mind your steam-pressed blues about that," she drawled.

"Let me know how that works out for you." Warren turned his attention to the crime scene. He was a few steps away when he wheeled around again. "Say, Miss Tindall, just how confident are you in your P.I.'s abilities, anyway?"

Dee's right eye barely twitched. "He's not 'my P.I.' He's my boss first, cousin second. As to our combined skill, as Noah said, I think we make a pretty effective team."

"Well, you seem to be in the gambling mood, considering this whole rental business." He approached us. "Since it sounds like Noah has just been hired, do you think you two could solve this mystery before my team can?"

Dee gave him a small smile. "Barring unfair advantage, yes, I do."

"Then I propose a friendly little wager."

"Dee…" I started.

She held up a finger to me. "Do tell."

Warren seemed to be enjoying this way too much. "The first one to find the murderer, and provide sufficient evidence for his or her arrest, wins."

"What are we wagering?"

"One thousand dollars. Out of personal funds, of course."

"Better yet," Dee replied. "Forget the money. If we win, our firm gets priority access to public police records, courtesy of a few well-pulled strings from you."

"And if I win, you take your," Warren made quotation marks with his fingers, "practice out of Seattle—to, let's say, Bellevue."

My jaw dropped open. He had to be kidding.

"Afraid of the competition, I see." Dee nudged me with her elbow. "There's one more condition, Lieutenant."

"Name it."

Dee blew the ever-present curl of hair out of her eyes. "You only get what you give. If either side gets more information from the other than they disclose, you forfeit."

Warren laughed. "Shoot, in that case, I'll throw in your first month's rent if you win."

My cousin didn't crack a smile. "That's only your side of the deal, Lieutenant. I am not betting money."

"Afraid?"

She waved him off. "Nah. I never wager in greenbacks."

True. She always had more interesting conditions in mind. I just wished she hadn't been quite so creative with this round.

Warren held out his hand. "You have yourself a bet, Miss Tindall."

My cousin might as well have slugged me in the gut.

* * *

"Colonel Mustard, in the dining room, with the revolver." Dee set the game piece in its proper place on the board. So far, Dee's apartment looked exactly how I had expected it. Neat, businesslike, and mind-numblingly modernist in its decor. So much had changed in my cousin since our Texas ranch days. Years ago, she would have dismissed this place as a yuppie den.

I tossed down the revolver card and drew another from the ghost pile. Back in high school, Dee and I had worked out a way to play the board game Clue with only two people, and we'd never played it differently since. "I can disprove your suggestion." I grunted. "You know, I would enjoy this game a whole lot more, if you hadn't gotten us into a high-stakes version with Warren."

Mischief sparkled in her brown eyes. "Believe me, before all is said and done, he'll be begging us for double or nothing."

"As usual, I don't follow you." I rolled the dice.

"Lieutenant Warren overestimates his own team. See, a lot of people won't tell law enforcement what they'll tell to a plainclothes individual. Thus, while Warren's waiting for warrants and whatnot, we've already got the drop on the trail. By the time he's bothered to actually ask us for information, we've already been able to chew on it for a while."

"Still, to wager our entire business?" I set Professor Plum in the library and searched the board for the wrench token.

"We're only wagering our location. I can just as easily move us to another city as I can to downtown Seattle. So, if we lose the bet, we're winning a fresh start, sans one police lieutenant."

"Maybe so, but I really hate Bellevue. It's so...hoity-toity." I shuddered at the thought of living there.

She flashed me a brilliant grin. "Which means higher paying clients, of course."

"You've got this all figured out, don't you?"

"As usual."

Here she went again, taking charge of my business. I pondered pulling rank, but couldn't quite figure out how to do it. My brain faltered for a response. I turned back to the game. "Hmm. Well, Professor Plum, in the library, with the wrench."

"I cannot disprove your suggestion."

At least something was going my way. I glanced over my game notes one last time. "Then I would like to accuse. Professor Plum, library, wrench."

Dee shook her head. "It's the study, not the library."

I smirked and flipped open the envelope, laying the cards out on the table. "Professor Plum. Wrench." I frowned. "Study."

"That's why I never lose at this game, Noah." Dee pulled the library out from under the stack of discarded cards. "I always keep track of ground covered."

Wednesday, April 28

I settled onto my stool at the breakfast bar, next to my cousin, trying to acclimate to the environment of her apartment. It was bad enough that she had conned me into carrying a cell phone three weeks before. Now my entire life was in upheaval. I already missed my desk, which we'd sold when it became clear that it wouldn't fit in this space. Paying storage fees wasn't worth it. "Maybe we shouldn't have been so fast to drop the old office. Working out of your apartment, Dee..."

"I worked out of yours. Deal with it." Dee's fingers flew across her laptop keyboard. "At least we have internet here."

"I'm just saying, I hope we get this whole mess cleared up soon. At least the manager is happy to hold the office for us. I doubt anyone else will want it now." I sipped my coffee and loaded a fresh piece of paper into my loyal typewriter.

We had just returned from Warren's office with an unofficial copy of the victim's identification, which had been found on his person. The Washington state driver's license identified him as forty-one-year-old Jonathan Conhue. The police were busy interviewing anyone who had been in the building around the time of the murder. Meanwhile, Dee and I had returned to her apartment to do some digging of our own.

At least, that was what Dee described it as.

I clattered out a couple more interesting details from the crime scene description. The response of the typewriter keys to my fingers gave me joy. "So, how are your new-fangled investigating techniques working out for you?"

"Not bad, so far." She pointed to the victim's grinning face on her computer screen. "It turns out that Mr. Conhue was an independent real estate agent."

Made sense. "That would explain how he got in there."

"Perhaps, assuming he had the combination for the key box. He doesn't work for the same real estate office as Praveena. Actually, he owns his own company."

"Is it possible that someone at Praveena's office might be involved? They'd have easy opportunity."

"It's possible, but it doesn't make much sense. They'd be taking quite the loss on a potential lease by killing another real estate agent. Not to mention, things would focus right back on them." She shrugged. "I mean, anything's possible at this point, but my suspicions lie elsewhere."

I made a note to find out who had access to the office, and how they'd have to get it. "At least we've ruled out our own real estate agent. Praveena wouldn't have shown us that office if she was guilty."

"I agree that she's unlikely, but of course, we can't jump to a conclusion of innocence at this point." Dee clicked something. "Hey, hey, what's this?"

I leaned over to get a better view of her screen. "What?"

"There was a recent lawsuit against Mr. Conhue for fraud. Our victim won, but from the looks of it...breach of contract, misrepresentation, some funny business with the commission..."

"He wasn't getting paid?"

Dee sat back. "Oh, he got paid. Three times."

I squinted at her laptop screen. "How did he manage that?"

"Claimed that he never received the first check, demanded another be sent registered. Then he complained it was written out to the agency and not to him, so he demanded a third. Then he somehow cashed all three."

My mind reeled. The victim had to have broken nearly every check fraud prevention rule imaginable. "How did he get away with that?"

"All his conversations with the client were over the phone, so he claimed that the client sent those as 'gifts.' Surprisingly, the arbitrator bought it. Conhue successfully counter-sued the plaintiff for slander and defamation of character."

It sounded like motive enough for murder. "Who's the plaintiff?"

"An area businessman named Alberto Verde. I'd say he would be a good person to talk to."

2

And Then There Were Three

"A Noah Clue to see you, sir." Alberto Verde's secretary maintained a sunny expression at us as she spoke into the intercom.

I folded my wet umbrella, and leaned it against the wall by the front door of the consulting firm office. The tiny waiting area barely accommodated two large chairs and a water cooler, alongside the massive quarter-circle receptionist desk. Frankly, the furniture seemed like it had been intended for a much larger space.

I caught myself pondering various furniture arrangements for the third time today. The delayed promise of my new office kept crowding to the front of my mind. I removed my black Stetson and gently shook the rainwater off of it before hanging it on the coat rack by the door.

"Mr. Verde will be just a moment," the secretary assured me.

"That's fine." I decided to study the woman's face instead of the office. Auburn hair, sparkling green eyes, rosy cheeks, slightly vacant expression as she pored over something on her computer screen. My best friend David had a near perfect memory for people—for everything, actually—but I really had to fight to even notice a face, much less recall it later.

"Send him in, Miss Florentina," came a man's tinny response over the intercom speaker.

The secretary motioned toward the closed door. "Mr. Verde will see you now."

I snickered to myself. Florentina was a perfect name for someone with a "rose leaf complexion" as the poetic types would call it. And her boss was named for the color green. What an odd combination. I entered first, Dee right on my heels. I stuck out my hand. "Thank you for making time to see us today, Mr. Verde."

Alberto Verde stood, a plump, five-foot-six-inch, nearly bald Spanish gentleman. A bushy strip of black and silver hair reached around the back of his head from one unusually large ear to the other. "What can I do for you, Mr. Clue?" He sat down.

I took the right-hand chair in front of the desk. "We understand you've done business with a Jonathan Conhue."

All the color left Verde's face. "What do you want?"

I checked my posture to make sure I didn't appear threatening. "We want to know what you can tell us about him."

Verde shook his head. "I can't say anything. There was a gag order as part of the settlement. I barely avoided another lawsuit when someone working for me leaked the details to the press."

That could provide even more motive. "When's the last time you had contact with Conhue?"

He narrowed his gaze. "Not since we met at his attorney's office over a month ago. Why? What is he accusing me of now?"

Dee leaned forward. "Conhue is dead. There's an investigation."

Verde's gray eyebrows arched in surprise. "And because I lost to that scum bag, I'm a suspect?" He bristled. "He nearly cost me my business. Conhue was a scam artist, plain and simple. Say, are you police officers?"

I shook my head. "I'm a private investigator. We're working in conjunction with the police on this case."

Verde shifted around in his seat. "There are sure to be plenty of people who have been taken in by this guy. Have you talked to any of them yet?"

"We're starting with you. What more can you tell us?" Dee poised her pen over her notepad, ready to transcribe any new information.

The man leaned back in his office chair and ran his right thumb against something in his palm. "Do you know why I'm stuck in this dinky space? I hired Conhue to help me find a larger office for my consulting firm. We're a small business, so his seemingly low commission attracted us. I settled on some square footage in Queen Anne. Four hundred square feet for thirteen dollars per square foot a year. Conhue brought the papers here to my office for me to sign. I was supposed to send him his commission in check form."

Verde sighed. "I sent the first check in the mail, but Conhue complained a few days later that he hadn't received it. So, I sent another check through FedEx, so it could be tracked. Then, Conhue complained that he couldn't cash it because it had been made out to his firm, and not to him directly. So, I put a stop payment on the first two and sent a third, which he cashed."

Frustration marred the businessman's face as he leaned forward on his desk. "Then, when we go to visit our new office space, someone else is moving in. I talk to the building manager to try and clear up the misunderstanding, and I find out that I had never actually rented the space. What I thought were the first, last, and deposit, had actually been just 'fees' for Conhue's services. When I got a look at the contract again later, I found that it hadn't been a lease at all, and the actual rent was twenty-three dollars per square foot. The papers I had signed in hiring Conhue stated that any disputes were to be settled by a predetermined arbitrator."

I couldn't help but marvel at the brazen genius of the plot, disgusting as it was. I couldn't contain my curiosity about Conhue's check trick, especially since he used it against an experienced businessman. "How did he manage to cash the other two checks?"

"That!" Verde huffed. "Turns out, at my bank, stop payments on checks only last six months unless renewed, and Conhue is good at waiting. When he cashed the other two checks, the bank decided the deposit was in 'good faith'. The legal burden is on me to prove loss. I tried to bring that up in the case, but as you know, I lost."

I frowned. "I am so sorry, Mr. Verde."

"It's my own fault. Of all people, I should know to read every contract before signing it. That's what I'm always telling clients, after all." He held up a pen with the name of a local credit union. "I also switched financial institutions."

Dee finished jotting down her notes. "If you don't mind my asking, but after everything, how much did Conhue get out of you?"

"Eight hundred sixty-six dollars in what I thought were first and last month's rent, two thousand in an alleged deposit, four thousand one hundred sixty in commission, three times over of course, and another ten thousand as a countersuit for so-called defamation of character. Grand total, over twenty five thousand dollars."

I whistled. If all this was true, it didn't surprise me that someone decided to knock off Jonathan Conhue. Still, murder was murder. "How did you manage to keep your firm afloat?"

"I borrowed heavily from personal funds to make up for most of the losses. The rest will even out with time. We're still bringing in more than enough business to stay open, though we've had to push back our move until next year at the earliest." Verde set down his pen. "As much as I lost, I'm sadder but wiser. Still, I'm not sorry to hear that Conhue is dead. How'd he go? Eaten by spiders, hopefully."

I weighed how much to disclose without compromising the case. "We're still waiting for the medical examiner's report. Is there anything else you can tell us?"

Apathy registered on Verde's face. "If you're looking for people that hated Jonathan Conhue's guts, you'll need to talk to his older brother." Verde scribbled something on a pad. "Major Robert Conhue. He could give you loads of dirt on this guy, I'm sure. I found out through all of this that Jonny had a long-standing reputation." He slid the note towards me.

I took it and stuffed it in my pocket. "How do you know this Major Conhue, anyhow?"

"He and I served together in 'Nam. We're old buddies."

Some friend. "And he didn't warn you?" I glanced at my cousin to see her reaction. As always, none presented itself. How had she learned how to be so stoic, anyway?

Verde frowned. "He'd said something once about his brother being a skunk, but I didn't make the connection until it was too late."

I stood to leave. "Thank you again for your time, Mr. Verde. We'll be in touch."

"As will the police, I'm sure." He leaned back and gestured around his cluttered office. "No matter, I have nothing to hide."

Thursday, April 29

"Jonny's dead?" Major Robert Conhue grunted. "Can't say I'll be attending the funeral." Little emotion marked his long, rectangular face. His short, graying hair offset his blotchy red skin. A well-groomed silver mustache perched beneath his nose.

"Not the usual reaction to losing a family member," I mused.

Major Conhue pushed back from his desk and crossed his study. "He was hardly family to me, as far as I'm concerned. A relative, yes, but not family."

"Why do you say that?" I took a careful sip of the hot coffee the major had offered us, and recognized the overtly acidic taste of a popular specialty brand from somewhere back East. I decided against drinking any more.

Major Conhue took a large sip of his own coffee before setting the mug down on a shelf with a little more force than I thought necessary. "I refuse to acknowledge someone who makes his living defrauding honest people. The only reason he moved here to Seattle was to get away from some legal troubles in Tennessee, where he'd been running an alleged music label under an alias."

Dee scribbled something on her legal pad. "How much do you know about his most recent operations here?"

Conhue stood with his back to us, looking out the window. He waved Dee off. "The less I know about Jonny's endeavors, the better. He comes...well, he came...over to brag to me about his latest scheme, and I'd have to throw him out before my temper got the better of me."

"And you never considered calling the police?" Dee's voice held that formal air that always seemed to let her ask the most awkward questions with impunity.

The major barely paused before replying. "I had no proof and didn't want the negative media attention on my family."

"Had you ever considered killing him?" I asked.

Major Conhue whirled around. "I despised him, but I would never stoop to murder."

I recoiled inwardly. How was it, my cousin could ask anything and never get a reaction, but I got rebuffed on a regular basis?

"Impressive gun collection, Major." Dee had left her chair, and stood by a glass case. "You're an enthusiast?"

The major's clouded expression cleared immediately. "Dare say I am. I've been collecting since my army days. My favorite is that one there. It's a six-inch Smith and Wesson Model 66 revolver. It was commissioned by the Rhode Island State Police in '76, but after only two hundred were made, the state police decided to swap to the four-inch. One of my army buddies was on the force, and he gave it to me when I retired."

Dee had really gotten Major Conhue off on a rabbit trail, although at least his anger at my question had been averted. He rambled on about his collection for a good eight minutes. I occupied myself by browsing the other items in his study. Ornate jars, teapots, and statuettes dotted the shelves. Most of them appeared to be bronze, but a few looked like jade or ivory. It would seem that guns weren't the major's only collecting interest.

I pulled us back onto topic. "Can you think of anyone that would want to kill your brother?"

Major Conhue turned around and scowled. "It'd be easier for me to list off who wouldn't. Almost everyone that ever knew him would kill him in a heartbeat, given a decent opportunity."

"But you wouldn't seek revenge?" I ventured, hoping to approach the subject from a less confrontative standpoint than last time.

"Not like that. I know that probably has your brilliant detective mind running a mile a minute..." Major Conhue made a spinning motion with his finger, "...but you'll find that I'm so far removed from whatever events occurred recently that my only connection is being unfortunate enough to be related to the scum bag."

Dee cut in. "On a different subject, what do you know about Alberto Verde?"

Major Conhue looked a bit surprised at the mention of the name. "Alberto? We're old army buddies. Good chap. Haven't talked to him in a couple of months, though. He said he was having some sort of legal trouble. Why?"

"How long did he know Jonny?" my cousin continued, deftly avoiding the inquiry.

"He didn't...at least, not as far as I know. Is there some sort of connection I am unaware of?"

Dee and I glanced at each other, gauging if we even had to tell him about Verde's troubles.

From the vibrant stream of expletives, it was safe to say the major had figured it out all by himself. "How much did Jonny take him for?"

"Somewhere in the ballpark of twenty-five grand," I replied.

Major Conhue spit out another curse. "I hope that son-of-a-gun died slow!"

* * *

Dee and I claimed a table on the curb in front of the Starbucks a block from her apartment. I nursed a cup of coffee, extra heavy on the cream and the sugar. "How does one get to the point of wanting their own brother dead?"

My cousin slung her free arm over the back of her chair. "I'm not sure, but we do know that Major Robert Conhue had motive."

I took another sip. "At least it swings a little in the major's favor that he didn't know about Alberto Verde's trouble with Jonathan."

My cousin shrugged. "That's what it looked like, but Major Conhue may also be a very good actor. We shouldn't rule him out just yet."

"What about Verde?"

"Motive there, too."

My pocket buzzed, and a Michael Bublé song sounded. I fished out the cell phone and flipped it open. "Clue, P.I."

"Never thought I'd be calling you on my own time, Noah." Warren sounded none too pleased. "I have some information that I feel I am obligated to share, to keep this game of ours entirely fair." He cleared his throat. "To be transparent, all of this was cleared for public release. The victim doesn't have any next of kin on file."

"Do tell."

I heard Warren rustling through some papers. "We got the official medical examiner's report in. Jonathan Conhue died from four copper pellets in his brain stem, and two in his heart, apparently fired point-blank."

"Pellets? I hadn't realized they could really kill a person."

The longer-than-normal silence almost made me question if the call had been dropped. "You don't get out much, do you? They're solid metal projectiles. Do the math."

"Estimated time of death?"

"According to the coroner, between 11:00 a.m. and 1:00 p.m. We talked to one of the front desk receptionists at the Colman building, though, and we have Conhue entering alone on April 27th, around 12:45 p.m. Since you found him around 1:15, that gives us a thirty-minute window. We can narrow it down further, though. A cleaning lady, Elissa Snow, was working across the hall, and heard someone enter the office in question at 12:23, and leave at 12:57, so whoever killed Conhue almost certainly came and went at those times."

"Assuming she was telling the truth, of course," I mused aloud. "Although why would a cleaning lady kill a real estate agent?"

"Weirder things have happened. We're treating her as a possible suspect, of course." Warren clunked what sounded like his large coffee mug down on his desk. "On the note of possible suspects, the victim's medical records did turn up that he had a history of psychological problems, for which he was seeking treatment. Heaven only knows who he could have ticked off."

It suddenly struck me that Warren's generosity equated to a play for information from us, or at least to trap us into a forfeit. I countered. "Our investigation turned up that Conhue had defrauded a major businessman by the name of Alberto Verde and got away with it. One of Verde's army buddies is Major Robert Conhue, the older brother of our victim. He doesn't seem that broken up by Jonny Conhue's death."

Warren cleared his throat. "Brother, huh? Good, that saves us some footwork. We never were able to find his next of kin. We found out about that legal funny business, too." He paused a moment, and then sighed. "I might as well divulge our suspects, as well."

I pulled out a pen and positioned it over my notebook. "Shoot."

"We're looking at two real estate agents that were directly affected by Conhue's scam: an Adriana Skye, and your own agent, Praveena Nayar." More rustling papers. "And that's all we've uncovered at the moment."

Not much, but it was a start. I debated whether the cleaning lady was an angle worth pursuing on my own, or if that would be better left to the police.

Lieutenant Warren broke the silence. "Nice having a civil conversation with you for once."

I grinned. "Amazing what you'd discover about me when you get to know me."

Warren's voice turned stony. "Yes, well, let's try and keep those discoveries to a minimum. Keep me updated." He hung up.

I slid my notebook across to Dee. "Warren's guys found a few more possible suspects."

"They're going to go interrogate them to pieces, no doubt, if they haven't already." Dee looked over the paper. "I say we go have a chat with Ms. Skye."

* * *

"Conhue? Yup, know him, hate him." Adriana Skye tapped her cigarette in the ash tray on her desk. "I hope you're here because he's on trial or something."

I studied an unusual ceramic paperweight on her desk which resembled crumpled paper. "Dead, actually."

"Better yet." Ms. Skye's voice held no emotion as she leaned back in her chair and brushed her dark chestnut bangs away from her face. "So, what can I do for you?"

Dee consulted her notebook. "How did you know Mr. Conhue?"

She took a long draw on her cigarette, blowing the smoke out from between her bright red lips. "He hijacked a number of my clients, getting them to sign off on properties behind my back, and taking the full commission. Of course, when things turned sour for those clients, many of them blamed me for not warning them. Several were under the impressed I'd referred them."

I waved the smoke away from my face. "Have you been sued by any of them?"

"No, but my reputation online is terrible, thanks to this. Business is way down." She snuffed out her cigarette in the ashtray.

Dee picked up one of Ms. Skye's business cards. "What do you specialize in?"

The woman sighed and leaned forward, sorting through the papers on her desk. "Residential, mostly. A lot of apartments. More recently, I've been shifting focus to professional properties. I think you can imagine why."

"How long have you been in real estate?" I took the card from Dee and pondered the raised black print. Nothing terribly enlightening presented itself.

"Eight years. The last two have been a nightmare for me, professional and otherwise." She punctuated the last word with an exasperated toss of her head.

Dee nodded. "Conhue?"

She glared out from under her dark, furrowed brow. "Among other things."

"Like what?" I prompted.

Skye bristled as anger flashed in her violet eyes. "Does this relate to matters at hand?"

There I went again, getting suspects angry. I scrambled to make the question relevant. "Let's just say, you're presently a suspect in a murder investigation."

Dee shot me a dirty look. Perhaps I shouldn't have said that.

Skye's laughter held derision. "Oh, this is a murder, is it? Curious detail to leave out." Her tone turned to ice. "You can speak to my lawyer if you have any further questions."

Dee lowered her notebook. "Ms. Skye, my very abrupt boss did not put that well. The police consider you a suspect. We, however, simply want more information about Conhue, and what kind of damage he has done."

"Nice save, lady. Look, I told you everything I know about the lout. My own personal life is entirely beside the point."

The buzzer sounded. Skye held up a hand to us and pressed the button. "What?" she snapped.

A voice crackled over the intercom. "Mr. Blanchett on line two."

"Thank you." Skye released the button. "If you will excuse me, I have some actual work to take care of. If you have any more questions, as I said, you can speak to my lawyer." She handed Dee a business card.

Dee took the card and studied it for a moment. "I don't think you meant to give this to me." She handed it back.

Adriana Skye blanched. "That's...that's a client. This is my lawyer." She held out another card.

Dee took it and closed her notebook. "Thank you for your time, Ms. Skye." My cousin grabbed me by the arm and dragged me out of the office.

Once we were in the elevator, I turned to her. "I'm still trying to get used to..."

She cut me off. "Just keep the quiet, hawk-eyed P.I. cover up, and let me do the talking from now on. As soon as you open your mouth, you become a liability."

"So, I'm more or less a brain on legs in this partnership?"

"Close. You're the face that gets me into places."

Ouch. "Good to know I'm appreciated."

Dee bowed her head cordially in my direction. "Thank you for having a P.I. license."

I opened my mouth to deliver a witty comeback, but the elevator doors opened before I could say anything. As we walked towards the front of the building, I noticed Dee was busy on her smartphone. "What are you doing?"

"Dr. Stephen Orchard is a psychologist in Queen Anne."

I tried to get a look at the screen. "And who is he?"

"That card she first handed me was for him, not her lawyer."

"Just because he's a shrink doesn't mean he's her shrink. She said he was a client."

Dee flashed me that annoying million-dollar smile again. "Then why did the card have an appointment time written on it for the day before yesterday?"

3

Crazy With A Side Of Fries

Dr. Orchard's receptionist, a heavy-set woman in her mid-forties, gazed at us over thick red-rimmed glasses. "Dr. Orchard is in with a patient right now. Would you like me to take down a message for him?"

Dee shook her head. "We'll just wait."

"Suit yourself." The receptionist retreated to hunch in front of her monitor. Her gray-brown perm bobbed with the force of her furious typing.

My cousin and I took a seat. After a moment, Dee leaned over and whispered in my ear. "Okay, Watson, time to work on your observational skills."

"Come again?"

"People watching." Dee nodded surreptitiously to the man sitting on the other side of the room. "Put that almost-Bachelor's degree in psychology to work. What do you observe?"

I concentrated on a man in his late thirties sitting next to the window directly across from us. He had his arms crossed while his right heel tapped out a rapid, steady rhythm on the floor.

The man glanced around the room, spotted me, and stared. I kept my gaze directed towards the window next to him. Finally, he slumped down in his chair, glancing at me occasionally.

"He's nervous," I whispered to Dee. "I think he's afraid of people knowing he visits a shrink. He doesn't want to be labeled as crazy."

"Very good. How about the woman in the corner?"

The woman in question had buried herself in a copy of *Vogue*. Her legs were crossed, and she barely moved at all. "She's hiding."

"How do you know she isn't just reading the magazine?" Dee whispered back.

"It's entirely too close to her face. All those perfume samples would be overwhelming." I puffed out my chest a little, congratulating myself on a good observation.

"Nice. How about the man sitting under the abstract painting?"

I scanned the room. "Dee, I don't see anyone else in here."

Amusement laced her voice. "Look behind you."

I turned around, expecting to see a partition and another section to the waiting room. My nose met an off-white, textured wall. "Dee..."

"And up, stupid."

My gaze fell on an abstract painting over my head. I slumped in my chair, fuming inwardly. "That's cheating."

The door opened. "Same time next week, Mr. Calderon?" the smooth male voice floated down the hallway.

"Thank you, Doctor." A man in his early fifties, with thinning white hair, snatched a card from the receptionist's desk as he hurried out of the office.

The receptionist nodded in my direction. "There's someone over there to see you, Dr. Orchard."

The psychologist studied us for a moment over his half-rim glasses. I wondered if his receptionist had picked up her habit from him. Finally, the doctor waved us over. I stood and approached, Dee right behind me.

"Come back to my office. I have about ten minutes before my next patient." The doctor led us down an accent lighted hall that smelled of pine and vanilla, into a side office lined with dark wooden bookshelves. Patches of books were interrupted by Avant-garde glass vases containing spindly decorative branches. Smooth river stones dotted the small glass tables. A dark red couch nestled against one wall, a matching chair sitting catty-corner to it.

"What can I do for you, today?" Dr. Orchard shut the door and sat down. His jet black hair glinted in the office's mood lighting. He rubbed his carefully curated mustache. Given his angular features, had he thrown in a goatee, he'd look remarkably like psychology legend Philip Zimbardo, albeit with a less prominent chin.

I decided to let my cousin do most of the talking, especially since she didn't tend to tick people off. She jumped right in. "This is Noah Clue, a private investigator. I'm his secretary, Dee Ann Tindall. Are you familiar with a Jonathan Conhue?"

Dr. Orchard closed his eyes, tented his fingers, and rested them against his lips. "I'm not at liberty to discuss patients."

"Including murdered ones?" I chimed in.

The doctor's dark brown eyes popped open. "Conhue is dead?"

I nodded, opting not to say anything else. Frankly, I was amazed that my cousin had managed to find the victim's shrink.

Dee continued unabated. "How about an Adriana Skye?"

Dr. Orchard sat stark upright. His mouth gaped open. "Don't tell me she's dead, too!"

My cousin shook her head. "No, she's fine. However, we understand the two were at odds, professionally."

The psychologist relaxed back into his previous pose. "I cannot speak for Adriana, but as to Mr. Conhue, he considered her clients fair game."

Dee scribbled a note. "How long was Conhue a patient of yours?"

"Two years, six months, and five days," Dr. Orchard recited without hesitation.

"Impressive memory." I pondered why someone would be that specific. Was Dr. Orchard lying to us?

The psychologist still had his fingers tented, which was starting to get on my nerves. He closed his eyes again. "Conhue is a hard one to forget. Classic case of sublimation. He was angry over his needs not being met as a child and he redirected that anger into taking money from his clients."

Dee jumped on that remark. "So, you knew about his illegal activity, then?"

"Of course, my dear. But I cannot break professional confidence, can I?" Dr. Orchard's voice remained smooth and level.

My cousin's demeanor didn't waver. "Were you aware that all of his sales were scams?"

Dr. Orchard sighed. "Jon's superego never had a chance to fully develop. His father was all but absent, and his mother was too busy to pay him much attention."

Oh great. A Freudian. That explained a few things. "So, you're saying Conhue was the victim in all of this?" I blurted out. I couldn't stand proponents of this outdated school of psychological thought.

Dr. Orchard nodded knowingly. "Hurt people hurt people."

Dee elbowed me. "Do you have any ideas on who might want to kill Conhue?"

"Oh, I'm sure there were many." He shrugged gently. "Not me, certainly. I only wanted to help him get better."

My cousin scanned her notebook. "Dr. Orchard, how is your professional standing?"

He bowed his head to her. "Stellar."

Dee tapped her notebook. "So, there is no truth in the APA's investigation of your practice?"

I blinked. When did she find that out?

Dr. Orchard drew in a sharp breath. "None whatsoever."

"Is it possible that Conhue was the one to report you?" Dee threw the question out as casually as a request for a coffee order.

The psychologist raised an eyebrow. "The thought never crossed my mind. But, even if he did, that would give no reason for me to kill him. The APA will find no evidence of those wild claims." He stood. "Now, if you will excuse me, I have an appointment."

Dee tailed him out of the office, with me on her heels. She continued her questioning like a journalist hounding a politician. "What motive would someone have to report you?"

"Good day, Miss Tindall." Dr. Orchard pushed open the door and waved a female patient over.

I pinned myself to the wall, trying not to knock over the vase of vanilla incense sticks. Dee didn't seem interested in leaving yet. "We will be in touch," she announced.

"I'm sure you will be. Hello, Elizabeth. How are you doing today?"

"Been better, Dr. Orchard," the woman simpered.

"Do tell, my dear." The two disappeared into the office.

I glanced at Dee. She held up a finger.

After a moment, faint giggling floated into the hall. Dee started towards the exit. I casually noted the office hours posted on the door. "Why would a psychologist close on Tuesdays?" I muttered to myself.

Once we were in the car, I turned to my cousin. "Okay, genius, I get why we came, but how did you know that was Conhue's shrink?"

"Total coincidence, but a lucky one at that. This just got a whole lot more interesting."

* * *

"What are you proposing, Miss Tindall?" Lieutenant Warren snapped the Manila folder shut. "We can just as well interview suspects at the station."

For once, I had to side with Warren. Dee was about to blow our strategic advantage.

"They all seem to be hiding something." Dee studied her nails. "They're all so intent on keeping their little secrets locked up, you won't be getting much information out of them."

Warren leaned back in his chair. "Hmm, you have a point."

She did.

"I have a friend who owns a mansion just outside of Seattle," Dee continued. "He owes me a favor. I've already talked to him, and he's more than willing to host for us."

"Still, a dinner party? Even if we get them all there, who's to say they'll give any more information in that context?" Warren did not sound convinced.

She gave a sly smile. "A little wine, social conversation, and one thing in common—a hatred for Jonny Conhue. Sooner or later, the subject is bound to come up."

Warren turned to me. "You're unusually quiet, Clue."

I shoved my hands in my pockets. "I'm just trying not to take your side, sir."

Dee rolled her eyes. "Let's put it this way: Noah, how many cases have you solved on your own?"

"Zero," Warren answered for me.

She turned to the lieutenant. "And how far along has police procedure gotten you in this investigation?"

"Not far at all," I replied. Warren shot me a dirty look.

"Well, then, boys, it would seem that since neither of you have a better idea, we might just give mine a try. What have we to lose?"

I couldn't think of anything. Apparently, neither could Warren. We both stared at Dee, trying not to look like deer caught in the headlights of a semi truck.

A Cheshire cat grin covered her face. She clapped her hands. "Good, so, that settles it."

Warren held up a finger. "Hold on one more minute, Miss Tindall. How do you plan to explain the police presence at this little event of yours?"

"I can't imagine that you'd be wearing your uniform to a formal dinner party." Dee waved to Warren and turned on her heels. "See you there!" She waltzed out of his office.

Warren put a hand to his forehead. "I'm not sure how I feel about her, Noah. At least I could shut you down."

I glanced over my shoulder at my cousin, who had already struck up a conversation with an office worker. "Ye-ah, I'm fairly sure Dee took classes in Jedi Mind Tricks."

"She's *your* secretary." Warren muttered.

"That's what I keep telling myself, Lieutenant. It really doesn't make me feel any better."

* * *

"Well, it sounds like you're making excellent progress," Curtis Daubney crowed over the phone. "Plenty of suspects already. I'm sure you'll have this wrapped up in no time."

My client seemed to expect miracles. I took a sip of coffee. "I appreciate your confidence, sir, but having a lot of suspects isn't usually a good thing in my line of work."

"Still better than none, is it not?" Daubney's voice became muffled, as if he had covered the phone mouthpiece. "Ah, Herschel! While you're up, can you bring me the estimate from the cleaning service? Thanks."

Daubney returned his attention to me. "You always read about crime scenes in the news, but you'd never believe how expensive they are to clean up after the cops are done."

I cleared my throat. "This is the office where we found the body, I'm assuming?"

"Well, I haven't had any other murders, so, yes."

I really didn't want to postpone our move into the new office. "If it helps, I don't really care about some carpet stains. We'll just put the desk over it and call it good."

Dee gave me a weird look as she handed me one of the printed invitations for the dinner party. "What do you think?" she whispered.

Daubney chuckled. "Well, we still need to have it properly cleaned for health reasons. I appreciate the thought anyhow."

"I understand." I pulled the phone away from my mouth and held up the thick white paper invitation with gold foil trim. "Expensive looking stationary," I murmured.

Dee grinned. "Of course. Read it."

I ignored her for the moment and focused on my client. "Well, I'll keep you posted on the case, of course. Good luck with the cleaning."

"Thank you. It should be interesting." Daubney sounded more amused than anything. "All the best to you in narrowing down your list of suspects."

"Thank you. I'll be in touch."

We exchanged pleasantries and I hung up. I turned my attention to the invitation. "You are cordially invited to a dinner party in honor of Mr. Charles Radcliffe's latest publication, *A Murder in Blue*." I looked up. "Why in the world would they attend this? Chances are, none of them even know this man."

Dee looked ready to burst with pride at her own brilliance. "Here's the trick, Noah: all of our suspects have known countless people over the years. They'll assume that this is someone they know. You don't turn down an exclusive dinner invitation when you're afraid of offending a forgotten wealthy acquaintance."

I tossed the card down on the coffee table. "Who is this Radcliffe fellow, anyhow?"

"My friend. He's a mystery author. You like detective fiction. You must have read some of his stuff."

I shrugged. "The name doesn't ring a bell."

"*Assassin on the Delta*? You have to have read that."

The memory registered, and my mouth fell open. "You're friends with *C. J. Radcliffe*?"

Dee grinned. "You should see how excited he is to be staging this whole thing. He's been reading our notes on them, and he'll pretend he knows them all. That will be enough to keep them from leaving."

I wasn't sure whether to hug her or run screaming from the apartment. "That is amazingly underhanded."

"Why, thank you."

I put a hand on my hip. "And when they figure out that they're all connected to Jonny Conhue?"

She nodded. "That's when things really start to get interesting."

"Did you consider that they might realize they've been snowed at that point?" A knot formed in my stomach as I envisioned the possible train wreck.

"Absolutely. I have that covered." She flashed me a grin. "Needless to say, this is one social event that isn't going to be worth missing."

I was already trying to figure out how I could miss it.

Sunday, May 2

I tugged on my collar, trying to get a little more breathing room. The black suit jacket and red tie felt like foreign garb. "I feel like a stuffed shirt, Dee."

"Well, you probably look like one, so that settles that." Her voice floated from the other side of the bathroom door.

I hunched my shoulders and focused my attention on straightening my pocket square. "Thanks a lot. You can insult my appearance without even looking."

"I have a vivid imagination."

"I had no idea," I murmured with full sarcasm. Teasing was fun in small doses, but my cousin usually didn't know when to stop.

Silence hung for a moment. "Ready?" she asked.

"If you ask me if you look fat in the dress, I can't promise a nice answer, cousin dearest."

"I'm not that stupid." Dee opened the bathroom door. The light glinted off of her sparkly red floor length party dress. She had pulled her hair back into a loose bun.

I shuddered. "I haven't seen you in that dress since the Wedding Cake Incident."

"Oh, come on, that was years ago." She brushed aside the ever-present curl on her forehead and tried to tuck it in.

"You don't forget things like that." I sighed. "Well, you look nice all the same."

She put a hand on her hip. "Well, thank you," she drawled. "You don't look too bad yourself. I retract my stuffed shirt statement."

"I appreciate it." I adjusted my tie. "This is quite probably the fanciest party I have ever attended in my life, and it isn't even real."

Dee's stubborn curl dropped back in front of her eyes. "Oh, it's real. Radcliffe is indeed celebrating his new book. He's just commemorating it by helping us solve a murder. He's weird like that. Besides, any excuse for fireworks, he says."

How much money did this guy have, anyhow? "He's paid for a fireworks show?"

Dee laughed. "Hardly. The guests are providing the fireworks. Radcliffe calls it research."

"Radcliffe sounds like he's out of his mind." I donned my black Stetson and studied my reflection in the mirror. Not bad at all.

"It's possible. After all, he says that writing is borderline schizophrenia for fun and profit." She plucked my Stetson off my head. "Cowboy hats aren't formal attire."

"Uncle Denby always said a gentleman rancher isn't fully dressed without his hat." I snatched it back from her. "So, we're attending a staged dinner party, hosted by a crazy person, with several murder suspects, and a disgruntled police lieutenant who is determined to end my career?"

"You can make anything sound bad." Dee snatched up her clutch bag, and we headed for the car.

"How did you meet this Radcliffe guy, anyhow?" I asked as I slid into the passenger seat of Dee's vehicle.

She buckled her seat belt and started the car. "Radcliffe came into my dad's law firm doing research for a novel. I answered a few questions for him. He subsequently asked me to dinner."

"So, you're in love with the guy?" I wasn't sure how I felt about the potential of another eccentric relation.

"We thought about it, but I could never be with an author."

"Why not?"

"Weird work habits, poor hygiene." Dee looked me over. "Actually, you'd make an excellent author."

I glared at her and hit the radio button. "You can stop talking now, Dee."

We found Radcliffe's house without much trouble. It was the only driveway gate in the neighborhood that was open. I stared up at the nine foot wrought-iron fence as we passed through. The dense trees along the property line gave way to carefully tended lawns and gardens. An impressive castle-like mansion stood proudly ahead.

I whistled. "When you said Radcliffe was rich, Dee, I didn't think you meant he was *this* rich. I didn't think authors made that much—not even bestsellers."

"Radcliffe is an eccentric, Noah. He dabbles." She pulled the car into a parking space near one of the fountains.

"Profitable dabbling." I pulled down the visor mirror and checked my appearance. "Now I can't wait to meet this guy."

Dee turned to me and clasped my shoulder. "Just remember, it is purely coincidental that our suspects are here. We have to keep them long enough for me to get my plan into place, at which point, no one goes anywhere for a good long while."

I brushed her off. "Okay, now you're starting to scare me, Dee."

A dangerous glint of mischief shone in her eyes. "Just leave everything to me."

That old, gnawing sense of being extraneous returned. "Isn't there anything you need me to do?"

My cousin nodded. "Keep your eyes and ears open. Put that P.I. training of yours to good use."

I grimaced. That would be a tall order for someone with abysmal observation skills.

4

Putting On The Fritz

Charles Radcliffe's reception room seemed cheerful and inviting. Cherry wood accented the warm cream wall tones. Various plush arm chairs and sofas dotted the room, giving an open invitation to comfortable seating. Tall ficus trees stood guard on either side of a broad archway. Beyond them, a tall, sandy-haired man sat apparently composing a tune at a black Steinway piano. Glass patio doors displayed a wide swath of Radcliffe's property. I moved closer to listen, leaning against the archway to the piano nook.

After a couple of measures the man stopped abruptly and faced me, a warm smile on his face. "Noah Clue, yes?" His voice held a definitive British accent.

"Um, yes." I held out my hand. "Good to meet you."

"Isaac Juniper," he introduced himself as he shook my hand vigorously. "Pleasure to meet you, Mr. Clue."

I couldn't contain my curiosity. "How did you know it was me?"

He pointed to my head. "The Stetson. You're famous for it."

I snatched the hat off my head, wondering why the servant who took our coats hadn't mentioned it. "I do believe you're the first to use the word 'famous' and a reference to me in the same sentence."

"In local literary circles, your name has come up a few times. Not many private investigators solve murders. Well, at least, not in the real world. Sir Arthur Conan Doyle basically invented the trope."

"He also invented forensic chemistry," I countered.

"True point."

"So, are you an author too?"

Juniper laughed. "Me? Not much. Just a few articles and such. I leave most of the wordsmithing to Charles. I'm usually playing Forster to his Dickens."

I tried to decipher the reference. "Come again?"

"Sounding board, draft editor, friend." Juniper chuckled. "Also, literary agent."

"Ah. And pianist?"

"Not really. I dabble." He played a simple piano melody with his right hand.

That was the second time that word had come up tonight. "I'm beginning to think 'dabbling' is the secret to life."

"It has its place. If you want to hear piano, ask Charles to play some time. I've been trying to talk him into recording for years, but he always laughs it off." Juniper turned back to the piano and began playing a classical piece.

A couple of uniformed men carried trays of hors d'oeuvres into the main reception room. I recognized one as the man who had taken our coats at the door. I excused myself from Juniper and approached him as he set the food on the long sideboard against the wall. "Excuse me, sir, would you mind putting this with my coat?" I held out my Stetson.

"Of course, sir." The man took my hat, and headed back out of the room. I shook my head in wonder. I'd always thought full-time house staff had gone away with the roaring twenties. Maybe Radcliffe just kept them on for special events? Your typical caterer wouldn't be taking coats and hats.

I perused the sideboard. Several platters of tasty-looking appetizers enticed me to try them. I popped a finger sandwich into my mouth, savoring the garlic and chicken. I'd have to go slow on these. I could easily clear the plate.

A man sang out. "One of those sandwiches is not like the others, who's going home tonight?"

I whirled around to face a tall, grinning gentleman in a sleek gray tuxedo and wild-patterned red bow tie. His long, jet black hair had been pulled back in a low ponytail, and a pair of rectangular-rimmed glasses perched on the end of his hawk-like nose.

I stared. "Excuse me?"

"I'm just kidding." He waved me off. "None of those are poisoned." His hazel eyes twinkled. "The punch on the other hand..."

My confusion gave way to understanding. "You have got be Charles Radcliffe."

"However did you guess? Oh, wait, never mind, yes." He rubbed his goatee. "You're Noah Clue, the brilliant detective. Say, can you tell me what I had for lunch?"

I took a wild guess. "Chicken salad?"

His eyes widened. "Ooh, you're good."

"Seriously?" That was a first.

Radcliffe laughed. "No. I had pasta with garlic sauce. Good try though." He patted my arm, turned on his heels, and walked off, whistling the theme from *Poirot*.

"Get a load of that guy," I muttered to myself.

Dee sidled up to me and rested her forearm on my shoulder. "Yeah, he's a real kick."

"After you." Warren's voice floated into the room.

A redhead in a floor-length, slinky, black dress glided in.

"And it looks like Warren has a date." I whispered to Dee. The lieutenant looked lost and somewhat bewildered in a rented black tux. At least, I assumed it had been rented. Somehow, I couldn't imagine Warren owning a tuxedo. But then again, I couldn't really picture him in regular civilian clothes at all.

Radcliffe intercepted my rival. "Gregg Warren. So good to see you. And who is this lovely lady?"

"How did he know him?" I whispered to Dee.

She leaned towards my ear, her voice still bearing that playful tone. "Remember when I went to get a coffee and didn't come back for two hours on Friday morning?"

"Yeah?" The hairs on my arms bristled.

"I helped Radcliffe memorize everyone, so he could pretend that he knew them. It helps keep them here."

My cousin's scheming ran even deeper than I first suspected. I kept my voice level low. "I'm still not certain they're all going to show up, Dee."

She didn't sound concerned. "Oh, I am."

"How's that?"

"Radcliffe spent Friday and part of Saturday dropping in on all of them and inviting them personally. My idea." Dee studied her nails. "Not bad planning for a little 'ol Texas gal, if I do say so myself."

Her audacity astonished me. She had all the makings of a real con artist. "So the two of you just hoodwinked everyone involved."

Dee's cheesy smile flashed. "Fun, huh?"

"You're sick."

My cousin raised her eyebrow. "Says the man who told our future landlord he could lease us an office with bloodstained carpet."

I had wondered when she'd bring that up. "He's having it cleaned anyway. I just never cared much about perfection."

Warren approached us, his date clinging to his arm. "Evening, Clue. I thought I spotted you lurking over here. Hello, Miss Tindall."

"Evening, Warren." I smirked. "Tonight should be interesting."

"To say the least." He turned to the young lady with him. "Emily, this is Noah Clue, the private investigator I told you about, and his secretary Dee."

Emily held out a gloved hand to me. "Mr. Clue. I've heard so much about you." Her patronizing tone revealed that Warren had told her nothing good.

Radcliffe's enthusiastic voice sounded again. "Welcome, come in, come in. So good to see you, Ms. Skye."

"Thank you so much." Adriana Skye swept in, wearing a royal blue satin evening gown. A tall, late twenty-something, blond man accompanied her. "This is my nephew, Andrew Heasley, a budding writer himself. Andrew, this is C.J. Radcliffe, an internationally famous mystery author."

"Good to meet you." Heasley shook Radcliffe's hand vigorously. Owlish glasses emphasized the young man's offset blue eyes. "I'd love to exchange writing techniques with you."

"So glad you could join us." Consternation crossed Radcliffe's face as he pulled out of the aggressive handshake.

Judging by Heasley's contorted nose bridge, I doubted he was as respectable as he tried to appear. Even his smooth, enunciated tone unnerved me.

"Auntie, dear, where did you meet Mr. Radcliffe again?"

"The funny thing is, I can't seem to remember." She laughed nervously. "I do mix with so many interesting people, after all."

Radcliffe smiled. "A book signing, wasn't it?"

She feigned a revelation. "It must have been. I've read quite a few of your books. Your last one was simply intriguing."

"Why, thank you, ma'am." Radcliffe bowed dramatically. He motioned to the right side of the room. "Please help yourself to hors d'oeuvres. Dinner is in half an hour."

As Skye and Heasley approached the sideboard, Dee wrenched me away. "Let's give it some time."

I gazed over my shoulder at the luscious finger sandwiches, and regretted the decision to pace myself. "But, the food…"

Dee patted me in that condescending way she used to use when we were kids. "You don't want to spoil supper. Ah, here comes another guest. Let's observe from here." She parked me out of the way in the nook. Juniper grinned at me as he searched through a pile of sheet music.

Radcliffe greeted the next guests. "Ah, Alberto Verde. Welcome. And the lovely Rosa Florentina, too. I am so glad you both could make it."

"Thank you for inviting us, Mr. Radcliffe." Verde looked ten years younger, and a few pounds thinner in the smart blue suit jacket. He beamed at the host.

Florentina smoothed a crease in her lavender lace gown. "Pleasure to see you again, Mr. Radcliffe."

"He brought his secretary?" I asked Dee under my breath.

"Apparently." She shot me a questioning look. "Why? Do you find that unusual?"

"For me, no. You're the better half of my brain. For him?" I watched Florentina fuss with her short auburn hair.

Dee rubbed her chin. "I think she fancies her employer," she whispered to me.

"The feeling is obviously not mutual. So is she also a suspect?"

My cousin shrugged. "Only time will tell. Stay put and keep your ears open." She strolled off, humming the *Diagnosis Murder* theme. Her love of crime shows almost rivaled my appreciation of Film Noir, except at least my interest didn't come with earworms.

Juniper got my attention. "Are you a fan of jazz?"

"Jazz is life. What do you have in mind?" I hoped he'd go for something from the forties.

"Something along these lines, I'm thinking." The pianist ran his fingers across the keyboard and launched into a piano rendition of Count Basie's *One O'clock Jump*.

While I loved the music, it hindered my ability to hear the guests. I scooted closer to the archway.

Radcliffe turned to the next arriving guest. "Dr. Orchard. How are you this evening?"

From my vantage point, I watched Adriana Skye blanch as she turned towards the entrance. She dropped into a chair by the window. Heasley took a seat on the blue sofa just adjacent.

The psychologist gripped the silver lapel of his dark purple tuxedo. The ends of his mustache curled upward, and his black hair was slicked back, making him look vampiric. A silver bow tie bobbed at his throat. "I am doing well. And you?"

"Fantastic. Love your tie." Radcliffe adjusted his own loud version. "Good to know I'm not the only one trying to bring them back."

"Ah, yes, of course." Dr. Orchard's words seemed stilted. "Book sales going well?"

Radcliffe shrugged. "For the first month, quite well indeed. It already made The New York Times bestseller list."

"I hear it is difficult for some authors to make it in writing these days," mused the doctor.

Radcliffe chuckled. "Not for me. Being internationally recognized, I have no trouble getting decent advances from any publisher."

Orchard simpered. "Naturally. You must have them eating out of your hand."

Radcliffe's jaw twitched. "Well, I do draw the line at making them grovel, of course."

The psychologist had obviously missed the clue. He patted the author on the shoulder. "Yes, there is a lot to be said for not overplaying your hand."

Radcliffe recoiled. "Indeed. Excuse me." He turned to the next guest. "Mrs. Snow, so good to see you. Come in."

Dr. Orchard spotted me and skittered over. "Mr. Clue. Fancy meeting you here. It really is a small world, isn't it?"

I glanced around for a means of escape. "Yes, I suppose it is."

"How goes the investigation?"

He'd get no hints from me. "We've, uh, hit a dead end." I tried to catch Dee's eye, in hopes she could rescue me from the conversation. No such luck.

Dr. Orchard clasped his arms behind his back. "Ah, that's a pity. I can imagine it is quite hard to rule out so very many suspects."

"It is at that." I slid towards the buffet table, hoping to put myself closer to the finger sandwiches, and further from the side order of crazy in front of me.

"Major Conhue!" came Radcliffe's cheery voice. "How are you this evening, old chap?"

"Doing well, considering." The major sounded irritated and exhausted, like he hadn't been sleeping well at all.

Dr. Orchard started. "Conhue? This evening is getting more interesting by the moment." He turned to view the newcomer. "Do you suppose he has any relation?"

I shrugged. "You could always ask him."

"Mm. I'd rather not bring up such an unpleasant topic as that at an event like…good grief, is that Adriana Skye?" Orchard approached the nervous real estate agent.

I scurried over to my cousin. "Dee, I do hope you invited some other people." I whispered.

"A few of Radcliffe's friends, just to make this seem coincidental." She gestured to Juniper still sitting at the piano across the room, talking with Mrs. Snow. "As soon as Jonny is mentioned among the guests, the clock starts."

My stomach churned. "The clock?"

"More like a time bomb." Dee looked at her watch. "I don't want to reach into my bag of tricks until the last possible moment."

This Dee-fueled plot sounded more like a disaster in the works by the minute. I scanned the room for exits. "Does our gracious host actually know these other people?"

"Oh, yes." Dee took a sip of champagne.

Warren ambled over. "You'd better have one humdinger of a game plan to keep this charade going, Miss Tindall," he murmured.

Dee's eyes seemed to sparkle brighter. "I certainly do." She kept her voice just above a whisper.

The lieutenant crossed his arms. "Just how confident are you?"

My cousin looked quite smug. "Fairly."

"Dr. Adams, glad you could make it!" Radcliffe greeted yet another guest.

Warren leaned in. "Enough to go double or nothing?"

Dee skewed her eyebrows. "Given our terms, define double."

"If I win," Warren counted off on his fingers, "Noah gets out of the P.I. business altogether. If I lose, I pay for your new office and Noah's new apartment."

"Cute, Warren, but I'm not that stupid." Dee sauntered away.

Warren's mouth dropped open. He snapped it shut and blinked. His gaze followed my cousin across the room.

I cleared my throat. "Can you keep a secret?"

He didn't avert his stare. "What?"

"I'm not really doing the P.I. thing," I whispered. "She does all the thinking. I'm just the face that gets her into places."

Silence hung between us for a moment. I could almost hear the cricket chirps in his brain. "You know, that explains a few things." Warren wandered off.

My stomach growled. I hurried to the buffet table and loaded a small plate with finger sandwiches. I hated the fact that my cousin saw me as a dismal failure. I wasn't sure why I let Warren in on that. Maybe he'd lighten up on us a little.

And then again, given his apparent blossoming rivalry with Dee, he might not. I moved to a nearby corner and turned my attention back to the other guests.

"Robert! I thought I recognized your voice. How are you doing?" Alberto Verde shook Major Conhue's hand vigorously.

"As well as possible these days, Alberto." The major's voice took on a somber tone. "I'm so sorry to learn of your troubles. I had no idea. Is there anything I can do to make up for it?"

Their conversation began to overlap with that of Adriana Skye and Dr. Orchard, and I decided to focus in on the latter. "I didn't think you read fiction. A waste of paper, I thought you said." Skye did not sound pleased to see her shrink.

Dr. Orchard kneaded his palm with his opposite thumb. "Well, I admit, the invitation came as a complete surprise to me. I don't remember meeting him."

I threw a few nervous glances around the room. Dee and our host were nowhere to be seen. This could go downhill fast.

One of the staff members cleared his throat. "Dinner is served!"

"Saved by the bell," I whispered as Warren came up beside me again to file into the dining room. I marveled at Radcliffe's classic sensibilities, right down to a waitstaff seemingly out of the Edwardian era.

"For once, Clue, I'm with you," he muttered in response. Warren looked around. "This whole affair has me on edge."

I patted the concealed carry holster under my suit jacket. "If it's any comfort, I'm packing my Smith and Wesson."

Warren quirked his mouth. "That ancient six shooter?"

I grinned. He really didn't know Texans. "I haven't missed a target with it since I was fifteen."

The lieutenant shrugged. "At least you've got that going for you."

* * *

As the guests slowly filed into the dining room, I stopped to study a rather striking painting of a little boy trying to lure a horse, while three girls stood by, giggling. Radcliffe stopped beside me. "Gorgeous, isn't it? It's called 'A Tempting Bait,' by Arthur Elsley. Just a print, but I do have one of his originals elsewhere if you want to see it later."

I smiled. "My Uncle Denby has a picture of a horse that looks a lot like this style."

"You should ask him what the signature on it is. Elsley is an absolute classic."

I hesitated. "I hope you don't mind the question, but I'm curious. The staff...are they just for special events, or...?"

Radcliffe chuckled. "You don't see that much nowadays, do you? A few of them live here. For the rest, this is just a typical nine-to-five. We host a lot of special events here at the estate, so technically, it is as much a business as it is a home."

I caught sight of Dr. Orchard's reflection in the glass. The psychologist looked around the room, and then quickly swapped a couple of placards near the head of the table. "I think one of your guests is promoting himself," I whispered to Radcliffe.

"Should be interesting. Who?" Radcliffe leaned slightly to see the reflection. "Ah, looks like he's just displaced Dr. Adams. I'll give my friend a heads up." He sauntered off.

I approached the table, reading the placards as I passed. Mine sat between Dr. Adam's place and the smug Dr. Orchard. I slid into my seat and waited for events to unfold.

After a few moments, Adams sat down next to me and unfolded his napkin. He gave a subtle wink in my direction, indicating that Radcliffe had filled him in on Orchard's presumption. I stifled a chuckle and watched the other guests take their seats.

Once everyone was seated, a pair of servants entered with a metal food cart. I leaned back as a hot plate of food was set in front of me. The patterned gold edge framed a steaming helping of poultry, grilled eggplant, and mashed potatoes. Another servant topped off my glass of champagne.

Major Conhue took a bite of meat. "Roasted pheasant. I haven't had this in ages."

"It is quite tender. What do you think, darling?" Skye turned toward her nephew.

He took a delicate bite of eggplant. "Delicious," he pronounced.

I couldn't help but notice that Heasley seemed primarily interested in appearing high-class, an endeavor at which he failed miserably. By contrast, Mrs. Snow, the cleaning lady from the building where Conhue's body was found, looked every bit the part of the high class lady without even trying. Her simple blue-patterned dress and string of pearls seemed to fit the scene better than Skye's evening gown. I regretted not being able to get to know Snow better, but the circumstances didn't lend themselves.

"My compliments to the chef. Also..." Dr. Orchard stood and raised a glass. "To my dear friend, C.J. Radcliffe. Congratulations on another successful novel publication!"

Dee held a napkin to her face, clearly trying not to laugh at the absurdity of the presumption. Juniper, meanwhile, looked thoroughly amused, wiggling his eyebrows in our host's direction.

"Cheers!" The dinner party clinked their glasses together in Radcliffe's honor.

Adriana Skye focused her attentions on Alberto Verde. "Tell me, have you read Radcliffe's latest book yet?"

The businessman dabbed at his mouth with his cloth napkin. "I confess, I have not." He settled his broad frame back into his chair.

"I have. Quite a thrilling mystery." Dr. Adams, sitting on my left, took a sip of champagne. "His best yet."

"The butler did it." Lee Fox, another friend of Radcliffe's, gave a sly, bewhiskered grin at Adams.

"Don't spoil it for us." I retorted.

Fox chuckled. "You're rather gullible for a private investigator. There isn't even a butler in *A Murder in Blue*."

"Actually, there is," Radcliffe interjected, "though he is a rather minor character. He first appears in, what, Chapter Seven?" The author laughed. "Don't let my friend rattle you, Mr. Clue. He does this to everyone."

Fox rubbed his scruffy gray beard. "Are you certain the butler didn't do it, Charles? He could have poisoned the champagne."

My stomach lurched. Hopefully Dee had anticipated protection for me, if any of our unwitting guests had planned to take me out.

Radcliffe shook his head, his black ponytail swaying. "I would like to think I know the story inside and out, but you know how it is. You don't make up the story, you only write it down."

"I wish things worked that way in the academic publication realm." Dr. Orchard mused. "It would save quite a bit of time."

Verde cast a suspicious look at the psychologist. "I would hope you don't *make up* anything in that field." He took another bite of roasted pheasant.

"Well, no, of course not." Dr. Orchard gestured with his fork. "But, you have to figure out how to put your thoughts together in a convincing fashion. Those peer review panels are always reading with a jaded eye."

"Especially when you're pushing regurgitated Freudian ideas," I muttered to myself.

Dr. Adams winked at me, and then nodded vigorously to Dr. Orchard. "They can be a hassle sometimes. So, have you been published yet?"

"Two or three articles." Orchard waved it off. "Nothing of significance, really. I stick mainly to clinical work."

"Mmm, I understand that," Adams replied, as if to his plate, as he hid the look of amusement on his wizened face. Had the good doctor already summed Orchard up as a moronic joke?

Dr. Orchard chewed thoughtfully for a moment. "I did write one article on the causes of sociopathy that got me some margin of recognition locally a few years ago, but you know how quickly that fades." He sighed. "And anyhow, I doubt anyone would take it seriously now, after Con…" He stopped mid-sentence and waved off the statement. "Well, never mind. Just the scattered musings of an old psychologist."

The mood at the table grew quite somber. I tried to enjoy the herbed mashed potatoes, but the near mention of Jonny Conhue's name had me on edge. I knew it had to happen sooner or later for the evening to be worth the trouble, but I didn't look forward to it.

"You know, your name does ring a bell." Major Conhue pointed his fork at Dr. Orchard. "You're the psychologist that tried to help my idiot brother, aren't you?"

Orchard stopped mid-sip of his champagne. "Ah, so you *are* related? I had wondered when I heard your name."

Skye pushed her plate away. Her cheeks turned pale. "Suddenly, I've lost my appetite."

"Jonny Conhue." Verde shook his head. "On the one hand, a pity. On the other hand, not in the least."

Dr. Adams set down his glass. "I do believe I've missed something. Who are you talking about?"

"My idiot…" Major Conhue stopped himself. "My brother. He had a rather sordid reputation over the last several years."

"Until someone offed him." Adriana Skye's red lips were twisted in contempt. "Something that belongs in one of your books, no doubt, Mr. Radcliffe"

Conhue looked over at me. "Which reminds me, why exactly are you here, Mr. Clue?"

Dr. Orchard leaned forward. "I was going to ask the same thing." He looked over at Skye. "For that matter, how did you know about Conhue, Adriana?"

"He scammed a few of my clients." Skye wrinkled her nose.

"He got me as well." Verde blew out a breath. "I figured he was safe, since he was the brother of my old army buddy."

Major Conhue shook his head. "I do wish you'd asked me about him." He paused. "It does seem odd to me that there are six people here with connections to Jonny. His shrink, two of his victims, me, and then Mr. Clue, and his secretary."

"Very small world." Radcliffe's bemused smile broke through. "It really does feel like a book plot."

Skye became visibly agitated. "It reminds me of a game." She threw up a hand. "Miss Scarlet, in the dining room, with the wrench." She set her jaw and made eye contact with me. "Know anything about this, Clue?"

I shook my head. "Interestingly, I got an invitation the same as the rest of you." Which was technically true.

"Where do you know Radcliffe from, anyhow?" Skye shot back.

Radcliffe responded for me. "It was my way to say 'thank you' for some help with researching a book." He nodded in my direction, and then at Dee across from me. "Thank you again."

I opted not to respond.

The author continued. "Frankly, these circumstances are as much a surprise to me as to anyone."

Radcliffe could have been a Broadway actor.

"Look, coincidence or not, we might as well make the best of it," Verde remarked. "We have a lovely dinner, fine company. Let's just put all talk of Jonny Conhue away for the night and enjoy ourselves." He took a large bite of eggplant.

Skye seemed to resign herself. She leaned back in her chair and let out a breath. Heasley patted her shoulder.

Radcliffe nodded. "A fine idea, Mr. Verde. Let's leave the murders to fiction for tonight, shall we? After dinner, what say I read a few chapters of my latest novel?"

5

Wined and Died

I stood in the corner, taking in the impressive sight of Radcliffe's library. A few logs crackled in the fireplace across from the double doors. Dark wooden bookshelves covered every inch of available wall space, locked glass doors protecting the contents of a few. A scattering of comfortable chairs dotted the room. A small red sofa rested invitingly at one side of the space.

The party had moved into the library, eager to hear a chapter of Radcliffe's book, but so far, everyone remained absorbed in their own conversations.

"More champagne, sir?" One of the servers held up the bottle.

I shook my head. "No, thank you. Water is fine."

"Very good, sir." He nodded to another server, who carried over a pitcher of iced lime and cucumber water.

I studied the scene. All of our suspects were still here. Elissa Snow had obviously brushed off the entire affair with Conhue, and seemed to be having the time of her life. The others had no idea that she was in any way connected, especially since she didn't speak up at dinner.

As to the rest of the suspects, they had taken to opposite corners of the spacious library. That is, with the exception of Verde, who was enjoying a vigorous talk of army days with Major Conhue and Lee Fox. Rosa Florentina stood beside Verde, listening.

"She looks so forlorn," I quietly observed to Dee.

She nodded. "The thought occurred to me over dinner. Florentina has as much motive to kill Conhue as anyone. She obviously worships the ground that Verde walks on. She could want revenge for what he did to her beloved."

"Mm, you have a point there." I sighed. "In all, though, this evening hasn't been very enlightening, I'm sorry to say."

Dee flashed me her mischievous grin again. "Oh, the evening is only getting started. Just be ready to play the part of the cunning detective. Put yourself in the shoes of one of the greats."

I hated improvisation. My stomach turned itself into a double knot. "I can try, but why? And when?"

"Oh, you'll know when. Excuse me." Dee approached our host.

I sought out Warren, who was having a lively discussion with Dr. Adams.

"That plays a significant role in a criminal investigation, in my mind." Dr. Adams chuckled. "But then, I'm no detective."

"Well, you have a point." Warren turned to me. "What do you think, Noah?"

I shook my head. "About what?"

"The role of lie detectors in detective work." The lieutenant sounded as if he expected me to have something to add.

I scrambled for an intelligent response. "Well, it isn't admissible in court, but one might argue it could keep one from barking up the wrong tree in some cases. It all depends on whether the subject had any psychological conditions that could throw it off, or knew how to fool it."

Warren gestured to me. "And that is, in my mind, the primary shortcoming of lie detection."

"I think that could be overcome with further research," Dr. Adams insisted.

Warren shrugged. "Only until someone figures out how to fool that. It seems like an endless chase to me."

I furrowed my brow. "Arguably, crime prevention could be labeled in the same manner."

Warren's gaze drifted back to me. He didn't seem to know what to say. "There is that," he said at last.

Isaac Juniper sauntered over. His sandy hair had relaxed out of its combed position, now drifting across his eyes. He brushed the distraction back with one hand. "Excuse me. Dr. Adams, could I have a word?"

"Oh, of course, excuse me." Adams nodded to Warren and me then walked away with the tall gentleman.

Warren turned to me. "I must admit, Noah, I wasn't expecting an intelligent response from you either time."

I shrugged. "Well, I was a professional student before Dad threatened to cut me out of the will unless I got a real job. He said, with a name like mine, I could never become a P.I., so I decided to prove him wrong."

Amusement crossed Warren's features. "I had wondered what got you into it. You're not exactly a natural."

I bristled. "You don't have to remind me."

"Anyhow, what did you need me for?" The lieutenant scanned the room. "Is something wrong?"

I lowered my voice. "Dee just said something rather cryptic to me. She says the evening is, quote, far from over, and she told me to act like a great detective. Do you know what she's planning?"

Warren seemed to wilt. "She's your secretary, Noah. If you don't know, we're both lost." He paused. "Which is a scary thought."

"I need your help, Warren. If we have any chance of figuring this out, we're going to have to follow her plan, but I just don't think I can fake this."

He put a hand on my shoulder. "Noah, if there is anyone on this planet capable of faking the role of a private investigator, it's you."

I marveled that he was able to say that with a straight face. I wasn't sure whether to be flattered or insulted. "Thanks, I think."

Warren seemed to skim the book titles on the shelves next to us. "Okay, who's your favorite literary detective?"

"I don't know. Sherlock Holmes, maybe?"

Warren rolled his eyes. "It would be. Okay, think like Holmes. Reveal bits and pieces of what you know about the case, while making them sound like your idea."

"And what if I blow something critical?"

"At this moment, nothing is critical, except maybe the part about this party being staged. How much can you remember?"

I rubbed my temple. "Quite a bit, I think. Everything from the interviews with the suspects."

"Great. Now focus on the alibis. Where was everyone on the day of the crime?" Warren drew a line with his fingers. "Drag it out like a detective movie. Make them sweat. Leave the thinking to Dee and me. I'll prompt you when I can."

I remembered the recent detective shows I had watched with Dee. "I can do that much."

"Good." The lieutenant glanced at his watch. "Now, when did she say you were supposed to pull this off?"

"She just said I'd know when." I glanced at the cleaning lady from the Colman Building, thoroughly absorbed in a conversation with Dr. Orchard. "By the way, what do you know about Elissa Snow?"

Warren held up a finger.

Emily latched onto Warren's arm. "We're going to ask Radcliffe if he'll read now."

Warren sounded hesitant. "We, meaning...?"

She bounced on her toes, her black high heels clicking on the hardwood floor. "Meaning Adriana and I. We're dying to hear it."

Skye came up just behind Emily, a slight smile on her face. She finally seemed to be enjoying herself.

"Well, if you can...you know...get him to, that would certainly be...delightful." Warren feebly patted her hand.

I pondered this shift in tone. Warren always had a hard, no-nonsense demeanor at work, but when he talked to Emily, he completely fell apart.

Emily turned around and approached the host. "Oh, Mr. Radcliffe, would you read us that promised chapter of your latest masterpiece now?"

Radcliffe smiled. "Naturally. I would be delighted to."

A voice sounded to my other side. "Would you like some more water, sir?"

I turned to the server, a bit puzzled. "I already have enough here, thank you."

Puzzlement flashed in his dark eyes. "I'm sorry, someone said that you were out."

Radcliffe approached us, glass in hand. "I, however, will require some refreshment before I read, Miguel."

The server poured the rest of the contents for Radcliffe.

The author took a long drink. "Ah, that hits the spot. Now, where was I? Ah, yes, a chapter. Where'd I put that book? Oh, yes, my desk." He left the room and returned shortly. As he reentered the library, he suddenly stopped and grabbed the bookcase. "Whoa." He shook his head and blew out a breath. "I'm...I'm a little light-headed."

Without warning, Radcliffe collapsed to the floor.

Emily screamed.

"Everyone, get out of the way." Dr. Adams rushed to Radcliffe's side. "Charles, can you hear me? Charles!"

"Dear me." Major Conhue looked on in shock. "Is he okay?"

Dr. Adams put two fingers to Radcliffe's neck, and put his nose close to the man's mouth. He turned around slowly. "He's dead. Poisoned, it appears."

The entire dinner party looked on in shock.

"Nobody leaves the premises!" Warren barked, clearly having snapped back into work mode. "I'm a lieutenant with the Seattle Police Department. Servants, shut the library doors. Is everyone in here that came to the party?"

Miguel was already two steps ahead of Warren, locking the doors with a key, which he dropped into his pocket. He turned back to the room, crossed his arms, and leaned against the doors. I had never noticed how imposing the little Hispanic man really was.

Dee came to stand beside us, counting people. "Yes, that's everyone, including the staff."

One of the servants took the blanket from the back of the sofa and put it over Radcliffe's body.

"That last serving of water was meant for me, and it was obviously poisoned. Someone intended to kill me." This was it. I turned around slowly. "Someone in this room wanted me dead. And I would suspect that whoever that someone is fears that I know they killed Jonny Conhue."

Adriana Skye sat down by the fireplace, her champagne glass still in her trembling hand. Major Conhue blanched and sank into an arm chair, his head in his hands. Florentina clung to Verde tighter than before. Dr. Orchard crossed his arms, an uneasy look on his face. Even Elissa Snow looked worried.

Then again, everyone seemed to be in shock from the murder.

Dr. Orchard piped up. "How do we know that Radcliffe wasn't the intended victim?"

"Because the drink was offered to me, and Radcliffe took it instead." I tried my best to make the guess sound like a definite idea.

The psychiatrist didn't seem convinced. "And how exactly do we know the servant didn't stage that?"

I turned on Orchard. "Why would he kill him here, in full view of everyone? Why not lace his water before bed so it would look like natural causes? No, the only reason someone would commit a murder at a dinner party would be if they figured that was the only chance they had to do it. And what better opportunity, than if five of your fellow suspects are at that same party with you?"

Dr. Orchard retreated to a couch. At least I had shut him up. Now, if I could only keep this going until we found the real killer. Which begged the question, how did Dee know this would happen? I knew she would never kill a friend just for a chance to catch a murderer. I had to wonder if the man under the blanket was really quite as dead as Dr. Adams said he was.

Murder or no murder, I wasn't about to pass up this opportunity.

I folded my hands behind my back and began to pace, like in the movies. "We all had equal access to that pitcher. Anyone could have slipped something in and mentioned I needed a refill." I turned to Miguel. "Tell me, do you remember who you last served, before me?"

The servant remained rooted to his post. "Major Conhue, if I recall correctly."

"Major Conhue." I approached the suspect slowly. "Let's talk about Jonny. You didn't get along with him, did you? In fact, I remember you telling me you hated him."

The dead man's brother glared at me. "As I told you before, I'd never stoop to murder."

I pressed in. "Jonny spoiled the family name—your family name—and ripped off a friend of yours to boot."

The major seemed confused. "I didn't know Alberto had been conned until you told me."

"Oh, you *said* you didn't know Alberto had been conned. But then, you also said you didn't know anything about his death. If one could be a lie, what's one more?" I paused, recounting the interview in my mind. "You're a gun collector. A former army man. You've had plenty of experience with shooting people."

The major sputtered, "But only in wartime, and not my own flesh and blood, even if he was a scoundrel!"

I kept my tone cool. "Where were you around 12:30 p.m. on the day he died?"

Conhue put a shaking hand to his forehead. "I...ah...at a pawn shop on First Avenue, I believe. Palace. I was purchasing an antique handgun for my collection." He looked up. "Call them. They'll be able to prove I was there."

Warren pulled a notepad out of his pocket and scribbled a note. "Nothing doing tonight, they'd be closed. But I'll take it under advisement and follow up as soon as possible."

I turned to Major Conhue's friend. "And then there is you, Mr. Verde. Out twenty-four grand due to Jonny Conhue's schemes. He could have ruined you."

Verde squared his shoulders. "I'm a resourceful businessman. What good would killing Conhue do me? I'd only risk losing everything if found out."

"Oh, everyone stands to lose something from a crime, but that never seems to deter people. Perhaps you figured you could get away with it, given your resourcefulness."

"I was at my office at the time." Verde pointed to his assistant. "Rosa can vouch for me."

I turned my gaze to the young woman. "Rosa Florentina, yes. Your faithful assistant, who wishes to be so much more to you."

Verde crossed his arms. "Our relationship is purely business."

"To you perhaps. Yet what you don't notice is that Miss Florentina would do anything to protect you." I studied her eyes. "Lie about your whereabouts. Kill a man."

Florentina threw up her hands. "I would never do such a thing, no matter how much I love..." She clamped her hand over her mouth, eyes wide with surprise.

Verde looked at her with some puzzlement. "Miss Florentina, what are you saying?"

I continued. "Truth is, both of you have motive, and as such, neither of you have an alibi."

Verde pondered this for a moment. "I had an appointment at that time with a client. You can contact him. He'll verify both Rosa and I were in the office at the time."

I turned away. "Warren, make a note of that."

"I'm on it. I will need that phone number, Miss Florentina."

"It's at the office," she whimpered.

I approached the psychiatrist. Oh man, I was going to have fun with him. "Dr. Orchard, you were treating Mr. Conhue for his sociopathy at the time."

Orchard tented his fingers, resorting to that same lethargic tone he used in his office. "I am not at liberty to discuss patients."

I ignored him. "But it didn't work, did it?"

He didn't move from his seat. "As I said, I am not..."

I gave him a patronizing smile. "Dear Old Mr. Freud can't get you very far these days, can he?"

That pushed his button. He jumped to his feet. "My patients all swear by my methods!"

"Oh, I'm sure they do. They pay you every week to sit in your office and talk about mommy. Sometimes those conversations go a little beyond psychology, don't they?"

He leaned towards me, fire in his eyes. "I'm not certain I like your inference, Mr. Clue."

Based on Dee's research and Orchard's mannerisms in his office, I took a guess. "The APA is investigating claims you've had inappropriate relationships with patients, which is a serious breach of ethics. Conhue found out, and was prepared to blackmail you over it. You had to shut him up."

"Utter nonsense!" Orchard pursed his lips.

"Where were you that day? Certainly not in your office. You're closed on Tuesdays." I had to admit, I was proud of noticing that.

Dr. Orchard stammered. "I...made an exception. My patient will vouch for me. I'll send the information once I get back to my office."

"Oh, no need. She's here, isn't she?" I spun around. "Ms. Skye?"

Adriana Skye sounded exasperated. "I have absolutely no idea what you're going on about."

I motioned to her. "Meanwhile, your reputation is in the tank thanks to Jonny Conhue, and you had easy access to the office where he was found dead. It's a simple thing to do—meet with him to show him the office, and then shoot him in the back."

She leaned back against a table. "Well, I couldn't very easily do that if I was with Dr. Orchard, now could I?"

I approached Skye. "Yet, why meet with him outside of office hours, yet still right in the middle of the work week?"

Dr. Orchard piped in. "It was a busy week for her. I made an exception. Anything for my patients."

I smirked. "Anything, including alibis? Once again, we don't know for sure where either of you were that day, especially since you two would have been the only ones at the office."

Skye growled her frustration. "Oh hang it all, we weren't meeting at his office."

"Adriana..." Dr. Orchard warned.

"Can it, Stephen. I'm not going down for your reputation." She stood with an air of defiance and brushed a wrinkle from her gown. "He was at my house. I think you can fill in the rest. My neighbor saw us both around 12:30, so there is no way either of us could have killed Jonny Conhue."

Not bad so far, clearing five suspects. "That leaves one person, Elissa Snow, the cleaning lady." I turned towards her, hoping I could make this look good. I knew next to nothing about her, and she didn't even make sense as a suspect. Why had Dee even bothered to invite her, anyway?

The older woman trembled a little, her curly white hair shaking along with the rest of her. She folded her arms across her small frame, as if she were cold.

Warren cleared his throat. "A private security camera in the office she was cleaning verifies her alibi one hundred percent. She did not enter the room in question."

I shifted my line of inquiry. "The office you were cleaning was located across the hall from where we found Jonny Conhue's body. Did you see or hear anything, Mrs. Snow?"

She seemed to relax a little. "As I told the police, I heard a door open across the hall at 12:26, and close at 12:37." She paused in thought. "Now that I think of it, I also heard a strange sound somewhere between there, rather like a staple gun."

That had to be the air gun.

Snow frowned. "Unfortunately, I saw and heard nothing else."

"That will do, thank you Ms. Snow." I turned back to the room. "So, it would seem we have alibis for everyone who had motive to kill Conhue." I scanned the faces of the suspects again. Dee had better be ready to solve this whole thing, because I was running out of ideas. What would Holmes do? I thought for a moment. "What are we overlooking? Who do we all have in common?"

My mind raced back to one of my legal classes in college. Many con artists would put an arbitration clause in legal contracts with their victims, to keep themselves out of a real court. I knew Conhue had fallen back on that. Could that be a clue?

I faced the businessman. "Verde, you sued Conhue, right?"

"Well, yes. Sort of." Verde tilted his hand back and forth. "We went through..."

I interrupted. "An arbitrator, you said."

He blinked. "Yeah. A Sand-hook, something or other."

I pivoted. "Ms. Skye, do you remember if any of your clients sued Conhue?"

She shrugged. "Yes, I think they did, and the name sounds familiar. Elias Sanhouk."

"Dr. Orchard, did Conhue mention any of this to you?" I narrowed my gaze at him. "And don't breathe a word about client confidentiality."

Orchard shook his head. "No, but he always bragged that no one could ever catch up to him."

We were getting warmer. "Major Conhue, you said that Jonny bragged to you about his latest scheme. Did he say anything about an arbitrator?"

"Just that he had a business associate covering his back." Conhue bit his lip. "I suppose that could be him."

"So all of our suspects here are accounted for at the time of the murder, but we've neglected one critical suspect: Elias Sanhouk, the arbitrator." I paused for a moment. Had I actually figured that one out on my own?

"I don't think I need to tell anyone, but the killer is not in our midst. I guess I'm not dead after all." Radcliffe sat up and tossed the blanket aside.

I looked at Warren, who stared back at me.

"Are you serious?" Skye threw down her glass. It shattered across the floor. "This was a game the whole time, Clue!"

I stepped back from the mess. "I didn't know Radcliffe was alive."

"And neither did I." Warren didn't sound pleased. "Needless to say, you are all welcome to leave, seeing as there is no real crime here." He nodded to Miguel, who had already begun unlocking the library doors.

"My career is over, thanks to you." Dr. Orchard snapped at me as he passed.

I wasn't going to let him have the last word. "Actually, your career is over, thanks to *you*. You made the decision to cross the line. It was only a matter of time before everything came out, whether I got involved or not."

The psychologist pursed his lips, departing without another word.

"I told you there would be fireworks." Dee grinned at me and Lieutenant Warren.

Warren glanced over his shoulder as the last of our suspects left. "Yes, there were. It was dangerous, ethically murky..." He lowered his voice. "But surprisingly effective. Did you figure out the part about the arbitrator yourself, Noah?"

I shoved my hands in my pockets. "I guess I kinda did."

Dee nodded. "Not to mention, the fact that Skye had an appointment with Orchard on a day when the office was closed. You might just stand a chance as a private investigator after all."

Radcliffe stood and stretched. "Well, that was invigorating. Nothing like faking your own death to remind you how much you enjoy life." He grinned. "Have fun chasing down your new suspect, Clue. Feel free to let me know if you need any more help."

I still had to wonder how they pulled it off. "Dee, were the other guests actually in on the plot?"

"Oh, absolutely. Radcliffe didn't want anyone walking into a potentially dangerous situation unprepared. Well, except the suspects, that is. Adams pronounced him dead to complete the deception, obviously. Fox had a concealed weapon, just in case things got dodgy."

"And Miguel, my faithful personal assistant, had the whole thing rehearsed." Radcliffe patted him on the shoulder. "As for my incorrigible publicist over there..."

Juniper leaned against a bookcase. "I just came to watch the show, really. An evening well spent, and for a good cause. I hope you catch your guy, Clue."

"Before I do anything of the sort, I think I'll go home and catch some sleep." I yawned. "Pretending to know what I'm doing really is exhausting."

The remaining guests all laughed, obviously unaware of how serious I was.

6

Suspect Number Seven

Monday, May 3

"Conhue...Conhue..." Elias Sanhouk scratched his head, making his already wild red hair stand at odd angles. "I'm trying to remember. Short, curly brown hair, slight limp?"

I shook my head. "Not even close."

"Ah, well, I must be thinking of someone else, then. You meet so many people in this job, you know? Impossible to keep them all straight." His round face could barely contain his large, greasy smile.

"Conhue was a client of yours," Dee replied. "You handled a number of cases involving him."

"Did I? Hmm." Sanhouk furrowed his brow. "If you say so, Ms..."

"Tindall."

His smile turned depreciating. "Yes, yes. You're Mr. Clue's secretary, are you not?"

"I am." She glanced at me. "More or less."

He folded his hands on the desk. "Then you know first-hand how difficult it is to keep dozens, if not hundreds, of people straight."

Dee didn't miss a beat. "I can't say that I do, Mr. Sanhouk. I rarely forget anyone."

Sanhouk looked a little uneasy. "Lucky you. If it weren't for my phone, I would be hopelessly lost."

"You've gotta love modern technology." Dee eyed the device on the desk. "Is that the newest model?"

"Nah." Sanhouk waved her off. "I find that smartphones are like comfortable pairs of shoes. You buy one you like and use it until it wears out."

"Well, to each his own, I suppose." Dee kept staring at the phone.

"I rather like my typewriter," I mumbled to myself.

"How old is that device?" Dee continued her inquiry.

Sanhouk leaned back in his leather executive chair. "Oh, I don't know. Two or three years."

She nodded to it. "Then you would have the contact for Jonny Conhue in there."

Sanhouk blanched. "So I would. I clean forgot."

I doubted that.

Sanhouk picked up the device and switched it on. After a moment, he held up the address book entry for Conhue. A small photo sat next to the name. "Is this him?"

I nodded. "Yup, that's the guy."

"I think I remember a little more now that I see his face." Sanhouk rubbed his lip. "He was a real estate agent, right? A few clients of his tried to claim he owed them money or whatever. Quite a bunch of bad luck there for a while, but at least things worked out well in the end." He switched off his smartphone. "So, were you trying to get in contact with him or something?"

I set my jaw. Sanhouk had to know why we were here, and he wasn't very good at stalling for time. "Not exactly. Conhue was found dead in an office he was showing. The police suspect murder."

The news didn't seem to surprise the arbitrator in the least. "Well, if you're looking for suspects, I can give you a list of plaintiffs that took him on. I'm sure they would all have motive to kill him."

"That would be very helpful, Mr. Sanhouk," Dee replied. "We appreciate your assistance."

"I'll have my secretary get right on that." Sanhouk hit the intercom button with a little more force that I would have thought necessary. "Miss Kahler, would you please find the records for Jonathan Conhue?"

"Right away, Mr. Sanhouk," came the reply.

"Sweet girl, and very efficient." Sanhouk glanced at Dee. "Nothing against you, of course. But, if you can't trust your secretary to get things done, who can you trust? Miss Kahler is only too eager to do whatever I tell her."

"A good secretary to have around indeed," I replied. All the same, I had learned that there was much more to a good secretary than someone who could take orders, at least in my case.

"I hope you don't mind the question." Dee glanced at her notebook. "Where were you at 12:30 p.m., April 27th? We just have to cover all of our bases, you know."

Sanhouk seemed to patronize her. "I'm actually glad you asked. It shows you take your work seriously." He leaned back in his chair and rubbed his lips for a moment. "Let's see now...that was a Tuesday, wasn't it? I was visiting my brother in Bothel. He was having a baby shower for his wife." The arbitrator took out a pad of paper. "You can confirm with him or any of his guests. Here, I'll write down his number for you."

"Thank you." Dee took the paper and folded it up. "We certainly appreciate the cooperation."

A knock sounded at the office door.

"Come in, Miss Kahler," invited Sanhouk.

A very pale secretary entered, holding a thick folder. "Here are the papers you wanted, Mr. Sanhouk."

He took them from her. "Excellent, my dear, thank you."

I studied Miss Kahler for a moment. Her blonde hair was tied into a shortish ponytail on the top of her head. She wore very little makeup, and a simple blue dress. Her rather average stature seemed shorter given her slight slumping posture. I guessed that she couldn't be more than twenty-three or twenty-four.

Sanhouk paged through the folder. He pulled out two stacks of pages, and handed one to Dee. "These are copies for you." He handed the other stack to his secretary. "Miss Kahler, would you run off some fresh duplicates for me?"

As she left, he shrugged. "I like to have two of everything. Saves time." He set the empty folder down on his desk. "Well, I hope that is helpful to your investigation. If you need anything else, don't hesitate to call me." He handed me his business card.

"Thank you, Mr. Sanhouk." I shook his hand. "We will be in touch, I'm sure."

* * *

I slammed the passenger's door shut. "Well, that was a washout!"

"I wouldn't say that." Dee buckled her seat belt and began skimming the documents Sanhouk had given her.

I held up my notes from the phone call to the arbitrator's brother. "I suppose those records might come in handy. Still, there goes my theory about Sanhouk. He has a rock solid alibi."

"We'll see." She started the engine. "Not all of the cards have been revealed yet. We still have time."

"Meanwhile, we'll have to tell Warren that Sanhouk is clear."

Dee looked over at me. "We aren't telling Warren any such thing, yet. I am still not sure about this guy."

"I don't follow. He was helpful, courteous, cooperative, and he was in Bothel at the time of the crime." I tried to find some loophole in the alibi, to no avail.

"Noah, all I know is what my intuition is telling me. Don't strike him off your list of suspects yet." She drummed her fingers on the steering wheel. "There is something he isn't telling us. He seemed far too nervous for that."

I was unconvinced. "Everyone is nervous around a P.I."

"Perhaps, but he was nervous at the wrong time—before we told him Conhue had been murdered. You have to admit, that isn't normal behavior."

I stared down at my notebook. "Time will tell, I suppose."

Dee nodded. "Time, among other things." She looked past me, out the window. "Hold on a moment." She unbuckled her seat belt and snatched her compact from her purse. "I will be right back." She got out and approached a beat up red four-door sedan a few spaces away.

I looked around. The parking lot was completely empty, except for us, that car, and a brand new Volvo. What could my cousin be doing? I watched her let her compact slip out of her hands by the red car's driver door. She slowly bent down to pick it up, pausing about halfway back up to standing. Then, she returned to our car.

I stared at my cousin as she tucked the compact away in her purse. "May I ask what all that was about?"

She started the engine. "We'll be having a little chat with Miss Kahler after work. The shopping list on her dashboard mentions a certain little grocery store near here. We'll be waiting for her there."

* * *

I sipped my coffee and scanned the store's parking lot again. "Are you certain it wasn't a slight assumption on your part that she would be here after work today?"

Dee didn't look concerned. "She might not be, but I have a feeling we'll see her."

"I certainly hope we'll be able to spot her if she does come. This parking lot is packed." I set my empty coffee cup down.

She laughed. "You might want to call it quits on that stuff for today, Noah. That's your third cup already. You won't be able to sleep a wink tonight."

"Fine, I'll switch to decaf." I stood up to approach the coffee bar again, but Dee grabbed my shirt.

"Sit down. There she is." Dee pointed to a young woman in casual clothes and a slate gray newsboy cap.

"Shouldn't we approach her?"

Dee held up a finger. "Not until she's inside. Makes it look more coincidental that way."

Miss Kahler picked up a hand basket and an ad before entering the store. After a few moments, Dee motioned for me to follow her. We entered through the other set of doors. I quickly caught sight of our target. "She's heading for aisle seven," I whispered.

Dee snatched up a basket. "Look disinterested."

We wandered down aisle six and circled around. Dee slowed down and suddenly developed an intense interest in snack food. After a moment, she left her post in front of the potato chips and wandered towards Miss Kahler.

"Well, isn't this a small world? Weren't we just at the same office earlier today?" Dee actually sounded genuine in her surprise.

"Oh, yes." Miss Kahler looked incredibly uneasy. "Fancy meeting you here."

"Say, I was meaning to ask how long you've been working for Mr. Sanhouk. He certainly brags about you." Dee's gaze remained occupied on the selection of chips as she spoke.

The girl put a box of cheesy crackers into her basket. "Oh, about three years. He employed me right out of school. He's an excellent employer." She moved down the aisle toward the chips.

"Yes, those are hard to come by these days." Dee smiled at her. "He was so helpful to our investigation." My cousin picked up a bag of veggie crisps and viewed the ingredient list. After a few uncomfortable moments of silence, she addressed our unwitting interviewee again. "I hope you don't mind my asking, but seeing as you're here and all, we might as well save some time. Would you mind telling me where you were at 12:30 p.m. on April the 27th? Just for the sake of being thorough and all."

The girl blanched. "Oh, I was...I was at home. My boss gave me the day off."

"Can anyone vouch for you?"

Miss Kahler seemed trapped. "Not really, I...I live alone. I..." Her breath caught. "I really have to go. Have a good day, ma'am. Sir."

"Oh, I didn't mean to upset you or anything. Perhaps this was a bad time to ask," Dee apologized.

"I really have to go." Miss Kahler hurried out of the aisle.

I cautiously followed. The young woman abandoned her basket. "She's heading for the door," I whispered to Dee behind me.

"She definitely has something to hide. We'd better tail her."

I nodded and headed for the exit, flipping open my phone in transit. I punched the speed dial for the lieutenant.

"This is Warren."

"Hey, Warren, Noah Clue. I'll be tailing a possible suspect—a Miss Kahler. No first name known at this time."

The lieutenant's voice held no emotion. "Thank you for letting me know. Make sure you keep it legal. No rough tailing."

"No problem. I'll keep you posted." I hung up as we reached the car. "Dee, give me the keys. I have to be the one driving for this."

Dee furrowed her brow at me. "I thought you didn't have a driver's license."

"I do, I just don't like to drive." I held out my hand. "Come on, time is money."

Dee pulled the keys out of her purse and tossed them to me. "You better not wreck my car." She ducked into the passenger's side.

I hurried into the driver's seat and buckled up, putting the key in the ignition.

Dee shut her door. "I think I spotted her vehicle, heading for the east exit of the parking lot."

"Seattle rush hour makes this hard, just for the record." I pulled out of our parking spot and turned towards the exit.

I spotted the red sedan turning left, and followed. Only two other cars separated us. Good, that would help prevent her from spotting me. If she caught on, I'd legally have to suspend my pursuit.

"She's turning right on 14th avenue." Dee announced.

"Thank you." I turned. At least this was a side street. I fell back a bit, so she wouldn't catch on. So far, so good. She made a left at northwest 45th street.

"I have to hand it to you, Noah. What you lack in powers of observation, you make up for in tailing skills."

"Thank you." I paused at the intersection, before turning down the side street my target had just taken. As I rounded the corner, I saw her parallel park. I pulled off to the side and stopped the engine.

Miss Kahler got out, took a quick look around, and then dashed into the house. I pulled out my cell phone again and called Warren.

"This is…"

I cut him short. "Yeah, it's Noah Clue again. Kahler apparently hasn't spotted us. She just went into her house; at least, I presume it's her house."

"Uh huh. Fill me in here. Who is she again?"

"Sanhouk's secretary. He has an alibi, but she doesn't. She appeared nervous when we spoke to her."

Warren's all-business demeanor deepened. "What are you saying, Clue?"

I paused. "You know, I'm not really sure. Let me hand you to Dee, and she can fill you in."

My cousin took the phone and switched it to speaker mode. "Sanhouk has a rock solid alibi, but I still smell a rat. He was only too obliging."

Warren sounded puzzled. "I don't get it. Wouldn't you want cooperative interviewees?"

"Well, yes," Dee explained. "Except this one claimed not to remember Jonny Conhue until I hinted that he would have the contact on his smartphone, and then he regained his memory and handed over all of the case files."

"You better not have asked for those," the lieutenant warned

"Of course not. He offered." Dee paged through the folder. "It does rather strike me as a potential breach of confidentiality, to be honest. But I figure the onus is on him for that."

"Better turn them over to us all the same," Warren asserted. "So, how does the secretary fit into all of this?"

Kahler's front door opened. Our quarry emerged with a black tripod bag. She set it on the backseat, looked around, and made eye contact with me.

I started the engine. "We've been spotted. I'm calling it off." I turned the car around and headed back to Seattle.

"Good call." Dee nodded to me. "Warren, we're calling off the tail. We'll touch base later." She hung up.

I cleared my throat. "Well, cousin, I have to hand it to you on this one. Whether she's our killer or not, she's definitely acting like she's hiding something."

"I may have identified her as a suspect, but you got us to Sanhouk." My cousin grinned. "I say we make a pretty good team."

A team. I liked the sound of that.

7

End Game

Dee joined me in watching an old movie on her television. I needed a distraction from the evening's frustrating events. If only we'd been able to maintain our tail of Kahler.

"Look, there was one alleged eye witness to this killing. Someone else claims he heard the killing, saw the boy run out afterwards and there was a lot of circumstantial evidence." Henry Fonda's character mused. "But, actually, those two witnesses were the entire case for the prosecution. Supposing they're wrong?"

I grabbed a fistful of popcorn from the bowl on Dee's lap. Butter-free was pretty lame, but it was better than the other cardboard-based snack choices in the cabinet.

"What do you mean, supposing they're wrong?" Robert Webber shot back at Fonda. "What's the point of having witnesses at all?"

The star's response was drowned out by Michael Bublé, singing about dragonflies and butterflies. I grunted, paused the movie, wrestled my phone from my pocket, and flipped it open. "Clue."

"Noah, it's Warren. You and Dee need to get down to the station right away. There's been an attempt on one of your suspects' lives."

He had my full attention. "What? Who? When?"

"Adriana Skye."

I had to admit, I'd expected it to be Miss Kahler. I'd need to rework a few of my ideas. "What happened?"

"We're not entirely sure. She refuses to talk to anyone but Dee. It strikes me as a little irrational, but panic does strange things to people." Warren paused. "We could use your mind on this too."

"That's nice to hear, Warren. You've never really paid my mind a compliment before."

"Shut up before I take it back, Clue. Just get your scrawny hide down to headquarters as soon as you can."

* * *

Warren showed us into the interview room, and shut the door behind us. I almost expected him to join us, but he had decided to observe our conversation from the other side of the one-way glass.

Dee took a seat across from Ms. Skye at the interview table. "You wanted to see me?"

"Oh, Miss Tindall, it was horrible. I came home to find my neighbor inside my house. She jumped me and tried to strangle me." Skye had red marks around her neck, where her assailant must have grabbed her.

The real estate agent continued, obviously shaken. "I fought and managed to get away. Escaped in my car and drove directly here to report the crime."

I couldn't help wondering why she hadn't called 9-1-1, but I decided to roll with the scenario. I needed more information. "Your neighbor broke in?"

Skye shook her head. "I keep a key under a flower pot. She sometimes feeds my cat when I'm going to be home late." She choked back a sob. "I thought I could trust her."

Dee maintained a soothing tone. "I'm sorry to hear about your experience, but what does this have to do with us?"

Adriana Skye leaned forward. "I think she killed Conhue. This is the neighbor that saw Dr. Orchard and me together. I didn't put two and two together until after that dinner party setup of yours. We saw her putting an air rifle into her car that day. The time it would take to drive to the office building where Conhue was found..." Skye choked up. "It would put her there at the time of the crime."

The logistic jump set off warning bells in my mind. A few months ago, I would have bought this whole story, but now it just smelled like a setup. It was almost too obvious.

"What's her name?" Dee took out her small notepad.

Skye sniffed back a few tears. "Catherine Kahler."

My heart skipped a beat.

Dee's sympathetic gaze remained on Skye. "Can you describe her for us?" she asked gently.

"Really pale blonde, twenty something, about my height." The real-estate agent wiped her nose with her wrist. Dee offered her a box of tissues.

Elias Sanhouk's secretary lived across the street from Adriana Skye? I debated whether this would even make a plausible coincidence. Just how well did Skye know Sanhouk?

My cousin wrote something down. "What time did this happen?"

"I came home tonight at 7:23 and found her waiting for me. She screamed in my face and tried to strangle me."

That had been six minutes after I called off the tail. I wished Kahler hadn't spotted me.

Dee glanced at me and quirked her eyebrow. "This happened at 7:23. When did you get here?"

"Oh, I don't know..." Skye hesitated. "About ten or fifteen minutes ago? I'm not sure."

Dee nodded. "So, it happened over an hour ago. How long were you fighting?"

Skye threw her hands in the air. "How would I know? I was fighting for my life!"

"And yet you remember exactly when the fight started." Dee leaned back in her chair.

I remembered studying this anomaly in psychology. "According to the theory of flashbulb memories, traumatic events cause us to remember more details," I mused aloud.

Skye waved her hand out in my direction. "See? The clock was nearby, so I saw the time and remembered it."

"And thus, you would also remember roughly how long you were fighting for," I added. "However, aren't you assuming that she had a motive to kill Conhue? She could have been going anywhere."

Skye shot me a look of disgust. "I'm not assuming anything. She's Elias Sanhouk's secretary. I know, because I recommended her for that job back before Conhue turned out to be a snake. You said yourself that Sanhouk was the only one without an alibi. He probably put her up to it."

So that was the connection.

Dee continued, unabated. "Where is Kahler now?"

Skye's face clouded over again. "She screamed that she'd kill me and Orchard. We both saw her that night, so maybe she figured we'd be key witnesses against her, since we saw her with the gun."

"Have you called Dr. Orchard to warn him?" I prompted. Her apparent decision not to call 9-1-1 made less sense by the minute.

She sniffed and dabbed her eyes with her sleeve. "Of course, and then I came here. I figured this was the only safe place for me."

Dee crossed her arms. "It's interesting that this event now eliminates your own alibi, Skye, as well as that of Dr. Orchard."

"I came here because someone made an attempt on my life, and you try to tell me that it didn't happen?" Skye stood, fire flashing in her eyes. "You really have some nerve."

The door opened, and Warren stormed in. A tall, black officer followed on his heels. "Sit down, Ms. Skye," the lieutenant commanded.

Skye collapsed in her chair again, a scowl on her face.

Dee pulled out her smartphone. "Let's see...from your neighborhood to here only takes about sixteen minutes without traffic, and there is no major traffic right now. So, unless you were fighting for an hour solid, we have some time unaccounted for."

Skye bristled. "Look, lady, I don't know. I called you down here to give you some additional information, not for you to accuse me of making things up. I thought you would be more sensitive."

My mind raced. If the alibi for both Adriana Skye and Dr. Orchard was Catherine Kahler, and Kahler was also Sanhouk's secretary, recommended by Skye... "Dee! How far is it from Skye's house to Orchard's?"

Dee furrowed her brow. "I don't know his address."

Warren cleared his throat. "We have it, however. Sergeant Dunn, please get the file on Stephen Orchard."

The sergeant nodded and departed.

"We won't need to wait for it." I turned to our suspect. "Skye knows it, don't you?"

Skye blanched. "I...I never got it."

"Of course you would have." I leaned forward against the table. "What kind of person gets into a precarious relationship with a man and doesn't know his address? I've seen your office Ms. Skye. You're a thorough woman. Now, you can save us a whole lot of time if you share that knowledge with us. After all, if he's really in danger as you say, why wouldn't you want to ensure help gets there faster?"

Skye hunched her shoulders and gave the address to Dee through clenched teeth.

My assistant tapped on her smartphone for a few moments. "Twenty one minutes without traffic."

I nodded. "There you go. Forty-two minutes round trip, plus the time to get here. About fifty minutes, plus ten for the fight."

Skye crossed her arms. "Now who's assuming?"

"I have to agree with her there, Clue," Warren added.

I shook my head. "Oh, I don't think it's an assumption at all. It's quite simple, really. Kahler is the alibi—the second alibi, that is. Orchard and Skye originally claimed they were at his office, but when that turned up false, she fell back on the neighbor story. 'I'm not taking the fall for you,' is what I believe she said to Orchard?"

I stepped back into the brilliant detective role, except this time, things made sense to me. "Ms. Skye, you had plenty of motive to kill Conhue, as did Dr. Orchard. Conhue was a threat to both of your careers and reputations, and you wanted him out of the picture. You were the only one with an obvious link to Conhue, so Orchard was a safe alibi, until we stumbled across him—thanks to you, I might add."

Skye shifted around in her seat. I had hit a nerve.

"You were also the one with the easiest access to the building. It has several spaces for rent, which is what you recently switched your professional focus to, so anyone who saw you in the building would probably not remember, because you were *supposed* to be there. You could unlock the room easily."

Sergeant Dunn returned with the folder.

"Yes, we went over this convoluted theory before, Clue," Adriana Skye snapped. She crossed her arms. "What does this have to do with your accusation that I made up the whole attack this evening?"

I smiled a little. "One simple thing—the neighbor who saw you with Orchard was Catherine Kahler, a girl so flighty and unsure of herself, I think it unlikely that she could smuggle a weapon into an office building unnoticed. Yet, there is one major character flaw that makes her a pawn in this: she'll do whatever she is told. All you had to do was give her the weapon to hide and cite her as the alibi. Everything was fine until today, when she panicked and took something—I'll wager it was the weapon—back out of her house in broad daylight with the intent to get rid of it."

I paused for a moment, taking in the looks of surprise on everyone's faces. I had even beat Dee to this conclusion. "You knew that she could blow everything, Ms. Skye. She had to be silenced, and the only way to do that was to resort to plan C: frame her. You bring her over to your house, probably knock her out, and drive her to Orchard's house. It's not hard to put strangle marks on your own neck. Then, while you drive to the police station to report the alleged assault, Orchard kills her and makes it look like a crazed break-in, which is what you implied she'd be doing next."

I let the silence hang in the air momentarily for dramatic emphasis. "So, in this little game of 'who killed Johnny Conhue,' I think I can safely make an accusation: Ms. Skye, in the office building, with the air rifle." Satisfied, I leaned back on the wall.

"Clue...you are..." Warren began. I waited for the inevitable compliment.

"...you are an absolute idiot!" He turned to Sergeant Dunn and ordered him to get units out to Orchard's location. Warren headed for the door. "While you're playing Sherlock, Orchard is likely attempting to kill Kahler, if he hasn't done so already!"

* * *

Warren had me ride along with him to Orchard's house. Dee rode with another officer. By Warren's logic, since the accusation had been made, and the cards were about to be laid on the table, all players in our wager should be present.

As we pulled up to our destination, red and blue lights danced across the front of the house, shimmering on the broken glass of the front window. Three other patrol cars and an ambulance filled the street. Paramedics guided a gurney into the house.

"Stay put." Warren jumped out of the car and headed for the battered door.

A group of neighbors gathered across the street. I scanned their faces in case I recognized anyone. No one stood out.

After a few minutes, Warren tapped on my window and gestured for me to join him. I opened the door and followed him up onto the curb. A defiant Dr. Orchard emerged from the house in handcuffs. I could hear his burly escort's no-nonsense recitation of the Miranda rights from where I stood.

Warren motioned toward the house. "The girl's inside. Badly beaten but still alive. It appears she had been tied up while he wrecked the house with a baseball bat to stage the break-in. The responding officers caught him in the act of strangling her."

Dee sidled up beside me. "I'm glad the officers got here in time."

Orchard snarled at me as he passed. "You're two for two on ruining my life, Clue. First my practice, and then this."

I crossed my arms. "Of all people, you should know that truth always comes out. After all, wasn't it Freud who said 'If his lips are silent, he chatters with his fingertips; betrayal oozes out of him at every pore.'"

Orchard ducked his gaze.

Once he was safely in the back of the patrol car, Warren turned to me and my assistant. "You may have had poor timing on your monologue, but thankfully you figured out what was going on. Since Skye is the most likely to have brought Kahler here, I believe we can safely say that your theory looks to be accurate so far." He held out his hand. "Thus, I officially concede to you both. You have won fair and square."

Dee shook Warren's offered hand, and I did so as well. I wasn't really certain what to say.

"So, as per our terms," Warren continued, "I will pay the first month's rent at your office. I never thought I'd say this, but Seattle is one lucky city to have you two around. I mean that." He looked me square in the eyes. "You may be a total klutz when it comes to investigating, but you truly do have the mind of a great detective. I'm sorry I've underestimated you."

I shrugged. "I think *I've* underestimated me. I didn't expect to piece that together at all."

Dee patted me on the back. "Well, you did, cousin. At this rate, we're going to be the best P.I. firm in Seattle."

Tuesday, May 4

Curtis Daubney shook my hand enthusiastically. "First rate work, Mr. Clue. I never doubted you for a moment."

I smiled at the complement and sat down. "I appreciate your confidence. It looked a bit dodgy there for a bit, but we pulled through in the end."

Daubney smiled. "Well, you'll be glad to know that, because of this, we're installing some additional cameras in the building, and tightening up general security. We don't want people wandering in and out of here unnoticed." He wiggled his eyebrows. "Probably useful with a high profile P.I. firm moving in here and all."

"I don't know how 'high profile' we really are, Mr. Daubney, but I appreciate the thought." I replied.

Dee cleared her throat and held up the copy of the Seattle Times she had purchased on our way here. "We made the papers. I say that's pretty high profile."

"You'll probably have no end of clients after this." Daubney set a stack of paperwork on the table. "Now, in regards to that office, here's the lease. As per our agreement, the rent is half price for the first year, and the first two months are free. You've done us a great service, Mr. Clue."

Dee leaned over the contract. "I'll go ahead and read this over, if you don't mind."

I pointed a thumb at my cousin. "Legal secretary. I let her handle the stuff I don't understand—contracts, agreements, wagers..."

Daubney laughed at that last item, clearly not realizing that I wasn't kidding.

Thursday, May 6

"Couch coming in!" Charles Radcliffe entered backwards through our office door with the new sofa. Mr. Reilly, a prior client and wealthy businessman, had heard about our latest case in the newspaper, and decided to invest in our firm, both in cash and in brand new furniture.

Warren brought up the other end of the red couch. "Between our bet, your client, and all your friends, Clue, you're doing nicely for a relatively new firm."

I smiled a little. "Yeah, it works out well. And I'm glad you're not determined to end my career anymore."

"No need to." Warren set down his end of the couch and brushed his hands on his stained blue jeans. "You figured out what your career is—the silent, thinking half of a detective duo."

"Well, mostly silent," added Dee. "He does the end case monologue quite well, when he doesn't butcher the timing."

I grunted. Would she ever let me live that down?

"So, fill me in here," my best friend, David, asked as he and Reilly entered with a large desk. "Your whole solution seemed rather circumstantial. How did you figure it out?"

I was starting to enjoy explaining my deductions. "Adriana Skye relied on several layers of deception to cover her involvement in the murder. At first she claimed Orchard was a client, and then pretended to barely remember the arbitrator, yet provided his first name. She also conveniently left out that her alibi was said arbitrator's secretary; a position that Skye had recommended the neighbor for. Once you strip away all the lies, she and Orchard were the only suspects without verifiable alibis."

Dee studied the spot where we had found Conhue. The stain was gone, thanks to the bioremediation service Daubney had hired, but the memory remained. "Hmm, let's put the desk right here."

The two men set it down. Reilly stood back and nodded. "It looks good there." He turned to me. "Who actually pulled the trigger on Conhue, then?"

"Adriana Skye, naturally. She had easy access to the building, being a real estate agent. She could conceal the air gun in a tripod bag, an object no one would think twice about her having if she was photographing a space." I pointed my thumb at the door. "Conhue arrived here at 12:26, according to the cleaning lady's testimony of hearing a door opening. He probably believed he'd be meeting a client. Skye comes in shortly after that. No voices are raised, so Conhue either suspected nothing or was caught by surprise." I shrugged. "Unless Skye confesses, we'll never know for sure what happened here that day."

"She gave the weapon to Catherine Kahler to hide, no doubt intending to frame the young lady as a last resort," I continued. "Kahler was easy to manipulate, the same personality flaw that made her perfect as a secretary for a crooked arbitrator. Skye had a ready-made backup alibi and scapegoat. Things only started going off the rails when I tailed Kahler. She panicked and tried to get rid of the weapon. Skye knew she'd have to be silenced before she could spill the whole story to the police, so she staged the fight, drove her to Orchard's house..."

Radcliffe cut me off. "Wait, how do you know for sure Skye drove her, other than the timing you mentioned to us earlier?"

"I can explain that one." Warren sat down on the couch. "In her panic, Adriana Skye overlooked one detail. When we sent officers out to her house to gather evidence, they found Catherine Kahler's car. Noah had given us the make, model, and license plate number when he tailed her before. That meant someone had to transport Kahler to Orchard's place."

David took a seat next to Warren, clearly enjoying this. "So, how does Sanhouk figure into all of this? I assume he's uninvolved?"

"It turned out," Dee replied, "that Sanhouk had been taking bribes from Conhue to rule in his favor. That's why he was so nervous when we talked to him. He had absolutely no connection to the murder, other than the fact that his secretary was involved against her will."

Warren nodded. "Kahler will be charged with accessory after the fact, but could get off easy if she agrees to testify. However, Orchard's put himself up a creek. When my officers arrived on scene, they found Kahler tied up, and Orchard attempting to strangle her after having destroyed the living room with a large baseball bat. The fact that he was wearing latex gloves doesn't help his case."

"Unfortunate for him," I added. "Since Skye pulled the trigger, Orchard might have gotten off with a mere accessory to murder charge in this case. Now he'll face attempted murder, among a host of other charges."

"It's rather poetic that you ended up with the office where you first found the body," Radcliffe mused.

I snorted. "Not so much poetic as frugal. Since I solved the case, he gave it to me at half price for the first year."

"Works out well for me, since I lost the bet." Warren added.

"Well, I think everything looks good." Reilly put his hands on his hips. "You're just about ready for business; ready to solve the next baffling case to walk through that door."

Dee brought in a bottle of sparking cider and began handing out and filling cups. "A toast, to our detective firm."

"Hear, hear." I took the cup she offered me. "My name, and our collective skill." I raised the glass. "To my assistant, who is the better half of my mind, the police lieutenant who is obligated to help us,"

Warren grunted, but he still smiled a little.

"To our two supportive, if mildly eccentric, investors."

Radcliffe snickered. "Mildly eccentric?"

"And to my best friend, who has stuck by me through the whole weird adventure thus far." I nodded to David.

Dee winked at me. "And to the guy with the P.I. license who makes it all legally viable."

"He does more than that," Warren replied as he held up his glass. "So, here's to us."

How To Get Murdered

In Three

Easy

Steps

To Dr. Ware,

Who observed that I put a little of myself

into every character.

I can trust him, he's a doctor.

I must make one doozy of a case study.

1

I Get Yet Another Secretary

Monday, June 14

Dee sat in one of the padded office chairs near the front desk and pondered her clipboard. We had just spent the past four hours interviewing for a secretary, and frankly, the results were underwhelming. If only Leah Lee, my prior temporary assistant, had still been available, but my recommendation of her to a former client had secured her a comfortable administrative position. I couldn't ask her to give that up.

My cousin scribbled something. "Okay, so there's the redhead."

I sipped my coffee. "Ginger?"

"Yes, who believes our office is haunted." Dee wiggled her fingers in a spooky manner.

"How nice. Next."

She scratched the name from her list. "There's the amateur magician and self-proclaimed paranormal expert who *insists* our office is haunted. Eighty-seven words per minute, but seems to be easily distracted."

"That'd be fun." I snickered at the possible jokes I could play.

Dee wasn't amused. "The haunting, or having a paranormal expert secretary shoving a ghost detector in our faces?"

"Let's skip that. She needs to be answering phones, not checking them for a dark past."

My cousin scowled at me. "Noah, you really shouldn't have asked her if she could levitate."

I shrugged that off. "I was curious."

She turned back to the notes. "There's the former flight attendant. Ninety-six words per minute. How do you get fired from a flight attendant position?"

"How do you know she was fired?" I sat back in my chair, hoping for some deep insight from my cousin.

"Maybe she wasn't, I don't know. She looked flighty." Dee paused. "No pun intended."

I wadded up a piece of paper and lobbed it toward the trash can. It bounced off the rim and rolled toward the couch. "And we're considering hiring her to answer phones in an apparently haunted office. Brilliant. Next."

"Alleged."

"Toh-may-toh, toh-mah-toh."

Dee picked up the wad of paper and tossed it into the trash. "The former school teacher with PTSD. Seventy-two words per minute."

I rubbed the back of my neck. "I don't know. Do you suppose we'll have to raise our hands to go to the bathroom?"

"She did seem a bit stern." Dee sighed. "Moving on."

"There was that one girl, Jean."

My cousin rolled her eyes. "Her résumé almost made her sound magical. One hundred two words per minute. What language was that again?"

"Sumerian." I took another sip of coffee. "She'd fit right in with the alleged poltergeist. Next."

Dee's eyes twinkled with amusement. "Maybe we should just hire the ghost instead?"

"Great." I laughed. "The only P.I. firm in the country with a fully-automatic typewriter. That would lead to a dramatic drop in quality clients, wouldn't it?"

My cousin shrugged. "On the other hand, just think of the publicity we'd get."

"You want Miss Ghostbusters to come back with her creep-o-meter?" I cleared my throat. "Moving on. The med school dropout?"

"Who said she quit when a cadaver turned out not to be."

I snorted coffee out my nose and grabbed a paper napkin. My sinuses burned. "When the cadaver sits up, class is officially over. Probably not the best fit, given our location."

"I can see that now, giving her the tour of the office." Mischief sparkled in my cousin's eyes. "'Yes, and this is where we found a dead body. Right under where your desk is now. We're leaving you here alone for six hours. Have fun!'"

"At least we got the place for half price." I reminded her.

Dee shot me a mock glare. "If my coffee starts pouring itself, I'm holding you liable." She tapped her clipboard. "I don't think any of these candidates sound overly qualified for the job."

I wasn't impressed. "No. About half are certifiable, though."

"Maybe not certifiable enough." She turned a page. "We have one more applicant: Bryan. He should be here in about three minutes."

"Great, just enough time to refill." I stood.

Dee held up her mug. "One for me, too, please, while I try to tame this curl."

"Good luck with that." While my cousin kept her hair in a bun during work hours, that front curl always had a mind of its own. Oh well. I headed to the kitchenette. Our new office was a serious improvement from the last location, except for the creepy history. It made for a handy conversation starter, at least.

I filled both mugs, and then reached for a low-carb brownie. It wasn't food, but at least it looked like it. We needed some real donuts, but Dee had banned them and several other of my favorite goodies. Since I had to rely on her to feed me right now, I wasn't going to buck the system. Besides, she promised that if I managed to avoid saying anything stupid during the next case, she'd start giving me an allowance.

Lest you judge me, remember that a man has to get his money from somewhere. Besides, I wasn't about to tell her that my last two trips to Starbucks also involved a pit stop to gorge myself on pizza.

"Hello?" A young man's voice floated into the office. "Is there anybody here?"

"Nobody here but us ghosts." I emerged from the kitchenette and set the two mugs of coffee on the desk. "Just kidding. You must be Bryan Gannon."

"I am." The stocky young man stepped forward and shook my hand. His short dark hair seemed to have a mind of its own. "And you would be Noah Clue."

"The one and only."

My cousin returned from her curl-taming mission, defeated. She plastered a smile on her face as she joined us.

I gestured to her. "Bryan, this is my assistant, Dee Ann Tindall." I'd been calling her that all day, for lack of a better term. What do you call someone who does half your job for you, but pretends that you're in charge?

The applicant shook her hand. "Miss Tindall."

"Bryan Gannon. Have a seat." Dee gestured to the empty chair nearest the door, and settled into her own chair .

I took my seat behind the desk and tented my fingers, trying to look like there was a point to my being there. Actually, I rather looked forward to the show.

Dee picked up her clipboard, starting the interview. "So. Bryan. How fast do you type?"

"Last time I checked, somewhere around seventy-two, seventy-three words per minute, about ninety-six percent accuracy. I write up a lot of essays."

She scribbled a few notes, her cool, placid interview demeanor firmly in place. "What do you currently do?"

"I'm a college student. Going for my degree in criminology."

Dee nodded without looking up. "What got you into that?"

Bryan shrugged. "I dunno. I like crime shows. That's why I jumped at the chance to work for you guys. I can learn a lot from you, make myself generally useful, and then do my homework when things get quiet."

Dee gazed at him. "Bryan with a y? Why a y?"

"What?" Bryan tipped his head to one side.

"Why a y?" she repeated.

Wariness filled the young man's amber eyes. "Why?"

I grunted and leaned back in my chair, resting my hands behind my head. "Who's on first?" Of course, my cousin's interview style no longer surprised me. We needed a secretary who could think on his or her feet, deal with difficult personalities, and of course, handle our own day-to-day banter.

Dee ignored me. "I just want to know why, that's why."

Bryan shrugged. "My parents named me. No reason."

"So, no why to the y." Dee's pen scratched across the paper. "Irish or Scottish?"

Bryan-with-a-Y seemed more confused than ever. "What?"

Dee put down her pencil and looked at him. "You don't know anything about your family history at all?"

"No." He paused. "Do...you?"

Actually, Dee knew everything about our family history, right back to the thirteenth century. She would have gone further, but it involved a trip to Great Britain, and Dee would rather swim than fly. I got comfortable as I watched my cousin dig in.

Dee continued. "Bryan is Irish. So is Gannon."

"So I'm Irish?"

"Unless the name was assumed." Dee took a sip of coffee. "Which I doubt."

Bryan rubbed his temples. "Does this have any relevance at all?"

"Not really, no." Dee made another note. "Any criminal history?"

"Clean record." The applicant seemed a bit unnerved. My cousin took getting used to.

"In your family?"

Bryan squinted. "Umm...not that I know of. Unless you're talking about distant history, at which point I already said I can't help you."

"Nope. Recent history is fine. My great-grandfather once had a drink with Bonnie and Clyde. Didn't know who they were at the time, of course." Dee turned a page. "Can you answer phones?"

Bryan looked thoroughly confused. "Hold the thing up to my head and talk, right?"

"Ours like to answer themselves," I chimed in. "They'll do all the talking for both ends if you let them."

I rather enjoyed the awkward silence that followed. For once, I wasn't the one who was out of his element.

Dee cleared her throat. "This office has had an unusual history. We found a dead body in here when we first saw it. In fact, the desk sits right over the spot where he met his demise."

Bryan perked up. "Really? Cool."

I liked this guy already.

We hired Bryan-with-a-Y on the spot, and since his afternoon was otherwise clear, we invited him to stay to see how we did things.

He now stared at the plate of low-carb brownies in the kitchenette, looked at me, and then back down at the plate.

"They look real, don't they?" I chuckled.

He grimaced. "It's a plate full of lies."

"Tell me about it." I opened the mini-fridge and snatched up a bottle of water. "You're just lucky you don't have to live with her."

"So, is she your..."

I cut him off. "Cousin. I'm staying with her until I get my living situation worked out."

Bryan nodded. "Right, so, I'm trying to figure out the roles around here. She doesn't strike me as merely some flimsy assistant."

"We, ah, never got the titles officially figured out," I explained. "Closest we figure, she's the eyes, and I'm the brain, although that's not quite it either."

Dee wandered into the kitchenette. "You're more like the Encyclopædia Britannica." She reached between us and grabbed another brownie from the plate. "Or, another way of looking at it, I collect the pieces, and Noah figures out how to fit them all together."

"Thank you, cuz. That's the nicest version of it you've come up with yet."

She gave me a side glance. "He's also the one with the P.I. license, so he's my passport into places. Ostensibly, I take notes."

Bryan nodded. "So, just to be clear, my job is mainly to answer phones and hold down the fort while you two are out on cases?"

I took a sip of my water. "Mostly. On occasion, you'll come along to take notes, freeing Dee up to do some snooping of her own."

"Right, I remembered that." Bryan reached for a brownie before thinking better of it. He withdrew his hand. "How busy do you guys usually get?"

"It varies." I led the way back towards the desk. "Thankfully, we haven't had multiple cases at once yet, although the chances of that happening is increasing, given our recent publicity."

Bryan's eyes shone with excitement. "Right, the Conhue murder! The news was all over that one. He's the guy you found murdered in here, isn't he?"

The door to the office opened, and in walked a tall, skinny man in a shiny, gold and silver suit. "Mr. Clue?"

"That's me." I greeted the newcomer, trying not to focus on the loud, clashing patterns of his suit. This guy looked like he belonged on the Vegas strip. "Can I help you?"

Between his disingenuous grin and his thinning, slicked back hair, I half expected him to try selling me a car. He seized my hand in a cold, clammy grip and shook it. "Patrick Sharp. I'm the director of the Awakening Dawn conference. You've probably heard our advertisements on the radio recently."

How could I miss them? Dee's talk radio station aired their commercial every ten minutes, promising health, wealth, and happiness to each attendee through their "groundbreaking series of lectures on how to live a fulfilled life." Curiosity had driven me to look up the unspoken price of a ticket—eight hundred dollars per person. Still, a client was a client.

Mr. Sharp continued without missing a beat. "One of our main speakers was just found dead in the green room. Of course, we called the police, but as soon as I heard one of them mention 'suspicious circumstances,' I rushed down here. The conference is in three days. The last thing we need is some negative publicity scaring people away, and I definitely don't want anyone else from my conference targeted."

"Wait, what?" I tried to process this information. "How long ago was the body found?" I glanced at Dee, who took a seat by the window, just behind Sharp.

"About an hour. The police are still on the scene." Sharp pulled a golden money clip from his inner suit pocket and riffled through an obscene amount of cash. "I will pay you a thousand up front to take the case right this moment, provided you keep this as quiet as possible. If you can find the reason for the speaker's death before the conference starts, I'll pay you three times your regular fee, and you can keep the thousand as a bonus." He held out a fan of hundred dollar bills.

I cleared my throat, trying to process the offer. What kind of person carried that much cash on their person, especially in downtown Seattle? "You want me to keep this quiet?"

"Yes, well, ah, of course..." he stammered, "aside from the police. Talk to them all you like. Witnesses, suspects, whomever you need. Just, keep a lid on it. Publicity like this could kill conference attendance numbers." He set the money on the desk and leaned towards me. "Discretion is the key," he enunciated in a minty-fresh conspiratorial whisper.

Part of me wondered if those hundred-dollar bills were even real, but I knew Dee would be checking that as soon as our visitor left. "I can't promise miracles, Mr. Sharp. Murders aren't as easy to solve as they look in the books." I had learned that the hard way, but this guy didn't need to know it.

Sharp pursed his thin lips. "Yes, I understand. In the worst scenario, just having a private investigator on the case will help calm things down, so I'll pay you your normal fee no matter what." He grinned again. "But I have absolute faith you can solve this before the conference starts!"

I approached the front desk. Bryan immediately surrendered his chair. I sat down and tented my fingers, trying to sound as objective as Dee. The offer made me tingle with excitement, but I wasn't about to show it, especially since this guy seemed to be a master of closing deals. "Mr. Sharp, we aren't even certain there is a murder yet. If the body was found less than an hour ago..."

"Then if natural causes are established, you get paid the bonus, and we all move on." He sighed and took the seat across from me. "But I'm certain that's not it, Mr. Clue. I've known the deceased in question for years. He had no major medical issues, no sign of depression, no reason to believe he'd drop dead in a green room. While it could be anything, I strongly suspect foul play."

I glanced over Sharp's shoulder at Dee, who raised her eyebrows in amusement at our client's confidence in his own theories. Still, money was money, and if this was an open-and-shut matter, it would mean a lot of money. In any case, I had a full grand sitting in front of me on the desk.

I took a deep breath. "We'll take the case. My assistant will get the paperwork going."

* * *

When we reached the Washington State Convention Center, Dee let me and Bryan out at the curb, and then went to park. Sharp's personal assistant met us, and took us back to the 'scene of the crime,' as he called it. I chuckled inwardly. We still weren't certain a crime had even occurred.

Once inside, it didn't take long for me to track down Lieutenant Gregg Warren.

Amusement twinkled in his eyes. "If you're here to finally fix your life, you're three days early, Noah." Warren and I had a bit of a rivalry going, but it had settled down to something much friendlier.

I shoved my hands in my pockets and lowered my voice. "Just between you and me, I wouldn't take the advice of these yahoos if they were giving it away on the street corner."

His smile turned wry. "You and me both. What brings you here?"

"The conference director just showed up in my office and offered me three times my usual fee if I could solve the mystery of this guy's death before the conference. Paid an advance in cash, no less."

Warren scribbled something. "Funny, since we don't even know if it *is* a mystery yet. Could be natural causes."

I shrugged. "In which case I get paid for doing nothing. Win win."

"True that." Warren peered around me. "Who's the new guy?"

"Bryan Gannon." I gestured for my new secretary to step forward. "We just hired him to man the office while we're out on cases. We brought him along so he can see how we work." I nodded towards the door. "Dee's parking the car."

Bryan shook Warren's hand. "Pleasure to meet you, sir."

"Gannon." Warren smirked. "Good name for a P.I.'s secretary. Reminds me of Dragnet."

"I get that a lot, sir." Bryan seemed unfazed by the comparison.

"Really?"

Bryan shrugged. "Criminology major."

"Ah." Warren consulted his notebook. "Well, it looks like we're working together, Noah. The usual?"

I had come to enjoy our banter. "Sharing notes and evidence?"

The lieutenant dipped his head. "As law permits."

"First to solve?"

Warren gave a tight smile. "Loser buys lunch."

I shook his hand. "Deal. So, who's the apparent victim?"

Warren pointed a thumb towards the taped off green room. "Thomas Petree. Thirty-eight years old. Of course, we don't know cause of death yet, but it looks like a heart attack or something of that sort."

Why would Sharp mistake a medical issue for murder? "Who found the body?"

"Apparently an employee of the conference. I haven't spoken to him yet, so you're welcome to join me. Bring your new Captain Hastings along."

A classy Poirot reference. Bryan may not have realized it, but he'd already gained some points with Warren. I'd learned the lieutenant only teased people he took seriously.

* * *

We found the gentleman in question—a short, notably round man with bright blonde hair—nursing a tall cup of coffee in one of the empty dressing rooms. He already looked rather disturbed, and no surprise, given he had just found Petree's body. I looked around, hoping Dee would catch up to us soon. My specialty was in putting the pieces together, not in finding them.

Warren approached the man. "I'm Lieutenant Gregg Warren, Seattle P.D. Homicide. I would like to ask you a few questions."

Bryan and I stood back. I'd get my chance to ask some questions before long, but I wasn't about to get in the way of the police investigation. I couldn't afford to get on Warren's bad side again.

My new secretary took out a small notebook and pen, ready to start writing.

The man nodded. "Sure, go ahead."

Warren flipped open his notepad. "Let's start with your name."

"Binn. B-I-N-N."

Warren jotted down the information. "And your first name?"

The man hesitated. "Clarence."

Warren nodded. "Clarence..." He stopped writing and looked up. "Clarence Binn?"

Binn blew out a long breath. His face took on a pained expression. "Yes."

I had to say something. I waved from my spot near the wall. "Noah Clue."

Clarence Binn turned his attention to me. "Punster parents?"

"My dad, yeah."

Binn tilted his head. "Don't tell me you're a cop."

"Private investigator."

He winced. "Ouch."

"And you?"

"Wardrobe assistant." Binn grimaced.

Warren cleared his throat. "Gentlemen, if we could get back to the issue at hand." He poised his pen over his notepad. "What happened this evening?"

Binn shuddered. "I was looking for a sewing kit, and I knew I kept one in that room. As soon as I walked in, I found the guy slumped over in a chair. I thought he was asleep, so I tried to wake him."

"How did you try to wake him, exactly?" Warren was still writing.

"Well, verbally at first, but when he didn't respond, I tried to gently shake his shoulder. He didn't move, so I felt the side of his neck—you know, like they do in movies—and I couldn't find a pulse."

Warren looked up again. "Do you know how to find a pulse on the neck?"

"Never tried before, but like I said..."

"You've seen it in movies." Warren sighed. "Was anyone else with you when you found the body?"

"Not directly, no. There were other people outside, and I left the door open." Mr. Binn shuddered. "He just looked asleep. That was really creepy."

"Did you know the deceased?"

Binn shook his head. "I was hired by Awakening Dawn a few weeks ago. I don't really know anyone yet."

Warren took out his card. "Please stay in the area for the time being. We may have more questions for you later."

"I have to ask, am I a suspect?"

Warren looked him in the eyes. "Mr. Binn, it's too early in the investigation to even consider suspects."

I had to admire Warren's no-nonsense demeanor. He and Dee had that in common. I stepped forward. "You said you were just hired a few weeks ago. What were you doing prior to that?"

Binn shifted his attention to me. "I volunteered as a wardrobe assistant at a community theater, and had a job at a sandwich joint to pay my bills."

"What does your current job consist of here, Mr. Binn?" I glanced at Bryan, to make sure he was still taking notes.

"Whatever the wardrobe manager wants. Sewing and mending, mostly. Fetching coffee." He shrugged. "Still beats sandwiches."

I nodded. "Thank you for your time, Mr. Binn. I'll be in touch if I have any more questions."

"Glad to help."

As we left the room, Warren asked another officer to get Mr. Binn's contact information, and then turned towards me. "What do you think?"

I furrowed my brow. "It's like you said: it's too early in the investigation to consider suspects. We don't even know that this is a murder yet."

The lieutenant persisted. "If it is, do you think he's a candidate?"

"I don't know. Probably not. He'd have too much to lose, assuming he was honest about his work history. Anyhow, he didn't have ample opportunity."

Warren patted my shoulder. "Good man, you were paying attention. Just testing."

"Well, we know the victim wasn't assaulted," Bryan piped up. "He was found with his eyes closed."

Warren and I both turned to my new assistant. "How did you know that?" the lieutenant demanded.

Bryan pointed to his notebook. "Binn thought the victim was asleep."

Warren raised his eyebrows. "Looks like you've got a live one there, Noah."

2

One Flew Over The Conference Center

"All right, fill me in." Dee sipped her coffee and leaned back in her chair. The four of us had reconvened at a secluded table in the atrium of the conference center. "What'd I miss while I was shaking off Clark Gable?"

I squinted at Dee. "Sharp took a liking to you?"

She crossed her arms. "Why, is that hard to believe?"

"No, it just strikes me as rather..." I trailed off.

"Unprofessional." Warren finished the sentence for me.

I still couldn't wrap my head around it. "You spent an hour and a half trying to lose the guy?"

Bryan set a plate of muffins on the table. "Two bran, three cinnamon apple, three banana nut, and three blueberry."

"Thank you." Dee selected a bran muffin from the plate. "Sharp's tenacious, I'll give him that. It wasn't all wasted time. I learned a whole lot more about this conference."

"Like what?" I snatched up a cinnamon apple muffin, glad to have a snack that didn't resemble packing material for once.

She shook her head. "I asked first. Spill."

Warren pointed at Bryan. "Your new assistant has already written half a novel on the topic."

"Four pages and counting." Bryan waved his notebook in the air.

"Yes, but how much of that is essential information?" Dee took the notebook from Bryan and opened it. She blinked. "Where did you learn Pitman shorthand?"

Bryan grinned. "My mother was a secretary. She made me learn it years ago."

"*My* mother named me after Gregg shorthand," Warren muttered. "Court stenographer."

I snorted. "I say we go talk to Clarence Binn about filing a class action lawsuit against our parents for stupid naming practices."

Dee ignored us. "So, Petree was seated alone in a green room, which anyone could see someone going into or coming out of." Her gaze did not leave Bryan's notebook. "He entered the room around 1:17 p.m. and was discovered dead at 1:25 p.m." She looked up. "That leaves a pretty narrow window if this *is* a murder."

Warren shrugged. "Medical examiner believes this may have been a heart attack."

Dee continued. "Several people reported that Petree seemed confused and agitated when he entered the conference center, and demanded to be left alone. That further lends itself to the heart attack theory."

I needed more information. "It also means that something could have happened to him before he arrived at the conference center. I'll be interested in the toxicology reports." I snapped out of my pensive moment and snatched up a blueberry muffin.

"Good thought, Noah, although we'll have to wait quite a while for those. However..." Warren flipped open his phone and dialed a number. "Davis, I want the surveillance video from the drop-off area where Petree came in."

* * *

"No, Mr. Petree was as healthy as a horse. He jogged three times a week, maintained a strict all-natural diet, no bad habits." Laura Godfrey, Thomas Petree's personal assistant, sat across from me and

Bryan at a café near the conference center. The thin, mid-forties woman spoke in a deliberate, almost monotone voice, enunciating each word nearly to the point of making it painful. She barely moved as she spoke.

I nodded. "Do you know of anyone who would want..."

Godfrey cut me off. "No, Petree got along with everyone." She peered over her slightly upturned nose at me. Even her trendy multi-length hair style punctuated her condescension.

"I find that hard to believe." I tried to keep my tone neutral. I suspected that Godfrey was not leveling with me.

Her intense green eyes remained aimed at me. "He practiced what he preached."

"Which was?" Couldn't she be a bit more forthcoming?

"Balancing your life. He spoke on the topic all over Southern California for years."

I glanced over at Bryan, who was still playing stenographer for me. Dee and I had divided up the interviews between us. Since Bryan could obviously pick up subtleties, we decided he'd fill in for my usual observational deficits well enough. I turned back to Godfrey. "Southern California. He didn't usually travel outside that area?"

"Never. Petree didn't like airplanes."

Curious fact. "Why?"

"His leg."

"Cramps?" It irked me that she needed so much prompting.

"Paresthesia."

I'd never heard of that before. "Come again?"

"Tingling and numbness in his leg." Godfrey seemed to be enjoying her imagined superiority to me.

"From?"

"Old hip injury."

I sighed. "Ms. Godfrey, we haven't yet determined the cause of death. If this turns out to be a murder..."

She cut me off again. Her strong cheekbones accentuated her permanent scowl. "It won't. He had no enemies, I already told you."

"You seem pretty certain."

"I am certain. You're wasting your time." She still didn't move. She didn't even bat an eyelash.

I wanted to scream "BLINK!" at her, but I was determined to remain professional. "I have to cover my bases. It's..."

Her eyes narrowed. "Sharp put you up to this, didn't he?"

I exchanged a frustrated look with Bryan. Laura Godfrey was about as uncooperative as someone could be. "Ms. Godfrey..."

"It's just like him," she continued.

"Ms. Godfrey..." I repeated.

She wasn't listening. "I assure you, there is no crime here."

"*Ms.* Godfrey, if you would kindly leave the conclusions to me, and just answer my questions!" I struggled to keep my cool.

Petree's assistant blinked in a slow, deliberate manner. She gave an almost imperceptible sigh. "I am answering your questions, and I'm wasting quite a bit of time to do so."

I recalled something a detective in a book had said. "Just tell me everything, and let me sort out what's important and what's not."

An obstinate look flashed in her eyes. "Where shall I begin?"

"You said Thomas Petree never spoke anywhere but Southern California. Why did he fly out to Seattle?"

"He got a call from Sharp, about 5:43 p.m. last Tuesday. The phone had "Party For Two" by Shania Twain as the ringtone. He flipped it open and answered it by saying..."

I cut her off. "Ms. Godfrey, I think you know exactly what I mean by 'everything'."

"Just checking, Detective." Her thin lips formed a tight, smug smile. "Sharp said that he dropped Adrian Law from the conference, and he wanted Petree to fill his spot."

"Adrian Law?"

"Another speaker. Petree and Law were pretty close friends, so if Law wanted to kill anyone over it, it'd be Sharp."

"Go on."

"Petree reminded him he didn't travel, and Sharp insisted. I don't know how exactly he talked him into it. Petree's never had trouble turning him down before, but this time, before Petree hung up, he had promised to arrive in Seattle by today."

"How did you get here?"

"I flew."

I rubbed my eyes. "Ms. Godfrey..."

"Yes, details." She still had that irritating, self-satisfied grimace. "I flew in a day early to make some preparations. Mr. Petree is very... exacting in how he likes things. I had to find restaurants that met his dietary needs, ensure the right brand of bottled water was put in his hotel room, dressing room, all of that."

"So, you organized his food and water?"

"Among other things." She hardened her gaze at me. "Don't you go getting the idea that I poisoned him. I only directly handled the bottled water, and those were all sealed."

I ignored her. "And you said that he had no enemies."

"None."

"How well did you like him?" I decided to follow up with some empty assurances. "Not to suggest you had anything to do with his death, but one's relationship with his assistant sets a pretty good benchmark for his other professional relationships."

Ms. Godfrey's expression didn't change much, save the passing of the defensive gaze from a moment before. She brushed back a dark red wisp of hair with her manicured hand, her first overt movement since she sat down. "Mr. Petree was no-nonsense. No hostility, but no warm fuzzies either. Our relationship served a business purpose, nothing more."

"So, you wouldn't call him a friend?"

"No more than you would call *him* a friend." She indicated Bryan with her eyes.

Bryan raised an eyebrow in my direction.

I shrugged back at him. "Ms. Godfrey, maybe you could answer the question in a less relative fashion."

Her brow shot up, and the grimace turned into a patronizing smile. "Oh, well, in that case, no, I wouldn't call Mr. Petree a friend, in that we weren't trading mugs at Christmas, or anything of that sort. Outside of work, we acknowledged each other's existence. Nothing more."

"And Sharp? You suggested that he put me up to this."

She slowly leaned forward and folded her hands on the table. A condescending smirk covered her face. "Mr. Clue, Patrick Sharp is a paranoid nutcase. He's been known to blame audio-video glitches on grand conspiracies, and suggest that his room is bugged by Russian government operatives."

Somehow, this revelation didn't surprise me. Sharp hadn't struck me as a shining example of mental stability. "If he's that bad, why would Petree work for him?"

"Same reason you took this job, Mr. Clue." She eased back into her previous position. "The cash."

* * *

"Needless to say, she won't be winning the award for Miss Congeniality at any point." I sat back on the sofa and sipped my coffee. "No apparent motive, limited opportunity. If this is murder, I'd put her pretty low on the list of suspects."

We had returned to the office to regroup. Dee leaned against the wall as she read through Bryan's transcribed copy of the interview. "I can already tell you that she lied about one thing." She flipped a page over.

I sat up straighter. "What's that?"

"She said he got along with everyone, but that doesn't match with what a few of the conference crew members said." Dee looked at me. "Thomas Petree's marriage was in bad shape."

I took another sip of coffee. "Are we sure that's true? That could be a rumor."

Dee set one of the pages on the table by her chair. "I have two separate accounts of Rachel Petree arguing with her husband at the previous conference, last Wednesday. She didn't want him taking the Seattle gig. They exchanged some pretty strong words, and she stormed out."

"How strong?"

"Strong enough to sound like motive." She picked up her coffee mug and took a drink.

Bryan glanced up from the typewriter. "I'd have to agree there. This line is almost identical between the two accounts: 'You want to go, then go! Do me a favor and get hit by a taxi while you're there, you so-and-so.'" He grimaced. "I'm verbally censoring that last part."

I took another sip of coffee. "Understood."

"This type of argument wasn't rare, either," Dee added. "Petree would always stay calm, stoic, and stubborn, while his wife would lose it on him. Apparently, he treated everyone like that. You know the type—walks all over you, and remains completely calm and collected while doing it, until you just want to strangle him."

"Well, that explains his assistant." Bryan muttered.

I picked up the page Dee had finished with. "If the wife was local, we might have something to go on, but it's tough if she's in California, which she probably is. Warren can check that. Anyhow, we can strike the 'no enemies' part. So why would Ms. Godfrey cover for him like that?"

"Birds of a feather flock together. That's my guess." Dee turned over another page.

"Well, that makes sense." I recalled my psychology class from my third attempt at a Bachelor's degree. "By downplaying his relationship problems, she would downplay her own. She probably borrowed his perceived license to patronize other people."

"So, we have another dead skunk, and we need to find out which car hit him." Dee blinked a couple of times. "So to speak."

"What do you think, then? Murder?"

"Inconclusive until we get the autopsy results, but I'd say I'm leaning in that direction." Dee handed the second page of the transcribed interview to me. "What do *you* think?"

I lined up the two pages. "I think that if Ms. Godfrey felt like exclusively tagging Patrick Sharp as a 'paranoid nutcase,' we'd better find out what makes that ol' boy tick."

Tuesday, June 15

Warren met me at my office door the next morning. "Greetings, Sherlock. Got something for you."

I unlocked the office. "Six in the morning. It must be important. Do tell."

"Uh uh, not until you hand over your stuff. That's the rule." Warren looked around. "Where's Dee and the Boy Wonder?"

"Dee's running an errand, and Bryan has class. Interview transcripts are on the desk."

Warren sat down. "So, it's just us. Have you tuned up your brain yet this morning?"

"I was planning to make the coffee here. Want a cup?"

"Black, and strong enough to climb out of the mug and slap me, thank you."

"I prefer to live past breakfast, so I'll meet you halfway on strength." I opened the top of the coffee maker, set a filter in place, and began measuring out coffee grounds.

"So, you are looking at the Seattle Police Department's newest captain." Warren crowed. "Violent Crimes section, Criminal Investigation bureau."

I peered around the corner at him. "Hey, congratulations. When did this happen?"

"Got the news yesterday. You're the first person I thought of telling." He puffed out his chest a little. "It feels good to be recognized. But, I will miss being in the field as much. It's generally a desk job."

I frowned. "So, I suppose we won't be running into each other very often, then?"

Warren tilted his palm. "Well, I'll still be involved. Practically the top of the chain of command, shy of the Bureau's Assistant Chief, and the Chief himself of course. So, if you get any more murders after this, you'll see me." He leaned back. "Now, I got the footage off the surveillance cameras this morning. It shows Thomas Petree getting dropped off via car at 1:15 p.m. We got the license number, and since the conference contracts with the chauffeur service, we have the driver's information."

"I'll want to talk to him." I filled up a glass pitcher at the sink.

"Naturally. His name is Luis Cagle. I'll get you more info after we talk to him."

"What time did Petree's flight get in?" I dumped the pitcher's contents into the back of the coffee maker and started the machine.

"12:30. The airport security footage shows him getting into the car at 12:46 p.m., meaning it took nineteen minutes to get to the conference center. That leaves no time to stop anywhere, so that makes life easier." He sighed. "Meanwhile, Patrick Sharp left six voice messages at the front desk for me. That's the main reason I'm avoiding the office right now. I don't have enough caffeine in my bloodstream to handle that man."

"And yet you can handle me." I sat down across from Warren, happy to let him use my chair behind the desk if it meant he'd work with me.

"I'm used to your brand of crazy."

"I'm touched."

"Yes you are." Warren thumbed through Bryan's transcription. "Laura Godfrey, Thomas Petree's personal assistant. She looks interesting."

"Yeah, she's a piece of work. To be honest, though, I'm more interested in Sharp."

"He hired you though, right?"

"Yes."

Warren grunted. "I don't know where you're going with that idea, Noah. You're all over the press for solving the Conhue murder. He wouldn't want a brilliant mind like yours on the case if he was guilty. That only worked with the Fredrickson case because you were a washed up nobody then."

I weighed Warren's phrasing, trying to sort out if he had just complemented or insulted me. "I'm not sure how it all works out, but I want to find out just how paranoid Sharp really is. I mean, don't you find it odd that he hired me while your boys were just starting to poke around the place?"

"You have a point."

The coffee maker beeped, indicating the first cup was ready. I habitually avoided it, since it was usually stronger than if I waited for the rest of the pot. I grinned at Warren as I stood. "It's for you."

He continued talking after me. "Petree's wife has motive, but I assume she's still in California?"

"Who knows?" I grabbed a paper cup from the cabinet and filled it. "I'll have to leave that line of inquiry to you. You've got access to the right channels for it."

"Right. My team will take Rachel Petree, you take Patrick Sharp."

I smiled knowingly. "You really don't want to deal with him yourself, do you?"

"No, I do not. Anyhow, it's a bit outside the scope of my job description to ferret out just how much of a nut job he is."

I set the coffee in front of him. "Drill-sergeant-in-a-cup, black, no mercy, for Gregg."

"Thank you." He took a sip. "Woo! Good stuff."

"I'm glad you approve." I slid one of the transcript pages Warren had finished with, and skimmed it. "While we're at it, do you want to look into Godfrey, or should I?"

"We'll have a chat with her, and I'll let you know if she deviates from this story at all." Warren waved the remainder of the transcript. "Naturally, either of us can do the background check."

I slid the page back to him. "Let's both do it, and compare notes."

"Good plan." Warren took another sip of coffee. "Mmm. If I make a habit of coming here in the morning, I might be able to cut my coffee budget in half."

I pulled out my notebook and jotted down a few reminders. "So, if Petree was dropped off by a chauffeur service, wouldn't there also be footage from inside the vehicle?"

"Not always, but in this case, yes. We're working on getting that." Warren smiled a little. "You know, you're pretty sharp when you want to be, Noah."

I shrugged. "I'm only good at drawing conclusions."

Warren stood and set the transcripts down on the desk. "Well, this will give me something more to go on, at least. Thanks for the coffee."

"Be sure to let me know what you find out about Rachel Petree and Laura Godfrey."

Warren raised his coffee cup at me in salute. "Believe me, you'll be the first to know."

* * *

"Mr. Clue! I was just about to call you. How goes the investigation?" Patrick Sharp bustled up to me as I entered his temporary office at the conference center. Except for a few scattered papers on the desk, the space was immaculate.

Before I could answer, Sharp turned his attention to Dee. "And Miss Tindall. A pleasure as always."

Dee shoved her hands in her pockets, no doubt to prevent Sharp from kissing one or both of them. "Mr. Sharp."

He turned his attention back to me. "Any leads?"

I kept my most professional tone in place. "As I've said before, Mr. Sharp, we aren't even certain this is a murder yet. We're still waiting on the results from the medical examiner."

The smile faded from Sharp's face. "It can't be natural causes, Mr. Clue. I've known Thomas Petree for years. He was one of the healthiest people I know."

"Maybe so, but there are plenty of cases of otherwise healthy people having heart attacks and strokes." I weighed my words, trying to determine how to bend my line of inquiry towards Sharp's own reputation without setting him off. "All the same, I've been asking questions, in case this is ruled a murder."

That seemed to satisfy Sharp. He leaned up against his desk. "And what have you discovered so far?"

I decided to leverage the question for that tricky subject change. "This isn't Petree's usual circuit, is it?"

The director hesitated. "Well...no, it isn't. He usually speaks in southern California."

I tried to sound mildly surprised. "Usually? How often does he travel out of state?"

Sharp pursed his lips and looked out the window. "Ah...never."

"So, why did he come up here to Seattle?" I knew the answer, of course, but I wanted to hear it from Sharp.

"I had an opening."

I nodded knowingly. "An opening, yes. Who got dropped?"

Sharp only frowned at me.

"You see," I continued, "that could be a potential motive. Petree replaces another speaker, that other speaker gets jealous..."

"Adrian Law."

"Right, and who is he?"

Sharp bit his lip and wrinkled his nose. "He speaks on holistic wellness." He reached into a box near his desk and removed a photograph. "Here he is."

I studied the photo. Law's face was bright, on a very dark background. "Why was he dropped?"

"Why do you assume I dropped him?"

I took a breath to calm down. I had already gotten too close to revealing what I knew. "If the speaker had canceled or gotten sick, you would have said so up front." Actually, I had just made that up on the spot, but it sounded like something Dee would say.

My cousin remained annoyingly quiet. The only sound coming from her was that of the pencil scratching on the notepad. I wished she would add something to this interview, because I felt like I was in way over my head.

Sharp still didn't seem at ease. His shoulders hunched slightly. "We had a disagreement." His hand twitched, as if waving off the matter. He reached up and scratched behind his right ear before opening his mouth. I waited for more, but he only sighed and squeezed his lips together again.

I handed the photo back. "Details would be really helpful, Mr. Sharp. I'm going to have to talk to Adrian Law at some point, and it would be useful to have the whole story so I can spot discrepancies."

Patrick Sharp nodded. "He has been trying to take control of the conference for a while. He figures he can do it better than me."

"Better how?"

Sharp shrugged. "I don't know. He's been talking to other speakers behind my back, spreading rumors. He probably figures that if he can turn them against me, I'll resign."

"Where did Petree stand on that?"

"I think Adrian has been talking to him as well, but he doesn't... didn't...seem to harbor anything against me." Sharp put a hand to his forehead. "It's all very stressful. I'm sure you can understand."

I nodded. "That must be difficult. These sorts of conflicts happen a lot, then?"

Sharp blew out a deep breath. "I hate to say it, but yes. People can be so petty and underhanded. I've had to fire so many over the years because of stuff like this."

I nodded to a framed photograph of Sharp and Petree on the desk. "But Thomas Petree stuck by you."

Sharp picked up the frame and sighed again. "I like to think so." He traced his finger along the border. "I just hope that isn't the reason he's dead now."

"How about his assistant, Laura Godfrey? Did you get along?"

The director looked up from the picture frame. "Godfrey? No one gets along with her. She's shrewd, efficient, but I wouldn't say she plays well with others."

"Surely Petree got along with her, though."

"Thomas tolerated Godfrey. He appreciated her ability to keep everything organized, but I believe their communication was all business." Sharp replaced the picture on his desk. "Why, is she a suspect in his death, too?"

Why was this guy so convinced Petree had been murdered? "I don't have any suspects, yet. I'm still in the fact-finding phase. Did you ever have any trouble with Godfrey?"

Sharp shrugged. "I barely saw more than an occasional glimpse of her. Like I said, she was brutally efficient." He shuddered. "Honestly, if anyone could organize a murder, it would be her."

3

Coffee and Hard Feelings

Adrian Law scoffed into his cup of coffee. "Patrick Sharp is a paranoid fruitcake."

I sat across from the man at a table inside Starbucks. So far, the venue had proven to be a pretty reliable place to conduct interviews. "That still doesn't tell me what the disagreement between you two was all about."

The young man's brown eyes flashed, not anger, but amusement. "He accused me of talking behind his back, conspiring against him, trying to take his job. I'm used to paranoia from him, but this was the end of the line."

"So he dropped you from the conference?"

Law scoffed again. "Dropped me? He'd like to think so. I walked before he had a chance."

I raised my eyebrows. "You quit?"

"Moving on to greener pastures." He flashed a ten-thousand-dollar smile at me. It faded after a moment into a grimace. "You probably don't believe me."

I cleared my throat. "I don't take anything at face value, Mr. Law."

"No, you wouldn't. I can't blame you." He fished into his jeans pocket for something.

I glanced at Dee, hoping she would say something, *anything*. Her silence was driving me crazy. I raised my eyebrows and nodded towards Law.

She returned the gesture.

Adrian Law set his smartphone on the table. "I've been speaking at the Awakening Dawn conferences for three years, Mr. Clue. I've watched Sharp fire A/V guys for technical glitches that he regarded as sabotage attempts. He gets this certain tone in his voice when he's about to go off the deep end, so..." he tapped the phone with a finger. "I started secretly recording conversations whenever that tone was aimed at me."

"You know that's illegal in the state of Washington, right?"

"So sue me." He held out a pair of earbuds. "If you want the proof that I quit, have a listen."

The ambient sound was exactly what you'd expect of a recording made from inside a pocket, but I could make out Sharp's voice as clear as anything.

"This has gone on long enough, Adrian. I cannot have you badmouthing me behind my back!"

"What makes you think I am?" Law's voice came through loud and clear.

"You can't fool me. I can see right through your entire plot to take my place."

"Take your place? I don't want your place, Sharp. I never did."

"The heck you didn't!"

"I don't. I'm not even sure I want to be here anymore. Keep your stupid conference, Sharp. You can find some other schmuck to take my slot."

The recording blipped, signaling the end. I removed the earbuds and handed them back to Law. "Very enlightening."

A smug smile covered Adrian Law's face as he switched off the smartphone and pocketed it.

"Not admissible in court, of course," I added.

Law's smile faded momentarily. "At least it can point you in the right direction."

I smirked. "One can hope." Actually, this now made less sense than it did before .

* * *

As we walked back to the car, I flipped through Dee's notebook. "Is any of this fitting together for you, cuz?"

She shook her head. "Every time we find a possible motive, it gets shot down. Sharp needed Petree to fill that spot. Even if he *is* paranoid, he didn't seem to have a beef with the victim."

"What about Laura Godfrey, the assistant?"

"He dies, she's out a job. If there's a motive there, I doubt she'll show it." She wrinkled her nose. "Although I don't think Godfrey would show emotion to save her life."

"And Adrian Law?"

"Either he's clean or a darn good actor." She sighed. "If only Sharp was the dead guy, we'd have our pick of suspects. But Petree? There's no passion when people talk about him! Love or hatred, I could work with, but everyone's lukewarm about the guy."

"Except for his wife."

"True, there's motive there, but not much opportunity."

I pulled out my cell phone. "Maybe Warren's got something fresh on that front."

Two rings, and then a dry introduction. "This is Warren."

"Warren, it's Noah. Any results on the autopsy?"

"Good timing. I was just about to call you." I heard him shuffle some papers around. "Thomas Petree died of a complete heart collapse. There was also saliva on the chin, meaning he was probably drooling when he died. They're still not sure of the cause."

"Did you talk to the driver yet?"

"Cagle? Yeah."

"How'd he describe Petree?"

"Agitated. Shaking a bit. Petree chalked it up to hunger, since he hadn't eaten since leaving California. He also wanted the heater turned on. Cagle said Petree seemed rather confused when he dropped him off."

"So, he was agitated, shaking, cold, and confused," I repeated, mostly for Dee's benefit. "Any word about how he was on the flight?"

"We managed to talk to one of the airline stewardesses. He was crabby, but no more than your run-of-the-mill airplane-hating businessman. He didn't eat or drink anything. He did stand up a lot and shake his leg."

"That's consistent with Laura Godfrey's account of Petree's paresthesia." I frowned. "When did the symptoms set in?"

"According to Cagle, about ten minutes into the trip. The vehicle footage confirms that, and rules out the driver as a suspect." More shuffling papers. "And, that brings you up to date – at least until our boys finish going over that car with a fine-toothed comb. Anything new on your end?"

"Further evidence that Patrick Sharp is a few crackers short of a barrel. He dropped another speaker, Adrian Law, from the conference at the last minute and replaced him with Petree. Law's got a recording of a conversation with Sharp that confirms the director is paranoid."

"Interesting angle, but it only serves to eliminate motive for both of them." I heard Warren shut a drawer. "As to Rachel Petree, she is indeed in California. Her four-year-old had a doctor's appointment for that day, so we have an alibi with witnesses. She actually seems quite upset about her husband's death. I'll let you know if anything else surfaces on that front." Papers rustled. "As to Laura Godfrey, would you believe we can't find her?"

The few fragments of theories I had worked out disintegrated. Why would she bail out in the middle of a death investigation? It didn't look good for her. "What do you mean? She left town?"

"Well, yes, she went back to California, but that's not what I mean. The police intercepted her at LAX, but we can't find anything about her. No driver's license, no state ID, nothing in the databases, and she's refusing to identify herself."

"Why would a personal assistant be using an alias?" I glanced at Dee and watched her eyebrows go up in surprise.

"That's what we're wondering. I'll keep you posted." Warren cleared his throat. "I'll have to let you go. I've got someone at the office door."

"Right. Thanks, Captain." I hung up.

Dee leaned on our car. "Laura Godfrey is using an assumed identity?"

"Apparently." I scratched the back of my head. "That makes this harder, and certainly doesn't remove her from suspicion."

My cousin nodded. "Meanwhile, we now know that Petree was fine on the plane, but agitated and confused in the car?"

I nodded. "Complete heart collapse. The driver, Cagle, is in the clear." I threw my head back and rubbed my forehead. "I feel like I'm chasing my tail. This looks like natural causes, steeped in a toxic work environment, but my gut tells me there's more going on."

"I'm with your gut." Dee opened the driver's door. "Shall we head back to the office?"

"Actually, I'm going to take a little lunchtime detour on my own if you don't mind. I need to think things over."

Dee gave me a reassuring smile. "Go for it, Noah. Maybe that'll give the clever part of your brain a chance to put the pieces together."

"The clever *part?*"

"Fill in the rest however you like. Need a ride anywhere?"

I handed back the notebook. "I'll get a ride later. See you at home."

"Right, catch you later. Have a good think." Dee got into the car and shut the door.

As she drove away, I flipped open my phone and hit the speed dial. "Yo, David, you got a bit?"

* * *

I sat across from David Sigfield, my best friend, at Northlake Tavern, our longtime favorite restaurant hangout. I bit into a hot slice of pepperoni, olive, and sausage pizza, catching the oozing cheese with my thumb.

David slid a piece onto his plate before sipping his soda. "It's been too long since we've done this, Noah. Outside of Game Night—that's tonight, by the way—I rarely see you anymore."

I set down the pizza and sucked the cheese and sauce from my thumb. "Sorry, I've just been swamped with cases. Also just picked up a new secretary."

"I thought you had your cousin for that stuff?"

"Well, you know Dee: she does half the thinking. So, if we're out on a case, no one's at the office to take calls."

David grinned. "How hot is the new girl?"

I raised an eyebrow. "*He* isn't hot at all. Bryan Gannon. Criminology student, sharp as a whip."

"Whips aren't sharp."

"Ah, yeah. It's a metaphor, I think."

"A mixed one, maybe." David bit into his pizza crust-side first. "So, what did you get caught up in this time, Sherlock?" he asked with his mouth full.

"Motivational speaker found dead in the green room from a heart collapse. Conference director freaked out, hired me to investigate a possible murder before the body was even cold."

"Freaky."

"Pays good, though."

"That's what matters." David took a swig of soda. "Motivational speaker, you say? He connected to that big to-do they've been blabbing about on the radio?"

"Awakening Dawn? Yeah, that's the one." I hesitated. "Mum's the word, of course."

"Sure."

"I'm serious. Client confidentiality is no joke."

My friend set his cup down and leaned across the pizza. "Noah, I have carried the secret of your gluing Professor Ware's textbook to the podium for three and a half years. I think I can keep this under my hat."

That was true. If there was one thing David was good for, it was keeping a secret. "Anyway, this is where things get weird. The dead guy, no one seems to care much about him either way. Complete lack of motive."

"Like watching a Mariner's game, eh?"

"Yes, well...no. Not even that strong."

"Ouch." David plucked a piece of pepperoni off the next slice. "Well, there goes the murder theory."

"Not quite. Something isn't sitting right with any of us about this whole thing. Even Warren smells a skunk. The director who hired me? He's kinda a nutcase."

"Nutcase how?"

"The type who would check his toothpaste for explosives."

"Well, that sounds about right for that conference." David pulled two more pizza slices onto his plate. "Most of their speakers are a bit out there." He accentuated that last part by wiggling his fingers.

I stopped mid-sip of my Mountain Dew. "You've been to it? How'd you manage to cough up eight-hundred bucks?"

David waved me off. "Not me, but do you remember Tina from COMM-108?"

I raised an eyebrow. "No, but you do, I'll wager."

"Sure. Long black hair, brown eyes, nervous giggle, always wore that red scarf? We had a date two years ago or so. Just friends now. She moved to Duluth sometime last August." He sipped his Pepsi as if he hadn't said anything particularly notable.

"I envy your memory, David."

"Well, anyway, she went to Awakening Dawn in Portland last March. Decided to leave after the first full day. 'Wasted eight-hundred dollars and twelve hours of my life,' was her review."

"The victim spoke about 'balance in your life,' but apparently his marriage was in dire straits." I helped myself to another slice of pizza. "Wife's in Cali, though, so she's an unlikely suspect. His personal assistant was using an assumed name, but again, she doesn't appear to have motive or opportunity."

"You said he died of a heart collapse, right?"

I nodded. "Yeah. He was agitated, confused, and drooling just before his death."

"Lovely lunch conversation."

"Sorry, you asked." I took another bite of pizza.

"So, no motive, no opportunity, probably natural causes." David sipped his soda.

"Except, things don't seem to add up to that." I sighed. "And thus, why I'm sitting here."

"Well, always trust your spidey-sense."

I nearly spit out my soda. "Spiders! That's it!"

"What's it?"

I pulled out my phone and speed-dialed Warren. "You'll understand in a moment."

The line clicked. "This is…"

"Warren, it's Noah. I think I know how Petree died."

"Really?" Excitement crackled in Warren's voice.

"His symptoms suggest a bite from a Sydney funnel web spider."

Silence. After a moment, Warren spoke again in a flat, dull tone. "You know we're not in Australia, right, Colombo?"

I took a deep breath. "Cagle described Petree as agitated and confused. He also said he was cold. Those are all classic symptoms of a Sydney funnel web spider bite." I noticed David's incredulous look. Even he didn't seem to believe me.

"Noah, how in blazes is an Australian spider supposed to get into the back of a Seattle chauffeur service vehicle?" The captain sounded more annoyed than anything.

"That's what I want to know."

Warren sighed. "I think you've finally lost it, Noah."

I couldn't let this one go. "Weirder things have happened." I squeezed my eyes shut as I realized I had handed Warren a perfect straight line. "Just pass it on to the medical examiner, and let's see if it pans out."

I heard Warren set his coffee mug down hard. "Fine. I'll pass it on, with *your* name attached. If this turns out to be as nuts as I think it is, you take the hit."

"Deal. Keep me posted."

He scoffed. "Oh, ab-so-lute-ly."

* * *

I arrived home at Dee's apartment a little before 6 p.m. She was already in the kitchen cooking our contribution to the monthly Game Night potluck that evening, so I quietly set up my typewriter on the breakfast bar. With Dee, and now Bryan, transcribing notes for me, I didn't have as much of a need to type, and I had found that I missed putting words on paper. I had dragged my fancy electric typewriter out of storage for the office, and left the other manual I had recently purchased on my work desk. That allowed me to bring home the old, reliable Royal Heritage my Uncle Tindall had given me. After work, I enjoyed writing down anything that came into my head. Recently, most of those ideas were imaginary cases and their outcomes. None of it was novel-worthy, but I enjoyed it.

No sooner had I sat down, Dee spoke up, her back still to me. "A Sydney funnel web spider? Have you lost your mind, Noah?" She set the bottle of olive oil down on the kitchen counter a little harder than I thought necessary. She stirred the corn, rice, and beef sautéing on the stove. "Warren couldn't stop laughing when he told me."

I brushed my overgrown bangs out of my eyes. "He called you?"

Dee nodded. "I really thought you were over the problem with wild theories, but I guess I was wrong." She tossed a measuring cup in the sink set into the breakfast bar.

"Well, pardon me for looking at all the possibilities, Miss Marple." I fed a blank sheet of paper into the typewriter.

"Noah, how would that even be a possibility? It's not even remotely plausible! Australia is, what, seven thousand miles away as the crow flies?"

"About that, but crows don't fly that far."

"Neither do spiders!" She flicked off the burner and began spooning food into a casserole dish. "Well, with any luck, Warren will laugh this off and it will be back to business as usual in a few days. You're just lucky no one else heard your hair-brained theory, or we'd be out of business."

I glared at Dee. "Can you absolutely guarantee that a Sydney funnel web spider could not show up in a car in Seattle?"

Dee frowned as she packed the casserole dish into an insulated carrying case. "Not absolutely, I suppose, no." She shook her head. "But by that token, I can't guarantee that elves don't steal socks from the dryer, either."

I stuck to my theory. "Here's an idea, then. How about we propose this theory at Game Night, and see how it goes over?"

My cousin sighed in resignation. "Fine, but don't blame me if they laugh."

* * *

"Ladies and gentlemen, we have an issue of deep philosophical importance before us," David announced to the group. "Samantha must decide which is more handsome: James Dean...or Roman Numerals."

Samantha Keppler, my friend in the SPD forensics department, tossed her flaming red braids back. "Is it really a contest, David? I keep telling you, I don't find James Dean that handsome."

"He's definitely better looking than, what, hot lava or chickens?" Dee straightened out the cards on the table.

Alexandra Meyer, the forensics chemist of the group, laughed. "It might be debatable whether he looks better than chickens."

"Not better than," David corrected. "More handsome. Chickens aren't handsome."

"You haven't met many chickens," I retorted, still feeling a bit suppressed. My spider suggestion hadn't been mocked outright, but everyone seemed a bit skeptical about the idea. I'd been quiet on the topic for the last two rounds.

"Sorry, I'm going with Roman Numerals." Samantha handed the green card to Allie. "No contest in my book."

David drew a green card and tossed it down on the table with a flourish. "Silly." He picked up his plate of Dee's Mexican goulash and dug in. "Wow me."

I studied the seven red cards in my hand. Knowing David, he'd choose whatever made him laugh the hardest, but humor wasn't coming easy to me tonight. I decided to open the spider topic again. "Look, SEATAC is an international airport, with flights directly from Sydney. What's to stop a small and generally non-aggressive arachnid from hitching a ride on clothing or in luggage, and winding up in the back of that hired car?"

Sammi put down her card first. "Best I've got is 'watermelons,' although I suspect those are only funny if Gallagher is involved." She turned to me. "Now that you mention it, that isn't so absurd at all."

Encouraged, I continued. "Now, suppose that this isn't accidental. How much less improbable would it be for someone to conceal such a spider in their carry-on, and release it at the right time and place to bite the victim? Tracing a spider would be nearly impossible."

Dee stared at me, card paused in mid-air. I waited for her to issue a snappy rebuttal, but she merely blinked. "Your mind scares me sometimes, Noah."

I tried and failed to determine if that meant she believed me yet or not.

Dee set down her card. "A bad haircut can look pretty silly."

David leaned forward. "So, let's go with that theory for a moment, it not being an accident and all. How would the killer be able to time the release of the spider to bite the target?"

"He'd have to be the person just before him in the vehicle." Allie ruffled the cards in her hand. "That would be hard to arrange, of course. Very easy to miss."

"Could he wait on releasing the spider until he saw the victim was next?" Samantha suggested.

"Sure." Feeling more centered, I skimmed my cards in search of something silly. "Perhaps the killer deposited it on his clothes or in his hair in passing. No need to involve the car at all."

"Well, that should be easy enough to confirm. There are cameras all over SEATAC." Samantha nudged Allie. "Were you going to play something, girl?"

"Oh! Right." Allie brushed her blonde bangs out of her eyes and set down her card. "Bell-bottoms can look very silly. At least to me."

I sighed. "I'll be the first to admit that the murder theory isn't the strongest. A spider may be an untraceable weapon, but it's also very hard to aim." I cleared my throat. "For lack of a better term."

"We can at least figure out how to eliminate the possibility." Dee leaned towards me. "I'm sorry I yelled at you earlier," she whispered.

I shrugged. "It's not entirely your fault," I whispered back. "It's a strange theory, however confident I am in it."

"I'm beginning to think, the stranger they are, the more likely." Dee chuckled.

"Waiting on you, Noah," David prompted.

I frowned. "I don't have a whole lot to work with here, guys." What would David even find funny among these? Hairballs, chains, a nine iron, mice, or Bangkok. I wouldn't really consider *The Godfather* or Jesse Ventura to be funny.

I set down "mice" and hoped for the best.

David glowered. "Crud, people, you ain't giving me much to work with here."

As Allie embarked on a brief dissertation on how silly bell-bottoms were, Dee leaned over to me again. "I honestly hope you're right. Warren's ego needs a kick in the teeth." She scribbled something. "And though I hate to admit it, I think mine does too."

I blinked a couple of times and stared at my cousin. "Your ego?"

"Don't tell me you haven't noticed."

"Well..." I rubbed the back of my neck. "I'd call that confidence."

"Ever since we started working together, I've prided myself on my detective skills. But, if we're honest, I haven't solved a single case." Dee's voice remained in a whisper.

"You've helped. I couldn't have figured anything out without your knack for tracking down clues and reading people."

"I'm a finder, Noah. I examine everything I encounter with a critical eye. You are always the one who puts the pieces together."

She sighed. "So, in a way, I think I've been taking credit for your brilliance."

I pondered this. I always did feel inferior around my cousin. Was that why? "I really would be lost without your help."

"I would be too, without yours. I don't think I've done a very good job of telling you that, though, and for that, I'm sorry."

I smiled. "Forgiven. Now, let's get on with this game before this gets any sappier."

"Yoo-hoo!" Samantha waved in our direction. "Dee, you want to make a case for bad haircuts, here?"

Dee laughed. "Nah, I'm good. I think they speak for themselves."

David picked up the green card and tossed it in my direction. "I have to say, mice are just funny to watch, so Noah wins that one."

For once, I felt like I was winning more than a party game.

4

Burritos and Consequences

Wednesday, June 16

Warren slunk into my office the next morning, a manila folder tucked under his arm. "I'll take a cup of strong black coffee to go with my platter of crow."

I stood up from my desk. "Morning, Warren. What are you talking about?"

He dropped the folder on my desk. "The medical examiner didn't think your idea was all that funny. He confirmed it."

"Really? When?" I made my way into the kitchenette to pour Warren's coffee into a foam cup.

"This morning. I got the phone call while I was on my way here, so I stopped over to pick up the paperwork." He tapped the folder. "It's all in there. Three spider bites found on Petree's leg, symptoms matched Sydney Funnel Web spider. The medical examiner confirmed that by finding the actual insect carcass in Petree's clothing." He slumped into the armchair nearest to the door.

I set the coffee on the stand next to him. "Spider's not an insect. It's an arachnid."

"Yes, thank you, Encyclopedia Brown." Warren took a sip. "So, now we need to figure out how an Australian spider got in the back of a Seattle hired car. Please tell me you've got an idea."

The door to the office opened, and Dee came in balancing a box of her favorite fat-free muffins. "Good morning, gentlemen." She disappeared into the kitchenette.

I grinned at Warren. "As a matter of fact, we have a few ideas."

"What's this about?" Dee emerged with a muffin and her own mug of coffee. "Medical examiner confirmed the spider theory, eh?"

"However did you guess?" Warren's voice remained flat, even more so than usual.

"You're moping in our office at eight in the morning, and there's a new folder on the desk." She slipped back into the kitchenette.

I sat down in front of my typewriter. "So, I figure there are a few ways a spider could have got to Petree. The first involves someone depositing it on his person, intentionally or otherwise, as he was leaving SEATAC." I pulled the notebook out of my shirt pocket to follow along with the theories Dee and I had cooked up the night before.

"Surveillance footage might be able to confirm or deny that theory." Warren sipped. "Then again, it's usually hard to see clearly on that stuff."

"Second possibility is the spider being dropped in the car itself." I set the notebook down. "Of course, that's hard to time. What if it bites the wrong person?"

Warren leaned forward. "While we're going for wild theoreticals here, couldn't it have been on the plane?"

"Maybe, but I'd think he would have started reacting sooner. Based on the timing of his symptoms, he had to have been bit either in or just before entering the car."

"Good point." Warren took another long sip of coffee. "I can check the SEATAC angle if you want to talk to Luis Cagle, the driver, yourself. He seemed pretty shaken up. Apparently he doesn't normally work that day, but he had swapped schedules with another driver. I told him you'd probably get in touch."

"Right, you got a number for him?"

"It's on the top paper in the folder." Warren stood and raised his cup in my direction. "Anyhow, I've got to get to the office. Nice work on the spider theory, Noah, and thanks for the coffee."

* * *

"Lousy time for a fire." I stood in front of the Starbucks nearest Luis Cagle's apartment, where we were scheduled to meet him. Wednesday wasn't normally his day off, but the chauffeur service company had switched his schedule to give him time to recover from the shock of the event.

"Maybe someone left a cappuccino maker on after hours." Dee mused as we stared up at the charred face of the business. "I wonder how long it'll be closed."

I grunted. "However long, it's too late for us."

I spotted a man approaching out of the corner of my eye. As I turned, he held out his hand. "Noah Clue, right? I'm Luis Cagle."

"Hi, Mr. Cagle, thank you for meeting us."

"No problem." He turned and looked up at the building. "I've been out of the loop for two days. Completely missed this."

"That makes two of us."

Cagle shrugged. "Ehh, this is Seattle. There's a coffee shop on every corner, and plenty of restaurants besides. How about lunch?"

"Yeah, I suppose."

He pointed to a place a few doors down from the café. "That one just went in a few months back. I don't know anything about it, but it looks cheap enough."

The three of us continued down the sidewalk towards the restaurant. I kept glancing over at Cagle, trying to read any emotion in his dark complexion. His round face looked like the sort that would normally be given to generous smiles, but now, dark bags hung under his brown eyes, suggesting a lack of sleep over the past couple nights. Who could blame him?

"Really should've noticed the café was closed," Cagle repeated.

I shrugged. "Eh, don't worry about it."

In the short time it had been open, the restaurant in question had already seemed to gather the dull haze of a neglected fast food dive. The empty metal tables still gleamed like they had just come out of the warehouse, but otherwise the entire place had a feeling of desolation, as if this were the absolute last restaurant to be found for miles. Still, Cagle had picked it—albeit experimentally—so I resolved to give it a try. Anyway, I was getting hungry.

A scrawny young adult male slouched behind the counter, sizing us up. His blazing orange-dyed hair stood in complete contrast to his pallid, acne-encrusted face. "Welcome to Taco Muchacho," he recited without any semblance of emotion. "Can I take your order?"

Cagle and Dee both turned to me, as if I were their ambassador to a strange alien being. I reinforced the social smile on my face, and tried to ignore the green-tinged fluorescent lighting glinting off his innumerable piercings. I noted his name badge. "Ah, what do you recommend, Deven?"

The lanky youth barely blinked. "I don't."

"Um, okay." I tried to weigh the reliability of this kid's warning. "What's your special?"

Deven turned slightly towards the illuminated menu board, which had already gathered a generous layer of grease-infused steam. "Two tacos for the price of one."

"What kind of tacos?"

"Bean, beef, or chicken," he replied without blinking.

I resisted the urge to bail out. I'd heard of restaurants that looked terrible, and yet had amazing food. "How's the bean?"

"It will haunt you later."

"The beef?"

"That'll haunt you too."

I half expected Deven to tell me, in that same unmoving demeanor, that the road had washed out, and we'd best spend the night in some creepy house out back. "You really don't like working here, do you?"

He shrugged. "My probation officer says a job is a job."

"Is there anything you'd consider edible?"

He grimaced. "The chicken burrito usually turns out fine."

"Ah." I nodded, trying to weigh the kid's definition of 'usually' and 'fine'. I glanced at Dee and Cagle, who seemed determined to leave the situation to me. "We'll take three."

"You want salsa with that?" This young man had monotone down to an art form.

I studied his expressionless face for a hint. "Do I?"

"No."

"Right." I drummed my fingers on the counter. In terms of weird experiences, this was definitely on the list.

He punched our order in on the register. "Anything to drink?"

"You got coffee?" I still had my mouth set.

He looked up at me with a glazed look. "So I'm told."

"I'll have that."

"Suit yourself." The kid poked another button.

Dee cleared her throat. "Water for me."

Deven took a plain white cup from a stack on the counter and shoved it at us. "That'll be $7.58."

I pulled a ten from my wallet.

Deven turned toward Cagle, who had managed to put enough distance between us to look like a completely unrelated customer. "Anything for you?"

He waved him off. "I'm good. Just water please."

I suddenly got the strange feeling I had just bought three burritos entirely for myself. I took a seat at a booth towards the back.

Cagle settled in across from me. "Lieutenant Warren said you would want to talk to me. You're investigating this guy's death too?"

"Yeah, I was hired to look into it." I glanced around for Dee. I needed her to take notes.

My cousin slid in beside me and handed me a white foam cup of coffee, which I set aside to let cool for a bit. I turned my attention back to Cagle. "I understand you didn't know the victim."

Cagle nodded and stared into his water. "You rarely know the people you drive."

"Would you mind recounting your entire encounter with Thomas Petree for me?"

Deep frown lines deepened on Cagle's pock-marked face. If he was indeed unfamiliar with Petree—and there seemed to be no reason to lie—then Luis Cagle was clearly someone who cared a lot for people. He brushed his dusty black bangs out of his eyes. "I had been hired to pick him up at SEATAC."

I ventured an early interruption. "Do you know by whom?"

The driver shook his head. "No, the main office took that call. You'd have to check with them."

I nodded to Dee. Petree's assistant, Laura Godfrey, would have almost certainly made the arrangements, but it was worth checking. "Continue, please."

"Well, I picked him up at the curb near the terminal, of course. He was pretty quiet. Mentioned that he hated flying. I said, 'I hear you, my friend. I like keeping my feet on the ground too.' He kind of grunted agreement, and then was pretty quiet for a while. I tried a couple of times to start a conversation, but he didn't seem to be in the mood, so I gave up."

Cagle hunched down and took a careful sip of water. I turned to face Deven's sullen, pierced face and tried to estimate how long he had been standing there. "Um, hi?"

He dropped the red plastic tray on the table. "Here."

"Thank you." I kept my eyes on the server as he shuffled off to his post behind the counter. Dee and Cagle both stared suspiciously at the limp burritos steaming on the tray between us.

"So, was Petree quiet the entire way?" I asked Cagle, trying to restart his story.

"No, about ten minutes in, he began hitting his left leg rather vigorously. I asked him if he was okay, and he said 'Yeah, just an old nerve condition. Been sitting too long.' I asked him what happened, if he didn't mind the question. He started talking about playing football in college and getting injured, but I noticed that he was repeating himself a lot, searching for words more and more. He seemed to be getting really confused."

I absentmindedly picked up my coffee cup and took a sip, immediately regretting the decision. It tasted as if Taco Muchacho found the cheapest coffee on the planet, brewed it as weak as they could while still getting the color right, and then reheating it repeatedly over several days. I made a face and set the cup aside.

Cagle hadn't noticed. "Anyway, then Petree asked if I could turn on the heater. This seemed surprising, so I looked back with my rear view mirror and noticed he was shaking. When I asked him about it, he just said 'that's what comes from skipping lunch.' I threw him a bag of chips I had left over from my break. He seemed restless, like he was anxious about something, but he kept saying he was just hungry and tired. That's the way I left him at the Conference Center."

I picked up a burrito. "Well, I paid enough, might as well try these. Anyone want one?"

Cagle squinted one eye. "N...no. I'm good, thanks."

Dee merely glanced at the food, and then at me, her expression wordlessly saying "you first."

I shrugged and bit into the burrito. "Hmm, not terrible." I turned my attention back to Cagle. "Do you happen to remember the person before Petree?"

Cagle furrowed his brow in thought. "As a matter of fact, yes. Kind of a medium build. Liked to talk a lot."

"What'd he talk about?" I glanced at Dee, hoping she'd jump in at any time. Normally, she'd be full of questions, so why not now?

Cagle gave a short laugh. "A better question would be, what didn't he talk about? The weather, the Mariners, computers, recent news."

"What'd he say his name was?"

"Bill Something-or-other. Platt, I think. He said he was a consultant. I asked him what he consulted about, and he shrugged, said something about software, and then started talking about how great for the Mariners actually win a game for a change, 'against the Padres no less,' he said. Went on and on about Ichiro's double play at the top of the ninth. Said it was great to see it in person."

"The Mariners were playing in San Diego over the weekend, and they won on Sunday, so that must mean Mr. Platt had been in

California." I pondered the implications. If Platt was the killer, then he may have followed Petree to Seattle. "Where'd you pick him up?"

"Actually, pretty near to Pike Place Market. Dropped him off at the airport."

"That's a pretty short time to be in Seattle, coming all the way from San Diego." I took another bite of burrito, weighing what to do with the other two.

Cagle shrugged that off. "Maybe he was waiting for a connecting flight. He never said where he was headed. He might have been killing time."

I reached for the coffee mug again, remembered the contents, and withdrew. "Anything else you can tell me about him?"

"Well, you can pull the car's video footage to get an idea of what he looks like." Cagle hesitated. "Well, maybe you can't. I don't know what the police let you access. I'm just not very good at faces in general. Mostly focusing on driving."

"No, that makes sense. Did you see him doing anything?"

"I don't think I did. He used his hands a lot when he talked, so I was pretty used to ignoring movement after a while." Cagle paused for a moment. "He apparently requested me by name. That's not unusual, though. I have a lot of repeat customers, although I don't remember this guy before. He might have been a referral."

I set down the burrito, deciding that it wasn't worth finishing, and pulled a business card out of my pocket. "If you think of anything else, please do let me know."

"Absolutely. And, I'm sorry about the restaurant. If I had known it was this bad, I would have never suggested we try it." Cagle stood up and started out of the booth.

"Ehh, it's my own fault for ordering so ambitiously." I picked up the tray and deposited the contents in the trash as we headed out the door. I glanced back at Deven, whose stoic face seemed merely to say "I told you so."

It turned out, we had parked nearly in front of Cagle's apartment building. I clutched at my stomach, which was now quite uneasy. "If I may be so bold, can I come up for a moment? If those burritos 'usually turn out fine,' I got the off-case."

Cagle raised his eyebrows. "Oh, absolutely. I suggested that restaurant, it's the least I can do." He led us up the stairs to his third-story apartment. He unlocked the door, and seemed to be studying the doorknob. "It's...around the corner. Door's on the right," he told me without looking up.

I heard Dee ask him what was wrong as I found the bathroom. As I flicked on the light, I heard a slight rustle from the shower curtain. The sound connected with Cagle's preoccupation with the door, and my encounter with the burrito ceased to be important. I pulled out my concealed .38 Smith and Wesson and threw open the shower curtain. "Freeze!"

A medium-sized young man put his hands in the air, still clutching an open switchblade.

"You've been watching too much Alfred Hitchcock, kid. Put the knife down on the floor of the tub, really slow."

As Dee and Cagle came to the bathroom door, I heard the chauffeur gasp. "That's him! That's the Bill Platt guy."

Platt set the knife on the tub floor and stood back up, his hands still in the air. A faint, three-tone beep assured me Dee was calling the police.

I stared the creep down. "I am a licensed private investigator, and I'm placing you under citizen's arrest. Step out of the tub. Keep your hands in the air."

The intruder compiled, and I ordered him to lay on his face in the living room. Dee had pulled out her own weapon, so I holstered my .38 and patted Platt down for any other weapons. A small handgun had been tucked into his waistband. I pulled a clean handkerchief from my pocket and removed it, setting the weapon out of his reach. "What are you doing here?"

"I'm not saying anything."

As if that would help his case. "Suit yourself. Mind watching him for a second, Dee?"

"No problem." She still had her gun trained on him.

"Good, I'll check the rest of the house." I turned to Platt. "Don't try anything, kid. We're both from Texas. We never miss."

After a quick search of the house confirmed that Platt was alone, I returned to the living room. "Good thing we came up, eh, Cagle?"

Cagle sat on his couch, staring up at his living room wall of photographs, obviously shaken. "No lie. Taco Muchacho just saved my life."

At that moment, the enemy burrito started a return journey, and I fled to the restroom.

* * *

I sat with Warren outside of the interrogation room at police headquarters, where Bill Platt – real name Joshua Cobb – was still being interviewed. He had declined to have a lawyer present during questioning, and talked freely. He was now repeating everything for the sake of verifying consistency.

"The online chatroom we use is anonymous. It's in the dark web, so there's virtually no trace. My client paid me five grand in cryptocurrency to kill Luis Cagle."

Cagle? I turned to Warren. "So, he wasn't out to hit Petree at all?"

Warren pointed to the one-way glass. "Doesn't sound like it, but keep listening."

"It was the first time I'd ever done anything like this. On my first attempt, I posed as a client," Cobb continued. "I had a Sydney funnel web spider in a glass tube, which I had purchased through the black market. I deposited it next to Cagle's seat, just before I left the vehicle, but apparently it didn't bite him."

"What did you do then?" prompted the interviewer.

"I staked out his apartment, waited until he left, and then jimmied the lock and hid in the shower. The next thing I know, that P.I. had me at gunpoint."

Warren elbowed me. "Nice work on that, by the way."

"Yeah, thanks." I turned these new details over in my mind. "So, we have our weapon, our killer, the intended victim, and the motive."

"Right, and since you got one out of four, and I got none, I concede defeat." Warren tipped his cap. "A good game, as always."

I turned away from the window. "I'm still not convinced we've wrapped this all up. Who hired Cobb, and why did that person want Cagle dead?"

Warren put a hand on my shoulder. "Unfortunately, I think that investigation is beyond the scope of your case. I'll handle that end. I'll let you know what I find out."

"Sure, you're right. It's probably unrelated. Cobb aimed for Cagle and missed." I sighed. "I just can't shake the feeling that this is still very much connected to the conference. Something about that environment is off."

I expected Warren to brush that off and shoo me back to my office, so I was surprised when he responded, "You're serious, aren't you, Noah?"

"Yeah, I suppose. I just don't know if I should be." I started towards the door.

Warren moved in front of me. "Listen, you've untangled three of the stickiest cases that have ever crossed my desk. I'm learning that your instincts are better hints than some of my best intel. If you think the conference is still connected, by all means, follow that rabbit down the hole. Heaven knows this case just paid you enough to afford it."

5

I Go Rabbit Hunting

Thursday, June 17

"Beautiful bit of work, Mr. Clue." Patrick Sharp shook my hand vigorously. "How in the world did you ever figure out it was an Australian spider?"

I shrugged. "I happened to have taken a course in toxicology in college, and the symptoms matched. The medical examiner would have figured it out without my help."

"Well, you've certainly earned your wage." Sharp felt in his pocket. "Hold on, I have your check around here somewhere." He began searching the desk drawers. "I swear, I'm always misplacing things. I can't tell you how many times I've missed the perfect shot because I forgot something or other."

At least that explained why every available space now seemed to have a photograph on it.

Sharp finally pulled a check out of a drawer and handed it to me. "Three times your normal fee, as per our agreement, and you keep the thousand from earlier of course."

I studied the check, enjoying the sight of so many digits residing near my name as payee. I could absolutely start looking into moving out of Dee's apartment into one of my own.

"It has been an honor working with you," Sharp gushed. "You're clearly one of the brightest minds of our age." He turned to Dee. "And, Miss Tindall, it has been a pleasure."

Dee shoved her hands into her pockets to prevent the client from kissing them. "I'm just doing my job, Mr. Sharp."

I quickly changed the subject to get the heat off my cousin. "You certainly have a lot of photographs."

Sharp looked pleased. "Indeed I do. I take a lot of them myself. It's a simple way to show my appreciation for all the common people that keep the conference running smoothly. Sound guys, janitors, whomever. Also good practice for using my tripod."

As we got into the car, Dee turned to me. "I do believe you've more than earned your keep, Noah. I'm sorry I ever joked about an 'allowance.' The firm's on pretty good footing, so I believe you should start taking your own salary again."

"Does this mean I get to buy the sort of food I want?"

Dee started the car. "You can eat greasy chow mein every night if you want."

"Ugh, no thanks." I began imagining a huge take-and-bake pizza baking in my own oven—a luxury I could only dream of in the old place. I snapped my thoughts back to the matter at hand. "I'm still not entirely settled about this case, though, Dee."

"You too?"

"I feel like Petree is still linked to all of this, but I don't know how." I turned to my cousin. "Wait, you had the same feeling?"

"Yeah, it feels like there's more to this case, just under the surface." She flicked on the turn signal. "What did Warren say?"

"That I should follow the rabbit down the hole if I felt I should."

Dee grinned. "Then let's go rabbit hunting."

* * *

Back at the office, I found a confused Bryan-with-a-Y sitting behind the desk.

Someone sat reading a newspaper by the window, legs crossed, face completely obscured.

"Noah, I'm glad you're back. This guy wanted to talk to you." Bryan motioned for me to lean over, and he whispered in my ear. "Between you and me, I don't think he's playing with a full deck."

Great, just what I needed. "Why?"

"Don't believe a word your secretary says. I'm perfectly sane." David Sigfield tossed the newspaper aside and picked up his cup. "Great coffee, Noah."

Dee laughed and disappeared into the kitchenette.

I raised an eyebrow. "David, what are you doing?"

"Just testing out the new hired help. He's too easy."

Bryan furrowed his brow. "Huh?"

I rolled my eyes. "Bryan Gannon, meet my best friend from college, David Sigfield." I swung my arm out in dramatic introduction. "Don't worry, he's harmless."

David crossed his arms. "Hey!"

Bryan relaxed into his chair. "Good, because as soon as he started ordering the sandwich, I nearly called the police. But then he said he'd wait for you instead, so I decided to let you deal with it."

I wasn't sure how to respond to Bryan's decision to leave a probable crazy man to me, especially since it had turned out to only be David. My scrawny friend always had enjoyed crafting bizarre first impressions. "Right, so, what brings you to the office on a Thursday morning, except to scare my secretary out of his wits?"

"I heard you have coffee."

Coffee wasn't that strong a draw. "Sure, David."

"Well, actually, there was something. Remember how I was telling you on Tuesday about Tina going to that Awakening Dawn conference in Portland, and how it was a waste of money?"

"Yeah?"

"You ever solve that case?"

"More or less." I wished David would get to the point, but beating around the bush was just his way.

"What sort of answer is that? Did you figure it out or not?" David took a huge swig of coffee.

"The spider theory was correct, and it turns out some hit man had put it in the car. He said he intended it to kill the driver, but it bit the wrong person."

"Ah, so I probably don't have anything useful for you." David paused. "So, if that's the more, what's the less?"

I blinked a few times. "We don't know who hired the hit, and I still feel like something's unresolved."

My friend nodded. "Okay, well, for what it's worth, I remembered something else Tina said. Apparently the director dude talked about relaxation techniques and emotional control, but then she watched him lose it on a chauffeur in the parking lot later."

"That's Patrick Sharp in a nutshell, from what I've heard," mumbled Bryan.

David shrugged. "Yeah, anyway, Tina felt pretty bad for the driver. She got to talking with him, and apparently they went out for coffee. 'Luis was the only good part about this whole trip,' she said."

I coughed. "Sorry, what did you say his name was?"

"Luis Cagle, I think she said his name was. I don't think they stayed together, though."

"You're sure about that name?"

David grinned. "As sure as you hate mushrooms, old pal."

"And thus why I keep you around." I flipped open my phone and hit the speed dial for Warren.

* * *

"Yeah, I got paid a sizable bonus to work in Portland last March, driving for Awakening Dawn. Why?" Luis Cagle looked from me, to Dee, and then to Warren. "Ohh, wait. Was the Petree guy a speaker there or something? I never really thought about it much. I drive so many people."

I nodded slowly.

Cagle looked uneasy. "Does this make me a suspect?"

"Not unless you hired a hit on yourself." Warren flipped back through his pocket notebook. "We've got the records and confession from Cobb to prove that. Petree definitely wasn't the intended target."

"Okay, I guess I'm really stupid then. What's the significance of my working at Awakening Dawn, aside from an ironic coincidence? Does that give you any idea why someone would hire a hit on me?"

Warren returned to his current notebook page and poised his pen. "It might. Did you have a conflict with the conference director?"

"Yeah, in Portland, he blamed me for picking someone up at the wrong time. Chewed me out publicly. I never got a chance to tell him that the office gave me the wrong information."

"What did you do?" Warren prompted.

"Well, nothing. I just never bothered to go out of my way to drive for Awakening Dawn again, since it's usually a rather high-stress job, anyway." Cagle gave a small smile. "Most of the rest of the people I drive more than make up for the trouble."

I glanced over Dee's shoulder at her notes. "Has there been contact from the conference since?"

Cagle nodded slowly. "A little, though not directly. A lot of people there like having me drive them. But I refuse to pick up Patrick

Sharp. He always was rather high-strung, so it all worked out. When I heard their ads on the radio, I hardly paid it mind."

Dee cut in. "What cities did you work in with the conference?"

"Aside from that one Portland trip? Just around here."

When it became clear that Cagle couldn't remember anything else about the Awakening Dawn conference, Dee and I left him with the police investigator to recount the rest of his employment and social history.

Warren accompanied us. "Looks like your instinct might be right again, Noah. We're right back at Patrick Sharp."

"He certainly had the money," Dee agreed, "plus a possible motive, to hire the hit. I just wish we had more to go on."

I followed Warren into his office. "You mentioned records from Joshua Cobb. What was that about?"

"We were able to seize his computer. He kept copies of his correspondence with the person who hired him, on an unencrypted part of the hard drive. Quite the rookie's mistake." Warren sat down and shuffled a few papers on his desk. "However, this was all through the dark web. The only information we have about his client is a screen name: 'af56f1ndr58'. Probably randomly generated. Finding anything else will take a while, since he was running the Linux TAILS operating system from a DVD and had the rest of the hard drive encrypted."

I skimmed the page Warren was looking at. "He had to have known enough about Cagle to find him. Was there a photograph?"

"Yeah, right here." Warren pulled another sheet of paper out of the stack and handed it to me.

Sure enough, Luis Cagle grinned out at us from the black-and-white photograph. "Was this in color originally?"

"Yeah, and high resolution besides."

I squinted at the background. "This looks like it might have been taken at the conference. You can just make out the Oregon Convention Center sign behind him, and I think it was cropped. Cobb got the original as a file?"

"Yes, he did. Our digital forensics team is analyzing it...or rather, they will be. It's in queue." Warren tapped another folder. "We needed them to shift to a higher priority case, but they'll get back to this in a couple of days."

I felt for my cell phone. "Is there any way I could get a copy of the original digital image?"

Warren bit his lip. "Mmm...yes, I think I could arrange that."

"Fantastic." I flipped open my phone and speed-dialed David.

"Of course, be sure to tell us what you find," Warren added.

"Obviously," I replied as David picked up. "Hey buddy, it's Noah. I need a favor."

* * *

"You really do have great Wi-Fi in this building, Noah." David sat under the far window in my office, clattering away on his laptop keyboard. It had taken all of half an hour to get the photograph, stored on a memory card, and meet my friend back at the office.

"I never knew David was an IT, Noah." Dee stood by Bryan, showing him how to finalize case notes.

David waved her off. "That's just my day job. By night, I'm a hacker."

Bryan looked up. "A hacker? Like, a cyber-criminal? Really?"

"I get that a lot." David stopped typing. "No, 'hacker' is a lot broader and older than infosec...erm...digital security and how to break it. It refers to finding unusual solutions to problems, especially when those solutions involve technology."

I chuckled to myself. David had written multiple letters to newspapers, websites, magazines, and even the local news station, setting the record straight on the definition of 'hacker'. Thankfully, his soapbox speech was cut short this time.

"Ha!" A smile broke across David's face. "Good news, the time stamp on this photo is way off."

I raised an eyebrow. "How is that good news?"

"It means whoever owns this camera knows very little about technology. This says March 13, 2000. The default is almost certainly January 1, 2000." David grinned. "That means there's a good chance he'd only owned the camera three months when he took this photo."

Dee pointed at my best friend. "He scares me."

"It also means," David continued undaunted, "That he wouldn't know how to get rid of the 'ex-if' information on the photo."

Bryan's concentration on his file-keeping lesson was now completely ruined. "Ex-if?"

"E-X-I-F. Digital cameras put extra information on the photos we take." He typed something else into his laptop. "In this case, the camera make and model, and...oh look, global coordinates."

"Seriously?" I set a refilled cup of coffee next to David and leaned over the side of his chair. I couldn't make heads or tails of the green text on the black screen.

"Yeah, this is one of those pricey digital cameras that have GPS built in." David flicked out of the black-and-green screen to a web browser. "What do you know, this photo was definitely taken at the Oregon Convention Center."

I pondered this. "So, that almost certainly confirms that this was taken when Cagle was working for Awakening Dawn in Portland."

"Yeah, but it's pretty odd that the GPS didn't update the timestamp. Usually it will." David flicked back to the green-and-black screen. "But then, I've never heard of this manufacturer. Probably an off-brand. Nakken SXD-915M."

This looked extremely promising. "So, if we find the camera, we've almost certainly found who hired Joshua Cobb to kill Luis Cagle." I jotted down the camera brand and model from the information David had highlighted on his screen.

Bryan piped up. "How do you know the photographer hired the hit? There are plenty of cameras at conferences. Shoot, even some attendees might have them. It's a pretty wide net to cast."

"It would be but for one thing." I held up the copy of the picture. "Very few people take photographs of random chauffeurs." I crossed the office. "Bryan, I need the list of conference employees that Patrick Sharp gave us."

"You got it, boss." Bryan wheeled across to the file cabinet.

I rubbed my hands together, enjoying the surge of excitement. "David, pack all that info up and send it on to Warren. His card is on the table next to you."

David mock saluted. "Sir, yes, sir."

"And Dee?" My rapid-fire thoughts died out. "I...have no idea what I'm doing."

A lopsided smile spread across my cousin's face. "Sure you do, Noah. You just don't realize it."

"Can I...speak to you...for a moment? Alone?"

Dee pointed to the kitchenette. "Let's go."

Once we were out of earshot of David and Bryan, I turned to Dee. "What are you doing? You're usually full of ideas, but on this case, you've seldom spoken two words together."

Dee crossed her arms. "I've said more than that."

"Okay, fine," I sighed, "you said a few things. It's still not much compared to your usual."

My cousin reached around me for a fat-free muffin. "I'm trying to cut back."

I furrowed my brow, trying to process this. "Why?"

She leaned back and nibbled at her muffin. "Since we started working together, I've never been shy about sharing my two cents. This time, I was just curious how much you could do on your own."

"Well, I'm not doing so great." I leaned back heavily on the counter and thumped my head against the cabinet. "You and I both know I'm no P.I. Without you, I'm lost."

"Mmm." Dee swallowed and pointed her muffin at me. "You identified when and how Petree was killed, without my help."

"I missed the whole Luis Cagle angle."

"Yeah, and? Everyone else did too." Dee sighed. "It's like I told you the night you cooked up the spider theory: you've ultimately solved every case we've taken. You may be more of a detective than you think, Noah."

I grunted. "Well, I'll have to take your word for it. Meanwhile, can you conclude your experiment and help me?"

"Sure, although there's not much to say. You've already locked onto our target."

"What do you mean?"

"Find the camera, find whoever hired the hit." Dee brushed past me. "And I have a feeling, we've already found the camera before."

"Really?" As I turned around, I felt the last piece of the puzzle click into place. "Bryan, cancel that list! I think I know where to find our suspect."

* * *

I caught Patrick Sharp backstage at the Awakening Dawn conference. The director didn't look overly thrilled to see me, but he plastered a pretentious smile on his face. "Mr. Clue! What a surprise. I hope none of my other speakers have bit the dust."

"No, nothing like that. I actually have another question for you."

Sharp frowned. "The case is closed. Hired hit, missed, killed Petree. I don't see how I could help you."

I held out the black-and-white copy of the photograph. "Do you recognize this man?"

Sharp frowned. "Luis Cagle, one of the drivers for the chauffeur service we contract with. Sure, I know him."

"The police believe he was the target of the murder-for-hire." I glanced at Dee out of the corner of my eye. She had opted to stay to the shadows, mostly to avoid Sharp's romantic inclinations.

"He and I have had our differences." Sharp took the picture from my hands. "He screwed up the timing on an important pickup, left a VIP sitting at the airport for over an hour."

"And what did you do?"

"Had a few words with him, naturally. Complained to the company." Sharp shoved the photograph back at me. "You're not suggesting I had something to do with this, are you?"

"I'm not suggesting anything. I'm just gathering information."

Sharp's tone turned icy. "Well, make sure you keep your eyes on the right target. I'm not paying you extra to find out who hired the hit on Luis Cagle."

"Understood."

Sharp squinted at me. "Who is, anyway?"

I crossed my arms. "I think you know I cannot disclose that sort of information, Mr. Sharp."

Sharp merely grunted acknowledgment and walked off.

I followed him into the adjacent green room. "Do you know anything about Cagle?"

"I didn't hire him, so I know nothing." Sharp waved me off and began taking down a camera and tripod. "You'd have to ask the chauffeur company for all that information. I have other things to see to."

"Do you know who might have taken this photograph?"

Sharp practically threw his red camera into its bag and turned back to me, his pallid face contorted in rage. He stuck a finger in my chest. "I didn't pay you to harass me, Mr. Clue. I have a conference to run. Go play detective somewhere else." He snatched up the camera bag and departed at a brisk pace.

Dee emerged from the shadows. "How does that line go, 'Methinks he doth protest too much'?"

"Hamlet, Act III, Scene II, though a bit removed from the original meaning." I smiled. "But I've got a better one: 'Suspicion always haunts the guilty mind.'"

"Shakespeare?"

"King Henry VI, Act V Scene VI." I pointed to the door. "Patrick Sharp was carrying a Nakken SXD-915M."

A sparkle ignited in Dee's eyes. "See? I told you you're a good investigator."

6

Everything Comes Into Focus

"Thank you for the ride-along, Warren." I sat in the passenger's seat of the Seattle P.D. squad car, sipping on a hot coffee. The slight haze of the city had an orange glow from the sunset.

"It's the least I could do. I know you like watching these things work out." Warren turned onto Cherry Street. "It's a wonder I didn't think of it sooner. Of course Sharp would be paranoid enough to hire the hit. The judge obviously thinks so, thus the warrant."

I adjusted the position of the cardboard sleeve on my coffee cup. "Hey, by the way, did you ever find out more about Laura Godfrey, whatever her real name was?"

"Actually, yes! In all the recent chaos, I forgot to tell you that she finally decided to come clean. She's a strong believer in keeping work and personal life separate, so she operates under an assumed name." Warren chuckled. "For all her attention to detail, she failed to consider that she needed to register it as a doing-business-as name. She now has a spot of trouble to clear up for flying under a false identity, but otherwise, that's that."

As we slowed down to turn into parking, I spotted a familiar vehicle leaving the garage and heading towards 3rd Avenue. "Warren, there's Sharp!"

"On it." Warren turned on the lights, but Sharp only accelerated and turned onto Third. Warren picked up the radio. "Six-Oh-Oh, code four-eight-two Third Avenue south from Cherry Street. Red and black two-door Audi." Warren rattled off the license plate. "Suspected driver, Patrick Sharp, has murder warrant. Over."

The dispatcher's voice came through. "Ten-four, Six-Oh-Oh. Be advised, no cars are presently available."

"Six-Oh-Oh, ten-four, over." Warren returned the microphone to its holder. "You've got to be kidding me. West Precinct, and everyone is tied up?"

"All the nut jobs must be crawling out from under their rocks for the conference," I mused.

"You may not be far off." Warren turned again and picked up the microphone. "Six-Oh-Oh, suspect is headed west on James Street. Just turned onto Yesler." He paused and turned again. "Now on First Avenue South, driving erratically. Over."

The dispatcher's response crackled over the car radio. "Ten-four, Six-Oh-Oh."

"He's heading for the waterfront, isn't he?" I leaned into the turn.

Warren kept his eyes on the road. "I think you're right. I'm almost sorry I brought you along."

"It's fine. Rather exciting." I held on as we turned onto South Washington Street. This was actually getting *too* exciting.

"You nailed it. Waterfront." Warren nodded forward.

Sure enough, Puget Sound lay before us. Sharp drove straight into the dock parking lot and leapt out.

Warren called in our position. "Six-Oh-Oh, suspect on foot on South Main docks. Requesting backup, over."

"Ten-four, Six-Oh-Oh. All units unavailable at this time."

"Blast it all." Warren stopped the car and got out. "Stay here, and for gosh sakes, Noah, don't do anything heroic. I think Sharp's going to try and dispose of evidence."

"Who's being heroic?" I muttered as the door slammed shut. I rolled down my window slightly to listen.

"Patrick Sharp, I'm with the Seattle P.D. We have a warrant. Don't make this harder than it needs to be!" Warren had already drawn his taser. I couldn't imagine why – a gun seemed more logical right now, but maybe Warren wanted to avoid this turning ugly.

Sharp reached the side of the dock and held a black laptop bag over it. "This is a frame-up!"

"Just put the bag on the dock and your hands in the air," Warren ordered. "We can settle this peacefully."

Sharp drew a gun with his free hand. "No, we can't!" His voice had reached a frantic pitch. "You don't get it! No one gets it!"

Warren froze. "You don't want to go there, Sharp."

"They've already won! Don't you see that? No matter what I do, they win."

"Who are you talking about?" Warren started moving his hand towards his own weapon.

"Keep your hands up!" Sharp screamed. "Don't make me kill you! Just keep your hands up!"

I grabbed the radio. "This is Six-Oh-Oh. Private Investigator Noah Clue, on ride-along. Suspect has Captain Warren at gunpoint. Over." I only hoped Sharp couldn't hear this over Warren's personal radio. If he knew backup was on the way, this could go south very quickly.

The dispatcher's voice crackled through. "Ten-four, Six-Oh-Oh. All available units, fast backup Six-Oh-Oh, South Main docks. Over."

One look at Sharp confirmed the man either hadn't heard or hadn't understood the radio chatter.

Another response sounded. "Whiskey Nineteen, en route. ETA seven minutes. Over."

I hung up the microphone. "Dang it." I began scanning the dashboard. From Sharp's increasingly incoherent yelling, seven minutes was going to be too long. I flipped the switch for the public address system. "Mr. Sharp, calm down and listen to me. I have to talk fast before they arrive."

Sharp glanced towards the car, but I had already ducked almost completely out of sight. I continued. "We know all about what they are up to, and we want to help you, but we have to make it look good so they don't suspect anything."

"How do I know I can trust you?"

I reviewed my old professor's lectures on paranoia in my mind. "We know all about the people at the conference who have been trying to set you up, who want to take your place. You had to remove Luis Cagle before he could turn on you. He's the most important of their pawns, isn't he?"

"He was the mastermind, arranging everything against me!" Sharp replied, his voice still bearing signs of his mental instability. "They were all working together against me."

"Sure, but you were smart. You had photographs of everyone. It makes you look friendly, posing with them, but you can use those if you need to. And you needed one of those photos to remove the threat: Luis Cagle. You hire the hit man to remove him before he can do any more damage to your hard-earned reputation."

"I didn't have any choice!" Sharp yelled, his gun still pointed at Captain Warren.

"We know. They are trying to remove you from the picture by getting you caught for Petree's death."

"Petree was my friend! My only friend!" I could see Sharp trembling from my vantage point. "I begged him to come up here so someone would be on my side, and now he's dead."

I continued, keeping my voice smooth and reassuring. "But we want to help you. We can get you to safety, out of their reach."

"What if you're lying? What then?" Sharp yelled.

"If you harm this officer, we can't help you. It'll look bad for you. They will have won." I took a deep breath, hoping this would work. "They don't want us to get whatever is in that laptop bag, because it'll help us catch them. Help us prevent that from happening." I knew I was lying through my teeth, but maybe Sharp would buy it.

Sharp looked uncertain.

I went for the final move. "They have already backed you into a corner, but we want to help you. What do you have to lose?"

Sharp dropped the laptop bag onto the dock, and then slowly bent down and set the gun beside it. Warren moved in and put the handcuffs on him. "I'll put you under arrest, just to protect you from them," he assured Sharp, following up my line of negotiation.

As approaching sirens rang in my ears, Warren spoke into his own radio. "Six-Oh-Oh, suspect is in custody. Over."

I sat back and breathed a sigh of relief as the dispatcher responded with confirmation.

* * *

Once Sharp had been placed in the back of another patrol car for transport, and the evidence secured, Warren and I departed for my office. We drove in silence for a while.

Warren finally spoke up. "You should have been a police negotiator, Noah."

I waved off the suggestion. "Nah, I'm not usually that smooth. I just happened to have studied enough psychology to know how to deal with paranoia. My professor, Dr. Ware, taught me a lot."

"Academically, or by example?"

I nearly snorted my coffee. "Academically. He's a lot of things, but crazy is not one of them."

Warren sighed. "I'm honestly sorry I've been so rough on you, Noah. Not only are you a crack investigator, but you also just saved my hide."

I shrugged. "No, you were right to be rough with me. I'm learning not to be so slip-shod."

"Like that breaking-and-entering incident a few months back?" Warren chuckled. "In your defense, you had the right guy."

"Just not the evidence to nail him."

Warren glanced over at me. "I think I can legitimately call you a friend, Noah."

I pondered this. "So, no more wagers?"

"I don't know, those are rather fun, even if I always lose." Warren chuckled as he parked in front of my office building.

* * *

"I'm not sure I understand this." Bryan Gannon had just finished typing up the last of the case notes. "If Patrick Sharp was behind the hit on Cagle, why did he hire you?"

"He simply didn't realize the two were connected." I handed a fresh cup of coffee to Warren. "He also had little fear of being found out about his own crime because he was confident in both his cover and motive. He used the dark web to hire the hit, and he overestimated the anonymity that gave him."

"But he wasn't quite as technically savvy as he thought he was," Dee added. "He never bothered to set the time stamp on his camera, and his computer must have still had logs of the correspondence with the hitman, or he wouldn't have tried to dispose of it."

I nodded, enjoying the feeling of all the pieces fitting together. "It's rather sad, really. Sharp considered Petree his friend, by all accounts. So, it turned out to be a case of the boomerang hitting the companion, instead of the quarry."

"Sharp's attorney will probably go for the insanity plea, which seems appropriate in this case." Warren set down his coffee and sank back into the sofa. "Just as well. He's probably a nice enough guy, sans his obvious mental disorder."

"One more thing I don't get." Bryan shuffled his notes around. "Finding the camera is great, but how did you know to go looking for it with Sharp?"

I grinned. "That was simple. Online screen names are rarely random. Sharp was an amateur photographer, but he mentioned always forgetting photography equipment. That's why the backgrounds in most of his photographs are too dark; he didn't have the right apertures. The screen name of the person who hired Cobb was 'af56f1ndr58', and that always struck me as odd. The middle part looked too intentionally like 'finder'. The first part, 'af56' almost certainly refers to aperture F-five-point-six, which incidentally is one size larger than what was used to take the photograph of Cagle."

"Rachel Petree told me she never liked Sharp." Warren shook his head. "But Thomas Petree wouldn't listen to her warnings about the director's mental instability."

"If only Petree had learned to listen to his wife's warnings, but it doesn't sound like he was in the habit of it." I picked up a muffin without thinking and took a bite. "Ick! Dee, we've got to talk about the snacks around here."

Dee smirked. "Weren't you just talking about always trusting a woman's intuition?"

"Yes, but that has no bearing on your dessert choices."

"Or does it?"

"Tell you what, Noah," Warren cut in. "I'll start bringing proper donuts as repayment for all the coffee I drink around this place. I don't like Dee's cardboard snacks any more than you do."

"Hear hear!" Bryan joined in.

"Savages." Dee snatched up the plate of muffins. "Fine, ruin your health, see if I care."

Warren chuckled. "Eh, go easy on him, Dee. I owe Noah anyway, after what it took to bring Sharp in."

Dee perked up. "I didn't hear about this."

"Noah talked him down." Warren shuddered. "Good thing, too. I hate being on that end of a gun, especially when backup is delayed. Your P.I. is a pretty good negotiator when he needs to be."

Dee blinked a couple of times and smiled. "He's always full of surprises, that's for sure."

I raised my hand. "Just for the record, can I point out that I'm still a bit unnerved by this many compliments from you two? It doesn't feel natural."

"I can take over insult duty, if it'll help, boss," Bryan chimed in.

Warren, Dee, and I turned to the new secretary. "Shut up, Bryan."

Murder
In G Minor

To Annie.

You taught me to think of this stuff.

I swear that's a good thing.

You also taught me crimes only belong on paper.

1

I Dust Off My Cultural Side

Wednesday, July 14

"A classical concert? Doesn't seem your speed, Noah." My cousin Dee Ann Tindall shook off the plate she just washed and set it in the rack. She had her nut-brown hair caught back in a ponytail. A few wayward curls lay defiantly across her forehead.

I adjusted my red tie in our living room mirror. "I'm a man of many diverse interests."

Dee dunked a coffee mug in the dishwater. "Yes, but classical? I've always heard you say the only reason a man listens to Mozart is if he can't find the jazz station on his radio."

"Well, Leah wanted to go, and I can afford the tickets. Who am I to turn her down?" I ran the comb through my dishwater blonde hair for the fifth time and debated whether to wear my black Stetson to the concert. "Besides, this isn't Mozart. It's something called *The Planets* by Gustav Holst."

My cousin snorted. "Ever since you started dating Leah Lee, you've been turning into a regular arts connoisseur. First the impressionist exhibition, and now this."

"Is that a bad thing?" I set the comb down and stared myself in my unremarkable gray eyes. If I was supposed to pass for a high-brow lover of the arts, I didn't look the part, no matter how much I tried. I frowned at the suit-clad impostor in the mirror. I couldn't wear my Stetson with this get-up. "Well, I plan to invite Leah to the jazz festival next month. We're just sharing things we appreciate with one another."

Dee set down the last plate. "Just be honest with yourself, and with her." She reached for a dish towel. "I have to leave for the airport in half an hour, so make sure you have your keys. If you forget them again, you'll have to wait a week to get into this apartment."

I pulled the keys out of the inner pocket of my suit jacket. "Right here, cousin."

"Good." Dee put a plate into the cabinet. "I'm glad for the opportunity to see my folks again. I just hope I don't have to deal with…" She trailed off.

"With my folks." I finished the sentence for her. "Why do you think I'm not going, Dee? There are few people on this planet that can tolerate being in the same room with Jack and Patricia Clue for more than five minutes, and fewer still that like doing so."

"And my father is one of those few."

I sighed. My father, Jack, was the black sheep of the Clue family, being estranged—or nearly so—from every blood relation. Yet somehow his brother-in-law, Bennett Tindall, was still his best friend. None of us could figure out why, since Bennett had a reputation as a straight-shooter—a rare trait in a lawyer. Dee's mother, Elizabeth, chalked it up to her husband's blind loyalty. She couldn't stand her brother's company any more than the rest of the Clue family could.

I leaned on the breakfast bar and watched Dee put the dishes away. "With any luck, my parents will stay put in Decatur, and yours in Waxahachie."

"I keep telling myself that." Dee restacked the mugs in the cabinet. "I fail to understand why Mom and Dad won't come and visit me here some time. I offered to pay their way, if only to skip the Texas sauna and you-know-who, but they wouldn't budge."

I grimaced. "Saying my father's name won't make him appear."

"Sorry, I'm just used to keeping family laundry in the bag." Dee thumped the cabinet shut. "Well, enough about that. I know I'll be brought up to date on all the latest Clue-Tindall drama the moment I step off the plane, so I'd prefer to avoid thinking about it now. You said you're going double on this date?"

I gave my cousin a wry grin. "Worst conversation transition ever. You already know the answer to that question."

She crossed her arms. "You never told me who David's date is."

"That's because I have no idea. David doesn't tell me much about who he's going out with."

Dee shrugged. "She obviously likes classical music, if the punk rock computer geek of the century is voluntarily attending a two hour Mozart marathon."

"It's not Mozart, it's Holst."

* * *

Leah hooked her arm in mine as we left the concert hall at the Salish Music Conservatory for intermission. Her deep blue eyes sparkled. "Did you like it?"

"That was phenomenal." I grinned, resisting the urge to stroke her short blonde hair. How could I have ever thought her dumb? She constantly surprised me with her quiet brilliance. "I still can't get that one piece—*Jupiter* was it?—out of my head."

"Legend has it," Leah continued in her soft, gentle voice, "When the piece was first performed, the servants at the concert hall danced backstage."

David Sigfield, my best friend, laughed. "I know I wanted to! I never knew classical music could be so...varied. I'm used to it all being stuffy highbrow nonsense." He pushed his long, dark bangs away from his eyes. His date seemed oblivious to us as her gaze drifted around the atrium.

"Yeah, I'm more used to jazz," I replied. "But I think this sort of classical music is growing on me. It helps that it's about something."

"Hearing it live makes a big difference, too. Just wait until you hear the second half of the concert. Dvořák's *New World Symphony* is incredible." Leah pulled a little towards a concessions stand. "Oh, let's get something to eat. The concert isn't over until 9:20, and I can't wait that long."

Melissa Draper, David's date, finally spoke up. "You go ahead, I'll be right back." She peeled herself loose from David and wandered off in the direction of the restrooms. She seemed as stuffy as her carefully coiled brown hair. What had my friend seen in her?

I noted the prices at the concessions stand and fished a twenty dollar bill out of my pocket. "What would you like, my dear?"

"The tomato caprese sandwich looks lovely."

"Right, we'll take two of those, and a couple of waters."

The young woman running the stand slid two prepared sandwiches into the toaster oven. She punched some buttons on the cash register. "That's eighteen dollars and seventy-four cents."

I handed over the cash. "Pretty fancy food you've got here."

She shrugged and placed my twenty into the till. "We've noticed that most patrons of the arts aren't interested in popcorn and Milk Duds. Nineteen seventy-four, nineteen ninety-nine, and a penny makes twenty." She dropped the change in my hand.

"Thank you." I pocketed the money.

The girl slid the cash register drawer shut. "So, it's more productive to drag this rig in here for concerts." She set two cold bottles of water on the counter.

David tapped the glass case. "Actually, a pizza-stuffed pretzel sounds pretty good to me." He glanced over his shoulder. "I wonder what Melissa will want."

I unscrewed the cap on my bottle of water and took a sip. The toaster oven beeped. The girl slid our sandwiches onto foam plates and handed them to me.

Melissa bustled over with a sense of urgency. "David, we have to go back to the car."

David winced as he turned away from the concession stand. "What? Now? Why?"

She put her hand to her left earlobe. "I'm missing an earring," she hissed. "I must have dropped it in the car. I look lopsided!"

If symmetry mattered so much to her, I wondered at her choice to wear an off-the-shoulder dress.

Disbelief registered in David's brown eyes. "Can we get something to eat first? I'm starving."

Melissa crossed her slender arms, her elbow-length gloves nearly blending into the gold lamé fabric of her gown. "All you men ever think about is food. Are you willing to pay two hundred dollars to replace my earring?" She glanced over at Leah for support, but my date had turned her entire attention to her sandwich.

David sighed in the direction of his desired pizza-stuffed pretzel before pulling out his car keys. "All right, I'll help."

I handed my plate with the second half of my sandwich to David. "We'll all help. Maybe we can find it faster that way."

David's eyes expressed his gratitude as he bit into the sandwich.

Leah nudged me. "I'll only be able to eat half of this, Noah. You're welcome to the rest. It's very filling."

"Thanks, Leah. You're a gem." I led the way to the double doors. "Let's find that earring and get back before the concert resumes."

* * *

"It must have fallen off while I was fixing my hair in the car." Melissa took the glittery gold-plated earring from me and pinned it in place. "I'm just glad to have it back." She started towards the concert hall.

"You're welcome," David muttered as he punched the lock button on his key fob. The car blipped an acknowledgment.

Leah gave him a light peck on the cheek. "I think you're a proper gentleman, David."

David blushed and sent a worried glance in my direction. I laughed. Leah was affectionate by nature, and twice as loyal, so I didn't mind the display. She crossed and took up my hand so I could walk between her and my best friend.

"A lot of fuss for nothing, though," I added in a whisper. "Those earrings aren't worth two hundred dollars."

Surprise flashed across David's face. "No?"

"Those are cubic zirconia, not diamonds."

"How can you tell?" David whispered back.

"Simple. Reputable jewelers don't put real diamonds in gold-plated settings."

Melissa must have sensed she was the subject of conversation. She slowed down and fell into step beside David. "At any rate, we'll be back to the concert hall in time for you to get one of those fancy sandwiches you wanted. That is, if you're still hungry."

"Yeah, I am, although the line is probably going to be super long now." He sighed. "No matter. At least we found your earring."

Two loud pops reverberated across the campus, immediately registering in my mind. "Get down!" I shouted.

"What?" David dropped to the ground, pulling an unwilling Melissa with him.

"Gunshots." I pulled out my cell phone and dialed 9-1-1.

"I don't hear any screaming." Leah raised her head a little from her spot beside me. "I think it was just the two."

I glanced at my watch. 8:16 p.m.

The line clicked. "9-1-1, what is your emergency?"

Melissa struggled to her feet and scowled. "Well, this dress is pretty well ruined."

"Melissa!" David hissed. "Not yet!"

I ignored them for the moment. "Shots fired at Salish Music Conservatory. We've only heard two so far."

Melissa grimaced. "I don't hear any more. It was probably just a car backfiring."

"Can you see the gunman?" asked the operator.

"No." I pulled the phone away from my mouth. "Stay down, all of you! Those were gunshots."

David and Leah obeyed my order. Melissa merely brushed at her gold lamé dress in vain.

As I surveyed our surrounding area, a young woman bolted out of the left hand building. She crossed and entered the other building without so much as a glance in our direction.

I spoke into the phone. "A woman just ran from one of the buildings, and entered the other. This looks serious. I'd better find out what's up."

"Sir, officers are on their way. Our first priority is to make sure you're safe."

A piercing shriek sounded above us. "He's dead! Oh my gosh, he's been shot!"

I scrambled to my feet and unholstered my Smith and Wesson revolver. "I am safe. I'm a licensed private investigator, and I'm armed. A woman just screamed that a man has been shot, and is possibly dead." I rushed towards the building entrance. David, Leah and Melissa followed.

"How long ago was he shot?" the operator asked.

"Only about a minute. We heard two distinct gunshots at exactly 8:16 p.m."

"And you say the man is dead?"

"That's what the woman screamed from the inside of the building. I'm going up to check on this. Just a moment."

I cautiously opened the door. Classical music emanated from a ground level office, just loud enough to hear in the hallway. Leah, David, and Melissa crowded behind me. As we passed the open door, I caught sight of a short, brown-haired woman in her mid-thirties, standing by her desk. I covered my phone's mouthpiece. "Ma'am, are you okay?"

"I...I don't..." she gasped. Fear filled her eyes and she trembled violently. She clung to the desk, as if for dear life.

"She's having a panic attack." David slipped into the room.

"How do you know?"

My friend faced me. "My little brother is autistic. He has these all the time. Go ahead, Noah, I'll take care of this."

I started up the stairs, Leah on my heels.

Melissa remained by the office door, looking trapped, slightly disheveled, and completely out of her element.

We found a short, plump woman with tight black curls standing over the man's body, sobbing. Leah put an arm around the distraught woman's shoulder and led her away. I knelt by the body and felt for a pulse on his neck. "Yeah, he's definitely dead." I reported into the phone. "Single gunshot wound to the head. It looks like he's holding the weapon."

"Possible suicide?" the operator asked.

"Looks that way. My friend is watching what appears to be the only entrance into the building. We had a clear view of the front door when we heard gunshots, and no one came out."

"Okay, sir, please stay there and remain on the line until police arrive. They're on their way."

"All right." I took mental inventory of the room. Seeing as I didn't have a habit of being overly observant, I would need to make special effort now. I might not get another chance.

The victim lay on the floor next to the desk. I guessed he had probably been facing the door when he fell. A look of surprise was frozen on his face. The gun rested in his right hand. Blood splattered the wall behind him. One bullet hole marred the plastic ceiling light cover above.

I noticed the open window through the mostly closed curtains and bent down to look out of it. A window opposite it in the other building was also open, an abandoned workstation clearly visible. Perhaps the young woman had been working there when the gunshots sounded.

I studied the man's uncluttered desktop for anything unusual. No suicide note that I could see—in fact, there were no notes at all, except for some routine-looking paperwork. I observed a well-filled pencil holder, a desk calendar, a watch counting up, and a stack of blank sticky notes. The trash can was mostly empty, except for a few moist wipes and a banana peel. Against the wall opposite the desk stood a large, well-organized bookcase. Various small, foreign musical instruments dotted the dark wooden shelves. Books on music history and theory were crammed from one end to the other.

The emergency operator's voice sounded from my phone. "Sir, are you still there?"

"I'm still here." I scanned the room once more, to see if I had missed anything. Satisfied, I returned to the hallway where Leah and the student waited. I muted my phone. "Can you tell me what happened?" I asked gently.

The student nodded, her tight curls bobbing. "I was working in the building across the way there, and I heard arguing coming from Dr. O'Connell's office."

"He's the dead man?" I ventured.

"Yes. Dr. Liam O'Connell, one of the professors here. Anyway, he was arguing with Dr. Susannah Coyle, the professor downstairs. She left and slammed the door. Then, a few minutes later, I heard the door open again. Dr. O'Connell started yelling, and then I heard the gunshots."

I wished Dee had been here to take notes. As if reading my mind, Leah took a notebook from her purse and began writing.

Perhaps this witness could give me more details. "Do you remember what he yelled?"

The woman nodded. "He said, 'What do you want, now?' and then, "No!'"

"Go on," I prompted.

"I immediately ran over here to see if he was okay, and found him dead."

I studied her for a moment. "You didn't think that you might also get shot?"

"I...I wasn't thinking at all. I just wanted to make sure Dr. O'Connell was okay. When I got here, Dr. Coyle was in her office."

"Sir?" The 9-1-1 operator broke in. "The police are arriving on scene now, so I'm going to let you go. If anything else comes up before they make contact, don't hesitate to call back."

I unmuted my phone. "All right, thank you." I snapped it shut and slid it into my inner coat pocket. "You said they were arguing?"

"Yes."

"Do you remember what about?"

The student shook her head. "Not really. Something about paperwork. I tried to ignore them."

I heard a new voice downstairs. "In here, I think." A short, well-built man in a two-tone blue Seattle PD uniform came up the stairs. He spotted me and picked up his pace. "Sir, are you the one who called this in?"

I noticed the badge pinned above his left shirt pocket. 'T. JONES' marched across the dark blue right hand pocket in white stitching. "Yes, sir. Noah Clue, private investigator."

"Good, good. I assume the scene is secure?"

I nodded. "Other than checking the body for a pulse, I haven't touched anything. No one else has entered since I've been here."

"Fair enough." The man passed me, peered into the office, and grunted. "Certainly not a pleasant thing to find." He turned back to me and held out his hand. "I'm Detective Thomas M. Jones with the Seattle Police Department."

"Good to meet you." I couldn't help noticing the slight bags under his bloodshot eyes. Given the scruffy shadow of a beard, I guessed that Detective Jones must be ready to quit for the day.

"Now, who found the body?" He moved a little closer to us to allow a couple more officers past.

The student raised her hand a little. "I did."

Jones removed a notebook from his breast pocket. "And you are?"

"Henrietta Dunlop. I'm a student here."

"Tell me everything you know."

She took a deep breath and recited the story again. I took the opportunity to turn each detail over in my mind anew, looking for anything helpful.

Jones grunted and scratched the top of his head with the end of the pen, making his already untidy hair stand on end a little more. "So, you heard shouting before the gunshot, you say? That seems to rule out a suicide."

I had heard of a few cases where people did shout before killing themselves, but I didn't know if this was the right time to bring it up.

The detective turned to me. "How'd you get involved in this?"

"We're attending the concert. My friend's date realized at the start of intermission that she was missing an earring, so we went out to the parking lot to look for it. On our way back, we heard two gunshots." I brushed a dirt streak from my suit jacket. "As you can see, we hit the ground."

"Mm, yes, I was wondering about that."

"Well, anyhow, I noticed this young woman come out of the building across the way and run in here. We heard her scream that someone was shot, so we came in to help. My date and I found the student standing over the body."

"Pretty straight-forward. Thank you, Mr. Clue." He turned to Leah. "Anything to add to that, Miss?"

Leah shook her head. "That's everything in a nutshell."

"Come on, guys," Melissa shouted up the stairs. "We're going to miss the second half of the concert if we don't hurry up!"

Detective Jones looked down at her. "I'm sorry, ma'am, but until we've finished analyzing the scene and ruled you out as suspects, I don't want anyone leaving this area."

"I wasn't even in the building at the time," Melissa whined. "Just look at my ruined outfit." She crossed her arms. "Anyway, the concert is in the area. It's two buildings over."

Jones narrowed his gaze. "I can't spare a police escort to make sure you don't leave. I'm sorry, but you're going to have to stay put for the time being."

I raised my eyebrows. I understood Jones's motivation, but this did seem overkill. Still, it didn't seem fruitful to argue with this police detective. I started down the stairs. "Just roll with it, Melissa."

Melissa scowled and plunked herself down in a chair in the hallway. "Some evening this is turning out to be."

I could still hear David softly taking to the woman in the downstairs office. She appeared much calmer now, although still clearly on edge.

Detective Jones pushed past me, and approached the woman in the office. "Ma'am, who are you?"

"Su...susannah Coyle." I could see her visibly tense up. "I'm...I'm a professor here."

"Did you hear the gunshots?"

Fear flashed across her blanched face. "Y...yes, I was right here in my office."

"Did you see or hear anyone come or go?"

"N...no. Yes. Just afterwards, the student c...came in, and then the private investigator and his friends. No one else." She took a couple deep breaths. "Ch...check the surveillance c...camera. It's p...pointed right at the front door. There's no other way in."

I moved a bit closer to see the inside of her office. The phonograph continued crackling at the end of the record.

Jones glanced at me and continued his questioning of Susannah Coyle. "Did you have an argument this evening with Liam O'Connell?"

"Yes, I did." Dr. Coyle's voice shook.

Jones loomed over her. "Tell me about that."

This line of questions didn't seem to be helping Coyle calm down. "He's the assistant department chair, and I report directly to him. He...asked me to take care of some routine paperwork today. I finished it all—took me six hours—except for the student evaluations, which I planned to do this evening, after the concert. When I asked for a break to catch the second half of the performance, since some students of mine are performing, Dr. O'Connell refused. He insisted I finish the student evaluations before 9 p.m. We argued, and when I could tell he wasn't going to see reason, I stormed out of his office. I came in here and put on some music to calm down."

"Did you now?" Jones's voice had taken on a new tone.

Terror flashed in Dr. Coyle's eyes. "Wh...what?"

"You were heard having an argument with him, and you're the only person in the building at the time of the gunshots."

Coyle looked more panicked than ever. "Are you saying he was m...murdered?"

"I'm saying, no one shouts a whole lot before they kill themselves." Jones took out his handcuffs. "Dr. Susannah Coyle, I'm placing you under arrest for the murder of Liam O'Connell."

Coyle slumped in a faint, and David had to catch her. My friend sent the detective a withering glare. "Thanks a lot, buddy. I just about had her calmed down, too." He turned toward me. "Noah, call an ambulance."

2

I Get On A Detective's Bad Side

Coyle regained consciousness just as the ambulance crew arrived. As she was loaded onto a gurney, Jones rattled off her rights, unabated. "You have the right to remain silent. Anything you say can and will be used against you in a court of law."

Melissa stood up. "Does this mean we can finally leave?"

"Can it, Melissa!" David snapped.

Jones kept blathering on. "You have the right to an attorney. If you cannot afford an attorney, one will be appointed for you. Do you understand these rights?"

Coyle barely nodded between gasps of air. She reached out to David, who grabbed her hand.

"I'm going with her," David volunteered.

"Sure, whatever." Jones waved him off. "Elliot, go with them. Once Coyle is released, transport her downtown." He jotted down some notes. "Show's over, folks. You can go back to your concert."

Melissa grabbed David's arm. "You can't abandon me, here!"

David pulled away from her. "Look, lady, I don't know if you noticed, but a man is dead, and an innocent women may be pegged for a murder she didn't commit. Don't you think that's more important than some concert?"

Melissa stared at him. I couldn't blame her. As far as I could see, there wasn't a way to answer the question without sounding like a total lout. Finally, she spoke up. "I didn't come out here to get caught up in some detective novel. I wanted a nice evening. I have nothing to offer you, and nothing to gain by trying, so if you don't mind, I'm going back to the concert. Alone, apparently, since my alleged date has dumped me for a total stranger. Good night." She stalked off.

I pulled a card out of my wallet and handed it to David. "Call this lawyer, Tabitha Harris Mitchell. She's a public defender."

He nodded. "Will do."

Detective Jones stalked past us. "Ain't a jury in the world who'll acquit her."

His blind and calloused attitude made my blood boil. He had violated every rule of criminology. I followed him out of the building. "Now hold on there, detective. Are you meaning to tell me you come in, ask a few questions, and then arrest a woman for murder without fully investigating the scene of the death or gathering evidence?"

Jones opened the driver's door of his unmarked car. "It's called efficiency, son."

"It's called jumping to conclusions."

Jones spun on his heels and slammed the door shut. He snarled, the ends of his faint mustache lifting. "Excuse me, are you telling me how to do my job?"

I stood my ground. "I'm saying, you blatantly arrested her for the murder. Not on suspicion of murder, not as a person of interest. You've already decided based on nothing."

His eyes narrowed. "I arrested her based on eye-witness statements. She's the only one with opportunity, barring some lone assassin who can fly. Besides, she couldn't answer me clearly and changed her answers."

I crossed my arms. "She was having a panic attack! And we don't even know if this is a murder, detective."

Jones rolled his eyes. "I know it's a murder. You don't even enter into it." He opened the driver's door again.

My mind raced. Jones was clearly convinced, but unlike him, I had studied O'Connell's office. The shouting alone didn't convince me it was a murder. I couldn't put my finger on it, but Susannah Coyle made an unlikely murderer. I needed to buy some time. "Detective Jones, wait."

He froze and shot an icy glare in my direction. "Why are you wasting my time, Clue?"

"I'm certain you're making a terrible mistake, and I think I can prove it."

Jones leaned on the car door. "And what if I don't *want* you to prove it? Some wannabe cop underfoot, interfering with an official investigation? No, thank you. Now if you will excuse me, I need to call in." He stooped down to get into the car.

"Call Captain Gregg Warren! If he tells me to back down, I'm out of your hair." I hoped he'd take me up on the challenge.

Jones popped back up again. "You reeeeeeeally want to play this game, don't you? Fine. Have it your way." He pulled a smartphone out of his pocket and tapped the screen. A moment passed. "Hello, Sir. This is Detective Thomas Jones. Yeah. I'm on a murder scene here at the Salish Music Conservatory, placed someone under arrest already. Mm hmm. Yes, well, there's a Noah Clue here, going on about how I've got the wrong person or something. Right. Okay, sure." He held the phone out to me. "He wants to talk to you."

I took the phone, noting the smug smile on Jones's face indicating that he expected me to get reamed. "Hello."

"Noah?" Warren's warm tone greeted me.

"Yeah. Hello, sir."

"Sir?" He chuckled. "That's a new one. I kinda like it. Listen, uh, Jones is a pain in my neck already. Chief likes him a whole lot, so I can't really get rid of him. How confident are you that he has the wrong person?"

One more look at Jones's superior smile, and I decided to keep my answers to words that wouldn't sound like Warren had taken my side. It would make the news of the captain supporting me more of a shock. "Very."

"Like, loser-buys-dinner confident or I'll-bet-my-firm confident?"

Darn, how to answer that without giving anything away? "Second."

"He's listening, isn't he?"

"Yes, sir." I forced myself to frown.

"Smug smile and the whole infuriating package?"

"Absolutely, sir."

I caught sight of David accompanying Coyle and the paramedics. My friend tossed me his keys. "I'll call you when we're done. Pick me up at Harborview."

I nodded. "Sure, buddy."

"Is the scene even taped off?" Warren continued.

"I didn't observe that, sir."

Warren groaned. "Look, I've been trying to find a way to bring this Philadelphia transplant back down to earth, and with your track record, I'd say you're the ticket. So here's the deal." He rustled through some papers. "It's a bit irregular, but I'm clearing you as an official police advisor. Chief shouldn't have an issue with it, considering the cases you've solved. That'll get some of the red tape out of your way."

"Understood, sir." I continued to feign a look of disappointment.

"You're officially advising on this case, so you're free to work your magic. Follow police protocol and the usual rules, except one."

"Sir?"

"Keep the sharing to a minimum until you've wrapped it all in a neat little package. If you're right about this, and I have little doubt you are, I want the solution to come from you."

I gave a heavy sigh. "If you say so, sir."

"Excellent. You've just made my day, Noah. Keep track of your billable hours. You'll be getting paid for this, naturally. Oh, and just one thing more?"

"Yes?"

"I'd recommend recording any conversations you have with witnesses, both for evidence and to cover your tail. Just be sure you let them know."

"Yes, sir."

"Now hand the phone back to Jones, so I can burst his bubble."

"I understand, sir. Thank you for your time." I set the phone in Jones's outstretched hand and watched him slowly lift it to his ear, his superior attitude dancing in his eyes.

"Hello, thank you, sir. I will...yes?" As Jones listened, his smile began to fade. "Sir?" The light went out of his eyes, as if someone had hit the wall switch. "Sir, are you sure? I don't..." He hung his head. "Fine, you're the boss. All right. I will. What?" His ears turned red. "Contaminated? Yes, I will. Right away. Yes. Bye."

Jones gave the screen a firm tap and made eye contact with me. "All right, Clue, it looks like you've got a free pass to play detective. But allow me to remind you, you're an advisor. Leave the crime scene alone, don't tamper with witnesses, and don't get in my way. If you want files or any such nonsense, call the captain. Now hurry up before you miss any more of your concert. You'll have time to bother me in the morning." He stormed off into the building, no doubt to properly secure the scene.

Leah joined me and slipped her hand into mine as we started walking. "It sounds like you're already pretty deep into this one, aren't you?"

I nodded. "Yeah, Warren just made me an official police advisor."

Her smile warmed me to my toes. "Congratulations."

"Timing couldn't be worse, though. Dee and Bryan are both out of town this weekend."

She shrugged. "I've filled in for Dee before. That's how I met you, remember?" Leah leaned her head against my shoulder. "I'm no detective, but I take good notes."

I had to give her that. "Are you sure, Leah? I don't know how deep this is going to get, and I can't wait until tomorrow to get started. I need to talk to the dean before Detective Jones gets to him with all his crazy theories."

Leah patted my arm with her free hand. "Noah, don't worry about this. I've got vacation time saved up, Reilly will understand, and we can always catch another classical concert. Let's go find that dean."

* * *

Dean Aletha Matheson wasn't in her office, as I should have expected. Her administrative assistant took us back to the concert hall, and had us wait in the atrium while she fetched her. After a moment, a tall, slender woman with short, chestnut-brown hair approached us, looking more concerned than annoyed. Her bright blue checkered summer dress gave me a headache.

On cue, Leah pulled her smartphone from her pocket and began recording.

"Dean Matheson, thank you for meeting with me." I pulled a business card out of my inner coat pocket. "My name is Noah Clue, I'm a private investigator. This is my secretary. I'm so sorry to pull you away from the concert." I nodded towards Leah's phone. "Also, if you don't mind, I need to record this conversation."

"That's fine, and don't worry about the concert. I've heard more than my share of rehearsals." Matheson looked down at my card. "Is something wrong? Noreen said it was urgent."

"I'm afraid it is. Less than an hour ago, one of your professors, Dr. O'Connell, was found dead in his office." I tried to word this as ambiguously as possible.

Matheson's hand flew to her mouth. "Oh my gosh! Liam's dead?"

"Yes, ma'am."

"What happened? Was he murdered?"

I kept my tone neutral. "We aren't sure. Is there a particular reason you'd think he would be murdered?"

She paused. "Not really, it's just you're here asking questions. That wouldn't happen if it wasn't suspicious."

The dean had a point. I moved on. "What can you tell me about Dr. O'Connell?"

She hesitated. "Liam's a rather eccentric and demanding individual, but an excellent teacher nevertheless. Many of his students have gone on to perform in major symphony orchestras around the world."

"Has he taught here long?"

"Goodness, yes. Dr. Liam O'Connell has been teaching music at this school since long before I got here. He's been the Assistant Chair of the Wind and Percussion Division and conductor of the Wind Symphony for the past ten years."

"And, in general, he's well liked?"

Matheson gave a slight chuckle, and then seemed to remember O'Connell was dead. "No, I wouldn't say that. He's a very hard man to please. The greatest compliment he'll ever give a performance is his silence. Students take him because he's an effective teacher, not because he's a pleasant person." She blinked back a couple of tears. "I'm sorry, it's hard to imagine that he's dead."

"So, he didn't show any changes in mood or behavior over the past few weeks or months?"

"Not really, but then Liam rarely showed much emotion at all. He only spoke up if he felt something needed to be addressed, and otherwise kept to himself."

I felt a little panic rising in my chest at the knowledge that Dee wasn't here to support me, but one glance at Leah scribbling away in her funny little personal shorthand gave me a boost of confidence. "Can you think of anyone who would want Liam O'Connell dead?"

The dean bit her lip and stared at the wall behind me. "N...no. Well, my full answer will sound strange to you."

"Go ahead," I coaxed.

"I'd say, 'everybody and nobody.' Liam got on everyone's nerves on a regular basis, on account of his demeanor, so could he have driven someone to want him dead? Sure, take your pick of suspects. We've all had it up to our eyebrows with him at one time or another. But has anyone seemed overtly hostile? No."

"Okay. What do you know about Susannah Coyle?"

Matheson's thin eyebrows shot up. "Susannah? What about her?"

"I just want to know what you can tell me about her."

"Great professor, also a little eccentric, but very sweet. Her students all adore her. Why would you bring her up?"

I debated how to best answer the question without leading. "She was in the building when Dr. O'Connell died, so we naturally have to consider her."

"Well, you can consider her out of the equation, Mr. Clue." Aletha Matheson's voice had taken on a hint of ice. "Susannah would never hurt anyone. I know her too well to doubt that." The defiant look yielded to one of confusion. "Actually, I don't understand how she could have been in the building. Several of her students are performing, and she would never miss that. Are you quite sure?"

"Yes, ma'am. I spoke to her myself."

A hint of disappointment marred her pleasant face. "Well, it's good to know now, I suppose. We were going to announce her new position after the concert. I counted on her being here tonight, so I didn't ask her specifically to come. I didn't want to get her suspicions up about the surprise."

"New position?"

Matheson nodded. "The former chair of the Wind and Percussion Division, Vaughn Ramakers, retired four months ago. Liam O'Connell has been the interim chair, but it is such a demanding position, and we didn't want to pull him away from conducting. So we unanimously selected Susannah Coyle as the new chair. We were intending to announce it tonight."

Well, this put a whole new angle on the case. "Who knew about her new position?"

Dean Matheson stared up at the ceiling. "Let's see...just myself, the board, my administrative assistant Noreen, and...no, yeah, that's it as far as I know." She faced me again. "But you know how information can leak out. So, 'everybody and nobody' again, I suppose."

I reached up to tip my black Stetson, but remembered it wasn't there. I flicked hair off of my forehead instead. "Thank you, Ms. Matheson. You've been most helpful. The police will want to talk to you as well, naturally."

"Yes, I'm sure. And if there is anything else I can do for you, just let me or Noreen know."

I weighed whether to break the news about Coyle now, or leave that to Jones. Given his tactlessness...

I sighed. "You should probably be aware, Susannah Coyle has already been arrested on suspicion of murder. I'm not convinced, however, so I'm going to keep digging for evidence."

The shock registered on the dean's face. "Susannah...oh my goodness." She grabbed my arm. "Mr. Clue, I assure you this is a mistake. We'll hold off the announcement, but please do everything you can. You have my full support in this investigation. I just know that when all the facts are brought to light, she'll be proven innocent."

"I'm doing everything I can, ma'am." I shook her hand. "Thank you for your time." As we walked away, I shoved my hands in my sports coat pockets. "Well, shoot, if we turned this whole mystery around, it would be a lot easier to solve. Susannah Coyle gets promoted, someone get jealous and shoots her. But, that's not the case we have."

Thomas Jones barreled through the atrium door and stopped short. "Aren't you staying for the concert, Clue?"

I shook my head. "I've got a case to solve, Detective Jones. Now, if you'll excuse me, we have some interview notes to type up."

"Interview?" He rolled his eyes. "Oh, let me guess. You talked to the dean?"

"Aletha Matheson. She's right over there." I motioned towards her as she ambled back to the concert. "She's already expecting you, more or less."

Jones glowered. "And I'm sure you've already given her the whole sob story about how I arrested the wrong lady?"

"I asked unslanted questions. You should try it sometime." I brushed past him, Leah right behind me. "Good evening, detective."

* * *

"He arrested her, just like that?" Dee's incredulous tone came through the phone line.

I lay across my bed and stared up at the ceiling, studying the weird patterns the lamp light made in the popcorn texture. "Yeah, and he barely even glanced at the room where the guy died."

"But Warren's on your side?"

"He must be, or else he wouldn't have made me an official police advisor. Although I suspect he's merely wanting to use me to bring Jones down a few pegs. He really didn't sound like he had much respect for the guy."

"I'd give Warren a bit more credit than that. He wants the case solved, and he knows you'll get to the bottom of it. Cooling this guy's jets is just a bonus." Dee paused. "What'd you say his name was?"

"Detective Thomas Jones." I replayed his introduction in my mind. "Thomas M. Jones, that is."

"TMJ. Isn't that a nerve disorder or something?"

"It's the jawbone joint. The disorder you're thinking of is called TMD, which affects said joint."

"What *didn't* you study in college, Noah?"

I yawned. "I'm not actually sure. I dabbled in a bunch of stuff."

My cousin snickered. "So, aside from a dead man, how'd your date go?"

"Phenomenal. I have a newfound appreciation for classical music, and for Leah. You should've seen her at the crime scene. Completely collected, as always." I kicked off my right shoe. "She offered to be my temporary secretary for this case, since you're away."

"That's sweet of her. I can't help but like Leah."

"She's hard not to like. Meanwhile, David went to the hospital to help calm Coyle down. I picked him up. On the way home, he said he wants to follow this case all the way through as well." I yawned again and kicked my other shoe to the floor. "So, what's new in Texas?"

"Absolutely nothing. Your parents showed up, as I dreaded. I don't want to talk about it." Dee sighed. "So, who was David's date?"

"Melissa Draper." I spoke the name in a dramatic tone. "She was disgruntled over the whole thing, not that she seemed to enjoy the music to begin with. I don't believe she was ever interested in David at all, actually."

"So, if she doesn't enjoy classical music, why did she say she wanted to go?"

I loosened my tie with my free hand, pulled it out of my collar, and draped it over the bedpost above my head. "Beats me. But get this: she had a conniption about misplacing an earring, and tried to claim it was worth a bunch of money. They look like diamonds at a glance, but I know cubic zirconia when I see it. Actually, that's what led us to be where we were to hear the gunshot."

"A missing earring?"

"Yeah. Found it in the car, though." I tried to suppress a third yawn and failed. "Actually, Dee, I'm beat. I'm going to hit the sack.

Jones threatened to be on the campus bright and early, so I asked Leah and David to meet me at Starbucks at five in the morning, so we have time to come up with a plan and be on campus by six. Figured we'd beat him to the punch."

Dee chuckled. "Sounds like fireworks are due. I'm sorry I'm going to miss it."

I loosened the top button of my shirt. "You've got plenty of fireworks there."

"Wrong kind. Goodnight, Noah."

"Night, cuz." I hung up and debated whether to change into pajamas. A fourth yawn sealed my decision. I switched off the lamp and fell asleep.

3

I Become Official

Thursday, July 15

I sat down at a table in Starbucks with a hot, black coffee. "Barely five in the morning. I must be crazy." I set my black Stetson on the seat beside me.

"Hey, it's logical to me, pal." David took a bite of his glazed donut.

I took a long whiff of my coffee through the hole in the lid while I waited for it to cool down. "You don't seem the least bit tired."

"Well, contrary to popular belief, not all ITs are night owls."

I stared at my best friend over the lid of my cup. "You're a morning person? Since when?"

"Since forever. I only did the late nights in college so I could socialize with you all. I'm up at four every morning."

"You never cease to amaze me, David. Every time I think I know you, you surprise me again." I stifled a yawn. "What do you even do that early in the morning?"

My friend polished off his donut. "Eh, it varies. Lately, I've been really into this indie computer game. One of my friends got me hooked on it."

"Another aliens-take-over-the-world thing?" I ventured a sip of my coffee and tried to ignore the burnt flavor.

David waved his hand. "Nah, it's this new thing called Minecraft. The whole world's made of blocks that you can pick up and move around. You can build whatever you want."

"Really? That's it?"

A wide grin filled his boyish face. "Yeah, except you also have to avoid getting killed by monsters while doing it."

"Of course."

David couldn't hide his excitement. "I'm kinda into this red ore stuff the guy added earlier this month. You can make all sorts of electrical circuits with it."

I raised an eyebrow. "Sounds like a nerdy sort of game. I'll bet you it won't even take off. Everyone seems to want games where you blow stuff up."

David laughed. "Oh, you can blow stuff up. It has TNT. Or you can just scare a creeper."

"Good morning, gentlemen." Leah sat down. She looked fabulous for this early in the morning. "Did I miss anything important?"

I smiled at her. "Not really. David was just telling me all about blowing things up." I took another sip of coffee.

"It's, ah, a game." David set down his second donut and wiped his fingers on a napkin. "Minecraft."

Leah leaned back in her chair. "Yeah, my fourteen-year-old cousin is really into that one." She caught my eye. "But, we're not sitting in a café before dawn to discuss video games. What's the plan, boss?"

I grunted. "Getting my brain to work is a good first step." I studied Leah, who seemed totally alert as she waited for her order. "Don't tell me you're a morning person too."

She shrugged. "I like to go jogging around sunrise, so this isn't much of a stretch for me."

"You know, as a night owl, I'm really beginning to feel quite alone in the world."

David grinned. "Join us. We have donuts."

"Order for Leah!" came the call from the counter.

"Or in my case, almond croissants. Excuse me." Leah stood up.

David leaned forward. "You really scored with finding her, Noah. Melissa turned out to be a real jerk. I'd blame it on the murder and all, but she wasn't really warm towards me to begin with."

"Yeah, Leah's a gem. As to Melissa..." I paused as Leah sat down again. "I really don't know what to make of her, especially after last night's behavior."

Leah frowned. "I suspect she had other reasons for attending that concert, besides the enjoyment of music."

"Really?" David furrowed his brow. "That would explain a few things, actually. No matter, I could never be with someone with no concept of priorities."

I took a long swig of coffee. "Right, let's get down to business. Where are we?"

Leah whisked out her notebook. "It depends. Are we working off the assumption that Coyle is innocent?"

I shook my head. "As much as I want to, we really shouldn't. Lack of objectivity is Detective Jones's style."

"In that case, we have the dean's testimony that Coyle couldn't have committed the crime, on basis of her character."

"Mmm!" David held up a finger and swallowed his bite of donut. "I can add some details to that. Coyle was afraid of guns."

I studied him. "She told you that at the hospital?"

"Yeah. The gunshots are what set off her panic attack. Apparently her parents died in a drive-by shooting when she was four. She was in the car with them at the time."

"Oh wow." Leah breathed.

I took another sip of my coffee. "We'd obviously need to verify that, but if it's true, it is pretty strong evidence in favor of her innocence. What else?"

Leah brushed her blonde bangs out of her deep blue eyes. "Coyle was being promoted to department chair, over O'Connell no less."

"You know, that's unusual to me. If anything, it creates less motive for her to kill him, not more." I pulled out my own notebook. "Don't mind me, I'm just going to jot down a few random thoughts too. It helps me think."

Leah smiled. "Whatever works for you, boss."

David leaned forward. "We know first-hand that there were two gunshots, right?"

"Right." Leah nodded. "That's what I heard."

David turned to me. "Did both end up in O'Connell?"

"I don't think so." I tried to picture the crime scene in my mind. "I noticed a hole in the ceiling, and blood splatter on the wall."

"That seems to point away from suicide to me. I mean, that and the yelling." David took another bite of donut.

"No, we can't jump to that conclusion. People do a lot of strange things to work up the nerve to shoot themselves." I scribbled 'suicide' in my notebook, followed by three question marks. "Who knows what O'Connell was thinking? The dean said he kept mostly to himself, and nobody really liked him."

Leah picked the last crumb of her croissant off her napkin. "That student said he was yelling at someone before the gunshots, but she didn't see anyone."

David twisted the cardboard sleeve on his cup. "Was she able to see Coyle in the victim's office earlier?"

I started a list of people I needed to interview. "Being in shock, Henrietta might not have described everything in the best detail. We need to talk to her again today. We should also speak with other students and faculty. I want a better picture of both Liam O'Connell and Susannah Coyle to work from."

David grunted. "Good thing we're planning on being there by six. Jones will no doubt be prowling around by then, and we need to get to witnesses before he skews their perspective. There's nothing like the power of suggestion to throw off personal perception."

Leah stared at her notebook. "That detective's initials are TMJ, aren't they?"

"Yeah. Isn't that a nerve disorder? I never bothered to take biology in college." David took a long swig of his coffee.

"It's the jawbone joint." I paused. "You know, Dee said the same thing to me last night."

"Catchy initials. He's certainly a pain in the neck." David chuckled. "You know, tetanus affects the TMJ."

I snorted. "I wish it would affect this TMJ for a while."

Leah crumpled up her napkin. "So, we have our game plan?"

"For now, yeah." I stretched. "We'd better get moving if we're going to beat morning traffic."

* * *

We found Detective Jones getting out of his unmarked vehicle in the Salish Music Conservatory parking lot. He caught sight of me and gave a depreciating little smile. "Well, well, my faithful little shadow, right on time." He slammed the car door shut. "I was hoping to get some work done before you got here, Clue. Are you playing cowboy today?"

I ignored his snide remark about my signature Stetson. "Did you get any useful information out of the dean last night?"

Jones scowled. "Of course not, after your little stunt. She cooperated only as much as she had to, and praised Coyle to the skies the whole time." He stuck a finger in my chest. "I told you not to tamper with witnesses."

"For your information, Detective, I recorded my entire exchange with the dean's consent, and we've already sent a copy to Captain Warren this morning."

As if on cue, Leah pulled her smartphone out of her handbag. After a few taps, my voice came from the device. "Thank you, Ms. Matheson. You've been most helpful. The police will want to talk to you as well, naturally."

The dean's voice responded. "Yes, I'm sure. And if there is anything else I can do for you, just let me or Noreen know."

After a moment, my voice sounded on the recording again. "You should probably be aware, Susannah Coyle has already been arrested on suspicion of murder. I'm not convinced, however, so I'm going to keep digging for evidence."

Leah stopped the playback and tucked her phone into her pocket.

Jones clenched his jaw. "You're not convinced? That's what you told her? Since when is opinion a factor in this job?"

"Since you made it a factor yesterday evening, by arresting a woman for a crime without so much as a shred of evidence, circumstantial or otherwise." I crossed my arms. "So either start playing by your own rules, or lay off."

Jones glanced at Leah, and then at David. "You know, I don't recall Warren giving clearance for *three* advisors."

"Leah is my secretary, and David is my assistant." I pulled out my flip phone. "But I'm happy to check on this."

Jones lost a little color as I speed-dialed the captain.

"This is Warren."

"Hey, Warren, it's Noah. Do I need written permission for my staff, Leah Lee and David Sigfield?"

Warren chuckled. "They're filling in for Dee and Bryan, I take it?"

"Yes, sir."

"Jones playing semantic games already?"

"Yes, sir."

"Hand the phone to him, please."

I held out my phone to Jones. "He wants to talk to you."

Jones took it with some hesitation. "Yes?"

I could hear Warren from where I stood. "I'm not sure how they did things in Philadelphia, but we don't harass our police advisors around here. The D.A. is already breathing down my neck over this one, and the Chief is not happy. They had to cut Coyle loose, thanks to your tremendous lack of evidence, and her attorney has hinted at a lawsuit. Clue is there since you obviously don't know how to run a proper investigation, and if this hits the fan, he may be the only thing keeping the department from looking like the wrong end of a mule. You're going to start doing things by the book, and Clue is there to ensure you do. Got it?"

Jones stiffened. "Yes, sir."

"Don't mistake me, Detective, I have no problem pinning this whole mess on you if it goes south. Lay off the P.I., or I'll have you busted down to parking duty so fast, you'll see stars!" Warren's tone regained its cordial professionalism. "Now please hand the phone back to Mr. Clue."

I took my cell phone back from Jones's trembling hand. "What can I do for you, sir?"

"You hear all that?"

"Hard to miss, sir."

"I really like this 'sir' business, Clue. You do your thing, and try to keep Jones in line. If you have any problems, give me another call." Warren cleared his throat. "I've got to go do damage control."

"Have fun with that."

"Indeed. Talk to you later, Noah." The line clicked.

I snapped my phone shut and slid it into my inner coat pocket. Warren's confidence in me was both inspiring and utterly terrifying. "So, who haven't we talked to yet?"

Jones responded in monotone. "Everyone but Dr. Coyle, the student who found the body, and Dean Matheson. Since you're apparently the resident genius here, who do you suggest?"

I felt in my pocket for my notebook. "For one, we were thinking of reinterviewing Henrietta Dunlop, the girl who found the body, to see if she's remembered anything else. Besides that, I want to get a better picture of both Dr. Coyle and Dr. O'Connell, so anyone and everyone might be helpful." I found the notebook, pulled it out, and flipped it open.

Jones didn't sound convinced. "Broad search area. You got a pattern in mind?"

David piped up. "We can start with the current students of both professors, especially those who might be assisting them in some capacity. Faculty who worked directly with them et cetera."

"Good plan, David." I glanced at Leah, who had already started a list. "Second, have we already pulled the footage from the building's security cameras?"

Jones scowled. "What good would those do? There was only one entrance, and according to your own testimony, you were in sight of the front door the whole time. No one came out after the gunshots were heard."

I shrugged. "I agree that it's unlikely, but that doesn't rule out escaping through a window or hiding in the building until the heat was off. We need to cover all our bases. Did your men search the building for anyone else last night, detective?"

Jones glared at me. "I didn't babysit them, so I'll have to ask. Forensics is still processing the crime scene, so your assistants need to stay clear of there. Do one of you want to get the student lists from Matheson's office, or should I?"

I turned to my friend. "You want to do that, David?"

He nodded, obviously happy for an excuse to get away from Jones. "Sure, no problem. I'll meet up with you in a few." He departed towards the administrative building.

The detective gave me an impatient look. "Fantastic. In the meanwhile, you want to micromanage forensics, Mr. Clue, or do you have something else in mind?"

I decided to play off the sarcastically-intended suggestion. "I prefer to leave the forensics to the experts. But now that you mention it, I would like to get a view from the window again, if I won't be in their way."

"You can ask, but they'll likely tell you to take a hike. Come on." Jones started towards the conservatory. I caught a comment just under his breath. "At least you leave *some* things to the experts."

* * *

I peered through the narrow gap between the beige curtains. I could just barely see Miss Dunlop in the opposite office. "Huh. She's back to work already."

"What's that, Noah?"

I turned to face Samantha Keppler, the forensics technician, who also happened to be one of my personal friends. "Henrietta Dunlop, the student who found the body. She's here today." I peered through the curtains again. "I'll have to go and talk with her."

"Is there something in particular you're looking for, Noah?"

I looked over my shoulder at the red-headed tech. "Not really. I'll know it when I see it." At least I hoped I would, but I didn't need to share that part.

"Here, would it help if I opened these curtains a bit? We've already processed them and the window screen."

I pushed the curtains aside. "Window screen?" For the first time, I noticed a two-inch tear in the mesh. "What caused this?"

"We don't know. It probably isn't important, but we'll see. We're just at the documenting stage right now." She sighed. "It wouldn't have taken this long, but Jones said 'swab everything,' so that's what we've been doing." She looked out of the window. "Yeah, that student is working hard on something. Maybe she has a paper due."

"Do they assign papers in music school?"

Samantha shrugged. "I don't know. I majored in forensics science. Closest I got to the arts was photography." She moved a bright red curl out of her eyes.

I looked back at where Liam O'Connell had to have been standing when he was shot, and traced a line to the window with my gaze. "I could see a little through the gap in the curtain in here yesterday, when we found the body. Supposing—and this is a wild theory—that someone else could be a witness. What window do you suppose they would have to be looking out of to see O'Connell get shot?"

"I'd think…" Samantha paused for a moment before pointing to a dark window two to the right of Dunlop. "That one, right there."

"I wonder whose office it is."

Samantha shrugged. "Only one way to find out."

* * *

I tapped on the door to the office where Henrietta Dunlop worked. She looked up from her workstation. "Oh, hi, Mr. Clue. Hi Ms. Lee." Her tone bore little emotion.

Leah approached Miss Dunlop's desk. "How are you doing, love?"

"Not great, but if I stayed home, I'd just keep thinking about it, so I figured there was no point missing work." She studied me. "What about you?"

I removed my black Stetson. "I was asked to advise on the case. I think I mentioned last night that I'm a private investigator."

"Lucky for Dr. Coyle. Do they even have anything on her?"

I bit back my first response. "I'm just in fact-finding mode right now, Miss Dunlop. That said, would you mind if I asked you a few more questions?"

"Sure, have a seat. And you can call me Henrietta." A bit of color rushed to her cheeks. "Actually, all my friends call me 'Hen,' so that's fine too."

I pulled out a chair for Leah, and then sat down in a blue office chair next to the desk. My temporary secretary tapped her smartphone screen and nodded.

"Miss Dunlop," I said, "we're recording this conversation. Is that okay with you?"

She shrugged it off. "Sure."

"Thank you." I smiled at her. "I wondered if you might repeat your account of last night for me. Perhaps you remembered something since then."

"Well, sure, but I doubt there's anything new there." Hen sighed. "I was working here last night, finishing up a poster for next week's wind symphony concert when I heard shouting from Dr. O'Connell's office. The curtain was drawn, so I couldn't see anything, but I could hear them arguing about paperwork."

"Do you remember anything specific about that argument?"

Hen shook her head. "Not really. I tried to tune it out. I think Dr. Coyle was mad because she wanted to go to the concert."

I couldn't assess whether she had overheard that from the argument or Coyle's initial interrogation. "While we're on the subject, didn't you want to go to the concert?"

"Naturally. My brother was playing. But Dr. O'Connell wanted the first draft of the wind symphony poster done that night. So, I planned to get it done, email it to him, and catch the second half. That concert is still a month away, so I don't know why he needed it so urgently."

Leah held up a finger. "Pardon me for cutting in, but I'm curious. Are you a work-study here?"

Hen nodded. "Yeah, for Dr. O'Connell. I've got some talent for graphics design, so he has me do a lot of posters and promotional stuff for events."

Leah turned her attention back to her notebook. "Okay, just wondering. Continue."

I picked up the conversation. "So you overheard arguing. Then what happened?"

"Well, I heard the office door slam shut, and then everything was quiet for couple of minutes. Then I heard the door bang open again. There was shouting, and then two gunshots."

"Do you remember who was shouting, and what they said?"

Hen paused and stared at a spot on the wall behind Leah. "Yeah. I only heard Dr. O'Connell. He said, 'What do you want now?' and 'What are you doing?' Then he started yelling 'no' over and over, and then the gunshots."

This testimony certainly didn't sound good for Susannah Coyle, but we had to get all the facts, no matter which way they pointed. "What did you do then?"

"Well, I was worried for Dr. O'Connell, so I ran over to see if he was okay." She sighed. "You know the rest, I think."

"Did you like working for O'Connell?"

She hesitated a moment. "Uh, sure. Why?"

I glanced at Leah. There seemed to be too much uncertainty in that answer. "Henrietta, I know this is hard for you given what happened, but we need to know everything."

Hen blew out a long breath with an air of resignation. "Dr. O'Connell was a hard person to work for. He never had anything nice to say about anyone. Did you see those posters for the concert last night?"

I nodded. "Those looked really nice. Did you design those?"

"Yeah. Dr. O'Connell had me make so many little changes and corrections to them. He's as much a perfectionist with posters as he is with performances. Finally, after a few dozen attempts, I ask him what he thinks. He just sorta stares at the computer screen for a minute, grunts, and just walks out of the office." Hen rolled her eyes. "If I hadn't been working with him for so long, I'd have thought he hated it and had given up on me. But that's basically just how he says 'it's good.'"

"And that was normal?"

"Oh, totally. That's why the argument between him and Dr. Coyle wasn't surprising to me. I figured, if he's going to keep me from the concert for some dumb poster that isn't needed until next week, of course he'd demand a bunch of routine paperwork."

"What about Dr. Coyle? Do you know anything about her?"

"Not much. I only had her for Theory One last semester. I just know she's always very sweet to everyone around her. If I want a compliment on my work, I go to her. She could have never hurt Dr. O'Connell, or anyone else."

I stood and planted my Stetson on my head. "Thank you for your time. If you think of anything else, let me know." I set my card on the desk in front of her.

Henrietta shook my hand, and then Leah's. "I will. Thank you both for looking into this."

As I reached the door, I turned back and noticed her struggling with the window. "Do you need some help?"

"Yeah. This stupid thing won't shut."

I came over and grasped the upper edge of the window pane. Try as I might, I couldn't push it down. "Is it always like this?"

"No, only since yesterday afternoon. Usually it slides easily."

"Excuse me." I slid the office chair out of the way and knelt down. "Anyone got a flashlight?"

"Yeah, just a moment." Leah rummaged around in her handbag. "I keep one handy, since I usually get home after dark and can't see the lock." She handed a penlight to me. "Here you go."

I shone the light up into the gap between the window pane and the frame. "What in Pete's sake is that?"

"What?" Hen tried to see around my shoulder. "What's in there?"

"I'm not sure. Something's stuck up there. Leah, I don't suppose you have a pair of pliers too?"

Leah laughed. "Tools aren't my speed."

Hen moved out of my way. "The best I could offer you would be a staple remover."

I flicked at a splinter of wood. "That won't help here." I peered across the street and caught sight of my forensics tech friend. "Yo, Samantha! You got a pair of pliers handy?"

Samantha spun around and gazed out in my direction. "Is that you, Noah?"

"Yeah. Something is jamming this window open, and I want to know what it is."

She waved. "Don't touch anything. I'll be right there!"

4

A Tragedy of Errors

My hailing of Samantha got Detective Jones's attention too, because both arrived in little more than a minute. Hen had pulled her chair completely away from the window. I handed the penlight to Samantha and stepped back. "There's something jammed up in there. Henrietta here said that it worked fine until last afternoon."

Samantha peered up at the splinter. "Son-of-a-gun. That's gotta be deliberate."

Leah tucked her notebook away. "Why would someone do that?"

"Why the heck would we care?" Jones shot back.

I turned around. "Detective, what do you see out this window?"

Jones stooped to see below the half-closed blinds. "The crime scene. Okay, I take that back."

I figured that was as close to a compliment as I'd ever get from Jones. "A great detective once said, 'there's no such thing as a coincidence.'"

Jones straightened. "A great *fictional* detective. I read Hillerman too, you know."

Samantha cut in. "Who all touched this window?"

"Anyone could have," Hen replied. "Me, Dr. O'Connell, plenty of other students and faculty. Even Mr. Clue, when he tried to help me close it just now. It's not like we wash it or anything."

Samantha frowned. "No, of course not." After a moment, she brightened again. I could swear her hair turned redder. "But who touched the frame?"

Henrietta shrugged. "I don't know. I don't think I ever have."

"If you wanted fingerprints, couldn't you just check for them on whatever is shoved in there?" suggested Leah.

"You're cute, darling," Samantha replied, not at all deprecatingly. "Rough wood doesn't give very good prints."

I stuck my hands in my pockets. "So, I'm going to assume we're in your way?"

"You aren't in my way until you're between me and the window, Noah." Samantha handed the penlight back to me. "But you may feel extraneous for a while."

Hen turned off her computer monitor and picked up her notebook. "I should probably get out of your hair, too, then. Mind if I work in the corner over there until you're done?"

Samantha laughed. "You can play the euphonium for all I care. Once you've spent four hours analyzing a crime scene on a busy street corner during a protest, nothing bothers you anymore." She stood and took her camera out of its case.

As Leah, Jones, and I started down the hallway towards the stairwell, I remembered the other office with the possible clear view of Liam O'Connell's death. "Don't mind me, Detective. I want to check on an idea."

"Suit yourself. I'll just stand by and observe, if you don't mind."

"Be my guest." I stopped at room 205 and knocked.

"Come in," came the bored response.

As I entered, I noted the name on the door. "Excuse me, Dr. Aaron Sanderson?"

A stocky, broad shouldered man looked up from a stack of papers on his desk. His silver fly-away hair stood at weird angles. "That's me. What can I do for you?"

"I'm Noah Clue, a private investigator. This is Detective Thomas Jones, Seattle P.D, and my assistant Leah Lee."

Dr. Sanderson shook my hand, and then Jones's. "What's this about? The O'Connell thing?"

Thing. What an odd word to describe a recent violent death. "Yes." I motioned toward Leah's smartphone. "Dr. Sanderson, we're recording this interview if you don't mind."

"Sure, what do I care?" He leaned back in his brown leather executive chair. "Ask away."

His mannerisms seemed quite strange given the circumstances. "How well did you know Dr. O'Connell?"

"I knew our grump-in-residence as well as anyone. In case you're wondering, I'm neither surprised nor upset about Liam's death. He obviously pushed someone too far."

It seemed odd that everyone I had spoken to gave the same assessment of O'Connell. "What do you mean, exactly?"

"Liam was a harsh, demanding, critical old mongrel."

"Sounds like you didn't like him." I crossed to the closed window. Yup, I could see right where Liam would have been standing when he was shot.

Sanderson's voice held no malice. "No, I did not."

I continued. "Where were you last night at 8:16 p.m?"

Dr. Sanderson frowned. "Unfortunately, I'm going to have to stick myself on your suspect list and tell you I was right here, and alone."

I turned around, almost expecting Jones to be pulling out his handcuffs at these confessions. "You didn't go to the concert?"

"Nope. I've heard *The Planets* too many times already, and frankly, I don't even consider it one of Holst's better symphonies. So I stayed here and worked on lesson plans. I've got no alibi, and I already handed you a motive, but for what it's worth, I didn't kill Liam O'Connell. Wouldn't be worth the effort, really."

Jones raised an eyebrow in my direction. Dr. Sanderson seemed a better suspect than Dr. Coyle given the circumstances, yet the detective seemed unwilling to consider any other possibility. "Did you hear the gunshots?"

"Once again I'm going to paint myself in a terrible light. Yes, I heard indistinct yelling that sounded like Liam's voice, and then two gunshots. After a moment, I heard a young lady screaming. At that point, I figured there wasn't any reason to get involved. Everyone carries cell phones these days, so I figured the hysterical student would at least dial 9-1-1. I decided that if I didn't hear sirens in the next few minutes, I'd call it in myself. But, the cops arrived, so I had no need to get myself all tied up in this." Dr. Sanderson still didn't look much bothered by any of it.

"And you're sure that's all you know?" I prompted.

"Yup, that's it. I'm happy to repeat it for you a hundred times over if you need me to, because it will always be the same." Dr. Sanderson gave a cordial smile. "Anything else I can do for you all?"

I looked at Jones, trying to give him room to ask his own questions. The detective seemed content to watch me work. I continued. "What do you know about Susannah Coyle?"

"Dr. Coyle? Polar opposite of O'Connell. Sweet gal, wouldn't hurt a fly, contrary to what *some* people think." He glared at Jones.

Jones coughed. "We just brought her in for questioning."

"Bull." Sanderson faced me. "Coyle had too much to live for. She was going to be the new department chair."

I furrowed my brow. "How do you know that?"

"You overhear things. It's nearly impossible to keep secrets on a campus this small." He pursed his lips. "I don't think she knew, though. I guess no one wanted to spoil the surprise."

"Who all knew?"

"Beats me."

I held out my hand. "Well, thank you, Dr. Sanderson. We'll be in touch if we need to know more. Meanwhile, if you think of anything..." I hated waiting for a handshake.

"I'll come looking for you. Sure." He waved us off. "Best of luck."

I stuck my neglected hand in my pocket. As we reached the door, I glanced at the window again. "One last question?"

"Yes?"

"How long has the screen been missing from your window?"

"Is it?" Dr. Sanderson stood and investigated the issue. "Huh, so it is. I knew it would fall out sooner or later. It never did fit right." He opened the window and peered out over the edge. "I guess the shim came loose."

"The shim?"

He pulled his head back in. "Yeah, little piece of wood I used to make the screen fit better." He tapped the window frame. "It's gone. So is the screen. I guess both dropped to the street and were mistaken for trash."

This could be a piece of the puzzle. "Would you be able to identify the shim if you saw it?"

"Probably. I really don't know. It isn't every day you get asked to pick a scrap of wood out of a lineup." Dr. Sanderson laughed at his own joke.

Jones glowered. "A technician will come talk to you in a bit."

* * *

"Dr. Coyle? Sure, I have her for oboe. This is my third semester with her." Stefan Ewart, a third-year student at the conservatory, had met Leah and me in the cafeteria.

We had spent the last two hours finding and interviewing students of both professors, and they all seemed to confirm what we already knew. O'Connell was a harsh-yet-effective teacher who never had a positive thing to say about anybody. By contrast, Coyle was gentle and supportive, inspiring all her students to achieve their best. Equally obvious, students deliberately sought to take classes with both.

Yet Stefan presented a whole new angle.

I studied the student's round, freckled face. His bleached-blonde faux-hawk gave his entire countenance a washed-out effect. "You're taking oboe? So far, all the students who had Coyle were studying theory or composition."

The young man chuckled. "I'm not surprised. Dr. Coyle doesn't usually teach instruments, although she plays plenty of them. I had to beg her to take me on as an oboe student."

I glanced over Leah's shoulder at her notes. Her incomprehensible personal shorthand made it impossible for me to read anything. "Why were you so desperate for her to teach you?"

Stefan grinned. "For the same reason none of the other students want her. She never lets you start or stop in the middle of the piece. You start at the beginning, end at the ending, and whatever mistakes you make, you let stand. No exceptions, ever."

Leah's gaze snapped loose from her notebook. "That's pretty unusual for a music teacher, isn't it?"

The student nodded. "Yeah, and that's why I like working with her. On my own, I tend to rehearse the first part of the song so much, the second half suffers. Dr. Coyle won't let me do that."

This seemed to be the first odd thing I'd heard about Coyle. "You said no other students want to take her for a musical instrument?"

"That's right. When I asked her to teach me, she said 'I don't think you know what you're asking, Stefan.' Those were her exact words. I kept insisting, and she finally said, 'I will teach you on one condition: every time you play a piece for me, you play it from start to finish. No stopping in the middle, no starting over, no repeating a section until you get it right. I don't want one word of complaint about this rule.'" Amusement danced in Stefan's brown eyes. "I still remember her face when I said, 'Yeah, I know, that's why I want you to teach me.' Utter surprise. It was priceless."

"And that's how you've worked with her ever since?" I began mulling over the implications.

"Yes, although I remember one close call last semester. I broke the reed in the middle of the song. Snapped it right down the middle. Couldn't play a note. Dr. Coyle always listened with her eyes closed, but she sat bolt upright and stared at me with a look that scared me half to death." Stefan looked a bit shaken by the memory, even now. "I explained the reed had broken. Quick as a flash, she pulled another out of her pocket, tossed it to me, and told me to continue exactly where I had left off. When I was done, she told me sternly to always carry a spare reed or two." Stefan patted his shirt pocket. "I've got one in a box right here, and two more in my case."

I discarded my theory about Coyle just being dedicated to her teaching style. If this story held water, it could expose a serious psychological quirk. But would it help her case, or hurt it?

* * *

I stared at the laptop screen. Matt, one of the investigators, had pulled the memory card from the surveillance camera and reviewed the footage from the evening of O'Connell's death. Jones had taken for granted that the building had been empty, but the video showed quite the opposite. A janitor had entered at 6:30 p.m, and hadn't left until 9:15.

I squinted at the blurry image. Surveillance cameras were really overrated sometimes. "So, do we have any ID on this guy?"

Matt shook his head. "I only know he was there mopping by the front door at 6:36, and doesn't leave until well after the crime." He frowned. "The stupid thing is, he would have had to slip past all of us to leave."

"You were occupied with the crime scene," David offered.

"Meanwhile, this little oversight is throwing a serious wrench in the works," Jones snapped. "Well, let's figure out who he is so we can rule him out."

I turned back to the computer. "We need to talk to him, obviously. Dean Matheson should be able to tell us who he is. Now, another question. Has anyone tested for gunpowder residue, et cetera, on the body and clothes? I'd think the pattern would tell us a lot."

"Ah, heh, there was a bit of a wrinkle on that front." Samantha had joined us. "An intern at the medical examiner's office apparently washed the wrong body."

I could hear Jones nearly choke on his coffee behind me.

"The clothing should yield evidence," she continued, "But we won't be getting anything off the hands and arms. You can bet someone is getting an earful today."

"I'll bet you Officer Elliot didn't swab Coyle for gunpowder residue," Jones growled.

I looked at the detective over my shoulder. "Did you ask him to?"

He scowled. "I shouldn't have to."

A sarcastic grimace crept across David's face. "I guess that sort of thing is outside of the scope of a lead detective to oversee."

Jones glared at him. "Why are you here, again?"

"Of course, it's too late to check the janitor for gunpowder residue either, unless he didn't change his clothes." Samantha rubbed her neck. "I really hope we can get forensic evidence off the scene, but that's not looking good either. Whoever shot O'Connell wiped the doorknob and gun clean with sanitizing wipes, which we found in the trash."

"We could use an eyewitness right about now." Leah mused.

I stared at the grainy image on the screen. "With any luck, our friend the janitor knows something." Otherwise, this case was about to get a lot more difficult.

Samantha nudged me. "By the way, Noah, I've got to give you major points. Dr. Sanderson positively identified the piece of wood jamming the window as his shim."

* * *

I turned to the second page of the criminal history. Jones had met us in the parking lot of the downtown police station and handed over this document without so much as a word.

"Impressive track record. Burglary, aggravated assault, wire fraud, evading arrest, at least fifteen counts of possession. This dude's done just about everything." I turned back to page one. "So, who is this Philip Kasey?"

"Janitor." Jones snapped.

"Any warrants out on him?"

"No."

Great. Now Detective Jones had switched to the sulky teen approach to communication.

"So, we have a man in the building at the time of O'Connell's death, and he has a rap sheet as long as Beethoven's 9th Symphony." I started walking towards the station. "Did you talk to him?"

"Yes."

"Any luck clearing him as you hoped?"

"No."

I decided to switch to exclusively open-ended questions for the duration of this bizarre conversation. "What do you have on his possible involvement?"

"Unknown."

"What potential motives do we have for him?"

"Unknown."

You had to be kidding me. We reached the sidewalk, and I turned to Jones. He looked considerably shorter than I remembered him. "You and I both know that inquiries never turn up *nothing*. What did Kasey say?"

Jones pointed to the building. "Pending."

I rolled my eyes. "So, he said absolutely nothing to you when you picked him up?"

The disgusted detective heaved a sigh. "He barely knew anyone at the college. He was cleaning in the basement and was wearing headphones at the time, so he didn't hear the gunshots or commotion. When he finished cleaning, he left the building by the front door."

"Did he clean O'Connell's office first, then?"

Jones shook his head. "O'Connell told him to skip it and come back the next evening, and Kasey agreed to do that."

"At least, that's what he said happened." I frowned. "So, we have a convicted felon in the building when O'Connell is shot, and no one seemed to remember that detail."

"Including your Dr. Coyle. I'll bet they were working together."

I rubbed the bridge of my nose. What sewer did this guy crawl out of? "You really don't understand how investigations work, do you? You find the clues, piece them together, and they lead you to your suspect."

Jones scoffed. "And you think that because that's how they do it on CSI, right? The clues just magically fit together to make an arrow that points right to the bad guy." He had traded the sulky tone for his usual condescending one. "That's not how it works in the real world, Clue. You find your suspect based on motive and opportunity, and then you gather all the evidence you need to convict them."

I couldn't believe this guy. "Have you never heard of 'innocent until proven guilty'?"

"Of course I have. Right now Coyle is considered innocent. I'm going to prove her guilty. Any further objections?"

How do you argue with someone who is immune to reality?

* * *

"Finally! Someone sane!" Warren gestured to the chairs across from his desk. "Shut the door and tell me what on earth is going on, because it seems the entire department has lost their minds."

I waited for Leah to enter before I closed the door to the office. "What other disasters are we looking at?"

"Well, which ones have you heard of?"

I counted off on my fingers. "The body getting washed, no one swabbing Coyle for gunpowder residue, or the lack thereof, and...well, basically Jones's entire career as a detective."

Warren grimaced. "Well, I'm afraid I've got one more. We have a broken chain of evidence on almost everything recovered from the crime scene. One of the rookies handed off to another officer without proper documentation." He smacked himself in the forehead with a folder and tossed it on the desk.

Great. "Almost everything? What do we have?"

"Only the murder weapon itself, and some random piece of wood that may or may not have anything to do with this." Warren put a hand to his forehead. "Please tell me you have some good news?"

"Honestly? I don't know right now. This isn't as simple as Jones first thought it was." I glanced at my secretary. "Oh, I'm sorry. Warren, meet Leah Lee. Leah, Captain Gregg Warren."

Warren shook her hand. "It's a pleasure to meet you." He raised an eyebrow in my direction. "So, what happened to Dee and the Boy Wonder, anyway?"

I jutted a thumb to the south. "Dee's visiting family in Texas, and Bryan is back east somewhere, presumably doing the same thing. Leah has filled in for Dee before."

The lieutenant nodded. "And David? I noticed your IT friend came in with you, too."

"Yeah, he's with Jones right now. He's basically acting as my assistant, which is handy since he has a near perfect memory."

"Well, I'm glad you're not solo. I know you work better when you've got support." Warren slid a folder to me. "Here's the transcript of Coyle's interrogation, in case you wanted to read it.

We've got the video, too. I have to agree with your gut instinct on this. The case against her is as thin as a promise."

I skimmed the papers. "It looks like she keeps repeating the same thing she told Jones at the scene. She had an argument with O'Connell over paperwork, went downstairs to her office, and put on some music to cool off."

"Detective Jones seems to think her demeanor at the time is proof of her guilt."

I rolled my eyes. "She was having a panic attack! David found out that she had a fear of guns. Apparently her parents were shot and killed in front of her when she was four."

"That would virtually rule her out if we could prove it." Warren tapped the desk with his pen. "They were murdered, you say? I can track that down, no problem. Given her name and date of birth, it's as simple as pulling a few records. CPS probably has some information on it too."

I continued. "Meanwhile, we've got this janitor."

Warren slowly shook his head. "Have you seen his rap sheet?"

"Yeah, Jones gave it to me in the parking lot."

"Apparently 'securing the scene' is a completely foreign concept to the responding officers, Detective Hot-to-Trot especially. Kasey makes more sense as a person of interest than Coyle."

"Well, besides him, I'm exploring another angle. Literally." I pulled out my notebook and scribbled a schematic of the scene of the crime. "See, O'Connell's window was open, which is how the student across the street heard the argument between him and Coyle."

"Right. That's the only shred of evidence in favor of Coyle's guilt, and even that's sketchy."

I held up a finger. "Well, it gets more interesting. See, the student, Henrietta Dunlop, couldn't see O'Connell or the unknown attacker. She could only hear them. But, someone else heard the argument, a Dr. Sanderson, whose window actually gave him a perfect view of the crime." I drew a dotted line between the two windows.

Warren perked up. "He's an eyewitness, then?"

"Well...no." I frowned. "Unfortunately, he was ignoring the whole thing, and his desk isn't positioned for him to see O'Connell's window. Assuming he's telling the truth, he saw nothing."

"Rats."

"But..." I continued. "The wooden shim he had been using to keep his loose window screen in place was missing. Someone had used it to jam Henrietta Dunlop's window open on the day of the crime, sometime before O'Connell's death."

"So, the killer wanted a witness?"

"It looks that way—but not an eyewitness."

"Risky maneuver. What if O'Connell said the killer's name before he died?"

I closed my notebook. "Kasey would have opportunity to jam the window, but again, the question is why? Why would someone want Henrietta Dunlop to hear O'Connell's murder?"

* * *

"You've reached Dee Ann Tindall. I can't take your call right now, so leave a message." The voice-mail beeped.

"Dee, it's Noah. I really need to talk to you. Give me a call as soon as you get this. Love you, cousin. Bye." I closed my phone and frowned at the typewriter in front of me. "What do I know?"

Leah had left me a transcribed copy of her notes, and David had rattled off all his thoughts and suspicions to me as he drove me home. I had all the pieces so far, right in front of me, but it just felt like a jumbled mess.

The obvious solution stared me in the face. The janitor had a criminal record going back to 1997, and he had opportunity. With O'Connell's penchant for being demanding and unpleasant, motive could be teased out of anyone. Samantha had explained that someone had cleaned the crime scene, wiping the gun and the door handles with disinfecting wipes found in the trash can. Forensic evidence would probably be scarce, but the circumstantial evidence against Philip Kasey certainly seemed sufficient. If it were simply a matter of closing the case, the state wouldn't have a hard time pinning O'Connell's death on him.

Still, I didn't want to take Jones's easy way out. I wasn't satisfied until all the pieces fit into place, and there was one that refused to snap in: the jammed window.

Why would anyone want a witness to a crime?

I shuffled through the notes, barely making sense of the words on the page. "Come on, Dee, where are you?" I adjusted the paper in my typewriter and tapped out "Jammed Window."

What else didn't make sense? I added "O'C Torn Window Screen" to the list.

If it weren't for the murder weapon being in O'Connell's dead hand, I'd have suspected a sniper from Dr. Sanderson's office. And anyway, for the bullet to ricochet and hit the ceiling light would be ridiculous. Still, I wrote "Missing Screen" and "Sanderson?"

I tried to replay the crime scene in my mind for what must have been the hundredth time. Nothing seemed out of place...except the watch on the desk. It was being used like a stopwatch, counting up. If I could only remember what time it had shown. Maybe the forensics team had noticed.

My cell phone vibrated, and I snatched it up. "Hey, Dee."

An automatic voice greeted me. "Congratulations! You've won a two week Caribbean cruise. Press three to..."

I punched the hang-up button and closed the phone. What a lousy time for my cousin to take a vacation. I added "Stopwatch" to my list and went back to staring. I had no idea how to add a piece of wood, two window screens, and a stopwatch together to get a killer. And yet, it looked like that was exactly what I needed to do.

5

The Waters Get Murky

Friday, July 16

"Still at it, Mr. Clue?" Dr. Sanderson met us in the hallway near his office. "I hear you picked up our janitor."

"Still only making inquiries, Dr. Sanderson," I replied.

He leaned on his door frame. "I assume you know that I identified that piece of wood as the one missing from my office."

"Yes."

"Well, if you find the window screen, let me know. I can find no sign of it." Sanderson shifted his position, still leaning against the doorframe. "Actually, you might ask the janitor about it. I've been noticing a few things going missing from my office."

This got my interest. "Really? Like what?"

Sanderson stared at me for a moment, before standing and indicating with a nod of his head for me to follow him in. I did, with Leah on my heels. David stood at the door and watched, which I was starting to learn was his preferred way of working with me.

Sanderson tapped a shelf. "I've got a small collection of musical instrument statues. As you can see in the dust, one's missing."

I picked up a gold violin statuette and turned it over. No hole, so I could probably rule out the statuettes containing anything of value. "Twenty-four karat gold-plated?"

"Yeah, it's not really worth that much, but it looks nice. Most of them are gifts from students over the years, so they mean a lot to me. Eventually, I hope to get the whole forty-eight-piece orchestra of them up there."

"Just the one is missing?"

"Actually, this is the third that's vanished from my office in the past month. That's why I asked the conservatory to install the security cameras. I would have preferred one near each office, but they felt that one facing each front door would be sufficient." He rolled his eyes. "Obviously it isn't, but what do I know? Anyhow, it may be worth asking the janitor about, since he's a felon and all."

I set the violin statuette down. "Let's not jump to conclusions, Dr. Sanderson. He hasn't been arrested or charged with anything in the past three years."

"Well, hear me out." A peculiar light danced in Dr. Sanderson's eyes. "Let's say he is stealing stuff from offices, selling it for pocket cash. Liam O'Connell finds out and threatens to turn him in. The janitor doesn't want to go back to jail, so he shoots O'Connell." He flashed me a lopsided grin. "Pretty good theory for an amateur, you have to admit."

"That's not a theory, it's a hypothesis." David mumbled from the doorway, barely loud enough for me to hear him.

I made a mental inventory of the statuettes present. "Dr. Sanderson, I don't know whether these missing items have anything to do with O'Connell's death or not. I'll look into it, but let's not jump to any conclusions."

Dr. Sanderson grunted. "Sure, do it your way. But mark my words, they're connected." He shook his finger. "I haven't liked that janitor since he started working here."

First Jones, and now Sanderson. Didn't anyone believe in due process anymore? I decided to change the subject. "Do you remember which ones are missing?"

"Oh, the statuettes? A saxophone, a clarinet, and most recently, an oboe."

"When did you notice the latest theft?"

Sanderson's lopsided smile returned. "The day O'Connell died."

* * *

"He noticed it gone two days ago, and he only just gets around to telling us?" David grumbled just loud enough for me to hear him over the classical music playing nearby. "I don't like Sanderson."

"He might have only just remembered it," suggested Leah.

I knocked on Hen's open office door. She looked up and brightened. "Mr. Clue! I saw Dr. Coyle this morning already, so I guess they let her go. How is the investigation going?"

"Yes, they turned her loose yesterday morning." If Coyle was on campus, I needed to talk to her myself. "We're slowly finding more information, but investigations take time."

"Oh. Well, yeah, that makes sense. Hold on." Hen turned off her music. "Sorry. I've had that piece in my head for two days. I don't know why."

"Turn it on again," prompted David. "I want to hear it."

Hen shrugged and started the music. David listened for a moment. "I can tell you why it's in your head."

Hen shut it off again. "Yeah?"

"That song was playing in Coyle's office when O'Connell was murdered. I remember, it was at the end of a violin solo where..." he frowned. "What's the term for 'going up'?"

"That would be an ascending run," Hen answered.

"Okay, sure." David shrugged. "Well, it doesn't really matter anyway. Noah's the guy that asks the questions."

Hen turned to me. "Yeah, what can I do for you?"

"Well, I don't know if you can answer this." I stuck my hands in my pockets. "Do you remember the exact time that Coyle left O'Connell's office?"

Hen shook her head. "No, I only remember that the gunshots were at 8:16 p.m., because I texted..." She trailed off. "Wait, I texted my friend. Hang on!" She pulled out her smartphone. "I remember complaining about them arguing, and then...yes, here it is! I said, 'Oh, good, they're done for now.' That was at...8:13 p.m."

This lead looked promising. "Do you remember when the door slammed open?"

Hen swiped through her messages. "No, I don't have that. But I don't remember it being that long before the gunshots. Couldn't have been more than a few seconds."

"Well, at least we now know there were three minutes between the argument and the gunshot." I couldn't tell whether that would be helpful, but it couldn't hurt. "Just one more thing. Has anything gone missing from this office in the last few weeks?"

"Here? No." Hen looked around. "I mean, it would be really hard to tell. A bunch of students share this space, so things change all the time. Nothing looks out of place, though." She smiled. "I'll let you know if I think of anything."

* * *

The forensics team had finished with O'Connell's office and cleared out. Everything that had been on the desk was gone, including the watch. The light cover with the bullet hole had also been removed.

David stood behind me. "They're thorough, I'll give 'em that. What were you hoping to find?"

"I don't know. Something that'll make this all fit together." I crossed to the window.

"O'Connell has quite the collection of musical instruments." Leah studied the shelf. "I wish we could find out if anything had vanished from this office, too."

"Any dust imprints?" David suggested.

She shook her head. "Nothing. Everything looks like it's in place. No odd spaces between pieces or anything to suggest an item had been removed."

I raised my eyebrows. I had always suspected that Leah was smarter than she let on.

The front door to the building opened. Expecting Coyle's arrival, I left the office and came down the stairs. Sure enough, I found the professor unlocking her office door.

I stopped at the bottom of the stairs. "Good morning, Dr. Coyle."

"Oh!" She jumped and turned around. "Mr. Clue, I didn't expect to meet you here."

"No? I'm investigating O'Connell's death, remember?"

"Yes, of course." She opened her door and slid the key into her pocket. "You can come in, I suppose. Pardon the mess. I just got out of a meeting, and I haven't had a chance to clean anything up in here since I got arrested so abruptly."

Leah slipped into the room. "Dr. Coyle, right? I'm Leah Lee, Mr. Clue's secretary."

"Glad to meet you, I'm sure." Susannah set her phonograph's tonearm onto its rest and removed the record. "Having any luck so far, Mr. Clue?"

"Hard to say. We're working on it." I noted the title on the album sleeve. "*The Four Seasons*. That's one of the pieces I'm familiar with."

Coyle picked up the sleeve. "Yes, it's one of my favorites. This is the 1976 recording by Itzhak Perlman and the London Philharmonic. You know, for most people, every recording of classical music sounds the same, but I find that different conductors add their own unique flavor to the piece. It's almost imperceptible to the untrained ear, but once you're used to it, you can't help but notice." She paused, before sliding the vinyl back into the sleeve and replacing it on the shelf, alongside thousands of other albums. "Well, no matter, I'm just babbling."

I looked around the room, noting everything I could. Floor-to-ceiling bookcases occupied two entire walls of the office. Vinyl records filled most of that space, with only a couple of shelves holding books. I noted only a few knick-knacks. Wood-and-glass double doors opened into the main hallway. All in all, the office appeared grander than what I'd imagine for a music processor. "No, it's fine. I'm more of a jazz enthusiast, but I can appreciate differences in performance. Anyway, I do love the sound of vinyl."

"I know, right? There's something about it that computers just can't offer. It feels so much closer to the actual performance." Coyle closed the clear plastic cover over her phonograph.

"Is there something special about *The Four Seasons* for you?"

"It's my bad-mood music. Whenever I get really rankled, I put on *Summer: Presto*."

"I figured. That's the piece we heard the night O'Connell was murdered, wasn't it?"

Coyle sat down behind her desk and stared at me. Her expression darkened. "What do you want, Mr. Clue?"

I leaned back against the bookshelf. "I'm trying to work out the timing for that night. There's a bunch of stuff that doesn't make sense, and I'm hoping to put together some semblance of a timeline."

Coyle rubbed her arm. "To be honest, after the way I've been treated over the past two days, I'm not so sure I want to help. No offense to you, of course, but you're a police advisor. I'd much rather my lawyer was present during any questioning."

"Naturally. I'm not really wanting to know much about you, actually. I've already read the police interview."

"All the same. You'll have to imagine, if I tell you something seemingly unrelated, and that detective finds a way to construe my guilt from it, I'm effectively testifying against myself." She waved the idea off. "I'm sorry, no lawyer, no questions."

"That's fair." I looked around the room. "Did the police even check your office, anyway?" I caught myself. "Sorry, that's a question, isn't it?"

"No, that's a bit different. They didn't. I refused to give consent, they had no probable cause, and the request for a warrant got shot down. At least the officers had the decency to lock it up for me."

"That's nice of them. Say, has anything gone missing from your office lately?"

"Actually..." Coyle hesitated. "I'm sorry, I'll have to put that in the 'questions I won't answer without a lawyer' category. You can't blame me for being too careful."

"No, that's fine." I grumbled to myself. I could understand Coyle's hesitation. She didn't want anything getting back to Jones. I wondered...

I turned to my secretary. "Leah, we're not recording, right?"

"Nope." Leah held up her smartphone.

"Shut the door for a moment."

Coyle watched with concern. "What's going on?"

I took out my own flip phone, still closed, so she could see I wasn't recording. "Look, I am happy to have this conversation with your lawyer present, but you need to understand something: I am convinced you didn't shoot Liam O'Connell. If we can talk, completely off-the-record, you might be able to provide information that can put me on the trail of the real killer." I took the seat across from Coyle's desk and set my phone in front of her. "No record, no police, no tricks. If you still want a lawyer, I'll go along with it, but then it might take too long to learn what I need to know."

Coyle tapped the desk. "You know, if you were anyone else, I'd refuse. You could be wearing a wire, for all I know. But for some inane reason, I believe you." She blew out a breath. "Fine, what do you need to know?"

"Has anything gone missing from your office in the past few weeks? Even something small?"

She looked around, her mouth twisted up in thought. "Not that I know of, unless I've got some books or vinyls missing that I haven't noticed yet."

"Is anything here that wasn't before?"

"Odd question, but a good one." She stood and crossed to her bookshelves. "Once again, not unless someone put a new vinyl into the collection." She stopped. "Wait, this is new."

"Don't touch it. I'll have it dusted for prints." I left my seat and rushed over. "I saw that a few minutes ago, and I had a feeling it didn't belong."

"How did you know?"

"Someone else reported some things missing. I'm not much of a believer in coincidence."

"Well, it definitely isn't mine." Coyle backed up, still looking at the statuette, and then returned to her desk. "I hate the idea that someone put that there. If your detective had found it, he'd be arresting me for theft too."

"He's not my detective."

"You are on the same team."

I took my seat again. "Not really. I'm trying to solve a murder. He's trying to...well, you know that part."

Coyle snorted. "Yeah."

"What do you know about the janitor who cleans this building?"

"Philip?" She wrinkled her nose in thought. "Ehh...he's all right, I suppose. I don't really know anything about him, and he's not much of a talker. Always has that dreadful rap music on in his headphones, so he can't hear anything."

"Did you know he was in the building when O'Connell got shot?"

Coyle blinked. "No, except I should have guessed. It never occurred to me. I heard the gunshots and panicked."

"David told me you had a fear of guns."

"Yeah. David was really great. He had me pretty well calmed down by the time we got to the hospital. He told me he was sure you'd clear this whole thing up, and that you'd said to call that lawyer. Thanks again for that." Coyle fidgeted with a staple remover. "Yeah, David was great," she repeated.

I noticed Coyle had completely dodged the question. No matter, Warren would confirm or deny the information she had given to David. I didn't need to dredge up the past for her. I changed the subject. "You know, your students have a lot of good things to say about you."

"Yeah?" Coyle continued fidgeting. Her mind seemed to be somewhere in the past.

"Including your one oboe student."

Coyle laughed absently. "Stefan."

"He really appreciated how you have him play through every time. That's pretty rare among music teachers, I understand."

"Maybe it shouldn't be, but yeah. Stefan is the only student who will put up with my policy." Coyle seemed to be returning to earth.

"You're pretty dedicated to the method."

"Well, what can I say?" She set down the staple remover. "I hate unfinished things. Living in foster care does that to you. You get a new house, new family, new school, new rules, new expectations. As soon as you get used to it..." She snapped her fingers. "You're on to somewhere else. Nothing ever finished. So I guess that made me sensitive to finishing things, and it spills over into my teaching. I'm glad it works for Stefan, though."

At least it cleared that lead up. "What all do you do here at the Conservatory?"

"Officially, I'm just a lowly professor. I teach theory, composition, and in that one case, oboe. Besides that, I was basically O'Connell's de facto lackey."

I guessed that Dean Matheson hadn't yet told her about the new position, and I wasn't about to be the one to spoil the surprise.

Coyle leaned back. "I miss Vaughn Ramakers, and not just because he kept O'Connell on a short leash. He was one of the kindest people I've ever met. I would help him out anytime he needed it, and he helped me in turn." Her expression clouded over. "When he left, Dr. O'Connell became the interim department chair, and he expected me to automatically assist him, the same as I had done for Vaughn. I think I was supposed to be the acting assistant chair, but O'Connell just did all the managing himself." She gave me a sly smile. "Not that I care, but this doesn't have anything to do with timing."

I had almost forgotten the point of this discussion! "Sorry, I was just curious. Okay, next question, you had that row with O'Connell about paperwork. I know you put on that music to calm down, but could you walk me through what all you did and heard?"

Coyle stood. "Yeah, sure." She crossed to the door. "So, obviously, I came in. I think I was still ranting to myself—I do that, you know—and I paced around a bit trying to calm down. That never works, but I always seem to try it first."

I nodded. "People are funny that way. We form habits that have absolutely no purpose, and hold to them like our lives depend on it."

"Anyway, then I remembered that music was the best way to calm down. I took Vivaldi off the shelf..." She pulled the record out without so much as a pause to look. "And I put it on." She removed the lid from the player, slid the vinyl from its sleeve, and set it in place. With a few deft movements, she switched on the phonograph and dropped the needle towards the center of the record. The piece David and Hen remembered resonated around the office.

"Can you hear anything outside the office when the music is on?"

"Not much. This old building has a weird layout and thick walls, so sound doesn't carry very well. It's a definite advantage, since we all listen to our own music." Coyle closed her eyes and took a deep breath. "It doesn't matter how many times I hear this piece, it never gets old."

"So, you were listening to this, and what did you hear next?"

Coyle's eyes popped open and she stared at the door. "Indistinct shouting, and then two loud pops. I recognized them as gunshots."

"What did you do then?"

"I froze! I started remembering..." Coyle began to look like she had that night. I decided to cut the scenario short.

"Right, and then we came in. I remember the rest. Thank you."

Coyle closed her eyes again, tapping along with the music. Her breathing slowed down, and color returned to her face. After a few moments, she gave me a shy smile. "I hope that's helpful to you, Mr. Clue, I really do."

"Actually, I think it is." I stood. "I'll call that statue in to the police, now." I dialed Samantha's number.

"Sure, thank you."

* * *

As Leah and I emerged from Dr. Coyle's office, I noticed David talking with a tall, muscular, young African American man. A large black instrument case sat on the floor at his feet. My friend spotted us and waved us over. "Noah, this is Andy Lowry. He was just telling me about Liam O'Connell."

"Really?" I shook his hand. "Hi, Mr. Lowry, I'm Noah Clue, private investigator. It's good to meet you. Are you a student here?"

"Yeah, cello player. I understand you're trying to figure out who killed Dr. O'Connell."

"Yes." I glanced around, only now noticing the glaring absence of Detective Jones. I hadn't seem him since we arrived on campus. "What can you tell me about the professor?"

"Well, I was just telling your associate, Mr. Sigfield, about an incident last week. Dr. O'Connell nearly collided with me and my cello in this hallway. He came unglued and yelled at me to look where I was going. I apologized, but he ignored me and started up the staircase he'd just come down."

"Really? That's odd." I glanced at Leah to make sure she was taking notes.

David held up his smartphone. "I'm already recording, in case you're wondering, Noah."

"Thanks." I turned back to Lowry. "So, then he just went back to his office?"

"No. As soon as he reached the top, he messed with his watch a bit, and started running down the stairs again. I heard him hit another button as he passed me, and then he ran out the door. I figured he had taken up jogging or something, although I've never seen someone start at the top of a staircase." Lowry held up his hands. "But I don't try to understand Dr. O'Connell. He's always been eccentric, as long as anyone's known him."

I recalled the watch on Dr. O'Connell's desk. "Have you ever seen him doing anything like that before or since?"

My phone vibrated. I checked the caller ID. Warren. "Excuse me. Thank you for the information, Mr. Lowry."

As I reached the front door, I answered my phone. "This is Clue."

"Morning, Noah. I've got some more information for you. First, the gun in question was reported stolen two years ago in Airway Heights. It's unregistered and illegally obtained. We have absolutely no way of tracing the sale."

"Shoot. Okay, so that's 'first'. I hope 'second' is good news?"

"Perhaps, depends on how you take it. We found gunpowder residue on O'Connell's clothing that may be consistent with him struggling for the gun."

I nodded. "I know the first bullet was fired into the ceiling. I just wish we had been able to check hands for residue. It would have made this easier."

"I agree. Well, finally, I have the medical examiner's report for O'Connell. He definitely died from a single gunshot to the head, at a rather awkward angle for a suicide. So, it's being ruled a homicide. However, it also looks like it was a waste of a perfectly good bullet."

"What do you mean?"

"Liam O'Connell had inoperable brain cancer. His doctor told him last month, and according to medical records, Liam refused treatment. He told his doctor that he was 'going out with a bang.' He wouldn't have lived more than a few weeks."

I leaned up against the building and tried to process this. "So, now I need to find who wanted to kill a dying man?"

"Basically, yeah. And you thought it was interesting already."

"Do you know if he told anybody?"

"Hey, that's your department to find out. It's why we pay you the big bucks."

Sure, but only if I could solve it.

6

Salsa In Dee's Flat

"In two hundred feet, turn left," crooned the GPS.

"Oh, sure, you say that now." David retorted. "I tell you, Noah, I don't trust these things. My GPS once asked me to merge onto the freeway over a six-foot concrete median with trees."

"Mm." My friend's banter seemed to be off in the distance as I scanned the medical report we had picked up from Warren. "There's an interesting note here from O'Connell's doctor. When he told him about the prognosis, O'Connell didn't seem very upset. He actually grinned at the doctor and said 'I'll be going out with a bang.'"

"I don't think that's the bang he expected," David remarked.

I turned back to the first page. "Maybe he was planning to take a vacation or something? I'll have to see if the forensics team has turned something up."

"It's nice of Sammi to keep us in the loop. Didn't I tell you strategic friendships would come in handy?"

"I still don't see it as strategic. Just a friendship that happens to come in handy." Even so, I had been a bit surprised to get Samantha's phone call, telling me forensics was wrapping up their search of O'Connell's apartment, and that I needed to get down there. Leah had returned to her apartment to compile a few notes, and we were going to meet back on campus in a couple of hours.

As we pulled up to the apartment complex, I noticed Jones's unmarked car.

"Huh. I had wondered where Detective Lockjaw had gotten to." David pulled in next to the detective's vehicle and parked.

The GPS chirped happily, "You have arrived at your destination."

"Yeah, yeah. Can it, already." David poked the screen, and the device went dark.

It took us a couple of minutes to find the staircase, but we finally located apartment 308. I knocked, and Samantha let us in. "Hey, Noah. David."

I removed my Stetson. "Hi, Sammi. Thanks again for the call."

"No problem. I'll give you the run-down before Jones gets back. He's talking to neighbors right now, trying to 'rule out' other potential suspects. You know him."

"Yes. Wish I didn't." I looked around, taking in the environment. A few small pieces of furniture were pushed up against one wall. The space was immaculately clean, possibly owing in part to the forensics team, and next to nothing was out of place. "What do you call this decor style, anyway? Minimalist?"

"I have no idea. Believe it or not, this is virtually how we found it." Samantha produced a stack of receipts. "We found these near the desk. It looks like O'Connell has been selling off his belongings."

I took the receipts offered to me. "That's not surprising, given that he had inoperable brain cancer. I was reading the report on the way over."

Samantha's shoulders drooped. "So, it's not an indicator of suicidal intent. Darn. I was really hoping we'd found a smoking gun that would clear Susannah Coyle. That's why I called you over."

"Well, it isn't a complete bust. Look." I held up a receipt for a local computer shop. "He sold his laptop."

David snatched the paper from my hand. "Hey, I know this shop. A buddy of mine owns it. I bet I could get access to the laptop long enough to run forensic data recovery on it."

"Go ahead and give him a call. We can't afford to have this laptop sold before we can get to it."

My friend nodded, dialed his phone, and wandered off.

I skimmed the other receipts. "What was he planning to do with all this money, anyway? Send it to family?" I spotted the name 'Westbrook Funeral Home'. "Oh, here we go. He purchased a bunch of stuff for his imminent death and burial. I never realized funerals were this expensive."

Samantha moved to look over my shoulder. "They are, but not usually that expensive. It looks like he was going out extravagantly."

"I wonder if this is what he meant by 'going out with a bang.'"

"Look at this one." Samantha pulled a blue receipt out of the stack. "He also bought a very expensive gravestone."

"More like a monolith! It's listed here as a 'large engraved obelisk.'" I shook my head in wonder. "Talk about your egotism."

The door to the apartment swung open. "Miss Keppler, did you..." Jones froze. "Oh, great, it's you. What do you want now?"

Lockjaw, as David had taken to calling him, just could not be cordial. "I'm collecting facts, as always. Did you learn anything interesting talking to the neighbors?"

"Same answer from them all. O'Connell kept to himself. The few who ever spoke to him didn't like him. None of them are overly concerned by his passing. Nothing else interesting." Jones eyed me with suspicion. "I didn't tell any of them about Coyle, or any other working suspicions, in case that's what you're thinking."

"I thought nothing of the sort." I turned back to the receipts. "Have you seen these?"

Jones blew out a long breath, walked over, and took the papers from my hands. "Pawn shop. Funeral home. Et cetera, et cetera.

Yeah, he knew he was dying, so he decided to make his own final arrangements." He handed them back. "If there's anything else to that, you'll have to tell me. I left my Captain Midnight Secret Decoder Ring at home."

"No, I think it's pretty much the way it looks. Based on my inquiries, O'Connell hadn't told anyone about his condition. All this just seems to strengthen the idea that he was murdered." A new thought entered my mind. "Did he have any family?"

"Yeah." Jones handed the receipts back to Samantha. "One wife, who divorced him seventeen years ago and moved to Florida. His only child, a thirty-eight-year-old daughter, lives in Boston. Neither of them claim to have had any contact with him in the past ten years." He pulled out his notebook. "Okay, so it looks like I'm done here. Anything else important, Miss Keppler?"

Samantha shook her head. "Nope, we're done. Just about to clear out, sir."

"Bravo. Well, I'm going to wrap up some paperwork at the station. If anyone needs me, you know how to use a phone." Jones strode out of the apartment.

Once he had left, I followed Samantha into the dining area, where she began packing up her equipment. "Actually, I had a couple of questions. Were you able to lift any fingerprints from the statuette found in Coyle's office?"

She placed her camera in its case. "Yes, two sets. They're still being identified. Next?"

"Do you remember the stopwatch in O'Connell's office?"

"Yeah. We've got it back at the lab, although I think you heard the chain of evidence is shot to pieces." She zipped the camera case. "What about it?"

"Did you get photos of it?"

"Of course."

"What time was on the watch?"

Samantha paused. "I don't remember off the top of my head, but I can find out and give you a call as soon as I get back to the lab."

"I'd appreciate that."

David sidled up. "Noah, we've got to get down to the computer shop before it closes in an hour. My friend said we can take the computer, as long as it's returned when the case is closed."

"Great, let's go."

"Hold on, you two." Samantha gathered her equipment. "I'd better go with you to ensure we've got the proper chain of custody procedures in place."

I nodded. "Thanks, Samantha, you're a gem."

* * *

The doorbell echoed through the empty apartment I shared with Dee. I turned off the burner under the taco meat. "Coming!"

I had been half expecting David or Leah, so the sight of Warren in jeans and a T-shirt, carrying a pizza box, caught me by surprise. "Hey, what are you doing here?"

"I was in the neighborhood, thought I'd drop by." He held up a folder. "Also wanted to bring this to you. I'm sorry I wasn't able to call earlier, but I didn't think you should have to wait until Monday."

"Come in." I moved aside to let the captain in, and shut the door behind him. "Wait until Monday for what?"

"It all checks out. Susannah Coyle's parents were killed in a drive-by shooting when she was four, and the car wrecked. She only sustained minor injuries, and went into foster care. A report from a state child psychologist matches what she told David." He set the folder on the breakfast bar. "Coyle gave written permission to release the records to us, and to you. I think you'll find the whole report quite enlightening."

"Well, I really appreciate the support." I returned to the kitchen and opened a can of refried beans. "What's with the pizza?"

"Yeah, that. You hungry?"

I chuckled. "Thanks, but I've got supper started already. Would you like to stay? I'm eating alone, otherwise."

"Sure, why not? I've never had your cooking, but it can't be worse than a five dollar pepperoni pizza. Anything I can help with?"

"Sure, you can wash the lettuce in the fridge and cut it."

"Cool beans." He set the pizza box on the counter.

I emptied the refried beans into a saucepan. "Not for long."

"I've been meaning to ask why you always wear that black cowboy hat everywhere." Warren set the head of lettuce on the counter. "You got something to wash this in?"

I opened the cupboard above my head and removed the aluminum colander. "Right here."

"Ah, thanks." He took it and the lettuce to the sink.

"My hat was a gift from my Uncle Denby. He owns a ranch just outside of Marietta, Texas, and I spent summers there."

"Texas, right. You might have mentioned it before, but I couldn't remember."

I watched the normally hard-nosed Warren separating lettuce leaves. "I don't think I've ever really seen you outside of work before," I remarked.

"Not except for when I helped you move into the office. Then there was that infamous dinner party that Dee and your writer friend staged, although we were technically still working that time. What's his name? Charles something or other?"

"Yeah, Radcliffe. That was a weird experience." I stirred the refried beans. "You could have dropped that paperwork by earlier, on your way home from work. That's not your only reason for being here, is it?"

Warren shut off the water and sighed. "You're really more perceptive than you give yourself credit for, you know that?" He spread the dishtowel on the counter and began laying out the lettuce leaves. "Honestly, I was hoping you'd let me come in, just to hang out for a bit."

The refried beans began to bubble, and I flicked off the burner. "Why me?"

"Because, you're the first person in years I really feel comfortable around. My world has always revolved around work, because I can't relate to people outside of it. And heaven forbid I try to talk to a woman, or I'll turn into a blithering idiot." Warren patted the lettuce dry. "Cutting board?"

"Above the fridge." I pondered this new angle on Warren. "You seem to be able to talk to Dee."

"I've never tried outside of work, and anyway, she's unusual."

"What's so comfortable about me?"

"I don't know. Maybe it's because you make awkwardness look so easy." Warren grimaced and dropped the cutting board on the counter. "I'm sorry, that didn't come out the way I meant."

"I suppose you mean I don't fit in, but it doesn't seem to bother me." I slid past Warren to the fridge. "It used to, and maybe it still does sometimes, but somewhere in my first year of college, I learned that if people didn't like me for who I was, they weren't really going to like me if I pretended to be something I wasn't." I yanked the cheese drawer open and struggled to get the oversized block of sharp cheddar unwedged from the shelf edge. "Or, as my Uncle Denby always said, 'if people don't like you without a hat, they won't like you with one.'"

Warren began chopping the lettuce. "He certainly sounds like a wise man."

"He made a small fortune from a natural gas deposit on his land in the eighties. He's the one who put me through college, and who kept sending me money to stay afloat as I started the firm." I wrestled the cheese loose.

"Did he have any kids?"

"Nope. He married his high school sweetheart in 1965, and she died two years later. Uncle Denby never got over her. In a way, I'm his kid. He was more of a dad to me than my own father."

Warren looked thoughtful. "My parents split up when I was ten years old. I lived with my mother full time, and visited dad for Christmas, Easter, and Fourth of July weeks. I think he enjoyed those visits, but his new wife always treated me like a stray dog. When I was seventeen, I just stopped going." He scraped the lettuce into a bowl. "Well, there's that. Want me to grate the cheese?"

I realized I had been staring at him and holding the cheddar this entire time. "Sure."

Warren took the proffered block and raided the knife drawer for a grater.

I tried to process what Warren had told me. "That's really tough. I wish more parents would just think about how their decisions affect their kids."

"Well, Mom was great." Warren continued. "It was tough for her, with her job as a court stenographer taking up most of her time. I spent many hours running around with friends, and often had supper at their houses." He shrugged. "But I knew she was just working hard to support me. When she was home, she made me feel like the center of her world."

"My mother did everything shy of outright disowning me in public. I didn't fit into the high-status society she pretended to be a part of." I returned to the fridge. "Medium or spicy salsa?"

"You have spicy salsa?"

I set the mason jar on the counter. "My Aunt Elizabeth makes it. Might as well finish this batch off before Dee brings the next two jars. Proper warning, it'll make you weep and breathe fire."

"Elizabeth. Is that Dee's mother, then?" Warren set the bowl of shredded cheese aside and began wrapping up the rest of the block.

"Yeah, Bennett and Elizabeth Tindall are her folks. He's a lawyer in Waxahachie." I began dishing the taco meat into another bowl. "Actually, he's the one who gave me my typewriter before I left for college. Mind getting the sour cream out of the fridge?"

"Not a problem."

I removed the tortillas from the oven. "Would you believe Jones is still insisting Coyle killed O'Connell, after everything we've found? David's taken to calling him Lockjaw, after his initials: TMJ."

Warren grinned. "Good name. Yeah, there's no cure for the common stupid." He set the sour cream on the breakfast bar. "*That* is a quote from my mother."

"My uncle would say he's all hat and no horse. What do you want to drink, Warren?"

He chuckled. "Warren is the curmudgeon down at SPD headquarters. Please call me Gregg."

"I just don't want to get into the habit and wind up calling you 'Gregg' on the job."

He waved me off. "I really don't care if you do. I call you Noah already."

"You didn't answer my question."

"Hmm? Ah, what are my options?"

"Water, milk, water, water, and water." I shrugged. "Dee still refuses to let me have soda in the house, and we're out of juice."

"Water is fine." He held up the pizza box. "What should I do with this, anyway?"

"Stick it in the fridge, I guess. I like cold pizza for breakfast."

"Man after my own heart." Warren slid the pizza onto the bottom shelf, across the carton of eggs and half-full container of leftover oatmeal. "Any leads on getting your own place?"

"I've explored a few options, but I don't want to be too hasty. I have to like the neighbors and be able to tolerate the landlord." I carried a handful of spoons and two plates to the breakfast bar.

Warren—or Gregg, as I was now trying to think of him—dropped a hot tortilla on his plate and began filling it with refried beans. "Do you know, this is the first time I've done this in over a decade?"

I scooped a bit of meat into the middle of my tortilla and watched with amusement as Gregg piled ingredients onto his. "What, make a burrito?"

"No, just hang out. I don't warm up to people very quickly. Like I said, outside of work, I'm completely awkward. Instead of trying and failing, I just keep to myself."

"That sounds lonely."

"It is." Gregg dropped a generous spoonful of sour cream on top of his mound of food and tried to roll the tortilla. The filling oozed out in all directions.

I handed a spoon to him. "You're going to need this."

"How do you even roll these things?"

I laughed. "Well, don't go overboard, for starters. Fill a line down the middle of the tortilla, fold in the ends, and then roll." I held up my tidy completed burrito. "Texas know-how."

"I'll have to try that next time." Gregg took a bite of his attempted burrito, grabbing a napkin to catch some wayward filling. "I like your way better."

"If you don't have to be anywhere after this, I was going to catch one of those old noir detective films on TV."

"Sure, sounds like fun." Gregg took another bite. While he chewed, I caught a glimmer of a tear in his eyes. At first, I thought it was from my Aunt Elizabeth's salsa, until I remembered Gregg had forgotten it on this burrito. He wiped it away with his wrist. "I'm...I'm sorry." He cleared his throat. "The last time I did anything even close to this was with my buddy Rick back in 1988. He and I did everything together, kinda like you and David."

"What happened?"

"We enlisted in the U.S. Army together in '89. Less than a year later, we shipped out to Saudi Arabia as part of the 24th Infantry Division. Rick and I stuck together through the whole thing."

A sinking feeling formed in the pit of my stomach. "Gregg, I had no idea you were a vet."

He nodded. "Our division had just taken two airfields a couple days before, and we were pushing east. We encountered entrenched Iraqi forces, and we had to clear out the bunker. Four hours in, there's no sign of the fighting letting up, but Rick's by me this whole time." Gregg's voice caught. "An RPG went off right by us. He was between me and the blast." He squeezed his eyes shut and clenched his jaw for a moment. "I would have been killed if it weren't for him, but I was barely wounded. There was nothing I could do for him, I just had to keep fighting." His voice took on a tone of resentment. "They gave me a Valorous Unit Award, and for what? Getting shot at for six hours? I couldn't even save my own buddy."

On instinct, I put my hand on Gregg's shoulder. What could I even say? All of the acrimony that had been between us seemed to make sense. I doubted he'd told many people that story, and I wondered at being one of the few he did.

He took a deep breath. "Okay, you know what, hand me that salsa your aunt makes."

Before I could respond, my pocket buzzed. "Mind if I get that? Might be Dee."

"Go for it." Gregg grabbed the mason jar of salsa, scooped out a spoonful, and stuck it in his mouth. "Whoa."

I answered. "This is Clue."

Samantha's voice came through. "Hey, Noah, sorry to call so late. I'm still at the office. We got swamped with paperwork. I found the photo of the stopwatch you asked about."

"Yeah? What's it say?"

"Okay, the photo was taken at 8:31 p.m. and fifty-six seconds, and at that time, the stopwatch displayed fifteen minutes and thirty-nine seconds. You care about milliseconds?"

"No, but that is awesome, thank you. You sure it was showing minutes and seconds, yes?"

"Yeah. Another photo a few seconds later, it's a little hard to see, but the watch still shows fifteen minutes, so I'm one-hundred percent certain about the units."

I could work with this. "Samantha, you are an absolute wonder! Thank you."

"You're welcome. Don't hesitate to call if you need anything else. I'm looking at working the weekend anyway. Paperwork. Always paperwork." She laughed. "Tootles!"

I pocketed my phone. "Where were we?"

"Noah," Gregg mumbled with his mouth half full, tears streaming down his beet red cheeks in earnest, "Your aunt's salsa is incredible, and you'd better pass that along to her."

* * *

By 9:30, Gregg and I were well into the movie. Ingrid Bergman sat, distraught, looking at something off the camera as her dastardly husband, Charles Boyer, ranted on. "You've forgotten him as you forget everything. But perhaps I'm wrong to try to handle this myself. The case is one for people who know about those things."

"What a creep," Gregg remarked. "After the jewels the whole time. Talk about playing the long game."

"You know, in psychology, we get our term 'gaslighting' from this film." I grabbed another handful of popcorn from the bowl.

"It really is amazing what the power of suggestion can do, isn't it?" Gregg indicated the screen. "I mean, Paula isn't really a weak-minded woman at all, but the constant admonishments that her perception isn't valid just wear her down. She really thinks she's going crazy."

"Actually, it reminds me a bit of Jones. That's the whole reason I wanted to interview witnesses before he could. His way of insinuating that Coyle was guilty could so easily skew their perspectives. A sweet, unassuming music professor suddenly becomes a monster."

"Thankfully, that didn't happen. No one at the conservatory would buy it." Gregg caught another piece of popcorn in his mouth.

"Watching this, I almost can't blame Jones for jumping to the conclusion he did. All the initial facts did seem to suggest…" I trailed off. The old feeling of pieces fitting into place rushed over me. I jumped to my feet. "That's it! I know who killed Liam O'Connell!"

Gregg held out his hands. "Who?"

"I'll tell you as soon as I can confirm it." I snatched my cell phone from the side table and scrolled through the call history.

Two rings, and then I heard, "Samantha Keppler speaking."

"Samantha, it's Noah Clue. I need another favor."

7

A Matter Of Timing

Saturday, July 17

Jones stalked into the downstairs hallway of the crime scene. "This had better be good, Clue! I've got actual work to do today, and listening to some hair-brained theory is not part of it." He caught sight of Warren and froze.

The captain made eye contact with him. "You had better make the time, Detective."

Jones immediately quailed. "Sir! I didn't expect to find you here."

"Obviously." Warren crossed his arms. "When Noah told me he'd figured out who killed Liam O'Connell, I wanted to be here."

Samantha joined them, holding two manila envelopes in her hand. Her green eyes sparkled with merriment as she viewed the assembled group. "Huh. We've got quite a reveal party started. This should be good."

Jones grunted. "I fail to understand why we can't do this down at the station."

Lockjaw really didn't know when to quit. I glanced at Warren and received an encouraging nod. "I felt it was important to do this here, because we need to reenact something." I removed a stopwatch from my pocket. "Dr. Coyle and Henrietta Dunlop have both graciously agreed to come in today and assist me."

"How entertaining." Jones leaned up against the wall across from Coyle's office door. "Do continue."

Annoyance flashed in Warren's eyes. I'd hate to be in Jones's shoes later. I decided to focus on the case-at-hand. "Here's what we know. Wednesday evening, Doctors Coyle and O'Connell were having an argument." I nodded to Coyle, who started up the staircase with David. "Henrietta is across the street, waiting for David's cue. Her window is open, just as it was on the evening O'Connell died."

Jones looked bored until Warren cleared his throat. The detective immediately feigned an expression of interest.

"Coyle left O'Connell's office at 8:13 p.m." I pointed to David at the top of the stairs. Coyle slammed the office door and came down the staircase, and I started my stopwatch, knowing David had done the same with his. "As you'll see, it takes twenty-five seconds to come down the staircase at a good pace and reach her office door."

Coyle reached her door in the expected time and entered. "I ranted for a few moments, until I remembered that never helps me calm down," she explained. "That was about twenty seconds, by Noah's timeline. After that, I decided to put on some music." As soon as I pointed to her again, she took down Vivaldi's Four Seasons from her bookshelf and began setting it up on the phonograph.

Jones raised an eyebrow. "Assuming she's telling the truth?"

I held up my hand. "I can prove this. Roll with it." I glanced at the stopwatch. "We just need to wait for the right timing. I've got this entire thing worked out, down to the second. It takes her about seventy-five seconds to start a record." I waited until my stopwatch displayed one minute and forty-seven seconds. "Susannah, start it in three, two, one..."

The music started. I indicated her office with my thumb. "That is the same piece of music that David and Hen heard."

Jones shrugged. "So?"

Warren snarled, "Jones."

I held up my finger. "Wait for it."

Just as my watch hit the three-minute mark, David yelled "Bang...bang!" I hit the lap button.

"That's the gunshot. It is now 8:16 p.m., and Hen immediately comes running. The security camera proves that she enters the building at exactly 8:16 and forty-six seconds. We checked the timing, and it only takes about thirty seconds to get here."

Hen came barreling into the building. She ran past us and up the stairs. As she reached O'Connell's office, she yelled "Oh my gosh, he's dead! Someone shot him!"

"We were just outside, and when we heard that, we came in." I nodded to the front door, and Leah entered. "Again, we have an exact time, 8:18 p.m. and fifteen seconds."

"I remember distinctly," David added, leading Hen down the stairs, "That the song was on that third-from-last violin solo, and I have a verified near-eidetic memory."

As the music ended, I stopped my watch. "The track finishes at 8:19 and nine seconds exactly. Then, you arrived, Jones."

The detective scowled. "Really? That's it? That's all you've figured out?" He turned toward Gregg Warren. "Sir, he's wasting our valuable time."

The captain seemed amused with the detective's cluelessness.

I played it cool. "Do you disagree with any timing I've demonstrated? Was the music playing when you arrived?"

"It's all fine. You demonstrated the obvious, and no, there was no music when I got here. So?"

I held up my stopwatch. "What does the last lap say?"

Jones squinted. "Three minutes, exactly. That tells me nothing."

Who had ever made him a detective? "It should tell you a lot. There was a running stopwatch on Dr. O'Connell's desk, and based on the time it displays in the crime scene photo, it would have to be exactly three minutes at the time of the gunshots. Doesn't that strike you as odd?"

"Not at all." Jones brushed past me. "All you've done here is played this out, as if O'Connell were shot by some invisible assassin. You've merely assumed Coyle is innocent."

Warren put out his arm and stopped Lockjaw from leaving. "Stay put and listen."

I flipped open my notebook. "In your investigation, you overlooked one little factor: Susannah Coyle cannot start or stop a song in the middle. That goes back to her parent's death when she was four. They had been driving along, listening to the radio, when a drive-by shooter killed her father and mother. According to police reports, the car crashed through a guardrail and into a ditch, destroying the front end. The radio stopped. The young child formed a strong association between incomplete songs and tragedy. This has been verified by a state child psychologist."

Jones raised an eyebrow. "How do you know she didn't outgrow that quirk?"

I continued. "Because of her modern habits. She only has one student for a musical instrument, despite being an accomplished performer herself, because she requires that all pieces be played through. She couldn't even bring herself to flee the scene at the sound of gunshots. Her fear of guns is equally well documented."

Jones threw his hands in the air. "Fine. She's afraid of guns and obsessive about music. Can you get to the point?"

"The point is, we've just proven that no more than fifteen seconds could have elapsed from the start of the song until the gunshots, or else you would have heard it. Your own testimony, and that of David, prove that fact. And since she couldn't have started it in the middle, and the song cannot be heard from the upstairs office, it is not possible for her to have shot Dr. O'Connell." I blew out a breath and waited for the detective's reaction.

Jones growled. "Fine! Coyle is innocent! Is that what you wanted to hear from me? Well, there it is!"

Warren rolled his eyes, but said nothing.

Jones crossed his arms. "So, assuming all this is true, who is the killer? The janitor, Kasey? Would he be able to escape in time?"

"Potentially." It amazed me that Jones remained defiant. "I agree that Philip Kasey is the most likely suspect for a murder here. He has opportunity, an extensive criminal record, and with O'Connell's personality being what it was, anyone could have motive. But, I believe he is cleared by another crime altogether."

Leah took a borrowed statuette of a violin from her handbag and handed it to me.

I lead the way into Coyle's office. "A statuette similar to this was stolen from Dr. Sanderson's office across the street, the same day O'Connell died. Sanderson has long suspected Kasey of petty theft, which is why the cameras were installed. Samantha, were you able to identify the fingerprints on that recovered statuette?"

"Absolutely." The forensics technician handed an envelope to Warren. "Sir, would you please read the results?"

The captain opened the flap and slid out the paper. "Aaron Sanderson and Philip Kasey. What's the significance of this, Noah?"

"Kasey only took one statuette at a time to avoid detection. He needed a place to stash it while he cleaned this building. As you can see, Dr. Coyle doesn't collect any type of knick-knacks in her office." I handed the golden violin to the professor.

She set it on her shelf. "Noah and I found the oboe statuette right here yesterday morning," she explained.

The detective shrugged. "Great, so Kasey is back to theft. I'd heard the boys picked him up for something yesterday, but how does that clear him?"

Just how dense was Lockjaw? I tamped down my frustration before continuing. "The fact he'd put something in Coyle's office, instead of just about anywhere else in the building, indicates that he didn't expect her to be in. She was supposed to be at the concert, so O'Connell would be the only one here. He wouldn't have made plans to kill O'Connell with everyone gone. The security cameras would implicate him as being the only other person in the building, and with his record, he'd be caught in a heartbeat."

I couldn't help but enjoy watching Jones lose it at this point. "Fine! He's clear! O'Connell was murdered by an invisible man! When everything else is eliminated, whatever remains, however impossible, must be the truth, right?"

"You learn more by listening than talking, Jones." Warren's voice held a warning tone.

Hen stood by Coyle. "Who did kill O'Connell? Dr. Sanderson? You said he had a clear view of the scene."

I shook my head. "No. The trajectory for the bullet in the ceiling is wrong, it wouldn't explain the yelling, and the bullet that killed O'Connell matched the gun in his hand." I couldn't hide my grin any longer. "The answer is: O'Connell wasn't murdered."

"Argh!" Jones thumped his head against the wall. "You. Aren't. Making. Sense. He's in the city morgue, you idiot!"

I held up a finger. "Ah, there you go, jumping to conclusions again. I didn't say he wasn't dead. I said he wasn't murdered. You took it for granted that no one yells before they kill themselves. Sometimes they do, except Hen's testimony seemed to indicate an attacker. However, that is only because that's the scenario O'Connell wanted us to believe."

Warren whistled. "Impressive."

Coyle stared at me in shock. "Liam shot himself? Why?"

I shrugged. "He had nothing left to live for. O'Connell never told anyone, but he had inoperable brain cancer. He would have been dead before the term ended. He was counting on a promotion to department chair to be the ultimate feather in his cap before he died, but the board hadn't selected him."

"That's right. Matheson told me last night that I was…" Dr. Coyle trailed off. "Oh my gosh, that's why he set this up, isn't it? He was jealous of me?"

I nodded. "O'Connell hated the idea that someone was being promoted over his head. He knew the new chair would be announced at the concert, so he conspired to keep you and Hen from attending. He used the shim from Sanderson's office to jam Hen's window open, just to ensure she'd hear the argument with you, Dr. Coyle."

"Another student had noticed O'Connell timing himself running down the stairs a few days before, and that he had hit a button as he passed Coyle's office. Liam O'Connell timed the entire fictional crime, and worked out that three minutes would be sufficient for Coyle to come down, get a theoretical gun from her drawer, load it, and return to his office to kill him. He wipes the door handle and gun in advance, to make it look like the scene had been cleaned, and then opens the door and starts an argument with his imaginary attacker. To reproduce a struggle, he positions the gun close to his body and shoots the light cover. Finally, he holds the gun at an angle that is awkward, but possible, for a suicide, and pulls the trigger. Unfortunately for his carefully timed plan, he hadn't counted on the music playing, knowing very little about Susannah Coyle, and he hadn't planned on the janitor being a potential suspect."

For the first time since I'd met him, Detective Thomas M. Jones had nothing to say. He merely blinked at me.

I looked at my notebook. "O'Connell had told his doctor he would 'go out with a bang,' which was taken to mean he'd be living it up in his last few weeks. Yet all Liam O'Connell did was sell everything he had to purchase a lavish funeral and headstone for himself, and then stage the downfall of an innocent colleague." I sighed at the irony. "The 'bang' was literally meant, and a total waste of an effort. Had he left well enough alone, he would have learned the real reason he hadn't been promoted: his work as a conductor was so appreciated, they didn't want to take him away from that. He would have died naturally, honored by the school he'd poured his heart and soul into."

Samantha held up the second envelope. "I have a copy of the fingerprint analysis from the unfired bullets in the gun, right here. Noah called me with his suspicions, and I was able to confirm: Liam O'Connell had loaded that pistol himself."

"Meanwhile," David added, "I know the owner of the shop where Dr. O'Connell sold his computer, so I was able to turn in a favor and run a forensic data recovery. Over the past two weeks, O'Connell did a lot of internet searches about murders staged as suicides."

Jones snatched the envelope from Samantha and opened it. "Very clever, Mr. Clue. I'm sure you must be congratulating yourself on solving this, so go ahead and take all the credit. You'll get all of it anyway, I'm sure." He handed the paperwork back to Samantha as he passed her on his way out of the building.

David laughed as the front door swung shut. "We haven't seen the last of Detective Lockjaw, have we?"

Warren grunted. "He'll be disciplined for his foul-ups regarding this case, but the chief still believes he'll make a good detective, so, I'm afraid we're stuck with the idiot for now."

"Well, who cares about him? We've got our own genius detective right here." Leah kissed my cheek. "And I'm proud to know him."

* * *

"I'm really touched that Dean Matheson would arrange for an encore performance, and invite us. I'm also glad that Dr. Coyle and Hen don't have to miss it in the end." I straightened my tie as Leah and I walked towards the concert hall. "Do I look okay?"

"Almost. Hold on." Leah stopped me and adjusted the tie. "There, now it's straight."

"Thanks. I mean, do I look like I'm trying too hard?"

She put a hand on my chest. "I've never thought so. You look like a gentle-natured Texas boy who isn't used to high society, and that's what I like about you. You don't look down your nose at people."

"Hey, hey." David called to us. "Wait up, you two!"

I turned to face my friend. He approached with a stately African-American woman, with fine, cornrowed hair. In her long blue dress and high heels, she slightly surpassed David's stature. They stopped, and David introduced us. "Noah, meet my date, Tabitha Harris Mitchell. Tab, this is Noah Clue and Leah Lee."

"Tabitha Harris...Mitchell?" I cleared my throat. "The lawyer?"

She dipped her head. "That's me."

David grinned. "We met the night Coyle got arrested, and we immediately hit it off."

Miss Mitchell shook my hand. "It's a pleasure to meet you in person, Mr. Clue."

"Likewise. Well, I'm glad you're finally dating women worthy of your attention, David." I gestured to the concert hall. "Shall we?"

Dr. Coyle, Henrietta, and Matheson met us just inside. For the first time since I'd met her, Susannah Coyle looked completely relaxed. "I wanted to thank you again all for your help. You are truly a Seattle treasure."

I removed my Stetson. "It was our pleasure, Dr. Coyle."

"Yoo-hoo!" Melissa Draper's shrill voice echoed through the atrium. "Hi, all."

"Well, that answers the question about why she came the first time," muttered Leah, just loud enough for us to hear. "She wanted to latch onto the soloist."

Melissa leaned against the black-haired gentleman beside her. "This is my date. He's a world-renowned violinist, you know. He was just telling me all about his European tour." She sent David a coy smile. "So, how are you holding up?"

"Just fine." David kept a level tone. "This is my friend, Tabitha Harris Mitchell. Tabitha, this is Melissa Draper."

"Ah. Ironic last name." Tabitha ignored Melissa's outstretched hand. "Funny, David's never mentioned you."

"Nothing worth mentioning," he replied.

Melissa blanched.

"By the way, darling," the lawyer continued. "I adore those cubic zirconia earrings you're wearing. Oh, I own a few pairs myself, probably from the same designer. They're inexpensive enough, I never have to worry about having them stolen." Tabitha pulled David towards the inner door. "Shall we find our seats?"

I exchanged a surprised glance with Leah as Melissa slunk off looking deflated, still clinging to her date's arm.

Once we were inside the theater, I stopped Tabitha. "Did David tell you about the earring incident?"

She shook her head. "No, but she marked herself as a social climber. I can read people pretty quickly. It's a vital trait for a lawyer to have, I've found."

As we took our seats, I leaned towards Leah. "I think classical music is starting to grow on me. I'm actually excited to hear *The Planets* again."

She smiled. "I'm glad. We're still going to that jazz festival next month, right?"

"You bet."

"Let's just hope there won't be any murders at that one," David remarked. "Everywhere you go, Noah, people are dying to meet you."

"Maybe so." I leaned back. "But not tonight."

All work and no play makes Jack a dull boy.All
work and no play maßkes Jack a dull boy.. All
work and n play makes Jack a dull boy. All work
and no playmakes Jack a dull boy. All wrk and no
play makes jack a dull boy. All work and no play
makes Jack a dull boy.

www.ingramcontent.com/pod-product-compliance
Lightning Source LLC
Chambersburg PA
CBHW051529100726

47898CB00005B/1631